"Jesus!", called Joseph, loudly bearded mouth, his smallish eyes peering helplessly and yet hopefully up and down the caravan. "Jesus!" he called again, louder and more frustrated. Then aside to his wife, who was temporarily and by chance standing next to him, "Where can he be? Why did you not see to your son, woman, when we left Jerusalem? Now we are a day's journey away, and we are missing our eldest."

The sun beat down on them mercilessly - there was no shade, no breeze, no hint of coolness in the air.

Mary, as usual when he was in this temper, took no notice of her husband's verbal sally, but walked off to continue her search among their kin for Jesus. She brushed her thick, brown hair back from her large, dark brown eyes as she went, careful to keep her tunic over her head so as to keep the sun off. This left Joseph with the chore of staying with the slow moving ass - still crawling along as part of the caravan - and the other belongings of the family, which did nothing to improve his disposition.

When the throng had departed Jerusalem early that morning following the annual census demanded by the Romans, Joseph and Mary had assumed that Jesus was among their relatives since he seemed mature beyond his years, and since they could not conceive of him not knowing the departure time. They had thought that he would turn up during the day, but as it grew later they became more concerned and began an earnest search for him.

"James and Simon. You will go together and search the train for a distance of ten minutes ahead of us. Joses and Judah, you will search the train for a distance of ten minutes behind us. When you have traveled so far, if you do not find him or find evidence of him, return to us."

Thus did James, at eleven years of age the first born son of the union of Joseph and Mary, and Simon, his youngest brother, find themselves running ahead of the family to search among the other travelers for their brother.

"James, why did Jesus not come with us from the city?" asked seven year old Simon, the youngest of the four boys in the family. He was of curly hair with a light complexion, a prominent nose and small mouth that he inherited from his father. As a lad he was impish, but extremely popular among his siblings for his good nature and ability to laugh at himself as well as others.

"I have no idea; I just hope that he did and that he merely did not do so in our company," said 11 year old James, of whom the younger boy appeared to be a copy, except for James' darker hair and larger eyes, which

1

he inherited from his mother, to his brother who, because of his shorter stride, was alternately walking and running a pace behind. While James hurried to move forward in the crowd ten minutes, Simon struggled to keep up with him. They weaved in and out of the people in the caravan, searching one side and then the other for their lost brother.

"I do not believe that he left Jerusalem," replied Simon, after a moment. "I have not seen or heard of him all day." James did not know whether to count this among the jokes that Simon liked to play on others, but after a moment's reflection decided that it could not be - sober and mature Jesus would not allow that to happen.

"This could be also," said he to Simon, "though I cannot think why he would stay behind."

The family - Joseph and Mary, four boys and two girls - had left Jerusalem early in the morning so as to head north toward Nazareth, their home city, with a large crowd also heading north, the better to be safe from thieves. Now it was toward evening, and the blazing summer sun was setting in the west, leaving a faint glow of comfort to the travelers who had toiled in its parched heat all day. Soon the caravan would stop for the night, and the travelers would feed themselves as best they could before settling down to a fitful nights sleep.

James and Simon weaved their boyish bodies among the throngs of donkeys, carts, oxen, wagons, goats, sheep and people, looking this way and that among the people, stopping now and again to ask an acquaintance or family member if they had seen Jesus, at twelve the oldest child, since the departure from Jerusalem. For the most part the men walked and allowed their wives and children to ride on the backs of the animals or in the carts and wagons, though here and there they could see a woman with no husband walking while her children rode. They wore long, loose fitting robes and pulled part of their tunic over their heads to shield themselves from the merciless sun, and resembled nothing so much as people who were hoping that although they traveled in the sun, the sun would not recognize them. Covered heads bowed before the heat, and even the children hadn't the energy to prance about. There was some desultory conversation, but little more than guesses about how much further they might proceed before stopping for the night. Here and there a baby cried, the only direct acknowledgment of the predicament of the company other than the bleating and lowing of the animals. With so many people and so much livestock and other possessions, it was a slow moving morass.

After what seemed like the appointed time the brothers stopped to assess the situation. "He must still be in the city. I can find no one who has heard of him," said James to Simon, while looking up and down the line while shading his eyes with one hand. "Somehow we have managed to leave him behind. Father will not be pleased, and let us hope that this time he is more swift in his punishment."

James and Simon made their way back to their family, only to find that Judah and Joses had even less respect for ten minutes distance than they.

"You have not heard of him either? Well then we have little choice but to return to Jerusalem to look for him. It is too late tonight, but we must start early in the morning." Joseph kicked at the dirt at his feet. "Two additional days travel because of that boy. Carpentry is not so profitable that I can afford to be away for so long."

The family continued on with the caravan in the expectation that it would stop soon for the night, and because they were still in need of the safety in numbers that it could provide. Presently they came to a small oasis, west and south of the town of Ephraim, much too small to accommodate the entire company, but the only comfort at hand. They found that those who had arrived earlier had taken all of the useful spots in the shade of the trees. Joseph laid out blankets for them to sleep on while Mary prepared a small repast of barley bread with olives and dried meat.

"James," whispered Simon, who lay down next to the elder brother when they had all finished eating and saying evening prayers, "what do you mean that this time you hope father will be more swift in his punishment of Jesus?"

"Jesus is the eldest, but there are times when it seems as though Mother and Father treat him as if he had no brothers at all."

"Do they love him more than us?"

"I do not think so, but they sometimes act as though he is better than the rest of us. Maybe this time they will realize that we are no less troublesome than he." With that they pulled their mantles over themselves to guard against the chill night air, and fell into an exhausted sleep.

Early the next morning they awoke to the sounds of the stirring animals, the smell of some morning meals cooking though there were few of these since the most of the travelers had not the resources to bring such food with them, and children with pent up energy scampering about the grounds. After breaking their fast with more bread and filling with dried meat, Joseph and his family set off once more for Jerusalem. As they departed the camp obviously heading south again they were forced to endure the taunts of those among their acquaintances and friends who saw them leaving.

"Joseph, the census is done; you may go home!"

"What can be the matter, Joseph? Forget to pay a bit of taxes to the Romans?"

"Leave someone behind Joseph?" called another, not realizing that he had the truth.

As an exasperated Joseph growled his responses back to his tormentors, Mary spied a cousin in the crowd, still eating her breakfast with her family.

"Ruth," called Mary, "you will listen for news of Jesus, won't you? He is not with us, and we are returning to Jerusalem to search for him."

"Let us hope for his sake that you find him first, and not his father," said Ruth, who knew of Joseph's stern nature with his children.

And so, after refilling their waterskins they were on the road to Jerusalem again, retracing their steps to the city. At first the road was open to them alone since no travelers coming from the north had yet made it this far south. But as the morning grew later they began to pass the straggling travelers from Jerusalem who, like them, had had to go there to take part in the census. An occasional troop of Roman soldiers passed them in both directions, some walking, others in chariots denoting their rank. It is not literally true to say that they passed the Romans; it is more accurate to say that they were forced off of the road by the Romans, who took no heed of the crowds on the road, but plowed right through them as though they were so many weeds.

After each time the Romans roared through, the travelers picked themselves up off the ground, dusted themselves as best they could, and resumed the journey.

Since they were not traveling as part of the large caravan that had wound its way out of the city the day before, they made better progress on the return trip, and so by late afternoon found themselves facing the northernmost gate of the city of Jerusalem.

This gate was the common entrance for the peasantry entering the city from the north, at least in part because almost immediately within it one found the magnificent temple built by King Herod (though a usable structure was in place, it would not be completed for many years). There the faithful travelers would go to give thanks for their safe arrival.

There were still travelers leaving the city after the census, though they were fewer in number now than the previous day. Otherwise the gate was thronged with sellers of various goods, everything from spices and cloth to jewelry, pottery and food. There were stalls set up on the back of wagons and carts selling prunes, dates, bread, melons and other fruits, goats and sheep, woolen cloth, lesser quality linens, and nearly anything else a person could want, and all being sold at the top of the trader's lungs. Tired though they were, the family of Joseph hurried in through the gate, ignoring the throngs, and began to search for the missing child.

4

Thinking that the search ought to be a simple one, they stayed together in the city, and began their search by going to the temple. The streets on the way to the temple were becoming more quiet with the end of the business day. Small children, cooped up all day because of the heat, played in the street, heedless of the trash, refuse, dirty washing water and the attendant rats. Some adults gathered outside the larger houses to re-hash the day or to plan for the morrow. This pleasant little chapter in the story of the city had long disappeared when they arrived at the temple, where, though the crowd was thinning, among the usual moneychangers, traders, sellers and hucksters of every kind in the temple courtyard they could find no hint of Jesus.

By now the sun was low in the west and the narrow passageways of the city were becoming dark with the late evening shadows.

"I will return to the inn to see if we may have our room" said Joseph. "You remain here and continue the search." Off he went towards the center of the city where they had stayed during the census. It was not an inn, really, but a house with two tiny, empty, unfurnished rooms on the upper level - rooms in which it was impossible for Joseph to stand upright - for the use of one of which Joseph and his family had been charged an outrageous sum. Joseph hoped that the price might have gone down with the census over and the demand for rooms less, but he was prepared to take it even so. It was centrally located, and would therefore aid in the fanning out over the city to look for Jesus.   At the temple Mary and the children settled themselves on the steps, two on a side, to keep watch. Once again James and Simon sat together on one side of the temple while Joses and Judah sat on the adjacent side. Mary and the girls patrolled back and forth between the remaining two sides. They did not sight him.

They returned to the room late at night in the company of Joseph who, having secured the same room for a slightly lower price, went back to the temple to retrieve them. The room was 8 feet by 10 feet so they had two reasons to spend a restless night: they had little room to stretch out, and son and sibling was missing.

When they began again the next morning, they split the children into groups to aid in the search, something they would not have done had the situation not been so desperate. They had lived all their lives in Nazareth and so knew few people in the city - it did not take long to canvas them to see if perchance Jesus had come to them. They were then reduced to simply wandering the streets looking for him, with frequent stops at the temple to see if he might have turned up there.

At day's end their efforts had been fruitless. They had no more idea about where Jesus was than they had two nights before at the oasis. By prearrangement they were to meet at sundown at the temple to pray.

Joseph, who had been searching by himself, and James and Simon were the first to arrive. They fell in exhaustion on the steps in front of the east entrance to wait for the others. They were tired and hungry since they had not the funds to buy more than one meal a day, and they had decided to have that meal in the morning. James was about to accost his father with the possibility of buying some food when they were accosted by a former customer of Joseph's. He was a large, bluff man, with a full beard hanging nearly to his waist, very thick eyebrows mounted atop huge, brown eyes that seemed to dance across his faith in their mirth. He was fully a head taller than Joseph, and much darker of complexion. He advanced to Joseph and embraced him with two huge, hairy arms, just as Joseph was standing up to greet him. He was so jolly that it was easy to forget that he was a dedicated member of the Zealots.

"Are you not Joseph, the carpenter of Nazareth? Of course you are! I never forget a face. You remember me, of course? While passing through Nazareth last year I hired you to fix my wagon. You did an excellent job - I am still using it in that condition today." Joseph could remember the man vaguely, but could not recall his name. Fortunately, he would have time to consider it. "It is beastly hot, is it not? I am sweltering. Ha ha, but there is nothing like the end of the day on the steps of the temple, is there? Presently we will thank God for this hot day and for the privilege of having been alive to enjoy it. Why have you not left the city to return to your home, Joseph? It cannot be inexpensive to stay here in the city now that the census is over. Where are your rooms? Surely you have found someone who will keep you for a reasonable sum. A relative perhaps, or another satisfied customer such as I? I cannot think what we are coming to when one must pay three denarii for the use of little more than a cell. But I would have thought that you would have left yesterday with the caravan that headed north, thereby pointing yourself towards Nazareth while in the safety of a large company. You remember my son Ananias?" he said, indicating a small boy, about James' size, standing next to him.

Here there was a brief pause in the torrent of words from the man, and Joseph took the advantage of the situation.

"I thank you for your kind words. We are only here because we seem to have lost our oldest. I..."

"Lost him have you? Let me tell you, there is no worse feeling in the world than realizing that you have managed to let one of the children get away. We lost young Ananias once, but only for a few hours."

"We have been searching for Jesus these two days, and it begins to look as though he is not in the city. Oh, and yes, I remember your son. He is a very serious boy, as I recall."

"Yes, he is that. I believe that one day he might follow me into the church. But he is a good boy, and I am proud of him. You will no doubt be delighted to hear that I shall soon be coming to Nazareth in another caravan. I shall make it a point to stop and see you. Are you still in the same situation? Looking for the eldest, you say? What happened? Did you not know that he was missing at the time of departure? Well, God save the boy, and devil take the Romans."

Joseph had listened to this monologue with a bemused smile. The man could talk a long time while saying very little, but Joseph had taken a liking to him the previous year, he remembered, because it appeared that the man had an endless supply of good will which he was careful to share with all those about him. It was the perfect mask for the Zealotry for which the man was well known, and, no doubt, his ticket to his position on the Sanhedrin.

As he and Joseph talked, the man's equally outgoing son sidled up to James, who had sat on the steps out of exhaustion, and who appeared to be close to his age, and sat down. He was small for his age, with a thin face and prominent nose dividing two close set, light gray eyes from one another. He had a jutting chin which looked as though it could not stand to be confused with the rest of the face, and a large mouth which took care not to waste any of the space on that chin, and which was blessed with an easy and pleasant smile. It was a mouth that he was not afraid to use.

"I am Ananias," he announced to James, who had given up standing by his father's side waiting to be introduced, "son of Ananas. What is your name?"

"I am James, son of Joseph, and this is my youngest brother Simon." Simon was asleep, stretched out lengthwise on the step.

"Who is it that is missing? An elder brother?"

"My brother Jesus, whom we have not seen since two days ago."

"Well, he will turn up. Have faith in God. You are from Nazareth?"

"Yes my father is a carpenter there."

"How do you like the city of David?"

"Very well. It is possible that I may come to live here myself when I am of age. There is little to do in Nazareth for those who are not the first born."

"It is the center of the Hebrew universe. Here are all the Scribes, the Pharisees, the Sanhedrin, the books of scripture - all that can matter in the life of the faithful. It is sad that there are so many who do not appreciate the things they have around them every day. I hope you would not be coming here for the sake of making money."

"That would be part of my goal. However much I may like worshipping at the temple, I must eat and I must feed my family."

"You will come to see that there is so much more to life than feeding and clothing and shelter. There is the knowledge and understanding to be gained from the study of the scriptures, the peace that comes from knowing God, and the calm that comes from having obeyed the law."

"That is all very well," said James, somewhat amazed at the religious focus of so young a boy, "but it is still true that the basics must come first."

"Then we differ only in what it is that we choose to call the basics," said Ananias. "What do we feed first? The soul or the stomach?"

"You see," they heard Ananas say, "he is a boy of serious bent. I should not be surprised to see him at the head of the Sanhedrin one day. How many twelve year old boys can debate what to feed first?" James and Ananias had not noticed that the two men had ceased talking momentarily to look at them, and happened to overhear the last of their conversation.

"It may surprise you to know that my eldest, Jesus, is very knowledgeable in the laws and the history of the Hebrews," said Joseph, attempting to keep the conversation alive.

"The one who is missing? Well, well, good for him. Let us hope that he is as knowledgeable at finding his way home and being more careful not to annoy his father."

Joseph felt he ought to take umbrage at this, but he could not deny the essential truth of it: Jesus was missing, and he was mature enough that he should not have allowed it to happen.

"Well Joseph the carpenter, I must be off. I will listen for news of your Jesus, and send word if I hear of anything. Meanwhile keep faith that God is looking after him, wherever he is. Come Ananias. Your mother will pitch me into the streets if we are not home by dark." As they departed, he said to his son, "It looks as though you may have found a new friend."

"Yes, it may be," said Ananias. "He is smart, and will make an interesting project."

The rest of Joseph's family straggled in over the next few minutes, all as tired and hungry as Joseph and the two boys. Joseph took stock.

"No news, eh? Well, there is little else we can do this night. Let us sleep and try again tomorrow."

"Father, how long will we continue to search for him?" asked Judah, the nine year old third son of Joseph and Mary.

"We will search for him until he is either restored to us, or we know what happened to him. He is one of us, and we will not abandon him." He said it without anger, but only tired resignation at the task still to be faced. Yet he said it with such conviction that no one thought to argue with him. They descended the steps of the temple, and made their way back through the dark, silent streets to their room, where they dined again on their travel fare of bread and dried meat.

After sleeping only a little better, they were all up early the next morning to begin again. Joseph decreed that they would meet at the temple at midday to assess what they had found out, and what to do next. Then they set out, divided as before, to scour the city for Jesus.

The air was hot and dry even at this hour of the morning. Dust swirled in the streets, riding on the zephyrs that twisted in and out from among the buildings. James and Simon set out into the eastern quarter of the city, south of the temple. They walked back and forth among the houses, the bazaars, the food cooking in the street, asking the merchants and dwellers if they had seen a twelve year old boy answering to the name of Jesus. None had. They followed the narrow, dark alleys that sometimes led behind the houses, ducked under the archways that occasionally crossed the streets, and followed the stairs that led on to the roofs of some houses. Once they found themselves on the perimeter wall of the city, and were immediately sent off by the Roman guards. Just as they stepped back on to the street they came across their new acquaintance.

"James! Simon. It is I. I was hoping that I might run into you during your searches," said Ananias.

"You wish to help look for my brother?" asked James, incredulously.

"Yes," said Ananias. "He is one of our people, is he not? Why should I not look for him? Better for us to find him than the Romans."

"What would the Romans do?" asked James.

"Maybe nothing, maybe the worst. You are not from the city where the Romans control our lives. There are not so many Romans in Nazareth. If they did not like Jesus, or he said the wrong thing in front of them, it is likely that you would never see him again. The Romans are proud of their laws and their civilization, but these things are not meant for the Hebrews."

The three boys continued on their way down the street, wending their way down the side streets and alleys that made up the city, slowly making their way back to the temple. James was glad of the company of Ananias, who knew every nook and cranny of the city, and who was not shy about asking people he did not know whether or not they had heard or seen anything of a strange boy named Jesus.

So narrow were the streets that, when the boys emerged into the courtyard of the temple they were momentarily blinded by the bright sunlight reflecting off of the gold and white stone of the temple. The nearly windowless walls of the city gave way to the magnificent open spaces leading up to the high gate of the temple. They left behind the dingy existence of the masses and approached the splendor of the temple that the taxes collected from the masses had built.

It was far and away the largest structure in Jerusalem, built - or being built - by Herod, who was serving the Romans as the titular king of Judea, to satisfy his own vanity, and, possibly, to ingratiate himself with the Jewish people. It stood just inside the northeast wall of the city, and was encircled by a colonnade. Within the colonnade were the courtyards, and in the midst of the courtyards, forming the crosspiece of a "T", was the temple itself.

The three boys entered through the High Gate and approached the stairs leading up to the west front of the temple - the appointed meeting place for the family. There they found that they were the last to arrive - all the other members of the family had already arrived and were waiting for them. All were tired, hungry, and discouraged.

They compared notes ever so briefly - there was little to report but failure - and then went inside the temple to pray. In contrast to the madhouse of dealers, sellers, middlemen, hucksters, beggars and thieves in the courtyards, the interior of the temple was relatively quiet, though it too was thronged with people.

There were people praying on their own in various poses, some meant to impress the other supplicants, others meant to impress only God. There was all manner of dress, from the wealthy in their colorful silks and linens to the poorest dressed only in the wool they made for themselves sheared from their own flocks. There were also members of the temple priesthood in their black robes bustling about on business or talking to the faithful wandering about. Near a column off to one side of the temple opposite his own family, James noticed a small knot of men being taught by what looked like a small or young man, but before he could observe further he was admonished by his father to keep up with the rest of the family. He attempted to look through and around the people between himself and the small group of men to see who the teacher was - his interest was piqued by the apparent young age of the man - but he could not get a clear look at the scene.

Joseph chose a spot in the middle of the temple floor where there were few other people standing at that moment, allowing the clan to lay claim to it, and began to lead the family in prayer. James' attention wandered now and then, and during a pause in the prayer he stole a glance toward the young teacher, and let out an audible gasp.

"James! Have you no respect for prayer? Have I not taught you that...." began Joseph.

"Father! There is Jesus!" said James in an excited voice, loud enough for the immediate passers by to hear. Needless to say they did, and looked in the direction of James' pointed finger, even though none would know Jesus. Joseph looked to where James was pointing, and saw that the young teacher was indeed his oldest son. His face betrayed his anger and relief as he began to make his way to where Jesus was standing. Mary also let out a sigh, but it was one of unrelieved joy, and, after hugging James, began to run to where Jesus was standing. The rest of the family followed. The other children in the family ran screaming in that direction until they were pulled up short by the stern visages of the men to whom Jesus was talking.

They approached Jesus from the side, so that at first he did not see them coming. His dark brown, wavy hair had just been trimmed, and revealed clearly the shape of his head. His dark brown eyes were averted as they approached, but his prominent nose, full lips and strong chin gave him a handsome profile. He was small for a twelve year old, though the others who were larger than he rarely seemed to take advantage of this fact. When he noticed the bustle he turned to look at them, but showed no sign of emotion, no relief at being found, and even, James thought, no sense that he had caused the rest of the family any trouble. Jesus simply looked from his mother to his father expectantly, as though he could not fathom what it was that they wanted.

Joseph could not speak immediately, since his first inclination was to admonish Jesus, which he did not want to do in front of the elders of the temple gathered there, and since he could not tell exactly what it was that Jesus had been doing in their midst. Thus Mary spoke first.

"Son, where have you been? Did you not know that we have been seeking you, sorrowing after you for three days?"

Jesus was unperturbed, James thought. "Why did you seek me?" he asked. "Did you not know that I must be about my Father's business?" James now expected an outburst from his father, knowing full well that Jesus could hardly be about the business of carpentry talking to men in the temple. But, and this somewhat to his disappointment, there was none forthcoming. Joseph and Mary only stared, and, it seemed to James, they appeared to understand what it was that he was saying to them. There was a moment of embarrassed silence while the family stared at Jesus and he looked back at them, as though expecting them to grasp what he had said, but this silence was broken by one of the elders, a thin white bearded man of sharp gray eyes, sitting on the floor near Jesus.

"You are to be proud of this son. He is brilliant in his interpretation of the laws, and well beyond his years in his understanding of the true meaning of the scripture. He appears to be more hopeful for the coming of the Messiah than we, but in all other ways he is to be commended."

This James could not fathom. While they had all studied the scripture at the feet of their father in the evenings in Nazareth, none were known as gifted scholars on the subject, and Jesus, it seemed to him, had shown rather less interest in the subject than some of the others. What was more, Joseph and Mary looked at the man with knowing eyes, as though they had some way of knowing what he said to be true. They thanked him profusely and then led Jesus away.

No one spoke until they were a short distance away from the elders, and, they assumed, out of earshot. There Mary broke into tears, and all members of the family hugged and kissed Jesus as though he had been missing for years, not days. He was glad to see them as well, and returned their affectionate embraces.

There were cries from the children of "Where have you been?" and "We've been looking for you everywhere" and "I saw him first" and "You did not - James did", and amid the cacophony from the children the voice of Joseph, demanding to know what Jesus had been about.

"We have spent three days looking for you," he said, in a voice that was not loud enough for those nearby to hear, but loud enough to convey his message to Jesus and to the rest of the family. "It has cost us time, money, and heartache. There was no reason why you should not have left Jerusalem with us at the appointed time...Quiet, you others - this is not the business of the entire temple... no reason for you not to send word of your whereabouts, no reason at all why we should have had to tolerate any of the last three days."

Jesus looked at Mary as though he expected her to mount the defense for his actions, but she, through tears of relief, only looked at him with a mixture of confidence and concern. He then said to Joseph:

"It is time that I begin to prepare for the purpose for which I was brought into the world." This brought no clarification for the rest of the family, and Joseph only glanced over at Mary to see whether she understood what he was talking about. It was clear that she did not. And yet, James thought, the response did not surprise them as it should have done. It seemed to him that Mary and Joseph were not surprised by the response, merely puzzled.

"Does this mean that you do not intend to follow me into my business as a carpenter, after all the time I have spent teaching you the trade? Is there some other line of work that you think you are more suited for? I have been teaching you because it is the right of the eldest to inherit the family business, but if you think that you have other plans at your ripe old age, then I can surely begin to train one of your brothers."

"I am learning carpentry, but it is not the purpose for which I was sent," Jesus answered, unperturbed.

"What is the purpose for which you were sent? To teach the elders in the temple the things they already know so well? Remember that they complimented you as a child - you will not always be so impressive. When you are grown and accountable for your own income, they will not pay you to say the things that were impressive coming from the mouth of a twelve year old boy." Joseph was confused. "What would you be - a teacher in the temple?"

"There are many who are in need of teaching, but the elders most among them. The Scribes, the Pharisees, the Sanhedrin - all these are established to protect the image of God with the people, but it is not the image of God that is in need of help. They cry for obedience before the law, but they do not comprehend the real meaning of the law."

"Do not comprehend!" Joseph began, his anger rising. "They have devoted their lives to the study of the scripture. How is it that they do not comprehend?"

"It is one thing to know the law, another to obey it, and still another to understand it. While they may know and obey it to the letter, they do not understand its purpose. I may write beautiful letters that are admired by all, but if I cannot form them into words that will educate those in my charge, then the beauty is for naught. Likewise, if I pray but the words come from an empty heart, then the prayer is useless and will go unheeded." Jesus said all this with a calmness that astounded James, since it appeared that Jesus did not understand the amount of trouble he was in. Joseph was apoplectic.

"Are you presuming to know which prayers will be heard in heaven and which will not? This is beyond endurance! We will discuss this matter more later. Let us get our belongings and begin the journey home - again."

Mary, not wanting to contribute to the public scene, had said nothing in the temple, but Joseph demanded her opinion once they had departed the city gate later in the afternoon. They were a few minutes only outside the gate, amidst the usual crowd of people coming and going from the largest city in the area, and just breaking clear on the road that would eventually lead them to Nazareth. There was no caravan departure on this day, and they would have to risk the trip by themselves, unless they could either catch up to, or be caught by, other travelers like themselves. Joseph and Mary were ahead of the children on the road, and Joseph looked back to see that all of the children were still with them. He saw Jesus walking in the rear by himself, looking at Joseph. Joseph turned his kindly yet troubled eyes toward Mary and asked:

"What am I to do with Jesus? Three days missing, three wasted days of expense and headache, and he does not even appear to realize that he has done anything wrong. Wait! And where has he been? I was so taken with his odd brand of teachings that I forgot to ask where he has been for the last three days. We have searched the city top to bottom and did not find him. Where could he have been that entire time?"

Mary was walking beside Joseph since the single donkey was loaded with supplies for the journey home and for business once they got there. She turned to him, smiling, and said: "He is well, and that will have to suffice for now. The truth will come to us in time, and you know that it is not good that we should test him too stridently."

"I no longer know what it is that I know about him," Joseph replied. "That he is a special child is undeniable. That he may be gifted beyond what we can know may also be true. None of that changes the fact that we just wasted three days looking for him, and that he made no effort to find us or to allay our fears."

"Trust God. It will all come to us as it should."

"You are right, as always. I will put it out of my mind for now. But we must watch the other children. They will not understand why Jesus is not punished for this." Pause, and then again with feeling: "And rightly not. He should not have disappeared for three days."

Behind him the children walked together, and took turns pillorying Jesus for the absence and the headaches it caused them all. James, being the next eldest, was by default allowed to go first.

"But where were you for three days?" he began testily. "It is not so large a city that we should have no word of you for three days while doing nothing other than searching for you. You must have been hiding to ensure that we would not find you. It is certain that you were not in the temple the entire time because we came there many times."

"I was within the walls of the city," Jesus answered, patiently. "I never left. I spent the time with the elders of the temple, discussing the law and the prophecies with regard to the coming of the Messiah, among other things."

"The coming of the Messiah!" James answered loudly. "How do you know so much about that? We have heard only parts of the story and the prophecies from father. It is not sensible that you should be able to discuss the matter with the elders. It may be that they were simply patronizing you."

"They were not," Jesus answered calmly, showing no emotion.

"And you are so sure, are you? It must be very comforting to know so much without ever having been taught," said James sarcastically.

"Knowledge may come from many sources," Jesus said, continuing to walk while looking at the ground in front of him. "It may come from the books that one reads, but it may also come on the wind as a gift from the Father. The elders have read all of the books, but they have understood none of them."

"And now you will tell us that the elders do not know what they ought to know - you, the twelve year old boy who has learned his scripture at the knee of a carpenter," said James, still testy at the effrontery of his brother. "You had best be cautious. God will not appreciate your elevating yourself in his eyes and at the expense of the elders."

Here Joses, the third oldest, fortunate to have his mother's eyes and his father's thick black hair, and the lightest complexion, joined the chorus. "But you see that even father does not punish him."

"That is true," said James. "As always, there are no consequences for Jesus' acts."

Judah, the fourth of the five boys, could not get over what he considered the central issue. "But where were you?" he asked again.

All of the brothers paused expectantly to hear the answer this time, so if Jesus had any plans to skip around the issue he quickly abandoned them.

"I was at the home of the high priest Gershim the first night, at the home of the elder Josiah the second, and would have spent this night at the home of Ananus had you not found me."

"What?" asked James, thunderstruck. "You planned to spend this night at the home of Ananus? We met him in the temple yesterday, and he did not mention that he knew you. In fact, he said he did not, but that he would help us look for you. When was this arrangement made?"

"Only last evening," said Jesus, "after he had heard me teaching in the temple yesterday."

"But that means that he made little effort to contact us after he had found you, when he promised that he would keep an eye out for you and report any findings to us." James puzzled over this news for a moment. "Why, I cannot understand it. Why would he not come and tell us the good news?" Realizing that he had just paid his elder brother, whom he was attempting to upbraid, an off hand compliment, he looked suddenly up. Jesus was looking him in the eye, and smiling in an understanding, conspiratorial sort of way. Embarrassed, James left the childish enclave and ran ahead to report to his father.

In answer to the implications of Jesus' revelation, Joseph could only say "Perhaps he was looking for us to tell us when we found him.

Perhaps he simply wanted to hear Jesus talk, and would have contacted us sometime later. There is no way to know. Put it behind you, for there is nothing we can do about it. Perhaps when I am nearer to my deathbed I shall ask him what was meant by these actions." James continued to walk with Mary and Joseph for the time being, attempting to work out in his mind what could be the reason for Ananus deceiving them in this manner. The other brothers, more lighthearted than the serious minded James, continued to taunt Jesus, wish for his punishment, and demand to know why he did not take them with him on his adventure.

After a few minutes James sidled back to the others and, in a break in the childish banter, said to Jesus: "Did you meet Ananias?"

"I did," said Jesus.

"What did you think of him?"

"He is smart and observant, but, alas, he will grow like the others, and be dazzled by the letter of the law. He will not understand what is meant by it, and he will not be able to apply it to the lives of the people who look to him for guidance."

Once again James was incredulous. "That is much to have learned in so short a time. How did you do it?"

"His eyes are cold and hard. Already he does not see the people around him as children of God, but as objects for him to bully into obeying the law. He will rise quickly in the service of the church, but he will be popular with his brethren on the councils, and not with the people."

James was amazed at this display of apparent knowledge on the part of Jesus, particularly since it appeared that Jesus had spent less time with Ananias than he had. He could not judge the accuracy of Jesus' comments, except to say that Ananias had seemed very pleasant and very faithful to him, and he looked forward to seeing him again.

CHAPTER 2

There was a steady wind blowing out of the west, which meant that, as designed, it swept through the carpentry shop of Joseph. The shop faced east, but it was open on three sides to take advantage of the prevailing winds. The weather in the area was much too hot for working indoors, though Joseph was forced to do some of his finishing work there because of the blowing dust and sand.

The shop was attached to the house where Joseph kept his family, but consisted of little more than a wood and straw roof supported by wooden pillars, without walls and with only a dirt floor. There were canvas "walls" rolled up and tied to the roof, which canvas could be lowered in case of the very rare rain or heavier winds. On this day the walls were up, and the shop open to the elements.

Joseph was not there, being out delivering an ornate chair made for the local rabbi. He delivered only to certain customers, it being to his advantage to simply wait for them to come to his shop to collect their merchandise. In that way they would not receive the product they contracted for without first paying their money. He delivered to the rabbi because he was a personal friend, because he trusted the rabbi to be able to pay, and because he liked to have his wares available for viewing in the rabbi's much frequented house.

While he was out, Jesus and James were working in the shop: Jesus completing another, simpler chair for a poorer customer, and James a small sled that could be dragged by a donkey. Jesus had an aptitude for carpentry, and worked faster and with surer hands than his brother, who had come to the trade late and so was still learning some of the basic skills that Jesus had been taught as a young boy. They worked at opposite ends of the outdoor shop, which was no more than twenty feet across, their robed but cloakless backs to each other, and for the last few moments, after some desultory conversation, they had been silent.

Suddenly there was a cry from James, and Jesus turned to look at him. "What is the matter, brother?" he asked, finding James clutching one hand with the other, apparently attempting to staunch the flow of blood.

"The knife slipped and scraped my thumb," James answered testily.

Jesus took several small steps across the small room to examine the patient, saw that the wound was relatively minor, and asked "Is there something that you would like me to get for you? You will need some water and a cloth to wash and cover it with."

"Thank you, that will not be necessary. It is only a small wound, and the bandages would get in the way of completing the work."

"You are a durable man, James," said Jesus. "You will make an excellent carpenter."

This comment rubbed against James the wrong way, and brought to the surface a resentment he had been harboring for a long time. "I have no wish to be an excellent carpenter," said he to Jesus, angrily but without raising his voice to ensure that their mother did not hear. Jesus looked at him sympathetically, but said nothing.

"It is you who was to be the carpenter, not I. I have always hoped to leave Nazareth and find my way in Jerusalem, but because you have shown so little interest in our father's business, he has been compelled to keep me here as well."

Jesus replied quietly and gravely. "I will be about my father's business soon, James. It is nearly time."

Both brothers had turned from their work and were now facing each other: Jesus with his hands reaching out toward James, and James standing with his arms akimbo. "It has been time these many years, Jesus. You should have taken the lead from our aged father long ago, yet you continue to dissipate around his shop without taking responsibility for it. You work on those chores which suit you, and leave the larger jobs to us."

"James," said Jesus, "you will remember that I said at age 12, when you thought me lost, that I must be about my father's business, and you expressed some doubt that I would have any business that would be related to the temple. Soon I will embark on the business for which I was brought into the world by my father."

"But why do you delay?" asked James, as he began to pace the floor in front of Jesus, increasingly agitated. "Why have you waited so long that I was forced to become a carpenter as well? Why could you not have made this decision years ago? You are now in your thirtieth year, and I am in my 29th. We are both late to be getting started in the business of life." Both were by now full bearded, though Jesus had lighter hair and beard than his brother. There were a few flecks of gray in the beard of James, even though Jesus, who was a year older, had none. James's large eyes were serious, intuitive, believing, particularly in the God of his fathers.

"I am not my own master, James. I exist to fulfill the will of my father," said Jesus, to the uncomprehending James.

"Our father has also been wondering why you have not made more progress in carpentry," replied James. "It will surprise him to learn that you have been delaying because he wanted you to do so."

"All will be made clear to you, brother, in good time. Have faith in me, your brother, that what I am to do I must do, and there is no other course available to me."

"Why should I need to have faith in you?" replied the exasperated James. "You act as though you are about to begin a mission that I would not understand - that I would not be able to believe was worthy of you. Your business is to be that of our father's carpenter shop, is it not? The only question for which I need faith is that which asks when you will finally begin."

Jesus looked at his brother with a sympathy and then sadness stealing across his face. "James," said he, after a pause while he gathered his thoughts, "James my dear brother, there is nothing more I can say to you at this moment. It is not yet the time for me to begin my ministry." He moved closer to James, putting his hands on James' upper arms, and smiling a pleading smile. "Please give your brother the faith that you owe him, and it will all be made clear to you."

James looked at his brother for a moment, before the implication of Jesus' last remark struck him. "Ministry? What ministry? Do you now say that you will not be a carpenter?" This was a frightening prospect for James, who, if Jesus did not go into the family business, would have to become the carpenter, which trade would probably trap him in Nazareth for the rest of his life.

Seeing that James would not comprehend, Jesus shook his head sadly, released him and walked back across the floor to where he had been working. His back was to James only for a moment, and then he turned again. "My ministry will be to the lost, the poor, the abandoned, the sick, the blind, the halt, the lame - all those in need of the comfort of God," said he, firmly but quietly.

"You intend to become a teacher?" asked James incredulously. "Why? What have you to offer? I have studied more diligently than you, yet I do not feel qualified to teach others. I am familiar with the Law of Moses, with the history of our people, with our hopes for the coming of the Messiah, yet I know that the elders are more qualified than I to teach. Why do you think you can do better?"

"I bring understanding - fulfillment of the law," replied Jesus calmly, in contrast to the steadily rising tones of James.

James was now beside himself. "You bring fulfillment? How can this be? What do you know of how the law will be fulfilled? How can you know when the Messiah will come? Even the High Priest does not know this. No one knows. What understanding do you have that others do not? And from whence does it come?"

"All will be made clear to you, brother."

"Again with this!" James was shouting now. "I want it made clear to me now. I am about to be trapped into becoming a carpenter, instead of going to Jerusalem to study with the elders as I would like, because my older brother believes he is a better preacher than he is a carpenter! This is the same elder brother who has trained all his life to be a carpenter, and has no training whatever as a preacher! Please tell me no more that 'all will be made clear to me.' Make it clear to me now!" James had forgotten all about he and Jesus long standing agreement that they would not disagree when their mother was present, and his voice could be heard in the street in front of the shop. It could also be heard in the adjoining house, and, as they had always feared, their mother heard. She came walking purposefully into the shop, dressed in a light blue robe, her long, dark brown but heavily grayed hair uncovered, and, at the moment, unkempt.

"What are my sons fighting about?" she asked, in her usual kindly manner, tinged with a firmness that gave both sons reason to believe that she would accept no less than the complete truth. Jesus stood facing his mother but said nothing. The enraged James turned his back on her, put his hands on the waist high work bench in front of him, and waited. Mary looked from one to the other, not caring who told her what she wanted to know, but it was obvious that neither was about to. "What are my sons fighting about?" she demanded again, this time louder and more firmly than before.

James wheeled around quickly, fire in his eyes. "I have just discovered that my plans for the rest of my life will not come to fruition because my older brother believes he will be a better preacher than he will a carpenter," said he, angrily and sarcastically.

Mary turned and walked the few steps to where Jesus stood, his hands clasped in front of him. "This is to be your father's business?" she asked calmly, and without reproach.

"It is," Jesus replied quietly. She regarded him for a moment, looking up into his eyes, searching from one to the other, possibly in hopes of answering some long held question.

She then turned slowly and walked back across the room to James, who still stood by his work bench, though he had turned around and his arms were now crossed in front of him. Her head was lowered, as though to study the dirt floor as she crossed it. She stopped in front of him, and slowly raised her eyes to his. She spoke pleadingly and apologetically.

"James, we must accept the will of God. I...I have never made all clear to you...your father and I have not explained." Here her voice tailed off, and she looked down at the floor again.

James was angrier than ever. "It appears that nothing has been made clear to me, and that nothing will be made clear to me! I am to remain in the dark all my life! But I will try again. I had no luck with my brother, maybe I will with my mother. Mother: what have you not made clear to me?"

Tears welled up in Mary's eyes as she looked up at James again, and she opened her mouth to speak, but she could not. She turned to run past

James into the house, but he sidestepped and got between her and the door that led to the house. "No, mother. Tell me what it is that you have never made clear to me. I tire of things around me, especially in my own family, not being clear."

"James," Mary said, as she began to cry in earnest, "do you block the way of your mother?"

James clenched his teeth in rage, and breathed heavily in an attempt to control his temper. He was so angry he could not organize his thoughts to speak, and he could not defy his mother. He pounded his right fist into the palm of his left hand in rage, turned and ran from the shop out into and down the street, eventually to disappear around a corner. Mary turned in the door to look at Jesus with a mixture of love and reproach in her eyes, said only "So difficult....so difficult," and then turned slowly and went back into the house.

After rounding the corner to get out of sight of his home James stopped running, partly because some of his anger was spent, and partly because he was winded. He continued walking down the street, now and then kicking the dust when some particularly injurious point occurred to him. As he walked he heard his name being called.

"James, James! Over here!" He looked up to see his friend Ananias, in company with his father and a small group of servants entering town from the east. His mood immediately brightened.

"Ananias. You are a sight for troubled eyes. Greetings to your father and to you." Ananias was now a large man like his father, though not as bulky, probably three inches taller than James and much more muscular. He kept his curly hair trimmed to some degree because he claimed that it made him hot, but his beard now reached midway down his chest, covering his prominent chin. His gray eyes danced as always, seemingly delighted with everything that passed in front of them.

"Greetings, James, to you and your family," said Ananus. He had of course grown no taller, but he was now rounder than when he had first met Joseph and his family outside the temple so many years ago. He seemed to be a little rounder even than the last time James had seen him, three months before. His hair and beard were now gray, and he appeared to be a bit stooped in his posture, but he was as merry and conversive as ever. "We have come from Capernaum, and are on our way to back to Jerusalem. It is good to see you again. I trust that God has been good to you?"

"That he has," answered James.

"Then what is this talk of troubled eyes?" asked Ananias.

"It is a minor family matter, and not important enough to trouble good friends with," answered James.

"I am prepared to wager that it has to do with your elder brother," offered Ananias, who knew of the occasional problems that James had with his brother. "What is it this time? More preaching?"

"It is a matter of preaching, and let us leave it at that," said James, with an air of resignation.

"We are on our way to your house, as we would not pass this way without greeting your family," said Ananus, seeing that the conversation over James's troubles would go no further. "They are all well, I take it?"

"They are," said James, "and they will be glad to see you. Let us hurry there, if you have no other business, so that my mother may prepare extra places at table." James began to climb on to one of the wagons being pulled by the oxen, but before he could do so Ananias jumped down from his donkey and began to walk with James.

"James, have you heard the news? My father is to be appointed High Priest in Jerusalem! It is the greatest honor that could come to a man."

"I am happy for you, Ananias. It is a great honor, indeed. This should do no harm to your own hopes of being High Priest some day."

"Certainly not. There can never be any harm in having relatives in the right places when one is in need of an important appointment. Let us hope that God gives him - and me, if I am to have the chance - the wisdom to preside wisely."

"He has already done so, Ananias, he has already done so."

"You and I have spent many hours studying the scripture together, James, and my father is aware of your knowledge and your character. Perhaps he will be able to secure a position for you there. It would not lead to your becoming High Priest, of course, but it would make a comfortable living and free you for more study."

James's eyes brightened at this prospect, if only briefly. He had wanted to live in Jerusalem since his first trip there long ago, and to be able to live there and devote himself to the study of the scripture would be the ideal existence. But his brow clouded over quickly, when he thought of the recent debate with his brother and his mother's reaction to it.

"Nothing would please me more, my friend," he said to Ananias, "and for you to have thought of me in this manner is more kindness than I can thank you for. But it does not seem likely for me. My brother Jesus means to become a preacher, and if he does so I will have to be the family carpenter."

"So that is the nature of the problem with your brother. You see how skillfully I wormed it out of you, and without even trying. So, Jesus wishes to preach." He paused here, absorbing the information. "What does he propose to teach?"

"I do not know. We did not get to that point. I believe that he is orthodox in his views, though it seems to me he is very optimistic about the

22

coming of the Messiah. But he may have a gift for it; you will remember what I told you about what he was doing when we left him in Jerusalem the time that you and I first met. Some of the elders appeared to be enthralled with him."

"It is unusual to hear any boy preach competently. They must have been patronizing him for that reason."

"Possibly," James replied, "at least that is what my father thought. There is no way to know. But it doesn't matter. He believes he can do it, and appears determined to do so. That will leave me with the carpentry shop, and force me to turn down your offer." Re-stating his dilemma irritated James again, and he let go with a rare oath.

"James! I have never heard you talk so. Well, well. There seems little that can be done if Jesus is determined. Have you not spoken to your father about Jesus' responsibilities? Can you expect any help from that quarter?"

"I have only just learned of his intentions, though I suspected all along that he would never take up the tools of the carpentry trade. I will talk to father, but I hate the thought of going to him behind Jesus' back."

"Here is another idea, James, but if you do not approve of it, say nothing to anyone and it will go away." Here Ananias lowered his voice to a conspiratorial tone, though there was enough traffic in the street that even James could barely hear him. "I could persuade my father to look for a position for you immediately, and, once the offer is made to you, your father will have to keep Jesus home to work in the shop so that you may go to Jerusalem to make the family proud of you."

"This scheme may work, Ananias, but it is devious. I will have to give it some thought."

By this time they had reached Joseph's house. The arrival of an entourage like that of Ananus and his son in a sleepy town like Nazareth does not go unnoticed, and they found that James' entire household was gathered in front of the house waiting for them. Greetings were exchanged, invitations to dinner extended and gratefully accepted, and the men settled down to talk while Jesus' mother prepared the repast. James glanced at Jesus and his mother once or twice, to see if he could determine what the result was from their clash of only a few moments ago, but he could see nothing. Indeed, it seemed to him that Jesus was making a particular effort to put the difference between them in the past. He spoke glowingly of James's progress in the study of the scriptures, made no mention of the incident in the shop, and expressed delight at Ananias announcement that his father would be High Priest and that he might be able to find a position there for James, since James, not being the eldest son, would have to find his own way in the world.

This suggestion caught James by surprise, but he was glad to have the issue in the open.

Joseph was happy that his son should have this kind of attention from the High Priest, but he made no commitment on James's behalf.

After the meal, Ananus and his son began their preparations for departure. They had decided to stay in Nazareth for the night, given the late hour, but there was simply no room for them in Joseph's small house. As they walked outside to go to the only inn in Nazareth, Ananus said to Joseph, "Remember, Joseph, my offer for James. He is learned in the scriptures, and should come to Jerusalem to continue his studies with Ananias."

"It is a princely offer, Ananus, and we are very grateful. But we will have to consider it more fully," replied Joseph. This was not the best answer that James could have heard, but it gave him some hope that an arrangement might be worked out. He had no desire to defy the wishes of his father, but that was a course that would have to be considered.

When the High Priest and his retinue had left, it was late evening. The heat of the day had dissipated, and it was cool enough that Joseph and the remaining two of his sons could sit down in the house to discuss the matter. Joseph would have insisted on as much anyway, since he hated to give any outsiders a chance to overhear family discussions. They sat on the floor where they had just eaten, facing each other. The room was dark save for the light of three oil lamps.

"Now," began Joseph, "we must decide what it is we are going to do about the carpentry business. I am an old man now, and it is time that I handed it over to one of my sons. Three of them I have already sent into the world on their own, thinking the succession to my own business secure. Now only my two eldest are left. In our tradition, it is the eldest that inherits. Jesus: are you ready yet to take up what I have built?"

Jesus looked Joseph in the eye and said to him, "You know that I must be about my father's business."

At this Joseph hung his head in disappointment, but he said nothing immediately. James sat silently as well, not wanting to rush the proceedings and make himself look selfish and greedy. Still, he was shocked to hear Jesus talk of taking up his father's business when he was in the room with his father and plainly had no intention of taking up his father's business. But this aspect of Jesus' comment appeared to have no effect on Joseph. He turned to James and said:

"What of you James? It is true that you are learned in the scriptures and deserve the chance to go to Jerusalem to study, but there must be someone here to keep the business going. Jesus has had his say. What is yours?"

"Father," James replied earnestly, "you know that I have always done your will. That is why I am still at home at my advanced age - I wanted to see that your business would have someone here to manage it when you are gone. Yet as you say it is not likely that I will have another chance such as this one, and it is my desire to go to Jerusalem to study."

Joseph sighed heavily at this, evidently anticipating the difficult decision that he would have to make. With a faint, resigned laugh he observed, "Have I produced such a poor family business that not even one of my sons desires it? My three youngest I have already given permission to seek their fortune, thinking that one of my two eldest would inherit my trade. And now the time is here, and neither of them wants to do so."

Jesus said nothing. James said, "It is your decision, father. I will yield to your wishes." There was a tense silence for a moment, as neither brother attempted to press his case. James did note that Jesus did not appear worried about the outcome of the discussion as he was - almost as though he would go his own way no matter what Joseph said. Joseph shifted his position on his cushion, as though doing so would aid in his decision making. It did not.

"The two of you are adamant, then. I must choose a career for both of my oldest sons, not merely the first." Pause. Then, with a worn voice, "It is thankful that I did not build some less respectable trade or you both would have fled from home by now." Another pause, another shift on the cushions. "Well, I cannot solve it at this moment. The question merely races around my brain without bothering to count the laps. I do not want to disappoint either of my beloved sons, but someone must stay. Still, there is no reason why the issue must be solved tonight. Let this be a happy time, and we will then take this issue up again."

With that Joseph turned the conversation to other matters, and Jesus seemed willing enough to allow him to do so. James joined in as best he could, but his mind was still on the developments of the day. He did not know how he would face the wrong decision by his father.

He did not have to wait long. Scarcely a week later, early in the morning after a hearty meal, James was standing in the street in front of the house talking to a neighbor when he saw Jesus, Mary and Joseph come out the front door of their own house. Seeing that Joseph and Mary appeared to have grave looks on their faces he quickly excused himself from the neighbor and went to where they stood.

As he walked up to them they all looked back at him, as though he were the only one not in on the secret, which was indeed the case. James looked from one to the other expectantly, to see which would break down and give him the news. Finally Joseph spoke.

"Jesus is leaving to begin his ministry," he began, with a touch of sadness in his voice, and as if in anticipation of James's reaction, he added, "and we must all wish him well."

The implications of this announcement went through his head so fast that, if asked to recount them, James would not have been able to do so. Jesus was leaving, apparently for good. That meant that James would either have to take up his father's business, or disappoint Joseph as Jesus was now doing. That in turn meant the end of his dream of moving to Jerusalem to study the scriptures under the tutelage of Ananus. Suddenly, in the space of a few seconds, James had gone from hopeful of a life in the temple studying the word of God to doomed to spending his life in the confines of tiny Nazareth chained, figuratively, to a workbench. The tedium, the long years in relative isolation, the absence of much in the way of mental stimulation, all hit James as soon as the words were out of his father's mouth, and he was too stunned to offer Jesus any word of congratulation.

He recovered himself within a second or two, and stammered out some words of good will, though it was difficult for him to feel them at that moment. Jesus appeared to understand, and stepped over to give James a hug around the shoulders and a look in the eye that James thought to be full of sympathy and love. As his mother and father hugged Jesus and wished him a safe journey, James for the first time gathered his wits about him. He noticed that, even though Jesus was apparently leaving at that very moment he had nothing with him - no food, no additional clothing, apparently no money (he wore no purse or belt for the purpose). This he could not reconcile.

"But where are you going," he asked Jesus. "Far away? You have nothing with you. How will you live?"

Jesus looked him firmly in the eye and said, "I will rely on the providence of God in heaven. He will look after me."

"You will rely on him for food? For drink? For the means to put a roof over your head at night? God is great, but he also expects that we will do our part."

"He does not fail to feed the birds or clothe the flowers in their finest," Jesus replied, "and he will not neglect me." Plainly Jesus meant to leave Nazareth and travel through the surrounding countryside without the means to care for himself for even a single night. This was great faith indeed, or it was brazen stupidity. This last did not seem likely to James. While he had had differences with Jesus in the past, he had always admired Jesus's common sense and his ability to see to the heart of any problem. It could not be that Jesus had simply not thought to take the necessaries with him - he was intentionally leaving all his belongings, and they were few, behind.

Perhaps he was intentionally following the example of John, called by some the Baptist, and of whom James had heard recently. This John, it was said by travelers, lives in the desert eating leaves and insects, wears only animal skins to cover himself, and ceaselessly preaches the word of God to anyone who will visit him outside of Jerusalem. This was a harsh example to choose for a prophet, as not even the likes of Jeremiah and Isaiah were ascetic to that degree.

Jesus interrupted his thoughts as though he had been able to read them faster than James could think them. "I neither need nor want any comfort of home, save the love that is there. These are but distractions to me, and I have no need of them. I will rely on the hand of God."

James could not be surprised with the fact that Jesus was leaving home to teach, but he was surprised to see it happen this soon. Mary began to cry openly at this moment, and it was Jesus who said,

"Don't cry for me or for yourselves. I will be about the work for which I was brought into the world. There are many lost sheep, and so little time for the shepherd." With that he hugged his mother and Joseph, turned to James and hugged him, and set off on his way.

James's dilemma was a difficult one - one that, like that faced by his father only a short time ago, he would not be able to decide immediately. He hoped that some event would spare him the necessity of making that decision, though he could only think of one: the return of Jesus. He did not believe this to be likely.

His bitterness over the situation slowly ebbed, though now and again he was reminded forcefully of the circumstances that brought him to this pass. There was the day when he was working in the shop by himself, an increasingly common occurrence, when a friend stopped by to see him.

"Eleazar, it is good to see you," cried James. "But who is this with you?" His friend was accompanied by a pleasant, beautiful young woman who looked familiar to James, but he could not place her. She covered her long, light hair with a veil, but she could not cover bright gray eyes and an open, happy expression.

"And you James. This is my sister Esther. You know her. It seems as though I have been away forever, when it has only been a few weeks. How is your father's health? How is the carpentry business?"

"Of course I know her, but I did not recognize her. She is a grown up young woman now. How old are you now? Nineteen? You are grown. And quite beautiful. You must have an intended or a husband by now. No? Well, it will not be long - believe me." And then back to Eleazar, "My father's health is not good. He continues to weaken, and you see that I am in the shop today alone. This is becoming more common. The carpentry business is good. We have more business than we can deal with most of the time. I should be happy with this situation, but I cannot say that I am." He smiled at

Esther, since he was somewhat embarrassed to be discussing this private matter in front or her, and she returned his smile but said nothing.

"So I understand," said Eleazar. "Speaking of which, I hear everywhere of your brother. He is becoming a famous preacher."

"What does that mean? I am prepared to believe that he is a traveling prophet without ever having heard him speak. What else do those who have heard him believe?"

"It's hard to say. Some that he is another Jeremiah or Isaiah, or that he is Elijah come to life. There is even some talk, which he has not discouraged, that he is the one to come."

James was a faithful Jew, anxiously awaiting the one to come promised by God. He had heard of others who claimed to be the one, but he never expected some one from his own family to make the claim. It irritated him highly that Jesus would allow such talk to continue.

"This is not to be tolerated," said he, enraged. "He hinted at something like this to me once, and I dismissed him out of hand. How is it that he resurrects it?"

"I did not say that he claimed it for himself. I have heard others claim it for him, and that he does nothing to dispel such talk."

"It is the same thing. One does not need to make the statement 'I am the Messiah' to have committed blasphemy. It is enough to lead others on. Blasphemy is a stoning offense! How can he bring such a trial on himself and his family?" The implications of the charge, beyond the obvious falsehood, occurred to James, and the ramifications for Jesus and the rest of his family suddenly came to him. The best that they could hope for would be merciless ridicule, but they might also be ostracized by their neighbors and friends, forced to pick up the stakes of their lives and move on.

"Well, well, it is minor," said Eleazar, as he examined the small table that James had just handed him, "at least for the moment. Pray that he either begins to discourage such talk, or that it does not get back to the High Priest."

James departed the house to walk off his dinner and to give more consideration to the problem. He walked the steadily darkening streets alone, paying little attention to the people around him. He knew most of them from a lifetime spent in Nazareth, and many greeted him familiarly, but he scarcely acknowledged them, so great was his confusion. At one point he walked down a narrow lane with his hands behind his back and his eyes firmly fixed on the ground in front of him. Rounding a corner he bumped into a woman carrying a load of fruit in her apron, knocking her and her entire load to the ground.

"I am so sorry, I didn't see you coming at all. Its entirely my fault," apologized James profusely. She had her robe draped over her head, shielding her face from James.

"I know it is entirely your fault, James," said the woman, in a pleasant voice. James stared intently to see who this might be, and after a moment she pulled back the robe to reveal Esther, the sister of Eleazar with whom James had become reacquainted that very day.

"Esther, you should not be so quick to condemn. After all, were I not the considerate kind, I could make a case for saying that it was you who bumped into me."

"That is true, yet this is the second time I have seen you this evening, and both times you were walking with your head down, studying the ground with all the attention that a cow studies it. I believe I would be able to find many witnesses to testify that tonight you have seen nothing but the ground, and so are at fault here."

"You have me there," said James, as the two finished picking up the fruit and restoring it to her apron, which was lying flat on the ground for that purpose. "Where is such a small girl taking such a load of fruit?"

"To my home, to be made into various tasty dishes," she answered.

"Then allow me to carry it for you," James offered. She agreed and they began the moderate walk to her home, with the apron carefully slung over James's shoulder.

On his return home, James was alarmed to see his mother highly upset and awaiting his presence. Joseph seemed to be breathing hard and laboriously, and his voice was thin and weak. James hurried over and knelt next to his father, opposite Mary.

"James," said Joseph, in a voice that could scarcely be heard, "James, my son. I fear that my time here is over. Take care of your mother, James. She is a strong woman, but she needs her son near her." He paused here for breath, and James took the opportunity to assure him that he would look after Mary. "James," he began again, "I have not told you what it means to me that you took up my carpentry business. It is a good feeling for a man to build something that his sons want to keep when he is gone." Another pause for breath, during which Mary and James said nothing. "You have succeeded far beyond what I had hoped for, and I am proud of you." Another pause for breath and to gather his voice, which had become more and more thin and raspy. James could feel tears welling up in his eyes, but he tried to cover them. Mary was crying openly.

At that moment there was a disturbance in the street outside the house, and James rose to see if it was the arrival of his brothers. As he stepped out of the front door of the house and attempted to adjust his tear marred eyes to the bright sunlight, he was accosted by his three brothers, Josias, Judah, and Simon, all of whom now lived in Jerusalem and had made the trek to Nazareth together. All three were married, but none had brought their families with them. All asked at the same moment after the health of their father.

"I believe that you have just made it in time, "said James. "Father is falling fast, and will not last much longer."

"Thank God that we have made it in time, then," said Simon, as the others agreed. The three new arrivals kicked off their sandals and made their way into the house, James bringing up the rear.
Joseph was whispering something to Mary, who was leaning down with her ear to his mouth. At the entrance of the three brothers her face, which was turned to the door as she listened, brightened noticeably.

"Your sons are here!" she called to him loudly.

"All of them? No? Josias! You are a sight for a sick man. Judah, my son! I have longed to look upon you. Simon! The youngest. All here, save Jesus. Well it cannot be helped. He is answering the call of God, and that must come before all. I am content now. I go to see the Judge ushered out by my family - the people I love most in the world." This long greeting appeared to tire him out, and he paused for breath once again. Judah, Josias, and Simon all pronounced their love for him, and their thanks at coming home in time to see him again. "Yes, yes. There is nothing more I could want," he rasped out, barely audibly, to his gathered family. Everyone knelt on the cushions as near to Joseph as they could, making a tight circle around him. Judah suggested they all step back to allow him more room to breathe, but Joseph would not hear of it.

"No! No! A little more air will make no difference to me. I would much rather be able to see all of my family at once, as a parting gift to me. Let my last glance at this world be of my family." With this his eyes rolled in his head just enough to allow him to focus on each of them, and then they gently closed, and his breathing stopped.

The death of his father did not cause James the anguish that he thought it might, probably because he had become mentally prepared for it over the last few weeks. His brothers had not been present to see the deterioration of their father, and so were more effected than he. His mother and sisters cried heartily. Joseph's talk of his family being present at the end made James's thoughts turn to Jesus, the only member who was not there. Where was he and what was he doing? Joseph had been forgiving about the fact that Jesus was not there, but James found it difficult. He had better be on a calling from God, thought James, to miss an important event such as this, and to have put himself in a position where his family could not find him.

Two weeks later James was in the carpenter's shop, which he was forced to admit was now his, working on some rush jobs. As usual on warm days, which most of them were, he had the shop open to the street, and he became accustomed to the hustle and bustle around him.

30

At the moment he had his back to the street, working on a small table where he did the majority of his finishing work. He worked the wood smooth with a stone, examined it, and then worked certain parts of it over again. When he was satisfied with the results he turned once again to face the street, and found himself staring at his brother, Jesus.

"Peace be to you, James," said he, in a quiet voice.

"And to you, Jesus," he answered. "You have surprised me completely. We did not know that you were coming home."

"I have come for a short visit. No one in the household knows that I am here, as yet." With this they both turned to go into the house. James did not know what to think. He wanted to chastise Jesus for not being there when their father died, for apparently allowing his followers, whoever they were, to refer to him as the one to come, and for all of the other failings in his life that James had conjured from his memory over the last weeks, but he found he could not.

As they went through the door to the house, James asked him, "Did you know that father died?" He thought that Jesus looked at him in an odd fashion.

"Yes," Jesus said after hesitating for a moment. "I heard the news sometime back from a traveler." James waited for a moment to hear some sign of remorse that Jesus had not been at home at the time, but Jesus said nothing else. James decided to push the issue a bit, to see what he could get Jesus to admit.

"Our father was a good man," he offered.

"He was, and he is with God."

"I think we may believe that that is true."

Jesus flashed a quick smile. "Yes, it is safe to believe that," said he.

Mary was overjoyed to see Jesus, and quickly prepared a meal for him. James joined in to hear what Jesus might have to say about his travels. Jesus did not appear any the worse for wear for all his travels, particularly when James considered that he still appeared to be traveling empty-handed - he brought nothing into the house with him. There even seemed to be a hint of freedom around his eyes, as though he had been recently relieved of a burden. His clothes did not appear to be the same ones he had left home in, yet they were not new either. He seemed calm and peaceful and at rest with the world. He talked easily and freely to James and to his mother, and it appeared to James that he went out of his way to make the two of them happy.

When the meal was over, and the food cleared away, James brought the conversation around to the subject closest to his heart.

"We have been hearing stories about your teaching," he began..

"I have no power save that given me by my Father in heaven," he said quietly, looking James straight in the eye. James was somewhat taken aback by this reference to his father in heaven, but he assumed that Jesus meant that God was the father of them all.

"It is even said," said James, "that you have followers, and that some of them believe that you are the one to come." Jesus looked at him steadily, with a bemused smile on his face.

"It is true that there are people who follow me, because I have told them the truth. Others I have sought because the message will have to be carried after I am gone. For those who have heard and believed, I have fulfilled the scriptures."

"Even to the extent of claiming to be the Messiah?"

Jesus paused before answering, never taking his eyes off of his brother. "Yes, even to that extent."

James heard the news with more bemusement than shock, and, while he had expected to be irritated by the announcement, if it came, he was more resigned than angry. "Jesus, you know that this is blasphemy. You can be stoned for making such claims, and if this claim reaches the wrong ears you will be stoned." He looked to his mother for agreement, but she sat staring at Jesus' face, less out of fear, he thought, than wonder.

"James, my brother, it is not for me to decide my fate based on the truth that I tell. My fate has been decided for me, and there is little that I could or would do to change it."

"But you are the son of a carpenter - a good man, but not God. How can you be the one to come?"

"How should I have come into the world? As a king riding in a golden chariot? This would not do because my kingdom is not of this world. I have come at the time and place where my message needs to be heard first. Those who believe will see."

James wanted to be calm, but this was too much for his strict faith. "The one to come will deliver us from our oppressors, free the Jewish people from their bondage. This much we have from the prophets. How will you, without power and without riches, achieve this?"

"The Son of Man comes to free all those who wish to be freed from their bondage. He offers eternal life to those who believe in him."

James was now irate. "Your kingdom is not of this world, yet you offer eternal life. This cannot be, and it is an insult to God and to the prophets for me to sit here and listen to blasphemy. I do not know from whence your ideas came, but they are wrong and dangerous ideas, and it would be best for you and for the rest of your family if you were to forget them. Mother, are you going to sit there and listen to this?"

"It is not for me to decry the will of God," said she.

32

"Then you believe what he says." James paused here for a moment to collect himself, then he went on: "You are both my family, and I will not hand in either of you to the High Priest for your blasphemy. But please speak to me no more on the subject." And with that he strode out of the house and back to the shop, where Jesus and Mary soon heard him pounding away on his work bench.

They heard James pounding on the bench, but if they had looked they would have seen that he was pounding directly on the bench - there was no work on it to be done. He was angry and frustrated, and could think of no other way to vent himself. His own brother a blasphemer! How could this be? And it did not appear that he had any intention of hiding this particular revelation from the people. He intended to go on preaching, and appeared willing to suffer the inevitable consequences. But where had he gotten the idea that he was the Messiah? Had he performed some sort of small miracle and been fooled by that? Had he been able to pique the interest of those to whom he spoke, as he had the elders in the temple when he was twelve years old, and then allowed their admiration to go to his head? It was all incomprehensible, and it could be the ruin of the family. He did not know what to do, and it appeared at the same time that there was little he could do.

James slept fitfully that night, and as a consequence was up all the earlier the next day, which was the Sabbath. He greeted his mother and his brother when they awoke, and made an effort to be amenable to his brother. He hated the thought that they should be estranged, and did not know what else to do but attempt to get along. They set off for the temple together, with Mary in the lead.

Nazareth was a small town, and therefore it had a small temple - it simply could not afford to compete with the likes of Jerusalem or even some of the larger surrounding towns. But Nazareth was an exclusively Jewish town, and that insularity meant that all of the town would be attending the service - no one wanted to be singled out as having missed.

The temple was a small ill lit affair with a low ceiling. All the men of the town could fit into the circular central chamber, and there was room for the women in the anteroom behind the screen that separated it from the main chamber.

James and Jesus left their mother in the anteroom and took positions on the crowded floor in the main chamber. James listened intently to the readings as he always did, and was particularly hopeful that today's service would have some reminder about the coming of the Messiah, since that topic had had his attention of late. He noted, with some degree of relief, that none of the people in the room seemed to be paying any attention to his brother, which suggested that the stories about his missionary work had not yet filtered out to the town as a whole.

After the lecture by the rabbi, there was the usual invitation for a member of the congregation to read. James was surprised, and alarmed, to see Jesus rise and walk to the lectern. This service among dedicated Jews was the last place that James wanted to see Jesus get up and declare himself the Messiah. Even if it were true that he was the Messiah, this would be the last crowd of people on Earth who would accept him as such. James hoped against hope that Jesus would confine himself to the reading and a conventional lecture. In the deepest recesses of his heart he knew that was not about to happen.

Jesus unfurled the scrolls before him, and began to read: "The spirit of the Lord is upon me. Wherefore he has anointed me to preach the gospel to the poor: he hath sent me to heal the contrite of heart, to preach deliverance to the captives and sight to the blind, to set at liberty them that are bruised, to preach the acceptable year of the Lord and the day of reward."

At the end of this passage, Jesus rolled the scroll up again, raised his eyes from the lectern to look at the people in the room, and said: "Today, in your hearing, is this prophecy fulfilled." There was a moment of expectant silence, as though the crowd were waiting for an explanation of this remark. When they realized that none was forthcoming, they began to talk among themselves.

"Is this not the son of the carpenter?" "Did he just claim to be the Messiah?" "Does not his family live here among us?" There seemed to be general agreement among them that they knew him, and that therefore what they had just heard could not be accurate. They then turned their attention to Jesus, who was still standing at the lectern.

"What do you mean by this?" one demanded. "Do you say that you are the one to come?"

"This is blasphemy!" shouted another, over the growing din. There were cries of "Throw him out into the street!" and "Stone him!" while others demanded that he explain himself. There was a general rising to the feet by the men who had been sitting on the floor in the main chamber, and among this number was James, who had had his worst fears realized.

Jesus raised his hands to quiet them and then said to them, "Doubtless you will say to me: physician heal thyself. We have heard that you do great things in Capernaum - show them to us here in your own country. Amen I say to you that no prophet is accepted in his own country. In truth I say to you there were many widows in the days of Elias in Israel, when heaven was shut up three years and six months, when there was great famine throughout all the Earth. And to none of them was Elias sent, but to Sarepta of Sidon, to a widow woman. And there were many lepers in Israel in the time of Eliseus the prophet: and none of them was cleansed but Naaman the Syrian."

This only angered the crowd more, and they began to surge toward the lectern. The press of the crowd was toward the door, and Jesus was caught up in this press as people pushed to get into the street first, or to get their hands on Jesus. James pushed through the crowd to be as close to Jesus as he could, though in fact he agreed with many in the crowd who were outraged at the claim that Jesus was making.

The shouting crowd pushed and pulled Jesus to the door of the temple. James noticed, as he had feared, that some in the crowd had now noticed him. "He is your brother. Is he the Messiah?" There were even cries of "Throw all of the family out of town! They do not deserve to live among us." This alarmed James for the sake of his mother, but he could do nothing. He was being pushed by the crowd toward the door, and could hardly turn his head, so intent was he on not stumbling, falling and being trampled by the crowd. He could not see his mother, and did not know her fate.

James saw some punches thrown at Jesus, and felt one or two, probably aimed at his brother, hit him a glancing blow. He also felt some kicks on his legs, though these did not hurt as much as they might have, given the excitement of the moment. Because the size of the crowd prevented them all from fitting through the door easily, and because he and Jesus were in the center of the crowd, they were a long time in emerging into the bright sunlight. They moved slowly and fitfully with the crowd, and were forced to endure the verbal stones thrown their way.

When they did finally emerge, the crowd seemed to James to turn uglier than it already was. The cries of "Stone him!" now seemed to drown out the others, and those of the crowd who were already outside began picking up whatever projectile they could find in the roadway, some of which included large stones. But one man called out, "Let us take him to the cliff at Namea, and throw him off." This met with the general approbation of the crowd, to the extent that the crowd could agree on anything.

James, who had not been able to make himself heard above the general din, attempted to sway the mob. "Brothers," he called out, "Listen to me. This is my brother. He has lived among you these thirty years. How come you to hate so soon? Give him time to explain himself to you." Only those who stood next to James could hear him, and they did not sympathize. "He had his chance," said one. "He is a blasphemer," said another, "and the penalty is death." This James well knew, and it was for this reason that he feared the crowd.

Jesus, who had been largely unresisting until that time, now suddenly shook off the hands of those who held him, and turned to stare at the crowd. The shouting suddenly died out as he did so, as though he had managed to cow them all into submission. He looked at them in sorrow for only a brief second, and then turned on his heal and began to walk out of town. There were cries of "Don't let him escape!" and "Stone him!" but there was no serious move on the part of anyone in the crowd to overtake his receding figure. He passed safely down the street and out of town.

This fact angered some in the crowd, who now turned their attention to the remaining object of attention, James. There were cries of "Arrest his brother until he returns!" and "Stone his brother instead!" but neither of these had any effect on the crowd, which began to slowly disperse.

The third day thereafter dawned bright and hot like most others, and found Mary and James on the road to Cana, a small village eight miles from Nazareth.

It was to be the site of the marriage of the daughter of a brother of Joseph, Gershim by name, who had made his fortune in trade. They made the trip without incident, though they spent much of the time speculating as to whether the events in the temple had carried so far from Nazareth.

The wedding was lavish by the standards of James and his family - the temple had been full of people, and it appeared that much of the village of Cana had been invited to the feast afterward. James saw some old friends there, and was surprised to see Jesus. He appeared calm and none the worse for wear for the ordeal in the temple three days prior, and it appeared that few at the feast had heard of the incident. James and Mary certainly did not talk the matter around, and since most of the other people at the wedding were family, there was an excellent chance that the news had not traveled this far.

The first chance James got he cornered Jesus to discuss the events at the temple three days previously.

"I cannot understand your actions," he said. "You stood before the people of your own town, and proclaimed yourself the Messiah. Surely you were not surprised when the crowd nearly threw you off a cliff?"

"I cannot help the way the people of my town react to my message," he said simply.

"I suppose not, but you could provide them with a message that is less likely to insult them."

"I can only provide them with the message I was sent here to bring."

"Who sent you here to claim that you are the one to come?"

"My Father in heaven sent me to atone for the sins of many. It was for this that I was brought into the world, and it is to this that I must be true."

"You are claiming that you have been called by God to proclaim that you are the Messiah? That you are the son of God? How can this be when you and I are of the same father?"

Jesus paused for a moment to consider his reply. "James," he said at last, "we are not of the same father. I am not the sire of Joseph of Nazareth. He is the instrument for my coming into the world, he was the light of his wife's eyes, and he was a good man who shall have his reward. But he was not my father."

"But I have heard mother talk of bearing you. I have heard the stories of your flight into Egypt soon after your birth. There is little doubt in my mind that my mother also carried you. With your claim you are saying either that mother and father were lying about our origins, or you are saying that mother was an adulteress. You must know what a sensitive claim this is." James anger began to rise, as he saw that Jesus appeared to believe what he was saying about himself, and if he continued to spread that message he would bring opprobrium upon the rest of the family, and call into question his mother's morals and the legitimacy of himself and his sisters. A mob that had been on the verge of stoning Jesus that recent morning might instead turn its attention to his mother.

"James, you are a faithful man. Do not judge God with the thoughts of man. Are not all things possible for God? Did he not create the world and all the wonders in it? Is it for the creatures of that creation to question whether God is living up to their standards? You suggest that my message cannot be because you do not understand how God brought it about. You are thinking as man thinks, and judging God by the standards of man. Believe what God wants you to believe, James, not only those things which you can see."

James calmed himself for the moment, realizing that he did not want his rising voice to draw any attention to the bizarre ideas he was hearing. It was better if the whole thing be allowed to drop for the moment. There were many people at the wedding that James would rather not have to face on this issue. In fact, he did not want to have to face anyone on this issue.

In a lowered voice he continued, "It is far too complicated for me to understand. My brother claims to be born of my mother but not my father, says that this does not make my mother an adulteress, and then claims that it is all the will of God that I should accept on faith. It is fortunate that you ask that such a string of non-sensical claims should be accepted on faith. There is no other way to accept them!" At this point they were joined by Mary.

"I can look at my sons from across the room, and know what it is that they are talking of. Do not discuss it here, I beg of you. There are people here who would not understand what it is that our family is going through."

"This is certainly true," James could not resist injecting. But a withering glance from his mother convinced him to drop the subject for the moment.

There was plenty of food and drink for the crowd, and there were many there who had more than their share of both. Most wore brightly colored tunics and robes in honor of the occasion, and many had the colors of their clothes supplemented by spillage. The food was set on low tables around the walls of the room, around which the celebrants gathered, while the wine was tended to by servers from large jars scattered around the room. The center of the room was reserved for music and dancing which competed with the conversation, so that none of the revelers could ignore the others.

James knew many in the crowd, since it was a family affair, and he made his usual effort to greet them all. James also met some men whom he had never met before, but who seemed to know Jesus, and who appeared to treat Jesus with what James considered extreme deference. They must have been some of the followers that he had heard about. But how came they to the wedding of a member of the family? And did they believe the claims Jesus was making about himself?

Jesus made the introductions, raising his voice above the din. Their names were Andrew and Philip, and said themselves to be from Capernaum. He did not explain to James what the connection between the three men might be, and James resolved to ask if he had the opportunity.

It was not long in coming. Walking around the outskirts of the feast to avoid the dancers, he came upon the two men talking to each other. He saw the opening which he sought.

They greeted him warmly, and then he asked them, "My brother did not mention your connection to him. How did you meet?"

Andrew, a short man with short black hair and beard, and who, James thought, was dressed in robes and mantle not suitable to the occasion, addressed him. "We were followers of John, called the Baptist. Jesus came to him for baptism, and, upon seeing Jesus, John said 'Behold the Lamb of God, who has come to take away the sins of the world.' We did not know what to make of this, but John told us that we should follow Jesus because he is the one to come. And so we are doing."

James was so thunderstruck by this reply that he could make no immediate answer to their apparently earnest statement. His jaw dropped and Andrew and Philip, seeing that he would say nothing, waited patiently, smiling.

"He is the one to come, you say?" asked James, after a pause. "What does that mean?"

"We do not know," answered Philip, the taller of the two, who had dark brown, curly hair which he appeared to take little notice of, and who was dressed in clothing as disheveled as that of his brother. "John, who was an upright and honest man, believed Jesus to be a prophet of some sort, we believe, and so he must be."

"Where exactly is it that you plan to follow him to?" asked James.

"Wherever he leads us," said Philip, to which Andrew nodded. James was about to ask when this trip might begin, and what it was that made them want to follow the son of a poor carpenter and many other things that crowded into his mind, but they were interrupted by a dancing group that came by and which pulled the two men in. James was left standing by himself, as puzzled as he had ever been in his life.

James was about to make his case more completely when they were joined by their mother Mary for the second time that day.

She greeted them both and then said to Jesus, "They have no wine."

This comment seemed as inexplicable to Jesus as it was to James, who could not see what she expected either of them to do about it.

Jesus said to her, "Woman, what have I to do with you? My time is not yet come." James was surprised at the cavalier tone of this answer, and assumed that his mother would be as well. But, surprisingly, she appeared to take no note, but only stood regarding him for a moment. She then waved her arm and summoned the head servant to her.

"Whatever he says to you," she told the man, indicating Jesus, "do it."

James knew that Jesus was notoriously unconcerned about money, and so would have none on him, but even if he were in possession of some he would not be able to purchase enough wine for such a multitude.

Jesus asked the servant what sort of containers he had available, and the man took Jesus and Mary to a small anteroom where there were six waterpots made of clay, each perhaps two cubits high. James followed along to see what he might be able to do to help, and he noticed that Andrew and Philip did the same.

Without regarding the waterpots very carefully, Jesus said to the servant, "Fill each of them with water." This command mystified the servant, who stood in place looking at Jesus as though there was some sort of explanation coming. It surprised James and the other two men as well, for they exchanged doubting glances. Seeing there was no explanation coming, the servant fetched five other servants, and the six of them carried off the bottles. They returned in a very few minutes with the pots filled to the brim with water.

When they had set them down in front of him, Jesus said to the head servant, "Now take a ladle and give some to the governor of the feast to taste." This command, just as the previous command had done, brought questioning glances from the waiter, who plainly believed he was being toyed with, but he obeyed, and fetched a ladle of the drink to his master.

When the man had gone, Mary said to Jesus, "Thank you," and then moved off to rejoin the festivities. Jesus did the same, followed by his two mysterious friends, leaving James standing alone in the anteroom, wondering what it was that he had just seen. The feast now had six full pots of water, minus a ladle, but it still had no wine, and yet his mother appeared to have been appreciative of Jesus' efforts.

When James walked out of the room he passed the servants re-entering it, and he saw them carry the pots out among the revelers. There was a cry from the governor that there was some fine new wine available, and that all of the guests were invited to sample some of it. When the other guests had had a chance to refill their cups, James dipped his into one of the pots to see what was it about the water that his brother had ordered that was worth being served at the wedding. He put the cup to his lips, and - nearly dropped it in surprise. It was among the best tasting wines he had ever sampled.

James quickly quaffed the rest of the cup of wine, to steady his nerves if for no other reason. He had just witnessed some sort of hoax, perpetrated by his own family. His mother had come to his older brother and reported that the feast had run out of wine, as though expecting him to do something about it. He had sent for water, in the presence of several witnesses, and then had sent the water out among the guests, though it was obvious that the pots had been full of wine, not water.

What could have been the point of this elaborate ruse? To make people think that he could turn water into wine? To take credit for saving the governor of the feast some embarrassment? Did he trust all the witnesses, including the servants, not to talk about what had happened? Worse yet, what had been his mother's role? Why had she, a woman he had always admired above all others for her moral steadfastness, taken part in so underhanded a scheme? Had the feast really run out of wine at all? One question crowded the previous one out of his head, and still James could think of no logical explanation for what he had just seen. He resolved to drop the matter for the time and enjoy the rest of the day, but he found he could not.

He wanted to ask his brother or his mother about the incident, but after one approach on each found that he could not face them. He resolved to seek out the servants who had been involved in the act, and convince one of them to tell him the truth. As he circled the room looking for the offenders, he heard several of the guests comment on the good quality of the wine, and how they had never tasted better so near the end of a feast.

James found three of the servants - all young men - talking together in the same anteroom to which they had fetched the pots of water on the command of his brother. When they saw him enter they started, possibly mistaking him for an employee of the bridegroom, who would surely have them punished for taking time off from the job. But James said to the eldest of them: "Come and show from whence you obtained the water."

The servant hesitated for a moment, looking as though he were the most put upon young man in the world. James enjoined him, "Come, come man. I will not report your behavior this evening. Simply show me the source of the water."

Wordlessly the man led James through the house. On the far side they came to a small courtyard, and in the middle of the courtyard there was a small pool walled with stone, formed from a small spring that ran through that end of the compound. The liquid therein was clear, and upon tasting it, James confirmed it to be water.

He straightened himself and turned on the servant. "You got the water from this pool? How came it to taste of wine when carried into the feast?"

"Indeed, master, I know not," said the sorely tested man. I only know that I was told to fill the bottle from this pool, and I did so."

"Was it this incident that you were discussing with the others when I entered just now? What do they say of the matter?" But the man could tell him nothing, and, as he appeared to be the more alert among them, James decided that he would get nothing from the others either.

He stooped for another taste of the water, just to re-confirm in his mind what he had found, before following the servant absentmindedly back through the house to the wedding feast. So deep in thought was he that the servant had to return for him twice, thinking that he had become lost.

The first distinguishable voice James heard upon re-entering the feast was that of one of the revelers praising the newly brought wine, a praise that made him wince. He looked for his mother and brother, and found them at opposite ends of the hall, in animated conversation with various members of the party. It appeared as though they had forgotten the incident already, though it was impossible for James to do so.

The next morning Mary and James began the trip back to Nazareth. Mary began the journey in high spirits, though her conversation tailed off as they grew weary. James said as little as possible the entire trip, doing the best he could to simply answer the comments of his mother, irritated by what appeared to be the treachery of his family, and fearful of betraying his feelings to them if he should talk.

CHAPTER 3

Jesus did not return with Mary and James to Nazareth, but it sometimes seemed to James that his spirit returned with them.

They began to hear everywhere of Jesus' teaching, his gathering of followers to himself, and the miracles he appeared to have wrought. And the incident in the temple was not forgotten among the more devoted followers of the faith. While it did not appear that the townspeople held it against James or Mary, neither were they allowed to forget it. In weathering this storm they were aided by James' long devotion to Judaism, and his many activities within the local temple. While not a member of the party of Zealots to which his friend Ananias and his father Ananus belonged, James was little less tolerant of the Roman rule, and only slightly more tolerant of deviations from the received applications of the scriptural teachings. He had become known around the town of Nazareth for his devotion and frequent attendance in the temple and for the decidedly unbusinesslike manner in which he managed the carpentry shop.

He decided that, if he were compelled to be a carpenter, he would at least be one who would be known to be in the service of God. It was not uncommon for him to allow the purchase of his wares on time but without charging interest - to allow the poor more time to pay. Any implements asked of him for the temple or for religious use in a home he provided free of charge. He fanatically refused to work on the Sabbath, even on projects ostensibly religious in nature. He gave alms to all beggars that he saw in the street, and was once seen to give one the cloak off of his back.

His generosity of spirit was appreciated in the small community, and, as will happen with amiable people, he was taunted now and again about his habits and his relationship with his brother.

"James," they would cry, on seeing him pass down the street, "there is a beggar in the next block who does not yet own a cloak of yours. Better see to him or your brother Jesus will smite you." These sorts of jibes irritated James in the early days after the incident in the temple, but gradually as the event faded into the background they also faded in James's memory.

As was inevitable with such generosity of spirit, James and Mary found that though James worked as hard as ever in the shop, they had less money to show for it. While they did not fall among the ranks of the poor, their money was stretched much tighter than it had previously been. James found that if he allowed the poor to buy on time he would inevitably be hounded by the wealthy to allow them to do the same. But if he acquiesced in this request he found that he had almost no money to show for his efforts: the poor would pay what they could when they could, though he often never received anything from them, and, it seemed, the rich were as bad, if not worse, than the poor. There were calls from among James's friends to end the practice so that he might return to prosperity, but he looked upon the trouble as the will of God and refused to change his ways. He did cease to allow the rich to buy on time, telling them that they had no need of such an indulgence, and their kind willingness to pay for the product in full when they collected it made it possible for them both to do a favor for the poor in the eyes of God.

Shortly after one such disagreement in his shop, James turned his back to the street to work on the bench behind him when he heard, "Are you not as kind to the comfortable as to the poor?"
He turned to see Esther standing opposite him in the shop, just under the roof and out of the sun. She wore a brown tunic which complimented her eyes, her hair was freshly combed and perfumed, and there were new sandals upon her feet.

"I try to be kind to all," he answered, "but I would like for those who can to pay at once, so that I may be more generous to those who have less."

"Perhaps then I will not be able to commission you for a child's chair. I haven't the money to pay for it today."

"You needn't the money today - you will need it when the work is finished."

"There is nothing due against the total today?"

"Not for friends of the family. But you did not dress like this to commission a chair. Where are you bound?"

"I do not see why I may not dress like this to conduct business with one of the most respected businessmen in the town."

"Who?"

"You, of course," said Esther, laughing. "Come, James. Do not think so lightly of yourself."

James laughed loudly. "If I am so well respected, why I am working day and night to keep up the house that my father built? Why have I not carved out an empire of my own? Why am I chided by attractive local women for not being kind enough to the wealthy?"

Esther bowed at the compliment. "Because you do not offer a sacrifice of money on the altar. You treat your fellows with respect. You obey the spirit of the law as well as its letter. Your rewards will come later. And none of this means that you are not respected. What event is there is town, business, pleasure, or religious, that James and his mother are not invited to?"

"You are very kind," rejoined James, "but those invitations may have more to do with the fact that there is no other carpenter in Nazareth, and the rest of the citizenry do what they can to make sure that I will never leave. It is a strange kind of welcome, but better than none at all."

"James, when did you become such a cynic? People invite you to events because they admire your work, your charity, your generosity of spirit. They want James at the table, not the local carpenter. I overhear conversations about you - people admire you for what you are, not for what you can make with wood."

"Well it is kind of you to say, and for the moment I will be happy to take your word for it. But let me hear more about this child's chair."

They conferred over the proposed article for a few minutes, but as it was to be a simple device James was soon in possession of all the facts he would need. He could not help asking one other question of Esther.

"I seem to recall that you are the youngest in your family. What need have you of a chair of this small size?"

"It is to be a gift for the daughter of my brother," Esther answered matter-of-factly. This satisfied James, and Esther went her way. James realized a few moments later that he had forgotten to ask her when she wanted the chair, but she was out of earshot by then.

A messenger came to James's shop in the early afternoon to announce that there would be a meeting in the temple that evening of select members of the congregation, and he was invited to attend. His initial inclination was to decline since he had some jobs on at the moment that promised to be profitable - something he was more in need of now - but upon mentioning this to the messenger, he said: "I am instructed to inform you that the subject of the meeting is the people who stand outside your home looking for the false prophet."

"In that case I shall attend," said James, knowing that the purpose of the meeting must be getting him - James - to deal with the problem in some manner. That being the case there would be many attacks on his brother Jesus, and it would be better for the family if there were some one there to control the damage.

That evening in the home of Rabbi Asa James found only a small crowd, made up of the Rabbi, the elders of the temple, one or two of the leading secular citizens of the town, and two priests - strangers that James had never before seen and who were the only two in the room unknown to him. They were seated in the smoke filled sitting room of the Rabbi's home, lounging on cushions or small chairs, and had evidently just finished their meal when James arrived. When James entered they got immediately down to business.

"Greetings, James," said the Rabbi, for whom James had just recently finished a piece of furniture, which he now saw the Rabbi sitting in. "May God be with you."

"And with you, Rabbi, and with you all." All those present nodded their heads in acknowledgment.

"James, these are Josaphat and Abidiah from the temple in Jerusalem," said the Rabbi, nodding toward the two strangers. James bowed to them slightly, and wished them well again.

Josaphat, the older and portlier of the two, who had a long gray beard, said "Ananus and Ananias send their greetings to you, as well as their hopes that you may help us in this effort."

"You may tell them to rest assured that I will do the will of God."

James hoped that this answer, besides being the truth, would help to ameliorate what he sensed was a tense atmosphere in the room. Instead, it seemed to surprise the two men from Jerusalem, who looked as though that was not what they wanted to hear.

When Josaphat had recovered from his surprise, he said, "You of course know that your brother Jesus is preaching all manner of things in the countryside to all who will listen, that he has a tax collector among his followers, and that he has supped with prostitutes and other wastrels, and that he has been supposed to work occasional miracles for the pleasure of the crowd." He would have continued but was interrupted by James.

"The miracles I have heard of, as well as the preaching in the country. I was aware that he has followers, but not that there was a tax collector among them. I have no way of knowing who he dines with. Surely all of this is rather harmless?" James found that all of this was out almost before he said it. He had not meant to irritate the people in the room, but he disliked the attitude of Josaphat, who was obviously condescending to both James and Jesus.

"What I tell you is true," continued Josaphat. "We in the Sanhedrin are keeping a close watch on your brother to see that he does not deviate from the law of Moses. But in the meantime we do what we can to prevent a legend from growing up around him. We have been told that there are frequent visitors to your home - visitors who come for the sole purpose of seeing the house where Jesus lives."

"It is true that there have been some people apparently looking for him."

"It is not desirable that his home should become a point on a pilgrimage map. It will cause unrest among the faithful to see their friends, neighbors, even family members following this false prophet. As faithful members of the temple it is our duty to see to it that the others members are allowed to worship without distractions of this kind."

"How can my humble brother be said to be a distraction to the faithful? He is not hurting them, and he is not preaching to them. He stays in the country and small towns."

"His listeners come to him from all over the area, and carry back his tales and false miracles to decent townspeople who know no better."

James could see that the man was angry, and decided that there was no way to pacify him. He tried another tack: "What is it that you want from me?"

"It has come to our attention, as we mentioned," began Abidiah, quietly and calmly while stroking his short black beard, a welcome contrast as far as James was concerned, "that there are people who journey to Nazareth to see the home of the prophet Jesus..."

"False prophet Jesus!" interjected Josaphat. Abidiah paused briefly as if to let the comment pass, but also give it a moment to sink in to those in the room.

"I say that your home has become a pilgrimage site for some, and we believe that this is not in the best interest of the temple and its faithful adherents. We would like to know what it is that these pilgrims are in search of, and what it is that they are saying about your brother."

James doubted that that was the reason these two personages had traveled all the way from Jerusalem, but he played along for the moment. "They want little and say little. If offered a meal they will take it and depart without a word of thanks or payment. If asked what it is they are looking for they will simply say that they wish to see the home of the prophet."

"Do you send them away?" asked Abidiah.

"There is little I can do when they are standing in the street. I tell them that Jesus does not live there any longer, and that he will not be back, so there is no need to wait."

"A sensible answer," opined Josaphat, calmer now. "And they do not wish to talk to the brother of the prophet?"

Ah! thought James: here it comes. Not only do they wish to discuss the pilgrims inspired by his brother, they wish to discover whether or not James is a follower as well. This is something the Rabbi could have told them in Jerusalem, if they had asked. Perhaps James had been so diligent about staying away from Jesus that the townsfolk had no idea what he believed about his brother the prophet.

"They care nothing for me, nor I for them," he said. "I can do nothing about the fact that they want to look at my brother's house, and there are so few of them anyway that they are easy to overlook."

This last comment pleased both men, but they were not finished yet.

"So you, James, are not a follower of your brother?"

"My brother is not my prophet."

"That is wise, that is wise," said Josaphat, who appeared to have re-taken the lead in the conversation. "But is not the stream of pilgrims a nuisance to a businessman? Would it not be easier to work elsewhere where you would not be bothered?"

What was this? Here was an unexpected tack on the part of the officials. What did they want him to do? Move?

"They are no nuisance at all, because there are so few of them that they are hardly noticeable. But even if there were more of them it would not distract me as I am busy and have no time for them."

"That is fortunate, then," said Abidiah, quietly. "We would hate to think that your own brother had caused you to lose business. But it may be that there are vacancies in other parts of the town that might suit your home and shop needs better."

"That is possible, but I have no need of moving. I have lived in the same house all my life, and have no desire to leave it."

"But if the house you are in now were torn down, it would save the townspeople the bother of seeing the pilgrims pass through to see it."

"Even if the pilgrims were traveling to tiny Nazareth just to see the house where my brother grew up, it is likely that they are bringing money with them to spend among the local merchants. Even so, I have heard no complaints from any of my neighbors."

"Well, well, we will leave it be then," said Josaphat, suddenly more jovial. "We are merely attempting to look after the members of the faith. You will keep the Rabbi informed if you hear of any stories about your brother?"

"My brother is not my prophet, but he is my brother. While I do not follow him, neither do I spy on him for the authorities."

"Understandable, understandable," beamed Josaphat. "Well, we will take no more of your time, James. God be with you."

As James departed the room it occurred to him that no one in the room had said a word save the two men from Jerusalem and the Rabbi, whose only contribution had been to provide introductions. Meetings between clerics frequently became contests to see who could present the most arcane knowledge of the Torah, but here all of the great minds of Nazareth sat silent. It must be fear, thought James. They did not dare express any thought on the matter of his brother's preaching because they were afraid to be on the wrong side in any dispute that might arise. No doubt they were all congratulating Abidiah and Josaphat now for the brilliant way in which they had handled the brother of the false prophet.

The visit by the officials from Jerusalem had not gone unnoticed in the small town, and the next day James was interrupted in his work several times by townspeople inquiring after his health, and wondering what it was that had been demanded of him. Among the callers was Esther, asking after her child's chair, other members of the local temple establishment who were not important enough to come to the meeting the night before, his friend Eleazar, and others.

He also noticed another of the small groups of pilgrims that had started the entire affair of the last evening, and resolved to speak to them, something he rarely did.

They seemed disappointed at not being invited in for a meal, but were cooperative enough to tell him that Jesus was at that moment in the area of Capernaum, alternately preaching and healing the sick and afflicted. In fact, a massive crowd had gathered in the area to hear him, and was following him in his travels.

Capernaum was just more than a day's journey from Nazareth, and James, after talking to his mother, decided to go there to warn Jesus of the high ranking attention he was receiving in Jerusalem.

He entered the city of Capernaum shortly after noon, and began immediately to inquire after Jesus. He was told by another pilgrim that Jesus was to be found on a hill outside of town with his followers, and that there had been word that he would preach that afternoon. James asked his informant for directions, and was given them, but he found that they were not necessary. There was a steady flow of traffic out of the city and toward the small prominence where Jesus was to speak.

There was a cross section of the people of the area: other Jews like himself, Moabites, Samaritans, Syrians. There were men and women in something like equal numbers, but few children. There was also a remarkable number of sick: blind, lame, deaf, dumb, those without their legs or arms, people being carried in cloth stretchers or on simple wooden stretchers, staggering forward on crutches or borne on the shoulders of comrades, and every sort of wailing, crying and moaning that the human throat could create.

James and the rest of the pilgrims trudged out of town through the north gate, and into the foot hills that surrounded the town on the north. The road led between two of the hills and into a small valley, itself surrounded by hills on all sides. The valley was grassy save for the occasional small stand of trees or bushes, and the day was brightly sunlit. James remarked to himself on the beauty of the scene.

James noted that people seemed to be gravitating toward a hill at the far side of the valley, and he followed them there. He had decided during the morning that he would not speak to Jesus until after he taught, since he had never actually heard Jesus preach. With that in mind he had also resolved that he would not let Jesus see him until after he had taught, so as not to distract his brother's attention.

It was apparent that the crowd thought Jesus would talk from a certain point at the summit of the hill they were all climbing, since they appeared to have cleared a spot for him there. James made his way there as well, but he was careful not to get too close, and not to get immediately in front. When he got to a position about 75 feet from the small clearing, actually a plateau jutting out from the side of the hill, which he was able to do only with a great deal of effort, since it appeared that many of the people had been waiting for some time, and to the right of where he guessed Jesus would stand if he stood in the clearing and looked directly down the side of the hill, he sat himself down as best he could, and waited with the others.

James sat in the sun for another hour, and the heat and the crowd were beginning to irritate him. He wanted to grouse to one of the other pilgrims about the conditions and the lateness of the speaker, but, strangely, he did not hear anyone else discussing the conditions. He forebore. He stood briefly, while carefully guarding his place on the ground, in order to size up the crowd, and he decided that there must have been about 4,000 or 5,000 people there. He wondered how his brother could attract them all, particularly since there was no way they would all be able to hear him.

Presently there was a stir at the top of the hill, to James's left as he faced the clearing, and a hush fell over the people around him. James immediately pulled his cloak over his head as a shade against the sun and to better protect against Jesus recognizing him. He looked to the top of the hill, and saw his brother emerge from a small stand of trees and walk slowly into the cleared plateau that had been left for him. He looked around him to all sides and down the hill, and when his gaze wandered too close to James, James ducked his head just a bit to ensure that his face remained covered. Behind Jesus were some other men, doubtless the followers that James had heard about. Among them were Andrew and Philip, the two men he had met at the wedding in Cana. They all sat down behind Jesus, who remained standing, facing down the hill. It was at this moment that James saw the black and white robed figures standing by themselves among the trees at the top of the hill, on the opposite side of Jesus from James. They were members of the Sanhedrin, and among them he recognized the large form of Ananus. Jesus must have seen them as well, and so James's trip was a waste.

Jesus stood there in the clearing, knowing full well that all eyes were on him - and waited. It seemed to James that he waited for an interminable time, but it might have been only a minute or two. It was plain that he was waiting for quiet, though James could not see what difference it would make, since no one in that throng any farther away than he would be able to hear.

Presently he began, and, to James's surprise, Jesus sounded as though he were standing next to James, rather than 75 feet away. It was as though Jesus were talking directly to him, rather than to the assembled multitudes. He looked around him to see if any of his neighbors had noticed this, but they seemed to be listening intently. He had come to the conclusion that he was the only one of his immediate neighbors who had never heard Jesus speak, because the conversation around him while they had all been waiting had been about other events in Jesus's teaching, healing of the sick, and other miracles, and it was equally clear that they hoped to see one this day. They appeared to pay no attention to the sound of his voice, as though they had heard the phenomenon before.

Jesus's first words surprised James as well. Rather than a quote from Scripture or a few remarks of deference to the members of the Sanhedrin, Jesus began teaching on what he appeared to believe was his own authority. Without preamble or anecdote he began:

"Blessed are the poor in spirit, for theirs is the kingdom of Heaven.

"Blessed are the meek: for they shall possess the land.

"Blessed are they that mourn: for they shall be comforted.

"Blessed are they that hunger and thirst after justice: they shall have their fill.

"Blessed are the merciful: they shall obtain mercy.

"Blessed are the clean of heart: for they shall see God.

"Blessed are the peacemakers: they shall be called children of God.

"Blessed are they that suffer persecution for justice' sake: for theirs is the kingdom of Heaven.

"Blessed are you when they shall revile you and persecute you and speak all that is evil against you, untruly, for my sake: be glad and rejoice, for your reward is very great in heaven."

Very impressive thought James - sensible rules to live by - though he could not recall where in Scripture such words were to be found. Still, other than that "for my sake", there was little harm in what he said, and little there to irritate the Sanhedrin.

James looked at the people immediately around him, and attempted to see as far down the hill as he could. It appeared that everyone present, even those at the bottom of the hill, were paying rapt attention. Could it be that they all heard his brother's voice as he did? If so, Jesus was a preacher of rare power.

And yet, why did he not ground his comments in the Scripture, to add to their power and meaning? Why did he not refer to the prophets, judges and kings for support of his words? Did he believe himself so powerful that his listeners should heed his words simply because he said them? There could be little doubt that few, if any, of the other listeners had the same complaint: all eyes were fixed on Jesus, taking in his every syllable.

"Do not think that I am come to destroy the law or the prophets. I am come not to destroy but to fulfill."

Again, powerfully said. Still no reference, but still no offense, either, though he was beginning to tread dangerous ground. There was the little matter over what he meant when he said that he came to fulfill the law - that could be the mission of no one but the Messiah - but he did not overtly claim that status for himself, which, James hoped, might be enough to turn away the wrath of the Sanhedrin.

Thereafter James gave over his ruminations on the teachings of his brother, and resolved to simply listen to the remainder. During the talk Jesus walked down to the front row of people sitting near him, and appeared to speak to them, though James still heard every sound he made. He walked around the entire cleared semi-circle surrounding him in this manner, as if to better see the intentions of those listening to him. He walked erect, calmly and serenely, yet without a trace of pride, thought James, not without pride himself. He did not stammer or stumble over his words, and he did not hesitate to speak his mind, even when it appeared to James that such speaking was the very thing that brought James to Capernaum in the first place.

He was alarmed, for instance, at the fact that Jesus called the hierarchy of the synagogue hypocrites. It was not actionable in and of itself, but it could only serve to heighten their suspicion and anger, and turn them more resolutely against him.

Jesus finished with an analogy of two men who built houses, one on rock and the other on shifting sand, and then have to suffer through a storm to see which house was the best. Jesus said that the house built on the rock is the better because it will not be blown down in a storm, but James did not understand what Jesus meant.

It was clear that Jesus had finished speaking, because he turned to face his followers, who gathered around him. The crowd surrounding James made no move, as though it were not convinced that the show was over. James took advantage of this to jump up and run to the spot where Jesus was standing with his friends - still on the small plateau on the side of the hill.

As James came striding up on to the plateau, two of the men with Jesus saw him, and moved to confront him, as though he were a threat to Jesus. But Andrew and Philip had seen him also and reassured the others as to his identity, and he was allowed to confront his brother.

Jesus' eyes lit up at the sight of him, and they embraced.

"My brother," began James, "you are a powerful speaker. You held the crowd enrapt."

"It is the power of our Father in heaven which engages them," Jesus replied.

"There are those who do not understand when you say such things, and they are becoming angry."

"Including my brother James?"

"What I think does not matter, because it is not I that am charged with enforcing the law of Moses. Those who have that responsibility believe that you are stepping outside of the bounds allowed even to a prophet, and are dangerously close to blasphemy."

"If it were not true, I would not say it," said Jesus calmly. "But what does my brother say of me?"

"I believe that you are a skilled teacher, and that there is much good in what you say. But I repeat, it does not matter what I think. I was summoned by some members of the Sanhedrin, others of whom you see here" - and here he pointed to the spot where the elders of the synagogue were still standing - "and asked to explain you, and I could not. They are concerned about you, and it will not take much to goad them into doing you harm."

"Others will also be goaded by my teaching, but that is the mission for which I was sent into the world."

"Can you not come home for a while, until the region is more settled - until the differences between you and the Sanhedrin have passed?"

"My dear brother: I have come to fulfill the mission that was given to me by my Father. It is not my mission to sew peace in this world, but in the next. Let those who have ears come to me and hear, and they will be spared."

"But already we have been visited on your account. Your followers come to see where you live, and members of the Sanhedrin have come to see what they can make of you."

"I teach in public every day. They have no need of going to Nazareth to see what I am about."

"So you defy them. You dare them to come and get you. What will you do? Use your followers to defend you?"

"James, my brother: I am in no need of defense. When they are ready to arrest me I will go quietly." Jesus said this with a calm that astonished James. It was as though he expected to be arrested; even as though that were his goal. James felt the crowd that he had run ahead of pushing and shoving to get close to Jesus, making their various demands on him, and it began to be difficult to talk.

"What is it that you want? To be a victim of Roman justice? To be a victim of temple justice? What purpose is served by that? And how will I explain it to our mother?" The crowd was insistent now, touching his garment, calling his name, asking for blessings on children, elderly, animals, elbowing each other out of the way to be closer. Jesus attempted to answer James, but he could not make himself heard over the din, and his followers came to rescue him from the mob. They escorted him up the hill, the crowd still following behind, and he disappeared over the top. The crowd was still surging past James, pushing him along in its bow wave. He did nothing more until the people had passed - and not all of the thousands who were there attempted to see Jesus personally - except attempt to keep his place and not be swept along.

James rose to begin the journey home, one that he knew would be long and hungry, since he had been relieved of his funds during the trip. He had at least made the necessary effort, and had heard his brother speak for the first time, and very well at that, so the journey was not a total loss. But he had nothing of comfort to tell the Sanhedrin if they approached him again, and he had nothing to tell his mother, who had placed so much hope on this trip. A fine diplomat he turned out to be.

CHAPTER 4

"Ananias, you are my friend and a respected member of the Sanhedrin, but sometimes your theories go to far. You know my brother: he could not possibly be less interested in political power. Let us have an end to this sort of talk. Very well, I will try once again, this time - I hope - with other members of my family. But please keep in mind that Jesus is headstrong, and that he will not likely allow himself to be talked out of his mission." Then with a hug and a good night they parted ways, and James began the walk back to his home.

He immediately regretted agreeing to go and talk to Jesus again, in part because he had already done it once without success, and partly because he knew that such an effort would have no effect. Still, he did love his brother as a brother, and it appeared that there was a danger in the land for Jesus. It was unlike Ananias, an otherwise sober man, to be so bothered by the fact of Jesus' preaching in the countryside. If he were representative of the attitude at the Sanhedrin, then Jesus might be in danger from the religious leaders of his own country, and not the mobs that Ananias seemed to hint at, and it did not appear that the Romans cared about him at all.

At home he proposed the project to his mother, and she agreed to it wholeheartedly. She also sensed the danger to Jesus, though James could not understand how she could come by the information, since she was not privy to all that he had heard.

James two sisters and his brother Joses still lived in Nazareth, and they immediately agreed to go. It was decided that the Nazareth branch of the family would go Capernaum, and that the other members of the family in Jerusalem were too far away to be contacted, or to want to make the trip. Plans proceeded apace, but James could not be as enthusiastic. He fully expected to fail, but on the other hand he could not talk himself out of going. However slim the chances of success, the situation was not hopeless, and therefore it was worth making the trip.

James' mother and sisters were anxious to leave immediately, and Joses was willing when the others were ready, but James was more circumspect. He stalled for a day or so claiming illness, and made the rounds of his friends in trade to find out whether any of them might be heading north. On the morning of the third day a caravan stopped through Nazareth, and James, who happened to be in the marketplace at the time, immediately went home to get his family, who were already packed and waiting impatiently for him, and they were off.

Capernaum, the small fishing town, was quiet, other than the bustle of those concerned directly with the arrival of the caravan. James' family arrived in mid-afternoon, and the bright, sunny day was hot and dry with a light breeze blowing out of the north. Dust swirled in the streets as James and his family wandered about asking after a room. There were small urchins playing here and there, women leading other urchins and carrying their laundry down to the Sea of Galilee, the usual merchants hawking their wares, all manner of human endeavor except people offering rooms for the night.

James and his family asked one after the other, particularly the merchants operating in the streets, until they finally heard of a room that might be available near the waterfront. They walked down to the piers to see what they might find.

They found another world that is part of all fishing villages: boats creaking at their moorings under the light breeze which was no longer blocked by the buildings of the town, the pervasive odor of fish, fish oils and human waste, and the noticeable change in commerce. Those merchants who had wares for everyman to sell confined themselves to the streets of the town, while those who wished to deal specifically with the fishermen set up shop on the waterfront.

It was now late afternoon, and, unlike the streets of the town, the marketplace on the piers was largely quiet. Dealing with fishermen was a morning and late evening business, when they would be fresh back with the catch. Now there was no one around to deal with, as the fishermen who planned to were preparing to go out in the evening, and the rest were elsewhere on business, or at home. No money was changing hands, so the piers were quiet, other than the usual loafers waiting either for a handout or for a job.

James asked one of the hangers on about the house with the room, and was pointed, after providing a menial bribe, in the direction of a two story home standing by itself one block from the piers. James and his family were shown a small, unfurnished room much like the one they had stayed in Cana. This room was equipped with straw on the floor, but it had such a low ceiling that James and his brother could not stand upright in it. They took it anyway for lack of something better, and, after arranging the few belongings they brought with them, they set off to find Jesus.

Everyone in Capernaum had heard of Jesus, and all had an opinion of him, but none seemed to know where he was at the moment. They wandered the quiet streets asking after him, and were finally rewarded by stumbling on one of Jesus' followers, who had been sent by the others to buy bread.

"Do I know him? Absolutely. I am one of his followers, called Judas. And who are you?" Upon being informed of their identities, Judas, a smallish man with a long, aquiline nose, a full thick beard just beginning to show some hint of gray, and piercing eyes, was at first pleasantly surprised, and said so. But this seemed to pass quickly, thought James, probably as the man figured what could possibly be their purpose. He covered it well, though, and soon agreed to take them to where Jesus was.

Jesus was at the home of another of his followers, Peter, when Judas brought his family to him. They found themselves at a small cluster of houses, one on each corner of a lot, of which one belonged to Peter. Between the houses there appeared to be a common courtyard, and this appeared to be filled at the moment of their arrival with every man from the town of Capernaum. Standing in the street outside the house they could see that the house itself was full of people, and they could see swarms of people sitting around the top of the fence that closed off the interior of the courtyard. James wanted to believe that it was a local party of some kind, but then he noticed that there was no noise coming from anywhere in the house or garden. He could see the people crowding the house and sitting on the wall, but none of them appeared to be talking. All were facing the courtyard between the houses and seemingly listening intently. It was an eerie silence that befell, and James could guess the reason for it: his brother was preaching.

Judas attempted to lead them through the house to the garden, but found that he could not pass. They then returned to the street to try the other houses, but they were also packed and had no room for the newcomers. Finally Judas took them back to the door of Peter's home, and bade them wait for his return. He then disappeared into the house and left them standing alone.

It was now late afternoon, and the sun was heading inexorably for the horizon, which in this case was the flat roofline of the houses across the way to the west. It was still hot and the sun shone brightly on the front of Peter's house, so James and his family moved around the south side to make use of what little shade resulted from the curve of the house away from the sun. They waited for what seemed a long time to James, who was about to attempt to part the crowd again, when a sweating Judas emerged once again from the house.

James could tell by the look on his face that Judas did not have news that they would like to hear. He walked slowly toward them, once he found them, with an apologetic look that belied the content of his message, if not the words.

Judas glanced quickly at their expectant faces as they gathered around him, and then studied the ground in front of him.

"Well? What has he to say?" asked James.

"You can see that there is a huge crowd to hear the master speak," Judas began, "and he is loath to leave them when they have waited long for him...."

"But we are his family, and we do not intend to steal him away, merely talk to him for a few minutes," James interrupted, as he could see where Judas's preamble was taking them.

"Oh, he will surely see you," Judas hastened to add, reassuringly. "Do not think for a moment that he has forgotten you. It is merely that he is teaching at the moment, and would prefer not to stop," he said, earnestly.

"Did you tell him that two brothers and two sisters are here, and that his mother is here?" asked James.

"I did, and he understands the effort you have gone to be here. But...."

"What did he say when you told him that we were here?" asked the increasingly angry James, who could tell that Judas was attempting to cover for the 'master'.

"This was evidently the question that Judas had been hoping would not be asked, since it caused him to paw the ground with his foot even harder. Presently, as if in answer to some new resolution, he lifted his head and looked at them.

"He said, 'Who are my brothers and my sisters? Are not all the people of the world my brothers and sisters? Are not the sinners who need me my brothers and sisters?" Here he stopped, though it was obvious that there was more he wanted to say. Again he looked studiously at the ground.

James was outraged. "What does he mean by this? That we are no longer his family? That we, who have sheltered him, loved him, covered for him with the authorities are no longer good enough for him? He now proposes to replace us with the sinners and tax collectors that he consorts with?"

Judas interrupted him. "Surely that is not what he meant. I have heard him speak of his family with love. He merely used the opportunity to make a point to those he is teaching. You cannot think that he has forgotten you."

"You are the one who tells us that my brother claims to be kin to the sinners of the world. He has redefined his family and left us out of his new world! I will go to see him myself." James attempted to push past Judas, who immediately began to plead with him not to make a scene, but James would have overpowered the much smaller man. He desisted only because his mother stood in front of him and grabbed his arms, and insisted that he not go in.

"James, don't, I beg you," said Mary. He is with his followers - let him be. We will see him later." James demanded to know how she, the mother of the man in question, could tolerate being treated in this manner, but she would not discuss the subject. "Do not make a scene, James, for my sake," she said.

As ever he could not refuse his mother, and so after another short pushing bout with Judas, he desisted. James wanted to wait for Jesus to come out, but Mary insisted that they find something to eat and then retire for the night. As they walked back to the waterfront, James chastised her.

"How can you allow Jesus to treat you this way? Is it not his duty to come when his mother calls?"

"I do not know his duty, only he knows it. Whatever he does, and whatever he says, he has a reason for it. Let him follow the path that is marked out for him."

"The path that is marked out for him leads to the cross - that is why we are here. If he does not cease the Sanhedrin and other enemies will find a way to do away with him." James was still indignant at having been turned away, and at the fact that Jesus had not even come out to see his mother.

"Maybe that is the path that he is to follow. I do not know, and neither do you. It is for us to allow him to go his own way."

"Then why are we here? Why are we not at home in Nazareth, allowing him to go his own way?"

"I am still a mother, even if I have been supplanted. I do not want to see him hurt or killed, and I will do what I can to prevent that. But I will not attempt to force him or shame him into obeying my wishes." James shook his head, but could find little else to say to his mother. It was obvious to him that she was still operating under the assumption that he was on some special mission from God, as were, it was safe to guess, most of the people crowding the house where he was currently speaking. His brother was a different story however, and he resolved to visit Jesus that night when the crowd had disbursed.

Accordingly, when the family had finished its small supper, James, under the pretense of going for a walk, went back to the house of Peter. He thought he detected a suspicious look on the face of his mother, but she said nothing, so he went his way. When he arrived back at the house the crowd was still there. It was just as silent as before, and appeared to be more crowded. There were now clusters of people gathered outside the house, though he knew from experience that it would be impossible for them to hear his brother from there.

He approached them to see what they knew of the length of the session currently underway, and was surprised to have them insist that he be quiet. He looked at them more closely, and sure enough they appeared to be listening to something, though James could not make out what. He asked, and was bidden to be quiet again by a man standing in the street outside the house, his eyes staring firmly at the ground, but his ears apparently cocked for some sound that James could not pick up.

James walked around the block of houses, and found it the same on all sides. All of the people in the street appeared to be listening to something, and none would carry on even the most rudimentary conversation with him. So James edged up to one of the doors in an attempt to hear better, but he could pick up nothing save the sounds that always go with a crowd trying to be quiet: the occasional shuffling of feet, muffled coughs, an occasional sneeze. He also became aware of the oppressive heat in the house, since all of those bodies blocked the normal air flow through it. He could see no way into the house, and after the failed attempts at conversation he decided not to try to force his way in. He retreated to the other side of the street to wait.

It was another hour before the crowd began to break up, and in all that time there was sign of weariness among the watchers and listeners in the street. None of them drifted off early, or gave up the vigil they had taken up so many hours before. Whatever else he might not like, he could do nothing but marvel at the power of his brother's preaching.

But, finally, long after dark, the crowd did begin to break up, and James sat up anxiously in his perch leaning on the house on the far side of the street, making sure not to miss the departure of Jesus in the ensuing exodus. When it was apparent, about 20 minutes later, that all of the crowd had left, and he had not seen Jesus, he once more approached the house.

There was a single lamp in the entry room, and apparently no one in the house. He could hear voices coming from the back of the house where the courtyard was located, and, in the absence of anyone to let him in, he proceeded through the door and to the rear of the house.

Behind the two sparsely furnished rooms he found a door that led to the courtyard, and he paused in that door to get his bearings. There was a low table set up in the courtyard, lit by a single lamp, and men were gathered around that table eating and talking. He recognized Andrew and Philip, the two followers of his brother that he had met at the wedding in Cana, and he could see his brother sitting at the table with his back to the door where James stood. The other men he did not know, though he looked carefully at them in the flickering lamplight for some sign of recognition. His reverie was interrupted by a smallish woman pulling on his sleeve.

"The master is not teaching any more today," said she. "Come back tomorrow." James brushed her aside, and, emboldened by her attempt to be rid of him, strode over to that table where the men sat. They all looked up at him unknowingly, save for Andrew and Philip, who recognized him and pointed him out to Jesus. Jesus looked up and smiled at him and said, "Peace be to you, brother. Join us."

"I must talk with you," was all that James said in reply.

"We will talk, as long as you wish. But you must be famished from the journey - sup with us first, and then you and I will talk." James did not

59

want to dispute with his brother in front of the followers, so after a moment's indecision, he sat down. He was handed some bread and wine, and Andrew made the introductions around the table.

James could not remember all the names, but there were two Simons (though one was apparently called Peter), James, Thomas, Matthew, Thaddeus, Judas, and others whose names he did not have time to commit to memory. He was greeted warmly and fondly by all of the company, but he could not do justice to the food he was given.

Conversation at the table consisted of the followers of James' brother asking Jesus what was meant by certain parables which had apparently been part of the speech that day. James could not follow the conversation exactly because he had not heard the speech, but he gathered that there had been parables concerning fruit trees, growers, and lost children. He paid little attention to this talk because he was trying to decide what he would say to Jesus when he had the chance. The family had come here to attempt to convince Jesus to come home, but James was now more incensed over their treatment that afternoon than he was over Jesus' ministry.

Presently Jesus rose, thanked the woman who had challenged James and who appeared to be the mistress of the house, since she hovered nearby looking after the wants of the men, and then, with a glance at James, indicated that they should repair to the far side of the courtyard.

They sat on a small bench under a tree on the side of the courtyard opposite where the others were sitting. Jesus smiled and looked at James expectantly, but said nothing.

"I..that is, we..came here to talk to you about your ministry and the danger you are in if you continue. You know that your mother and sisters are here with me? But first, I have to ask why you refused to see us this afternoon. No, that is not even the problem. The problem is, why did you not even acknowledge that we are your family? Why did you claim that those around you are your family?" James could feel his indignation rising over the afternoon slight, and his voice began to rise as well. "You and I have not been as close as we might have been, but you should have no reason to speak thusly of me. But that is something that I can live with. What I cannot understand is how you can allow such talk to come back to our mother. Do you not know that you must have devastated her? How could you be so cruel to her? And to our sisters, who have never been anything but kind to you?"

"James, my dear brother, there is no one I love more than my family, save our Father in heaven. But I am come to call sinners, and it was to sinners that I spoke this afternoon. You, Joseph, Mary, and all my brothers and sisters are already with me - I have no need of coming to you. I did not say that you are not my family - merely that there are also others who are part of my family the church. If a shepherd should lose a calf, will he not leave the others to find the one that is lost? Today I was looking for those who are lost, and calling them to me."

"Calling them to you - and not to God? I believe you are talking to me as though you are the Messiah, and we have had that discussion already. I cannot think where you got such an idea, and I cannot force you to give it up, but it is putting you in danger with the Sanhedrin, and now it is in danger of coming between you and your family - your earthly family."

"Nothing will come between me and my family. They will be with me always, and I with them. But I must call those who are not with me - who have not heard the good news - and it is to them that I must devote the remainder of my time here. Mary understands this already.....yes, she does.....and you, my brothers and sisters will come to understand it."

"What do you mean by 'the remainder of your time here?' Are you aware that you are in more danger now than when I spoke to you last? That is why we have all come: to persuade you to come home before a trap closes around you."

"My time here is limited - that is the will of the Father. But it is not a danger to me - it is simply the will of the Father. I go where he directs and teach to all who would listen. The hypocrites in the Sanhedrin will not listen to me, and because of that it is they who are in danger."

"It is they who may kill you, and not you who will kill them."

"They cannot kill me, just as they cannot kill anyone who heeds my words. Those who will sacrifice themselves for my sake will have everlasting life. The Sanhedrin will also fulfill the will of the Father, though it will win for them everlasting torment."

"If you do not care what happens to you, think of your mother. She has come this far to beg you to come home, to keep yourself safe for her."

"She has not come this far for that purpose - she knows what I must do, though she may not yet fully understand how it will all be carried out. She hopes yet that my mission here will not come to the conclusion she fears, and to that end she is willing to attempt to sway me, but she knows in her heart that I cannot be swayed."

To James' dismay, that statement seemed to echo the truth. Mary had always been a willing participant in this trip, but never an enthusiastic one. It would explain much if he could believe that she were only along to observe, since she did not believe that Jesus could be swayed. James paused for a moment, and shifted his position on the hard stone bench on which they were seated.

"You are beyond appeal," said he finally. "You do not even care for the health or the good opinion of your mother. How is any person to reach you?"

"You are wrong there, dear brother. I care very much for my mother's health, but I am come to fulfill the words of our Father in heaven. It is not for me to throw over my mission for the sake of my mother. Do you think that I am not aware of the pain that I have caused others? I am, but, as I have told you many times, there is nothing I can do about that pain. You will be made to understand all in good time. The question is this: do I spread my message - a message that could lead to the salvation of the world - or do I cease and stay home for the sake of my mother and my brothers? There is really no question of what the answer must be."

This was certainly true. How could James hope to sway Jesus with worldly concerns when it was apparent that Jesus believed himself to be on a mission from God? The two of them were talking at two different levels, and there was no way to reach Jesus on his.

"If you will not take the concern of your mother into account, then consider your own safety. There are those in the Sanhedrin who are calling for your head, and there is no doubt that such people have allies, maybe even among the people who follow you."

"I have no enemies among my immediate circle of friends, and the rest I cannot control. James: what will be, will be. I would no more try to avoid what is coming than I would submit to the devil himself. I put the same faith in the Father that you should put in Him, and in me."

James rolled his eyes at this last, and said, "It would be easier to place faith in you if you did not claim to be the Messiah. You know that I cannot believe that."

"Yet there are many who do, and for them there will be eternal life. There is no way to the Father but through me, my brother, but you must first open your eyes to see. I am the true path, but you cannot follow me until you see who I am."

"We have been through all this before, and you have not convinced me, and you will not do so now. How many false prophets have there been in our history? Have we not been warned to be alert for them? I find that I must be alert against my own brother."

"I am the way, the truth, and the light. All who would have eternal life must obtain it through me. I have been sent by the Father to bring the good news of salvation to all the world. It is through me that he will redeem the sins of man, and through me that man will be reconciled to the Father. All this will be made clear to you James."

"So you always tell me, and now I wish to hear no more on the subject. I have done all that I can, and, I believe, all that can be expected of me for you. Your mother, three brothers and two sisters have journeyed here from Nazareth to see if we could make you understand the situation you have placed yourself in. I have now been to see you twice, each time with the same result. While I will always love you as my brother, I can do nothing other than wash my hands of your fate."

"You will not be the last."

With this James rose from the spot where he and Jesus had been sitting in the corner of the yard, and for the first time noticed that he and Jesus were the last ones in the courtyard. The night was now chilly, and far advanced. James stretched himself and began to walk toward the door that led to the street. Jesus followed after him. James should have been tired, but he did not feel it; he seemed to have a feeling of dread, as though this parting with his brother were somehow different from the rest. He knew that Ananias would not be happy at the failure of his mission, and he could only hope that Ananias would be disappointed, not angry. He didn't fear for himself, but for Jesus, who did not appear to understand the forces gathering around him.

His report to his family the next morning was mercifully brief. It was quite apparent that Jesus could not be talked out of his ministry, and there was no amount of pressure or guilt that the family could bring to bear that would sway him. There was some discussion about whether they should all try to go see him at once, but James' detailed answers to their questions about the conversation the night before convinced them that there would be no point in it. So they packed up their meager belongings and began the trip back to Nazareth.

They arrived in the late evening and, after a simple supper, went straight to bed. The next day after opening his shop for a while early in the morning, intending to close it at midday and go to the home of Simon to report his failure. But soon after he opened Simon appeared at the shop inquiring after the mission. James recounted the discussion briefly, leaving out the other details of the trip, including the size of the crowd of people listening to Jesus. Simon listened with interest but without surprise, and, after a short discussion of more mundane matters, departed. James knew that it would not be long before Ananias had a complete report.

Simon had not been gone five minutes when James, who was working with his back to the street, heard someone enter his shop. He turned to find Esther smiling at him.

"Where is my chair?" she demanded, in a mock serious tone, smiling all the while.

"It is here," James replied, turning back to pick up the piece he had just been working on. "You see that it is almost finished; in fact it might be complete now were it not for this interruption."

"I hardly think that, carpenter. I see that my chair is such a low number on your list that you have time for travel rather than finishing it." As she talked James noticed that she was dressed very well this morning, with a blue cloak and a white veil surrounding her pretty face. Her eyes fairly shone, and her smile was infectious. James glanced ruefully down at his dirty brown cloak covered with sawdust and sweat.

"Don't feel badly for your appearance," she told him, answering his actions. "I would not expect anything else from a successful carpenter. But as long as you are looking, you have it in your hair also." James reached up and ran a hand through his hair, and found that he could hardly do so, so thick was the mess there.

There was an awkward pause, broken by the ever resourceful Esther. "How was your trip? Did you bring your brother home with you?"

"No, I...that is...we did not. I told him on parting that I now wash my hands of him. I have tried twice to talk him into his senses, once at the cost of a robbery and both times requiring long trips, but he does not heed. He likes playing the part of the prophet in the desert. He likes having the people surround him, listening to his every word. He will not come home or tone down his words, and I have done all that I can. He will have to look after himself from now on."

"I think your brother is a good man. He may be a misguided prophet, but he is harmless. Leave him to his own devices."

"I would gladly do so, but I have been enlisted twice, by powerful figures, to go to him and talk him out of his work. They seem to believe that he is dangerous, though they cannot convince me of it. It is true that he is in danger, because the men who prompted me to bring him home do not like his message or his presence. When they talk to me they always cite the Romans as his enemies, but the Romans do not care about him. It is the Sanhedrin that he has to worry about."

"But how is James the carpenter? Is he ready to get on with his life now?"

"It is too late for that. You know that I intended to go to Jerusalem to study, and only became a carpenter out of love for my father. Jesus should be where I am. I am ready to go on with the rest of my life to the extent that being a carpenter is my life. There is little else I can do now."

"So why have you not accepted fate, and moved on? Stewing over it will not help."

"I am trying to put the matter in the past, but it is difficult. The difference between studying one's God and carpentry is stark, and there is little I can do at the one to assuage the feeling of loss over the other."

"Well, I will help you. Wash your hands, and help me devour this lunch that I have brought. And please spare me your claims about how much work you have to do: if my chair is not done because you have time for travel, then you have time for lunch."

"If I am to be dragged out to lunch, the chair will be delayed."

"The chair is already delayed. If you do not go with me, I will consider the account in arrears." With this threat James put down his tools, washed his hands, allowed Esther to attempt to comb some of the sawdust out of his hair, and accompanied her to a small square in the middle of town where they could eat in the public eye without the presence of a chaperone.

They sat down on a low stone wall surrounding the well at the center of the square. Esther had packed bread and roasted lamb, a bottle of wine, grapes and some cheese. James found that he enjoyed the lunch immensely, though he irritated Esther by refusing to drink any of the wine.

"Why not?" she demanded. "Is the bottle I have brought not up to your high standards?"

"The bottle is to my liking, but I am slowly coming to the conclusion that a religious man should not touch spirits. They tend to alter one's condition - to give one a sense of happiness that is false because it does not come from God. I am going to stay away from wine for a time to see if I am not the better for it."

They passed a pleasant half hour watching the people come and go in the square, talking over the news of Nazareth - a relatively small town where many of the people knew each other - and never once mentioning the chair. James finally pleaded that he had to get back to work, and Esther walked back to his shop with him. James was vaguely sorry to see her go when she turned to head up his street toward her own home. He stood leaning on the pole supporting the roof of his outdoor shop watching her disappear in the crowd when he heard his mother behind him.

"You have been gone for some time," she said. "I trust you needed the rest?" He turned his head to her, without turning his body away from the street.

James noted the wry smile on her face. "I did not need the rest or the time off from my chores. But I did enjoy the lunch."

"There is more to the world than work, food, and sleep," said Mary, "and I am beginning to think that you need to find those other things."

James looked back up the street to see if he could still see Esther. He could not. "I am not settled enough to provide for a wife as yet, mother. There is still time."

"It is time to get over your disappointment at not being able to study in Jerusalem. You are a good carpenter - you have a fine business. Why can you not be happy? Many people in the world are much worse off than you, and they did not have the choice of going to Jerusalem to study or following in the family business. It is very likely that the rich and powerful are unhappier than you - because no one will find happiness in the things of this world. Look to God for your answers, James, not in your profession or in anger at your brother."

"It was in God that I hoped to find happiness - studying his law in the synagogue."

"Studying God and loving him are different things. The Sanhedrin, who have now put you up to two trips to talk to Jesus, study God, but they do not love Him. He is their excuse for keeping hold of the reins of power. Do not fall into their trap, James. You are too good a man for that."

James wanted to object that he was not like the Sanhedrin, but decided against it. He turned to Mary, kissed her on the cheek, and went back to his work. He worked feverishly that afternoon, finally finishing the chair for Esther and other smaller items for various denizens of the city. He skipped supper and fell into bed exhausted late at night.

CHAPTER 5

The next time he saw Ananias, which was a few weeks later as once again his friend passed through Nazareth, his friend and member of the Sanhedrin in Jerusalem asked him about his association with the Zealots, and was given an earful on the subject. They were standing and talking outside the temple, where they had met while James was on his rounds among the poor.

"I am done with them," said James. "They claim to be Zealots in defense of the Hebrew nation, but their zealotry consists in meeting and eating and drinking." James told Ananias about his efforts to interest them in charitable undertakings, and the response he got from them.

Ananias laughed heartily. "They are not the same as their brethren," he replied. "The Zealots give us more trouble than the Romans. They are fanatic about an independent Israel, and constantly agitate the people to get them to join the cause. Any situation, any meeting with the Romans, any small disturbance where the Zealots are present could be turned into a conflagration that would be ruinous for us all. As I told your (that is to say their) meeting, there is simply no way that we are going to be rid of the Romans any time soon. We must find other alternatives to the violence that they frequently advocate. You are fortunate that you became involved with a harmless crew. Not all are like that."

"I consider myself a level headed man. I cannot account for why I would condescend to go to even one of their meetings (though the food was good). They differ little from other groups in the way that they interpret the Scriptures according to the law, which is really what matters anyway. I will return to my Pharisaic roots, and be done with all those who would twist it to suit their own ends. I cannot help remarking, though, that your father was a Zealot."

Again Ananias laughed heartily. "That he was, and it was a mistake on his part that I will not make. James, James! I am sympathetic! What we do not need are more people telling us how to interpret the Scripture. This is the role of the rabbi and the elders. God himself set up one of the tribes of Israel to be priests to his people. It is not for every man to read the Scripture and then tell his brother what it meant." There was a pause, and James sensed Ananias looking at him in a quizzical manner. He looked at his eyes, and then realized that he must have been thinking about Jesus.

"No, you cannot hold that against me, my friend. As you know, I have done what I could about my dear brother. I wish more than you that he had stayed home and followed in our father's footsteps, but he did not. He is now preaching in the countryside and in the small town of Capernaum, but he is not offering revolt against the established order, nor is he attempting to overthrow the law of Moses. He is harmless to you and to the nation. I am his brother, not his keeper."

Ananias smiled patiently. "We differ on how accurately he interprets the law of Moses, James, and we differ on how much benefit he might derive from abasing the law. But there can be little doubt that he is a force to be reckoned with, and no longer a countryside preacher trying to scratch a living. He arrived in Jerusalem the day before yesterday with his followers, to the great joy of a multitude that sang his praises and spread palm branches before his donkey.

"Palm branches? Donkey?" What is the meaning of those things?" asked James.

"That is hardly for us to say. You know that he never speaks clearly about what he is talking about. He speaks in parables and stories that I am told even his followers have to have him interpret later. Yet day before yesterday he was the subject of a huge throng that turned out to see him ride into Jerusalem on a donkey, and laid palm branches before him, yet! Whether you like his teaching or not, you must agree that he is a man with power, and he is to be reckoned with."

"I can hardly think that you have listened to my brother's teaching, if you think him to be a man of power or influence. These are the last things on his mind."

"Power and influence do not necessarily have to be on his mind. If they are on the minds of his followers, it may be enough to incite them. You know the corrupting influence of praise and glory being heaped on one man: it could sway him to take up the cause of the people - or, for that matter, the Zealots - and then we would be in a pretty fix. No matter how powerful a speaker he is, he is likely to be a poor general, and he would certainly be a general without an army and without supplies. Such is the danger of religious fanaticism."

This time it was James' turn to laugh. "I really think you are being too imaginative. My brother loathes the idea of power - you know that. And whatever else he has done, he would not lead the people in a revolution on Rome."

"It is difficult to say what he might do. I am told that there have been incidents already, and he is only in the city for seven days thus far."

"Your information certainly travels quickly. Have you not been out of the city for two days?"

"I have, but I have had the good fortune to come across other travelers who have relayed information to me, and they are people that I trust to tell me the truth." Suddenly his mood brightened, and he let out one of those merry laughs that he was known for. "But enough of this James. Let us have no more on your brother. I am sure that you are right, and that we will

68

have no trouble from him. I was sidetracked when you mentioned the Zealots: I did not congratulate you on your return to traditional teachings of the law."

"I have never left the traditional teachings of the law. I did not give up any beliefs in order to sit in on meetings with rich old men. I was irritated at the Romans over the search of my home, and allowed myself to be beguiled into thinking that there was something that could be done about them. That is obviously not the case, and, even if it were, it would not get done by the local Zealotry. They cannot be counted upon to get out of bed in the morning if there is any risk in the enterprise. Without those of the Zealots who might have participated I have less resources to distribute, but nothing that I can get my hands on goes to waste."

"It may interest you to know that your charitable efforts have reached the ears of the Sanhedrin. No, no, it is true. Travelers have brought word of the man who closes his carpenter shop two days a week and spends his time among the poor and downtrodden. I understand that your mother is involved with you as well? You see, some travelers bring complete information. In fact they mentioned two women who assist you: an older one, whom I took to be your mother, and a younger one that I could not place."

"That would be Esther, who is a daughter of a friend of the family."

"Well, all three of you have the attention of those who work with the poor. I have heard you referred to as 'James the Just.'"

James colored slightly, in embarrassment. "That is very kind of you to say, though I insist that I had no idea of gaining any renown for myself."

"James, there is no need to justify yourself to me. Have we not been friends for nearly 20 years? Do I not know my James after all this time? Was I surprised when these reports of a just man working among the poor in Nazareth reached my ears? When I first heard the reports, without the name of the man being given, did I not assume that the man was my friend James? For some there is reward in this life as well as the next."

This was all very flattering to James, and yet he felt somewhat cheapened by it. Whereas he had been content to work privately, he now was afraid that people would think that he had been doing it for the attention. It was a form of payment for having done a favor, and it was payment that he could not help but resent.

It was late in the afternoon when James and Ananias broke up on the steps of the temple in Nazareth, and James extended the priest an invitation to come to his home for dinner, an invitation the man heartily accepted.

"I would not miss the company and home of your mother for all the world," said he. "So much is this true, that I am altering my plans to leave for Jerusalem this afternoon."

"In that case you will of course stay with us the night," offered James.

"Nothing could be better."

The next morning early Ananias departed for Jerusalem, and promised Mary and James to see to the welfare of Jesus, to the extent that he could. Immediately after his departure, an invigorated James went to the temple courtyard, where he hoped to gather goods for the poor.

Such was his reputation by this time that occasionally people would bring items to him for the poor. He was known about the area, greeted by all, and frequently stopped on the street with the offer of an old cloak, some well worn sandals, money or some other item that the owner thought might be of use to the poor. It was for this reason that he always repaired to the temple first before beginning his rounds among the poor: his own depleted resources were not enough to sustain the enterprise by themselves.

The courtyard of the temple was crawling with business. There were venders of every sort, selling crockery, cloth, fruit and vegetables, prepared food, bread, fresh and cooked meat, live meat such as sheep and goats, and obviously used items such as clothes and cooking utensils. They operated from various positions and contraptions, the most popular being the cart that could be opened into a small shop, and then folded and carted away again at the end of the day. Others simply laid their wares on the ground, others across the backs of donkeys. The air was thick with the smell of human perspiration, animal excrement, cooking fires, the competing cries of the venders seeking attention from the passersby as well as the calls for alms from the beggars.

He sat on a corner of the steps of the temple, and waited to see what would come to him. There was money, goods of many varieties, an occasional encouraging word from a passerby, an occasional poor person attempting to dip into the accumulation before it was theirs for the asking. James was inclined to politely fend them off, in payment for their bad manners, if for no other reason, but the thought of his actual mission around him startled him back to reality, and he agree to share some of the early wealth with them.

James observed the scene for a few moments, wondering only vaguely to himself if the courtyard of the temple were the right place for such enterprise, when out of the crowd stepped Esther.

"James," said she, "it is pleasant to see you here this morning. Your reputation has preceded you, and your generosity is known about the town. I have heard that you come here to collect items for the poor, but I had not been able to find you near. You have chosen a convenient corner, I see."

James had established himself on the northwest corner of the steps leading up to the temple itself. He commanded an excellent view of the entire

70

courtyard. "Yes," said he, " I was fortunate today. There have been other times when I could hardly squeeze in the gate, and others when I could find no place to sit other than on the ground among the shells of the venders. I always try to sit someplace high like this so that those who have something for me can find me easily. I am afraid that if they look too long, they will give up without leaving anything for the poor. Where are you going?"

"I am just out for a walk in the most colorful part of the town. It is sad to see the temple in this condition, but where else can one see such an aggregate of the people of the world?"

"If you would care to see this aggregate pass by you, instead of you by it, sit with me here. I should be here for another hour." Esther happily accepted this offer, and sat beside James. James remarked to himself that she, as beautiful as ever, seemed out of place in this den of thieves. She was as clean and fresh as the first breeze of the morning, and the surroundings were rank, dirty, and foul.

After a few weeks of waiting somewhere in the temple for handouts for the poor, James' reputation had grown to the extent that people intending to donate something to the cause would bypass the actual beggars in the street to give their item to James. There eventually came the day that James had been fearing, though he could not put a name on it, when the first poor person had attempted to retrieve something from the store brought to James.

A burly, gray bearded man dressed in very fine coat and cloak came walking down the street, fighting his way amongst the venders and money changers, bearing an armload of clothes, obviously, even from a distance, intended for James. The man passed several likely beggars on his way to James, and, after he had handed the items to James and the two exchanged pleasantries, one of the bypassed beggars rose from his spot and came to James and asked for one of the items that the man had brought.

James was about to give it to the man, when the donor stopped him. "I have come in good faith to give these clothes to the poor," said he, "and I'll not have them worn by dregs who get their living off the backs of others."

"But sir," said James, fighting to make himself heard above the din, "is he not the poor for whom this fine cloak was intended?"

"I know not who he is. He may be the most lazy, impractical man that God has ever created, and he may be the most industrious. But it matters not: I seek you out to give donations to because I believe that you will filter out the undeserving - those who will not support themselves, no matter how able - and give to those truly in need. I do not know this man, and so cannot be expected to give to him the gifts that I have accumulated over the years. Let me instead give to the poor through you."

"I appreciate your comments about any merits I might have, but will say no more on the subject. Leave the items to me, and I will see that they go to the right people."

"If I had wanted this man to have them, I could have given them to him when I passed by. I want to know that they are going to people who deserve them - who cannot make their own way in the world. It is my understanding that this is what you do."

"I make every effort," said James, in his calmest voice. "I do not claim to succeed all the time, but I always make the effort." This seemed to mollify the man, and he went off through the crowds toward the temple gate. After seeing that he was gone, James gave the item to the man who had asked for it. Then he thought again, and took it back. "No, I cannot let you have that item, it would almost certainly get back to the man that I had disobeyed his wishes, and he would give me no more goods. We cannot have that, so you" he said, turning to the mystified poor man "will have to make do with something else." The two of them looked through the pile of clothes that had accumulated, and the man, who had never said a word, picked another cloak and left, silently as he had come.

"Esther smiled at this transaction. "Is it always so contentious?"

"Not often, but it is also true that there are more debates over the issue of giving items to the poor than you might suspect. There are many like this man who want their donation to go to certain kinds of poor, if they can be found; there are others who do not want it known that they give to the poor, and so I am sworn to secrecy; still others have come to me wishing to exchange a poor cloak for a better one, as though I were in the business of buying and selling. It is sometimes tempting to dismiss them all and say that I will take care of matters, but I cannot afford to be so incautious. I need their support if I am to keep this up."

"Why is it so important to you? You could give to the poor through the temple as everyone else does. Why do you make a personal affair?" asked Esther.

"I am compelled, by God, I believe, to do it. There are times when I wonder why I continue, or why I got started, but each time I tell myself that it is time to give it up, I cannot. I do not know why God has chosen me; I see that there is work to be done, I am anxious for final favor from God, and so I have chosen a method whereby I can help others and myself. I only pray to God that I read his intentions right."

After another hour it became apparent that James would get no more contributions that day, so he and Esther gathered up what he had and headed out into the city. Strangely, they were not bothered by the poor begging in the temple. James speculated that it was because they hoped for money, and they knew that James had little. Nevertheless he put a coin in each cup that was offered to him on his way out of the temple, so that by the time they reached the gate he had nothing left. In response to Esther's jibe that that would slow down business for the rest of the day, he declared that he always brought a certain amount for giving himself, and when that supply was exhausted there was no more until the next week.

James wished to visit the south end of the town, where he had not been for some weeks. He and Esther decided after a very short walk, that they could not carry the goods they had amassed that morning that far. They stopped by the house of a man that Esther knew, and borrowed a small wooden cart that the man used to carry goods to market, placed the goods in that, and continued on their way.

When they reached the destination that James had in mind, James set the front end of the cart down, and said to Esther, "Let us try something new. We will leave the cart here, and let the poor come to us. In the past I have sought them out, but since there is no money to give today, it is better that they all be given equal chance at the goods. Since I know where they are, I will fetch them. You stay here with the cart to see that it does not disappear with one person."

James then walked the narrow streets in this outskirts of Nazareth looking for the people that he knew to be in need. Some simply slept in the streets, others had various rudimentary shelters, but little else. All lacked the necessary niceties such as clothes and sandals. James looked into their various hovels, lean-tos, tents, and caves and summoned those that he could find to the spot where he had left Esther. Word spread quickly, so James made his way back to Esther. On the way, just as he was entering the town proper, he heard a woman scream. Thinking that it sounded like Esther, even though no discernible words were spoken, he ran to the spot. He found her lying on the ground and the cart overturned, but no one else about. There was a cut by her left eye, but she was conscious and appeared to be only moderately in pain. He picked up her shoulders and held her, and used his cloak to stanch the flow of blood from the wound.

In answer to his demands for explanations, she said that a man had attempted to take some of the goods off of the cart, and that when she had asked him to wait for the others to gather, he had become insolent and insisted on rummaging through the items on the cart for anything that would suit him. Esther had insisted again that he wait, and he refused. She had then tried to stand between him and the cart, and the man had pulled her hair to get her out of the way. It was at that moment that she had screamed, and in the next he had struck her, taken something off of the cart, and then fled. He was a bearded ruffian in clothes so threadbare they barely clung to his back, but other than that she could remember nothing. Nor did she desire to, when James acted as though he intended to try to find the man.

"We would have given the things to him anyway, would we not? What sense is there in punishing a man for doing something that five minutes later we would do for him?"

"You have had an early initiation to the problems of helping the poor. You are quite right that we might have given the man the same cloak five minutes later, but it is also true that we might not have. We will attempt to see who needs what the most. The problem is that if people are allowed to run to the cart and take what they want, we will be in the position of allowing the biggest, or the strongest, or the earliest, or the luckiest to dominate. We attempt to be fair to all - the strong and the frail - and because of this we must have order. I would not be pursuing the man to punish him, but to show the others that they will not be allowed to steal from the others like them. If we were to follow your thought to its end, we would simply pull the cart down here, leave it in the street, and let the poor fend for themselves. In fact, we had better begin to deal with them now."

As they had been talking a crowd had been gathering around the cart, sampling the wares, (which were mostly clothes, some cooking utensils, sandals, bags and the like) trying different things to see if they fit or if they worked, and James did not like the look of the crowd. They were the usual lame, halt, and blind that he was accustomed to seeing on his jaunts through the city, but they seemed more ugly and surly on this day.

He immediately began to assert some control over the crowd, who were pushing each other to get closer to the cart, pushing the old and the weak out of the way, fighting over the most desirable items, and in the process damaging them. James pushed them away from the cart, took the goods that they had already taken away from them (he was younger and in more vigorous health, so they were hardly in a position to resist), and told them to stand back.

"We will do this in an orderly manner," said he. "We will try to see that all of you get that which you need, but we will not allow you to overpower those weaker than you. All of you stand there to one side in a group, and I will call you out by what appears to be your need." He then sized up the crowd, which was about 20 people, and called forward an old woman covered with ragged cloth and a shawl. James told her to pick through the items on the cart until she found a cloak that would fit her. Esther helped her with this, as the woman herself was so weak that she could hardly move one item on the cart to look at the others. The rest of the crowd was sullen over James' choice, and he kept a wary eye on them as the woman made her selection. Once or twice younger men in the crowd edged closer to the cart, and James ordered them back, fearing that they might trigger a stampede.

In this manner did James conduct the dividing up of the charitable contributions, but he noticed that as each selection was made, all based on his assessment of who left in the crowd was the most needy, he could see that those left were less and less patient. At each selection there was a larger murmur from the remaining crowd, another attempt to edge closer to the cart, another loud grouse about how all the best items were being taken. As the crowd grew more surly, James noticed that Esther grew more nervous, but he also admired the fact that she did not allow this to deter her from helping those who needed her. She scampered about the cart, sifting through the goods for the weak and the blind, helping them to put on selections of clothing, trying not to gag at the sight and smell of them, and being careful not to humiliate them.

Finally there were only a few paltry cloaks and ragged and torn sandals left, but there were still eight people who had not yet had a chance to select from the cart. Among these were the younger men that James feared the most (because they might hurt Esther). When James was ready to choose the next person, one of the men, a seedy, bedraggled, curly haired and long straight bearded man who smelled of body odor and urine from 15 feet away, and who had only a few teeth left in his mouth, the upper lip of which was covered with sores, said to him, "Where are the things for the rest of us?"

"There was simply not enough to go around this time, my friend," said Esther. "We will be back another time, and you shall choose first."

"What is that to me, if I have no cloak to keep me warm at night? Should I just go cold until you come back?" said he menacingly.

"There is nothing else to give you," said James. "We simply have no other gifts. We will try to return as soon as possible, as the lady says, and bring more with us next time."

But the mob was concerned only with the minute. "There is nothing that can be done now, anyway," said James. "Let us have peace," he called as they crept closer. He and Esther were on one side of the cart while the crowd was on the other, but the cart provided no protection to them, and for the first time that day James became nervous. It was obvious to him that they waited only for a leader to make the first move.

He whispered to Esther, "I will pick up the cart and begin running with it. You jump into it and allow me to push you through the streets. Do not fight with me about this." Esther nodded while never taking her eyes off of the men.

"Now!" he shouted. "Jump in!" As he said this Esther grabbed the waist high sidebars on the cart and vaulted into the cart. James began to move it at the same instant Esther climbed into the cart. But then, reasoning that they might follow he and Esther, instead of pushing the cart away from the men and down the street back toward the middle of town, he pushed it directly at the crowd, knocking some of them down and scattering the rest out of the way. By this device he was able to give themselves enough of a lead that none of the men followed them.

After he had pushed the cart a few hundred yards, James stopped for a breather. As he leaned on the side of a house on a street corner he said to Esther, "Well, I won't blame you if you decide not to come with me on my missions any more."

"It is a little more excitement than I was prepared for, but worth it. I need to get out more. I have to admit that it was very exhilarating."

"Exhilarating, you say? Do you have any idea how close we came to being beaten up over some old rags that we were trying to give to the poor?"

"We did give them to the poor, don't forget that. It may be that some of the poor were willing to fight for the better rags, but we did help those who cooperated with us. By the way, how do you plan to manage the situation the next time you go there? If you apply the same logic as today, you will be giving the best rags to the same poor people, based on the fact that they appear to be more in need. The rest are likely to resent that, since in effect it would mean that the worst off got something from you twice in a row, and the others got nothing twice in a row."

"Maybe we will reverse the process and give to the others next time, but it is likely that we will not see many of the same people next time."

"Why?" asked Esther, still sitting in the cart.

"I have noticed that the poor are a very mobile class of people. I seldom see the same ones in the same place more than a few times. I don't know why they move - perhaps they fell too far behind in their rents, perhaps they were thrown out of their lodgings, perhaps they have died or moved for some other reason. But, no matter which is correct, many of the people that we saw today will not be there next time. Let us just hope that it is the troublemakers who have moved on."

There were still a few rags in the bottom of the cart - those which had been left when the beggars started the trouble. These they gave to the next beggar they saw, and began the walk back home.

On the way, in a lull in the conversation, James searched his mind for a way to broach the subject of marriage. He had been considering the matter since Esther had first mentioned it, and the more he thought of the matter the more he wanted to take Esther for his wife. There was the little problem of family position but James determined that he would make the effort to overcome that. He did not really intend to ask for her hand this day - he merely meant to sound her out on the subject, and then see what followed.

She provided him with the opening he needed only moments later. She spied a dirty child by the side of the road, and commented on the inattentiveness of the child's parents to leave it out there by itself.

"You would never allow that to happen, would you?" he asked, he hoped playfully.

"Certainly not. I would never allow a child to be that dirty and ill kempt. It is criminal neglect." Panic set in on James: he could not think where to proceed from here. Any comment about marriage might be misconstrued, and he certainly didn't want the conversation to go beyond generalities for the moment. Once again, Esther to the rescue.

"And you, James? Will you be the best father that ever was?"

"Of course, of course," he answered hurriedly, afraid to look at her directly. "But first I believe I will get married."

She laughed joyously at this small witticism, a laugh that James always loved to hear.

"You will be a fine father, James, and a good husband." Panic again! The situation obviously called for him to return the appropriate compliment, but he couldn't get it out. He literally could not open his mouth until the moment had passed, and then he was embarrassed to try again. He was pulling the cart, and Esther was riding in it behind him, and while he was careful to avoid looking at her, he could feel her eyes boring into the back of his head. He felt her look down. But once again, it was Esther into the breach.

"When will you marry, James?" This was much too close for comfort, but his answer was out before he gave the matter enough thought.

"When I have found the right woman, and she will have me."

"What will she be like? Will she be beautiful?"

Much too close, but what to do? "I am not too concerned with beauty, because I know that in the long road of life it does not carry much weight. If she is beautiful in addition to other traits, then so much the better."

"What other traits, James?"

Was she toying with him? "She must be faithful to God, and to me. She must have the ability to run the home properly. She must love children very much, and she must be patient and contented with her lot, because she will never be rich married to me."

"Those are not very difficult traits to find, surely. Many women could measure up to such standards. You have but to ask the one of your choosing."

"You know very well that it is not so easy as that. I do not know very many women - in fact none so well as you. And before I ask, I would like to be reasonably certain that she would accept."

"There is no way to discover that except to ask."

James paused for a moment, having seen the opening that Esther had steered him to. He was struck by sudden resolve, stopped the cart, and turned around to face her.

"Very well, then, I will. Esther, will you marry me?"

"Yes, James, I will."

James was so struck by her sudden answer that he hardly comprehended what she had said. "What?" he asked after a moment's pause.

"I said, 'Yes, James, I will."

"Good. Good then, I am glad to hear it," he said, after another brief pause. Not knowing what else to do he picked up the cart again and continued on his way. But he felt much different than he had only a few seconds ago. He was elated at the fact that she had accepted, and with no hesitation at all. It was true that she also accepted without a hint of surprise, as though she suspected the question might be coming, and had given the matter a great deal of thought. She laughed from behind him.

"Is that it, then? Is there to be nothing else to seal the bond between us?"

In answer, James put down the cart again, lifted Esther out of it, and carried her down an alley between two houses on one side of the street. There he put her down, leaned her against the wall, and kissed her passionately. She returned the favor, and James could not think when he had been so happy. But once again, as always seemed to be the case, it was Esther to the rescue.

"I have loved you for so long James, that I cannot tell you when it began. Almost as soon as I met you, I believe. I do not think there is a better man on the face of the Earth than you, James. I have never been happier than I was today working side by side with you - that is, until now."

"You steer very well. I fell right into your trap, but that is where I wanted to fall anyway, so I end up where I belong. I have long loved you, but there was a time when I thought that I might not marry, in order to go to Jerusalem to study. But now the opportunity for that has passed, and I find that I am glad that it has. Otherwise I would never have been able to enjoy this moment. But you know that there are problems to be faced, and the first and most important among them is your family. They are not likely to take kindly to their daughter marrying a poor carpenter."

"James, I am certain that they will not mind. You are widely known and respected in Nazareth, and my family will believe that I have married well. I see that you are worried about how much money I will bring to the marriage, and you are afraid that my family will think you some sort of gold miner. Fear not: there is not as much there as many seem to assume. Do not forget that I am the fourth child, and by the time the money makes its way to me, much of it is gone. But we will not be poor anyway. You are a good carpenter, and I will see to it that you do not waste time on children's chairs which do not pay very well." At this they both laughed, kissed again, and returned to the street. James lifted Esther back into the cart, and he began pulling it back to where they borrowed it.

James could hardly pull the cart, for the giddy happiness that he felt. It was as though the cart weighed only a few pounds, and that Esther was not in it. He could hardly help himself from breaking into a run. The world looked brighter to him now, all the people happier, all the children cleaner and quieter, the sun brighter in the afternoon sky. He had no worries to think about, and none forthcoming.

CHAPTER 6

James dropped the cart and then Esther at their respective homes, and went in with her to discuss the marriage with her family. Her father was deceased, so her brother was head of the family, and he readily gave his consent to James. In fact, he agreed with such alacrity, that James had a difficult time understanding what was said. "What?" he asked again.

"Certainly, James, you may marry her. You are a fine man and will be a welcome addition to the family."

"I thank you, but you may not know the storm that I am. I have not much money, and I have to work many long hours for what I have. I also spend much time working with the poor. In addition there is my brother Jesus, who now and then has caused the curious to seek for him at our door, and who, though he means well, is a source of pain."

"All of this can be forgiven James, if you will love and cherish my sister, and take care of her, which you will do. Let us share a glass of wine on the occasion." James was elated at the ease with which he was accepted by the much more wealthy family of Esther, and praised God for it to himself over his first glass of water - even at this celebration he would take no spirits. What a day this had been, and what a change it had brought to his life, he thought to himself. He could hardly contain the satisfaction he felt. He forced himself to leave for his own home long after dark.

As he entered his own house, he found his mother in conversation with two men whom he did not recognize in the dim evening light. But they jumped up to greet him, and when they came to the door, in which he was still standing, he could see that they were Mordecai and Menim, two childhood friends of his who had moved to Jerusalem to set up a trading business together. Neither had ever been sorry for the decision.

The two travelers told such tales of Jesus, and the effect that he was having on the people that he met, that James and Mary decided to set off for Jerusalem to see if they could have any influence on him. James felt he knew the answer, but did not want to disappoint his mother. But before retiring for the night he passed on his news to her.

"You will be surprised to learn that I am to be married."

"To Esther? I am glad to hear it. I am surprised only that the announcement should be today, not that you are engaged to her. I have watched the two of you stall over that chair for too long to think that nothing would come of it. I am very happy for you. She will be a fine wife and mother." Finding all of his thunder stolen by his mother, James merely accepted her hug of congratulation, and retired for the night.

They packed and left the next morning, and made the trip to Jerusalem. James was careful to pack their funds in several different hiding places, to fool any thieves they ran into on the road, but they saw none and so arrived in Jerusalem intact, late, hot, dusty, tired and in need of a room. Because of the Passover feast the city was filled with pilgrims like themselves, but James went to the home of Mordecai, who had made the offer while visiting with James and Mary, and secured a room there for the two of them. Mordecai himself was not home from his business trip, but he had left word with the household to prepare for two visitors.

It was nearly dark, and the heat of the day had dissipated. James and Mary set off through the city to see if they could get word of the whereabouts of Jesus. They talked to several who had seen him during the day, but none that knew where he was at the moment. One even suggested that he and his disciples disappeared at night, and must therefore have been evil spirits.

The city was quiet, with most of the families eating their Passover meals, and James and Mary keenly felt the absence of such a meal for themselves. When they gave up on finding Jesus that night they returned to the house of Mordecai, and found a simple Passover meal laid out. They were invited to join, and ate heartily. They then went directly to bed to prepare for the morrow.

The next morning dawned bright and hot, under a fiery yellow sun in the East. James squinted at it when he and Mary emerged from the house to begin their search, to get his bearings. He then suggested that they set off in the direction of the temple to see if Jesus might still be there teaching, as they had heard was his wont.

They arrived at the temple to find that it was already crowded with pilgrims, merchants, traders - all of the people they thought Jesus had thrown out only days before. They went in to the courtyard through the main gate, and found that it was as crowded as the street outside. There was the usual bustle of food sellers, thieves, money changers, tax collectors, and all manner of buyers and other thieves attempting to make their profit for the day. James was unsure why, but he had half expected the crowd to be smaller, based on what he had heard about his brother. He casually mentioned this to a loiterer standing near one of the stalls, as a prelude to asking about Jesus.

"I thought I had heard that a prophet threw all of the businessmen, money changers and tax collectors out of the temple the other day. It did not take them long to find their way back, did it?"

"You are speaking of Jesus of Nazareth? Why should it not?" the man snarled in return. "That prophet has no authority here. And the merchants know that he will not be back to bother them, since he was arrested last night."

James was thunderstruck. "Arrested?" he demanded. "By whom? On what charge?" Mary sucked her breath in with a small, high pitched cry, her eyes wide.

81

"I see that you are a follower of the man," James' street side acquaintance shot back. "It will do you no good. He will be found guilty, and punished for his sins."

"I am not a follower of the man, I am his brother, and this..." he indicated Mary, who was standing off to one side, "is his mother. We have come to find him. But you have not told me who arrested him, and upon what charge."

"He was arrested by the Sanhedrin, on the charge of blasphemy. It is entirely possible that you can still find him at the house of Caiaphas, the high priest, where he was taken early this morning." James demanded directions to the house of the high priest, and he and Mary went on their way. They wove their way through the busy streets of the city until they came to the high stone structure that was the home of Caiaphas. There was a functionary from the temple wearing a black robe standing outside the door as though he were a guard, and James walked up the steps to him immediately.

"What has become of Jesus, who was arrested last night?"

"He was tried and found guilty of blasphemy, and is on his way to the court of the governor to have sentence carried out," said the man, in a gravelly voice.

"What sentence?"

"You do not know the sentence for blasphemy?"

"It is death, but that can hardly be what they have meted out to this man. He was nothing but a preacher wandering the countryside."

"He was a blasphemer who claimed that he was the Son of God. If that is not blasphemy...."

James interrupted him. "Of course that would be blasphemy if he had ever said it...."

This time he was interrupted by the guard. "He did say it. I heard him myself, last night." James stared in disbelief, but the man continued: "Why do you not go to the governor's house and see for yourself? What are you, a follower of the man?" James ignored the question, ran down the steps to tell his mother what he had been told, and then rushed off with her towards the house of Pontius Pilate.

The streets were crowded with the commerce of the day, and they had a difficult time making headway. When they arrived at the home of the governor, which fronted on a broad street, they found a small crowd gathered outside the gate, apparently watching the proceedings within. James and Mary skirted the crowd and circled the wall around the governor's home, looking for another way in. There was a back gate, but it was also closed and heavily guarded. There was no crowd there, so James assumed that it must be away from the action in the front. He could not convince the guards to let him in, so he and Mary circled back to the front of the house and attempted to push their way to the front of the crowd watching by the gate. They could not, and were physically rebuffed by some of the ruffians in the crowd.

As they stood on the outskirts of the crowd wondering what to do, there was a sudden cry from the crowd: "Crucify him! Crucify him!" This sent a chill through James' spine, because he had a sinking feeling about what was happening inside the wall. There were other cries of "He is a blasphemer!" and "Make him pay the price!", and one or two small voices attempting to make themselves heard over the others saying "Release him! He has done nothing wrong." James was glad to see that his brother had some support, but he could see that it would not be nearly enough if the crowd had anything to say about his fate.

He and Mary pressed up to the edge of the crowd to see if they could hear what was going on within, but they could not. James got as close to one side of the gate as he could, and picked out a reasonably smart looking man to ask questions of. The man was staring intently toward the gate, though there was no way he could actually see in, since he was in front of the wall and not the gate.

"What is happening within?" asked James, the crowd quiet again for the moment.

"They are trying the man called Jesus, who has been accused of being a blasphemer," said the man.

"What are these cries to crucify him?" asked James.

"The governor says that he can see nothing that the man has done wrong. Pilate does not understand our ways, or he would not have that problem. The crowd is attempting to steel his nerve for him."

Suddenly there went up a cry from the crowd: "Give us Barabbas! Give us Barabbas!, along with the same small ones demanding that Jesus be released. There was some pushing and shoving among those who disagreed on what should happen to Jesus with the result that those who were loyal to Jesus were pushed to the fringe of the crowd.

"What now?" demanded James of his new acquaintance.

"In accordance with our custom, Pilate is offering us a prisoner of our choice to celebrate the Passover. The crowd is demanding that Barabbas be released."

"What is the crime of this man Barabbas?

"He is a murderer and a seditionist."

"And he is considered the equivalent of a preacher?" asked James, incredulously. "Are they suggesting that releasing a murderer and a seditionist is the same as releasing a teacher? This is absurd."

"Oh? Are you a follower of the man Jesus?"

"No, I am not. I am his brother James, and this is his mother Mary."

"You are his brother, and yet you are not a follower?"

"I am not, but he is my brother, and I do not wish to see him punished unjustly." He was interrupted here by more cries of "Barabbas! Give us Barabbas!" and "Crucify the blasphemer!" and then a short silence, followed by wild cheers from the crowd. These cheers made James' heart sink, suspecting as he did that they meant that the governor had decided in favor of the crowd.

His acquaintance turned to him and sneered: "He is to be crucified by order of the governor. Save the blasphemer now if you can."

He forced his way through the crowd to see what was happening on the other side of the gate. Those people who would not move aside for him when he asked were forcibly thrown out of his way. When he had ensconced himself at the gate he could see the courtyard to the house of Pontius Pilate, the Roman governor of Judea. It was a large house with two stories, and on the second story there was a balcony overlooking the courtyard. James could see that people were just leaving this balcony, and disappearing back into the house. Below was a large open area, surrounded on three sides by the wall and on the fourth by the house. There were various small outbuildings attached to or near the wall, a small grove of trees near the house, and nothing else in the area.

He could also see a crowd of people, not unlike that standing with him at the gate, surging toward the gate. Apparently those on the outside had not been the entire spectating committee at the trial of his brother, but had been only those who could not gain entrance to the courtyard. As James was absorbing this realization, a guard appeared to open the gates to allow the crowd out. James and the others on the outside were forced to yield to the mass of people being escorted out forcefully by the guards.

It proved to be several hundred strong, for the courtyard of the house of the governor was among the largest open areas in the city of Jerusalem. For the most part they appeared to be in an exultant mood, openly rejoicing at the prospect of the death of Jesus. There were some who appeared to be downcast, and James guessed these to be Jesus' only supporters in the mob. He stopped one of the latter to ask what was up.

"The governor has condemned the prophet Jesus to death, at the instigation of the Sanhedrin," the small, elderly woman, bent over from years of toil, told him. But her fires were not yet out. "They will live to regret it!" she exclaimed, the light shining in her eyes.

James grabbed her wrist. "What are they doing now? Where is he?"

"They led him away through the house. He is to be crucified on Golgotha, which is on the east side of town, and more easily reached from the far side of the governor's place." She said this calmly, taking no note of the grip that James had on her.

"They are taking him there now?" asked James, his panic rising.

84

"Yes, they will crucify him immediately. It is a little early in the day for a killing, but possibly they want to get it done before the Sabbath begins."

This galvanized James to action. He ran back to where his mother was standing, still sobbing quietly, and told her the news. She simply asked, "Is there anything that we can do?"

"Not here," James replied. "You follow the crowd to see where they take him, and I will attempt to find Ananias to see if there is anything he can do."

At that moment they heard the voice of a woman calling Mary. When they turned they saw a young woman running toward them, dressed all in black from head to foot, and wearing a white veil over her head. It was Mary Magdalene, a woman of Jesus' acquaintance whom James had met once before. She had appeared to be a devoted follower, but James did not know how she came to know Jesus, or what his hold over her was. She was crying and sobbing, and leaned on Mary the mother of Jesus for support.

"They are going to crucify my Lord," she sobbed. "How can this be? How can God allow this to happen?"

Mary the mother of Jesus, who began crying more severely at the sight of Mary Magdalene, nevertheless tried to comfort her. "God's will is not known to us: He does not tell us what His plan is, or who will carry it out, or when it is to happen. He may yet intervene."

"He will have to do so quickly - they are taking him to be crucified now," Mary Magdalene sobbed, still clutching the other Mary around the neck and barely able to support her own weight. The crowd wound its way around the house of the governor to be at the other gate when Jesus came out, and James began to fear that they would be left behind.

"Mother and Mary follow the crowd and Jesus to see what happens. I will go to Ananias and try to have this injustice undone." He set off at a run for the home of Ananias, but it was a slow trip because of the traffic on the roads. He had to dodge among the sellers, the walkers, the animals being led to various places, some for their own slaughter, others weighed down with the commerce of the day.

Ananias' home was not so grand as that of the High Priest or the Roman governor, but it was a substantial home, all on one level, surrounding a small courtyard and a grove of trees that looked like nothing so much as an oasis in the desert. When he reached the house he was breathless, but he ran through the courtyard, approached the main door and pounded on it.

"Open up immediately," he demanded desperately, at the top of his lungs, out of character for him. "I must see the priest Ananias." A small boy servant opened the door, but was on the verge of refusing entry to James when James simply ran past him and into the house.

Not knowing which way to turn, he stopped in the first large room he came to. "Ananias! Ananias!" he called as loud as he could. "Ananias - I must speak to you! They are about to kill my brother!" He could hear footsteps running through the house, and after a few moments other adult servants came to see what the commotion was. "Send for your master," James ordered them, though they had no reason to obey him. "Tell him that James of Nazareth is here, and must see him at once." The servants paused momentarily, eyeing James suspiciously and wondering what to make of him. This enraged him. "Well? What are you waiting for?" he hissed. "Find your master, and tell him that there is an emergency! Run!" The servants still did not show the haste that James wanted to see from them, and he wanted to run after one of them to kick him into action, but he could not decide which to pursue. His indecision cost him: by the time he had overcome his own inertia, they had all disappeared. He continued to call Ananias on his own, and presently the owner of the house shuffled into view.

He was dressed in nightclothes, and looked as though he had been up all night: it was clear from the expression on his face that he had not been near the end of his rest. "What is the matter here?" he demanded, looking about the hall and the room for his servants, before recognizing James. James ran to him, and grabbed him by the shoulders.

"Pilate and the mob have condemned Jesus to death, and he is at this moment being led away for crucifixion!" he stated emphatically, nearly yelling in the ear of the priest.

Ananias was still trying to get his bearings after being wakened after a short sleep. He paused for a moment, rubbed his eyes in the black robe he was wearing, and looked James squarely in the eye.

"I thought that it might happen, but I did not think it would be this soon."

"You thought it might happen, and yet you are doing nothing to prevent it?" said James, still holding the priest by the shoulders and glaring at him only a few inches from his own face.

Ananias reached up and removed James' hands from his own shoulders, carefully re-arranged his clothing, and then began.

"Your brother was arrested last night, after the Passover supper. There were those in the Sanhedrin who wanted to wait, I among them...."

"You mean to say that you are part of this travesty?" James demanded angrily.

"All members of the Sanhedrin must take some of the credit, though for the fact of his trial I will own less than the others."

"Trial?" James demanded. "What trial? On what charges?"

"He was brought in at the urging of some of the members of the Sanhedrin who were afraid, after the events of this week, that he was a threat to the safety and well being of the city."

"That is nonsense, Ananias, and you know that it is."

"I said that this was the opinion of some members, not all of them," said Ananias softly. "I am inclined to agree with you, but once the accused is brought in and the vote for a trial taken, there is little that can be done."

"What did you try to do?"

"I attempted to have the session postponed until all members could be there, but it was to no avail. The hotheads were all in attendance, and they voted the verdict that they wanted."

"Verdict on what charge?" the still flustered James stammered out.

"Many crimes were suggested as possible offenses, but no one could agree on what he had done to warrant such charges. I called a number of witnesses myself, just to see that his side was given a hearing."

"And...?"

"The charges that were originally brought could not be upheld by the evidence on hand."

"And....?" asked James again, more insistently.

"I have been trying to speak carefully, out of regard for our long friendship, but the fact is that your brother hung himself."

"How did he do that? He had been preaching about the countryside for three years without hanging himself. How could he have suddenly done it in a single night?"

"In the midst of the questioning Caiaphas stood up and said to Jesus, 'There is only one issue that matters. Are you the son of God?' And Jesus, before the entire assembly, said that he was. What else could be done? This is blasphemy, and you know the punishment for blasphemy."

"A man in the midst of the Sanhedrin, at an early hour of the morning, and after intense questioning makes such a statement, and the assemblage assumes that it is the truth? Anyone might have reacted thus. He must have been tired. But what is the rush? Why has he already been before Pilate, and why is he now on his way to Golgotha to be crucified? Surely another day or two can hardly matter."

"James, you are one of my dearest friends in the world, and I understand your pain over your brother, but he committed blasphemy. It is the most serious crime there is. What would you have the Sanhedrin do? Lock him up for a week, and give his followers a chance to come and rescue him? If there were some doubt about whether or not he had committed the offense, I would agree with you. But there is none. He committed it in front of the entire Sanhedrin. It could not have been more plain. There were those there who supported him, and tried to make his case for him, since he would not make it himself, but even they were silenced when he claimed to be the son of God." Ananias reached out and grabbed James by the shoulders. "He is being punished in the same way that anyone else who made the same claim would be punished. It is difficult for you to accept, but there is nothing else that can be done. You know the law."

"I came here," said James, in exasperation, "in hopes that you might help me forestall this travesty. I see that you will not."

"I would if I could, but you know what the law says about the offense of blasphemy. What am I, a priest of the faith, supposed to do for a man who commits blasphemy in front of the entire Sanhedrin? Insist that he be shown mercy because I am a friend of the accused's brother? What would become of the law of Moses then? You above most others know that for the law to be effective it must be enforced. Who is Jesus, other than the brother of a friend, that he alone should be spared the consequences of the law? It has been over 2,000 years since we were given the law, and the law has been the savior of our people. Without it we would have ceased to exist as a people long ago. To ask that mercy be shown for this man for this most heinous crime is to dishonor all of our ancestors who have followed the law to the letter."

James heard all that Ananias said, but at the same time he was considering his other options. He could attempt to see Caiaphas the high priest to beg for the life of his brother, but he knew in an instant that this would be a mission of folly. Ananias, so far as James knew, was among the calmer members of the Sanhedrin where Jesus was concerned, and it was likely, given his reputation, that Caiaphas was among the least forgiving. In all likelihood it was Caiaphas and those on the Sanhedrin like him who had orchestrated this entire trial in an attempt to rid themselves of Jesus once and for all. Had they not sent James, not once but twice, to talk to Jesus in an attempt to convince him to give up his ministry, and retreat to the home where he could be a safe, quiet carpenter?

James could see that he was getting nowhere with Ananias, and he had half convinced himself that Ananias was not feeling all the grief that he was showing to James. He talked the sad talk, but he hadn't the look in his eye of a man who knows there is an injustice being done. James decided that it was an act put on for his benefit, and he resented it. It was also true that this interview was taking up time, and for all he knew Jesus might already be on the cross. Without a word he turned and ran from the house of Ananias into the street, dodged the crowds in the now busy streets, and ran out the gate of the city to the place known as Golgotha.

The place was a small, barren knoll immediately outside the gate, and no long distance from the house of the governor. When James arrived there the procession escorting his brother had already arrived, and there was a knot of people just drawing back from the figure of a man lying on the ground. As he got closer he was horrified to see that the man was Jesus, and he had already been nailed to the cross. James had seen men crucified outside the city before - it was not an uncommon practice among the Romans in their attempts to keep order - but this was the most ghastly sight he had ever seen.

Someone had formed a wreath with thorns, and placed the wreath on the head of Jesus, and, to make the matter worse, pushed the wreath down so that the thorns punctured the skin on his head. He bled profusely, so that almost his entire face was red with his own blood. There were rivulets of blood racing down his arms from the wounds on his wrists where the nails had been driven through, and similar rivulets running down his feet from where the nail had been driven through them and to the ground. He was naked, having been stripped of his robe by the soldiers, and he was covered from head to toe with bruises, welts and the marks of a very thorough lashing. He seemed to be red all over, the only distinction being between that blood which had dried in the course of the morning, and that which was still flowing from freshly opened wounds. He was conscious, but he had a vacant look in his eyes, as though he were attempting to remove his mind from the circumstances of his body. His eyes were half closed, but other than a moan that escaped now and then, he made no sound.

As James watched the soldiers finished their preparations and gathered at the head of the cross to stand it up in the hole prepared for it. As they lifted it and Jesus' weight came to bear on the nails in his wrists and feet, he let out a cry of pain that sent James' heart to his feet. As the cross fell into the hole that would hold it up, it landed with a shock on the rock bottom of the hole, and again Jesus cried out with pain. As the soldiers blocked the cross in the upright position with small stones, Jesus cried out again. Then the soldiers moved away to admire their handiwork, and only then, with the attention focused on the upright figure, did James notice that there were two other men being crucified with Jesus, neither of whom were known to him.

James was dumbstruck with sadness and grief. It hardly seemed possible that this was his own brother hanging from a cross outside the holy city, accused and convicted of blasphemy. He was rooted to the spot where he stood - he wanted to run to someone for help, but he knew there was no one there who could help. He wanted to let his brother down from the cross gently and take him in his arms, but the Roman soldiers were not letting anyone close to the cross. He just stood there, sweating in his robes from the run through the city, unable to think clearly, unable to move from the spot where he stood, unable to even take in the enormity of it all. He simply stared, mouth hanging open, wishing that it were all a bad dream.

He felt some irritation at his elbow, and attempted to brush it away, but it refused to go. He tried again to swipe at it, but it persisted. Only after a third swipe was he actually able to pull his eyes from the scene in front of him and look, and he discovered Mary of Magdalene pulling at his sleeve. She was weeping profusely, her face streaked with grime and tears, and only then did James notice that holding on to her was his mother Mary. She stood next to Mary of Magdalene, her face buried in Mary's shoulder, so that no part of her skin was visible. Her body was convulsed with crying, and her sobs were audible. But James had no solace to offer. Mary pulled at his sleeve gently, but she said nothing, and James said nothing to her.

The sun was now up brightly, and James was facing directly into it as he looked at his brother. He was therefore forced to move, and led the two women around to the south of the hill. James scanned the small crowd - no more than 100 people - but saw no other familiar faces. He and the women attempted to get closer to Jesus, but like the others they were rebuffed by the soldiers.

Jesus hung there quietly in the heat of the late morning, saying nothing and making no sound other than his labored breathing. Blood continued to drip from his many wounds, particularly those on his hands and feet, beneath which there were small puddles forming on the ground. The strain of his hanging body re-opened some of the wounds on his body, and blood flowed from these as well. Both Marys had cried themselves out for the moment, and fell silent each standing under one of his arms their faces buried in his chest, but the entire scene was now too much for James, who quietly wept for his brother.

A Roman soldier propped a ladder against the back of the cross, and nailed a sign to it above Jesus' head. The sign said "This is Jesus, King of the Jews." With each blow of the hammer Jesus moaned in pain.

When he had recovered after a few minutes, James felt the presence of others around them, and noticed one or two of Jesus' followers with them, as well as other women who appeared to have followed the procession from the home of Pilate. Among the followers of Jesus was the one named James, whom James had met once or twice when he came to Nazareth. This James stood in front of James and the two Mary's and had attempted to offer some comfort a time or two, though he had little to give. He glanced around him once, and James the brother of Jesus said to him, in a fit of pique and with no one else to lash out at, "Who will you follow now?"

The other James looked at him sadly, and said without reproach, "I do not know what I will do now." James felt his own inadequacy, and said "I am sorry. I do not know what to say." The other James nodded his head slightly, as if to say that he understood, but said nothing.

The hour grew later, and it appeared that the news of Jesus' crucifixion was spreading about the city, because James noticed that the crowd was growing. There was a steady stream of people coming out from the gate of the city, and making their way to Golgotha. The early watchers had been those attached to Jesus in some way, either emotionally or by blood, but now those who would be his opponents began to filter out, and among these were the members of the Sanhedrin who had condemned him.

As these new arrivals grew in numbers, they took courage from each other, and began to murmur among themselves. James could not hear them, since the crowd was not so large that all the people stood together, but he could feel the change in the mood on the knoll. The murmuring grew gradually, and soon turned to mocking. There were calls of "Others he saved, but himself he cannot save." and "Where is his father now?" and "If you are the son on God come down from that cross that we may believe in you." Each of these sallies brought laughter from the others of the crowd who sympathized, but only sullen silence from those who were supporters of Jesus.

As James watched the reactions to the scene - the mockery, the crying, the stunned silence - he felt himself to be an outcast. He did not believe the claims of his brother like some of the others, including, apparently, his own mother, but he did not understand the need for crucifixion for the crime of blasphemy, assuming that his brother had committed such a crime. Jesus was a man to him, his own brother, and he did not want to see him pay such a price. He was at worst a harmless man, and it appeared to James that this was the work of those on the Sanhedrin who somehow felt that Jesus was a threat to them. His helplessness angered him. His brother was hanging painfully on the cross, after a night of torture at the hands of the Romans, and now the Sanhedrin and their followers were coming out in the mid morning to view and laugh at their handiwork.

James looked over the crowd. There were young and old, many women, all economic castes, and many people from the temple. There were scribes and Pharisees, other lesser lights, and even, it appeared, some of the beggars and businessmen who usually graced the temple grounds. What could be their motivation, he wondered, other than to ingratiate themselves with the temple officials, or to jeer at the man who had thrown them and their businesses out only a few days before.

The Sanhedrin, resplendent and obvious in their black robes with black head coverings with white edges, gathered together directly in front of Jesus. The crowd, which now numbered several hundred, gathered around the Sanhedrin at a respectful distance - not so near as to be too familiar, but near enough to be able to hear and join in the fun. The Sanhedrin took advantage of this, and directed their jabs at Jesus loudly enough that all of the surrounding hangers on could hear.

One of the Sanhedrin noticed the sign above Jesus head on the cross, which said "This is Jesus, King of the Jews." "Who placed that sign?" he demanded. A member of the crowd informed him that a Roman soldier had nailed it there soon after the cross was erected. "It is not appropriate. He is not the King of the Jews." He turned to one of the Scribes and said "Send to Pilate. Tell him that this man only claimed to be King of the Jews. Change the sign to say 'This is Jesus, who said that he was King of the Jews'". The man scurried off and the mocking recommenced.

"It has been said that you can cure the blind. Let us see if you can come down from the cross." Laughter. "If you are a king, why are you on a cross, and not on a throne?" More laughter. "Why do you wear a crown of thorns, and not one of gold?" Derisive cheers. As James watched the crowd, he noticed Ananias among the Sanhedrin. He appeared to be laughing and joking with the others, a far cry from the apparently reluctant priest he had talked to in his home...some time ago...James had no idea how much time had passed since then.

Both Marys were standing on their own now, so James sidled nearer to the Sanhedrin, to see if he could distinguish what was being said by the individuals. As he got nearer he was passed by the Scribe who had been sent to Pilate. The man ran directly to the priest who had sent him and reported that Pilate would not allow them to make the change.

"What was his crime?" one of the bystanders asked a Scribe.

"He committed blasphemy, and at his trial in front of the Sanhedrin, no less," answered the Scribe.

This did not appear to make the necessary impression on the others standing about, so a priest added, "There is no more serious crime to be committed. This man is receiving the punishment of death demanded by the law of Moses." There were nods of agreement among the other members of the Sanhedrin and their hangers-on, and James, who was hiding himself to the extent possible behind another man, noticed that Ananias appeared to be scanning the crowd in search of doubters. Another man asked, "Why are the Romans involved?"

It was Ananias who answered: "Roman law does not allow us to put our own people to death. We needed the permission of the governor for even so heinous a crime as this."

An old woman who had been standing nearby watching the scene turned to Ananias and asked "What if he was the Son of God? It would not be a crime to claim it then?"

At this Ananias and the other members of the Sanhedrin turned to look at the woman, and Ananias, thinking he had the crowd on his side, said, "If he were the Son of God, do you think he would allow himself to hang on a cross? Would he not free us from the Romans?" There was laughter and general agreement at this, with nodding of heads and snickering at the gall of the woman.

But she was not deterred. "How could a mere man have cured the blind, or the lame, or raise a man from the dead?"

Ananias laughed uproariously at this, and glanced around the crowd to ensure that the bystanders joined him in his mirth. "You believe those ridiculous stories? No man could do those things. These stories were made up by the fools who followed this man to justify their following him. He...."

But the woman would have none of this. "I am a foolish follower of this man, and I saw him heal the blind man in the temple, and I saw him raise the dead man in Bethsaida. These things happened. We could not fake them, even if we wanted to. He did these things because he has the power of God. No one else could do them."

Ananias laughed uproariously at this, and addressed the crowd, rather than the woman: "A crowd of people follows a wandering minister in the countryside, and believes that he can raise the dead and cure the sick and the lame. What could be more natural?" This got him the hoped for laugh, and after allowing it to simmer for just a moment he continued, "This man is not the Son of God. I repeat, would the Son of God be hanging from a cross? If he can cure the blind and the raise the dead, why can he not save himself?" The woman attempted to say something, but Ananias would not let her begin. "I do not intend to argue theology with you," said he. "There would be no point in it. You and I are not able to deal with the problem on the same level. This man claimed to be the Son of God, he is not, and he is paying the price demanded by the law given us by God. We in the Sanhedrin have been watching this man for some time, and we have warned those who would listen that they should not be paying attention to all of these itinerant preachers who come along and claim that they have all the answers to life's mysteries. God has given us these answers, and we in the Sanhedrin will help those who wish to stay true to the faith." The woman would have said something else, but she was shouted down by the mob around her. At that moment the man in front of James moved, and as James was only a few feet from Ananias, he was immediately spotted. Ananias raised his hands and his voice to the crowd, asking for silence.

"Here!" he called, indicating James, and causing the crowd between them to part. "Here is the very brother of the man. Would the Son of God have a brother who is as human as you or me? Here is the brother of the man, both of them born of the same mother. Look at him! Does he look to be the brother of the Son of God?" Laughter among the crowd, and anger in James. How could his friend use him against his own brother? But he could think of nothing to say, and so stalked off.

James rejoined his family and friends. It was now late morning, and James began to regain his senses after the initial shock of seeing his brother crucified. He estimated that Jesus had been on the cross for about three hours. The crowd began to thin out again, as all of the people who had some emotional stake in seeing Jesus crucified went back to their own business. There remained only the family, some friends, and some people who were apparently followers of Jesus. James and the others immediately around him tired, and sat down to await developments.

After a few minutes, as James chanced to be looking in their direction, the little knot of members of the Sanhedrin broke up, with most of them heading back toward the city. But Ananias broke off from the group, and walked slowly over to where James was sitting. James rose as he walked up.

"James, my friend," he began apologetically, reaching out to hug James, "I am sorry that I put you in that position. As soon as I did it, I knew that I was wrong. This is a hard day for you, and I should not have used you against your brother." James did not know what to say. After a brief pause, Ananias said, "Say that you forgive me for my selfishness, and I will leave you alone." James could only nod. "Thank you, thank you, my friend. I could not have lived with myself otherwise. Now I will go. When this is over, come to see me. Let us talk, and re-establish our friendship." Ananias turned back toward the city. After he had walked a few steps he turned back to James and waved with his left hand, but James managed only a weak nod in return.

There now settled on the knoll an anticlimactic time. After the initial excitement (for the crowd) and pain (for James, his mother, and other of Jesus' friends) a reaction sunk in, and all on Golgotha seemed to fall into lethargy. One or two of the Roman soldiers looked as though they would sleep, if doing so would not get them into trouble, and in fact early in the afternoon the Romans relieved the guard. The rest of the crowd melted away, leaving only those most committed, one way or the other, sitting on the knoll waiting for developments. Jesus hung quietly on the cross, moaning now and then, pushing himself up with his feet to relieve the pressure on his chest. The heat of the day began to build, and the insects were a bother for those waiting with Jesus.

It suddenly occurred to him that, after seven or eight hours on the hillside watching, James was not sure if his brother knew that James and his mother were present. He reminded his mother of this fact, and she said that he had seen her on his way to Golgotha from the home of Pilate, and had spoken to her and to some other women present. James said that he would attempt to make Jesus aware that he was there, and both Marys and the other James said they would walk the short distance with him.

Because of the early morning sun they were not sitting directly in front of the cross, but just a little off to one side, and once the sun was no longer a problem, they had been in such a state of shock that they had never moved from the spot. They now rose, and walked, at a short distance from the cross so as not to antagonize the guard, around to the front of Jesus, so that he might see them. James was fumbling in his mind for the right words to say as they stopped in front of Jesus, when suddenly Jesus raised his head and looked at them.

The blood on his body was dried, and it no longer dripped from his wounds in his hands and feet. He was caked with dust and sweat and blood and grime, so much so that it was difficult to identify his race. His breathing was extremely heavy and labored, his chest, and indeed his entire body heaved with the effort necessary to obtain enough air, and it was apparent that he was in his last stages.

But before any member of the group said anything, he knew that they were there, and he looked at them, first as a group, and then each in turn. James could see his eyes struggling to meet the eyes of each member of the group, and when Jesus came to him, when Jesus looked into his eyes, James seemed to see all the pain, all the love, all the suffering that his brother endured, and once more his own tears flowed. He could not bear to look his brother in the eye, and he looked down.

But Jesus eyes seemed to have bored into James' brain, and he could see them still, even as he closed his eyes and turned his face to the ground; he could feel the long suppressed rage rising within him, and suddenly it burst out, utterly out of his control.

He had been standing at the back of the group, but with a cry he raced around them, and attacked the Roman guard leaning on his spear. He knocked the man to the ground, and wrestled the spear away from him, all the while screaming, "Take my brother down, do you hear? He has done nothing to deserve this! He is an innocent man!" He stood up, found himself holding the spear, and threw it down, but continued to rage at the surprised guard, who still lay on the ground, unhurt. After a moment the guard jumped up, and James was suddenly seized from both sides by two other guards, and held by the arms. The guard that he had knocked down walked up to him, and punched him once in the stomach and once in the face with his right fist, and then the two guards threw him to the ground. He lay there gasping for air, and attempting to spit the dirt out of his mouth at the same time, and the guard said to him, "It is a crime to strike a Roman soldier!"

At that moment a Centurion, new to the scene because James had not seen him all day, arrived, and intervened. The guard told the Centurion what had happened, and the man nodded sternly. He said to James, "I could have you arrested and placed beside your dear brother. But I will not. But do not come to me with your problems. Your brother has not broken any Roman laws. We did not put him here. Your own people demanded it!"

The other James, the Marys, and some other people picked James up and dusted him off to the extent possible, and helped him recover his breath, and insisted that he be calm. He glanced up at Jesus on the cross, and noticed that Jesus had raised his eyes enough to be able to see what was happening, and for an instant it appeared to James that Jesus was looking at him in a disapproving manner. He could hardly credit this - had he not simply had an outbreak of emotion over the sight of his brother being tortured by the Romans? There should be some credit in this. But Jesus head fell again, and James decided that he had imagined the whole thing. Another man gave him a drink of water, the first he had had all day. He asked for some for his family and friends, and it was granted them. They then sat down again in front of Jesus, but Jesus' head only hung in front of him.

Very suddenly it began to grow dark. Thick black clouds quickly filled the sky, seemingly appearing out of nowhere since James had not seen them roll in, and the air was full of foreboding. James looked at the clouds, at the people around him, at his brother on the cross, and could not help but think to himself that the events might be connected. But he dismissed this as the thought of a man too caught up in a family tragedy.

Those others still keeping vigil noticed the clouds as well, and there were comments on them: "I have never seen it this dark at mid-day." "Surely this is not a judgement on this man." "Of course it is not - he cannot even come down from the cross. How could he control the weather?" "How can it be this dark, and still not rain?" James had never seen it this dark at mid-day either. It wasn't like the darkness at twilight, where all about one is gradually hidden. The sun was still high in the sky, and one's surroundings were still clearly visible. At night it was sometimes difficult to tell whether or not the sky was cloudy, but that was not the case this time. It appeared as though there were a black canvas covering the Earth, held up by the gray walls of the horizon.

After a few minutes Jesus seemed to rouse himself, and the party of his family and friends rose and went to stand as close to him as the guards would allow. Jesus raised his head painfully and regarded the small group. The other James was standing, for the first time all day, next to Mary the mother of Jesus and James, and James was standing at the back. Standing next to the other James was a disciple of Jesus whose names James could not remember. Jesus looked at his mother, then at the other man, and said, "Woman, there is your son." He then looked to the other man and said, "There is your mother." No one said anything, but they looked at each other and then back at Jesus, as if there were to be more. James could not believe his ears. What did he mean that Mary was now to be the mother of the other James, and the other James to be her son? She already had other sons, one of whom she was living with and who was supporting her. Still, it was difficult to argue with a man in the last stages of death by slow asphyxiation; perhaps he had lost his head, or could no longer see clearly, and so was mistaken about who he had been addressing. James tried to overlook the matter, but it would not go away.

Later in the afternoon, when James was still brooding over this matter, there came a plaintive cry from the cross. James and everyone else on the knoll was startled by the noise, and so not sure what was said. The people waiting looked at each of their own allies to see if anyone else had understood, but it appeared that no one had. James looked to Jesus, just in time to hear him say "I thirst!" with what appeared to be a supreme effort. After the cry he sunk down on the cross and breathed even heavier than before. James, who had not left the hill since his initial arrival early in the morning, had nothing to offer. He rose and ran up to one of the soldiers to ask permission to fetch something for Jesus, but the soldier pushed him away. Just a second later, another man, from among those who had been taunting Jesus, ran up to the guard with a sponge soaked in some liquid that James could not identify. The guard smelled the sponge (James wanted to also, to see what was being offered, but was again rebuffed by the guard), stuck it to the point of his lance, and offered it up to Jesus. Jesus offered at it, but with the first taste spit out the substance and refused any more.

This brought the crowd back to life. The man who brought the sponge and his coterie laughed and taunted Jesus. "He thirsts but he will not drink! Very choosy for a son of God!" This sally aroused the wits in the crowd from their torpor. "I thought perhaps that we might see a show when he caused it to get dark, but I see that we will be disappointed." "It would appear that the darkness is only the weather." "Perhaps he can make it rain to cool himself off." "And us! What about us? Should we not be rewarded for entertaining him in this manner?" This type of banter among the hangers on irritated James, and he thought of another frontal assault, but he saw that he was seriously outnumbered and therefore likely to do little good, and he could not rid himself of the notion that Jesus had looked at him disapprovingly when he had tried it against the Romans before.

But he could not stay long away from what he considered a personal insult. After all he had suffered at the hands of his elder brother, here was the final insult, apparently within minutes of Jesus' death. How came he to speak on something that, within a few minutes, would be completely out of his control? And why would he, in his moment of hubris, choose one of his disciples to look after their mother, rather than his own brother? How dare he disown, in effect, James from the care of Mary? James bristled at this designation and was on the verge of contesting what Jesus had said, when his mother turned round to look at him. She said nothing, but the look in her eyes was very expressive: she seemed to be pleading with him to do and say nothing, and she did so with love and sympathy that told James that perhaps she saw something else in what Jesus had done which James had not. While he did not regain his temper immediately, he decided to leave it to Jesus' condition for the moment, and revisit the matter later.

He had not another moment to consider the matter because things began to happen quickly. Seeing that Jesus had roused himself, one of the two men crucified with Jesus said to him, in much the same hoarse, pained voice Jesus had used, "If you are the son of God, save yourself and us!" But the man on the other side rebuked him, saying, "You and I are paying for our crimes, but this man has done nothing wrong. Leave him be." When he had recovered sufficiently from this outburst, he turned his head to Jesus and said, "Jesus, remember me when you come into your kingdom."

Once again Jesus gathered his breath and his strength, and said to the man, "I assure you, this day you will be with me in paradise." This seemed to please the man, who lowered his head and said no more. Jesus also lowered his head for the moment, and made another effort to push himself up with his feet to relieve the pressure on his chest. But he hadn't the strength for it, and he fell back heavily. James could only think to himself, "At least he is consistent. Here he is dying on the cross for the crime of blasphemy, and yet he continues to grant access to paradise as though he were the keeper of the keys." He shook his head in bewilderment, but admired Jesus' faith, however misplaced.

There was a brief period of quiet. It was now mid-afternoon, and it had been dark for some hours, though James did not know exactly how long. There seemed to be no movement in the clouds, as though they had been sent to hang over that particular spot on the Earth until the drama they were watching played itself out. Perhaps God did disapprove, thought James, though he could not say which aspect of the picture He would disapprove of.

Suddenly Jesus rallied himself again, and cried out in a loud voice, "My God, my God, why have you forsaken me?" There was a gasp in the crowd at this, with various among the present thinking that he had called on a prophet, and others thinking that he was blaspheming even to the end. But there was no apparent response to his call, and all fell silent again.

The crowd waited expectantly, a tad too expectantly James thought, for people who claimed to believe that Jesus had no power. But Jesus rallied again, and, after gathering his breath once more, called out, "Father, into your hands I commend my spirit!" His head then fell once more, and this time he could not raise it. After another brief pause he said, more quietly this time, "It is finished." Then his entire body went limp on the cross, and all life passed out of him.

All of those in the group with James were moved to tears once again at this final act, including James himself. They had known this moment was coming all day, and yet they were unprepared for it, as though it had been sprung on them at the last minute. At that moment there was a flash of lightning and a booming thunderclap that seemed to reverberate back and forth from the walls of Jerusalem, and most of the crowd, now numbering only a score of people, began to run for what they thought would be the safety of the city walls. James and the others who were with Jesus stood their ground, though James felt a touch uneasy at the remarkable coincidence of the thunder and lightning beginning at the exact instant of Jesus' death. James even felt as if the earth shook. It was eerie, almost as though his brother had actually been right all this time.

The Centurion who had happened on the scene when James attacked the Roman soldier had been standing at the foot of Jesus' cross when Jesus had begun to speak. He looked up now at the dead figure on the cross, and then at the dark, ominous heavens and said, "Surely this was a righteous man." Those who would have contested his view of the proceedings were already running back toward the city, so there was no one there to contradict him.

The Centurion, apparently afraid that the weather was about to turn, and seeing that the two men crucified with Jesus were not yet dead, called one of the guards over and told him to break their legs. This the man did with a heavy wooden hammer, and, without the ability to push themselves up with their feet to relieve the pressure on their chests, they quickly expired.

The guard, unsure of what to do about Jesus, since he had been specifically told to break the legs of the other two men, turned to the Centurion for guidance, but found him distracted by a messenger from the city. He looked to the others of his own rank there, but they did not know what to do either. The guards were anxious to depart themselves, so one of them stabbed Jesus in the side with a lance. So depleted was he that very little blood spilled out. It happened so quickly that neither James or any of the others with him had a chance to prevent it.

With this act the guards and the Centurion abandoned the scene, leaving the bodies to a small crowd of onlookers who remained. James knew that it was not uncommon for the Romans to leave bodies on the cross for extended periods of time as a supposed lesson to passersby, but neither he nor any of the other friends of Jesus wanted this to happen to his body. As they stood there mulling the situation, a member of the Sanhedrin along with three other men, apparently servants, approached from the city. He was a small, elderly man with a white beard and hair peaking out from his black and white striped robes. He had friendly, alert brown eyes that seemed to dwarf his nose, and a large mouth that gave a hint to the booming voice that would emerge.

"Are you the family of Jesus?" he asked the small knot of people that included James. No one answered since they did not trust the motivations of the man, so he continued. "I am Joseph of Arimathea, a member of the Sanhedrin as you see. I have petitioned Pilate to be given custody of the body of Jesus that I might bury it properly. Forgive me, but I did not know if Jesus had any family here to look after him or not." Still no response from any member of James' small group. "I intend to put him in the tomb that was cut for my own burial - there." He pointed to a cave cut into the rock on a nearby hillside.

James finally roused himself and introduced those who were with him to the man, and said, "That is very kind of you. Forgive us, but we found it hard to believe that any member of the Sanhedrin would have the interests of my brother at heart. I believe that we would all be grateful for your help in laying Jesus to rest. We do not live in this area and so have no place to put him." With that Joseph signaled to the men who were with them, and they picked up the ladder the Romans had left there and began to take the body of Jesus down from the cross.

When the servants had brought Jesus down, his family assisted in wrapping him in the linen which Joseph had brought. This was the first time they had the opportunity to examine him up close, and it was a painful experience. He was covered with cuts, bruises, welts and puncture marks, and his body was more red on the outside than flesh colored, for the amount of blood that he had lost, and where he was not red with his own blood he was brown with the accumulation of dust and dirt over the last day or two. James wanted to recoil at the sight, but he did not, mostly because his mother did not. She and the other Marys cried quietly while the two James and the other man, who introduced himself as John, worked with the servants to clean and wrap Jesus in preparation for burial.

This done, they discovered they had no way to carry the body to the gravesite. Joseph was on the verge of sending back to the city for a wooden slab of some kind when James suggested that they could use the ladder that had been left there by the Romans. This was readily agreed to, and Jesus was laid carefully on the ladder, and the ladder was carried by the servants of Joseph to his tomb.

It was an awkward walk over rock strewn trails and slightly uphill most of the way, carrying the body as level as possible at all times. Upon arrival James was happy - as happy as the circumstances permitted - to note that the tomb was a large one, carved out of the hillside for Joseph's own use. It was at least ten feet side by six feet long and tall with a stone slab hewn out of one wall on which to place the body. It was entered through a small doorway, and near the door was a huge stone intended to be rolled across the entrance when the burial was complete.

The family and friends carefully placed Jesus on the slab, adjusted his linens to protect his body, said a short prayer led by James, and then walked back out into startling sunlight. All of the black clouds that had been hovering over the area for the last three or four hours had disappeared. The servants of Joseph rolled the stone across the entrance to the tomb, and, with a last prayer, the party departed for the city. James was suddenly overcome by exhaustion, and had not the strength to cry. This must have been the case with the rest of his party, because they said not a word on the way to the city, and even Mary his mother was no longer weeping.

Upon re-entering the city James and Mary went straight to the home of Mordecai. They were too tired and drained of emotion to want food or company, but the other James promised that he would call on them later with food. Left to their devices they retired to their room to sleep.

But after lying down for a while, both discovered that they could not sleep. In a matter of hours they had watched their world change drastically. The oldest son of Mary and James' older brother had been crucified for - it was said - claiming to the son of God. He had apparently been arrested in the middle of the night and brought immediately to trial, no one had interfered on his or their behalf, and the sentence was carried out early in the morning. They had then watched him die a slow and painful death. James felt that he had been done many injustices by Jesus, but he did not wish for this. He suddenly felt alone and empty, and life felt more dear to him, seeing how quickly enemies could arrange to have it taken away. He resolved to see Ananias the next day to get from him all the particulars of the arrest and trial of Jesus.

CHAPTER 7

James and Mary gave up the effort to sleep after a while, and sat up to stare at the walls. They were surprised by the arrival of the other James, the follower of Jesus. He brought them some simple bread to eat, along with some dried fish and lamb's meat. James and Mary ought to have been ravenous, since they had not eaten since the night before, but they found that they had little appetite. After eating enough to maintain their health, they both quit, over the objections of the other James.

"Where are the other friends of my brother?" asked James of the other James when they settled down.

"Many are afraid and are in hiding. They do not know how they will be treated by the people and the Sanhedrin after this terrible incident."

"Surely none of them is claiming to be the son of God?"

"No," said the other James, ruefully. "None of us will ever make that mistake."

"You do not believe that my brother was the Messiah?"

"I do not know what to believe at the moment. I believe that he possessed the power of God - that God was working through him - but I cannot see how the son of God can be crucified by evil men." The other James was obviously tired and dispirited. He sat slumped on the floor of the simple, sparsely furnished room, leaning on the wall. His hair was tossed and unkempt, his clothes dirty, but his face and hands clean. His eyelids appeared to be too heavy for him as he watched Mary and James pick at their food.

"What of the others?" asked James. "How do they perceive him?"

"Some say that he is the son of God, others that he is a prophet. But all may change now that he has been crucified. We have seen him perform miracles, have seen him cure the blind and the lame and raise the dead, and yet he has been crucified by the Sanhedrin. We will all have to re-think the matter."

"Did he actually claim to be the son of God to the Sanhedrin?"

"I do not know. None of us was there."

"How came he to be arrested and tried in the middle of the night? Surely there was no emergency."

"One of our number betrayed him to the Sanhedrin. We do not know why it was timed so - it may be that they simply wanted to do it in the night when any possible support for him would not know of his trial."

"Do you mean that one of his own followers turned him over?"

"Sadly, yes. Judas escorted the crowd to the garden where we were praying. I do not know why he did it, or whether the Sanhedrin might have given him a bribe. All that remains is that the man I revered above all others is now crucified, and there is no one left who can carry on his work."

"But what was his work?" asked James.

"To call all people to God through him. He said that he was the son of man, and that no one who would go to heaven without going through him. With his miracles it was not hard to believe this, and yet we see that he is gone at the hands of the Sanhedrin and the Romans, and some common criminal released in his place." At this he began to cry. James could sympathize with his pain, though for different reasons. Here was a man who had apparently given up everything in order to follow Jesus, and here he was disappointed: his leader crucified and he with nowhere else to turn. It appeared that he had placed his faith in the wrong person, and now, in the wake of the crucifixion, he would have to find his own way again.

After a respectful moment James asked him, "What will you do now?"

"I will meet with my brethren to decide what is to be done. We cannot give up yet I think, but it is difficult to know how to carry on. The message of Jesus was a strong one - he had many followers outside of Jerusalem - and we cannot allow it to die."

"Do you know where the others are?"

"They are in a certain room on the other side of the city that I know about. They will stay there until the time is right to venture out."

"You mean to say that they are in hiding?"

"You may call it that. How are we to know what the reaction of the people of Jerusalem will be to us, now that they have done in our teacher? What will you do?"

"I will return to Nazareth and take up my trade again. I have merely closed the shop for a short time."

"You do not believe in your brother?"

"That would depend on what you wanted me to believe," replied James. "Was he a preacher? Yes. A prophet? Perhaps. A blasphemer? I hope to find out the details tomorrow. The son of God? How could I credit such a claim?"

"But you have heard of the miracles he has performed. Could a mortal man do these things?"

"Anything is possible with God, and you know yourself that he has worked through prophets before. It is possible that He chose to work through my brother, but I cannot see why he would do so."

"But there is more to him than this," said the other James, earnestly. "Have you heard him preach? Yes, you have. I saw you on the day he gave the sermon on the side of the mountain outside Capernaum. Can such words come out of the mouths of men?"

"They can do so if God wills that they should. Have not the prophets spoken equally well?"

"No, they have not. They warned us to stay the path that would lead us to God, but Jesus told us what that path was, and where we may find it. There is peace in his words that are not to be found in those of the prophets."

"Are you trying to convince me that he was the son of God, or yourself?" asked James, somewhat testily.

"I admit that I am less sure that I once was, and yet, even after all that we have seen, there can be no question that he was a special man, and that God has some plan for him," answered the other James, paying no attention to the tone of James' voice.

"You will get an argument from the Pharisees, the Sanhedrin, and some others on that."

"True, but that is because they have not listened to him over time, and seen his great works. To them, he was a threat to their precious position, so they got rid of him in the only way they know how. He brought peace and healing to so many - this cannot be the end of his story."

"You are a man of faith. I hope it is not misplaced."

"I hope that I am a man of faith, because that is what he told us to be. I also hope that it is not misplaced." With that they lapsed into silence.

After a few minutes James asked, "How are the other followers of my brother accepting this?"

"Some better than others of course, but I believe that they are with me: today is not an end, but a beginning. I would invite you to join us tomorrow to see where we might go, but I do not gather that you are really one of us, and in these trying times I would not invite anyone into the circle without the permission of my brethren."

James smiled at this. "I thank you for the thought, but you are right: I am not one of you. My brother was a good man, and possibly an effective teacher, but he did not teach the law, and while he may have had some healing power, he was not the son of God. So you see that even if your brethren welcomed me, it would not be for long."

The other James smiled at this and shook his head, but said nothing. "I must go," he said, after a moment, rising. "The others will be concerned for me. I will try to look in on you tomorrow, but I cannot guarantee that you will see me."

After he had gone, Mary, who had said nothing the entire time, said to James, "It is sad, my son, that there are others with more faith in your brother than you."

"I admire and love my brother, mother, but his friends and he claim too much for him. Surely you do not still believe that he is the son of God?"

"I do."

"How could that be? Would God allow his own son to be tortured and crucified in this manner? How we have seen him suffer this day! This can hardly be the handiwork of God."

"Do not judge the Lord, James. We do not know his will."

"This is true, mother," said James, lying down to sleep, "but we do know the law, and it will have to sustain us until a proper Messiah comes."

Mary walked over to where James had lain down, bent down, and kissed him. "Do not close your eyes to the power of God, James." James was finally able to sleep that night, and slept the sleep of a dead man. He did not awake until nearly mid morning on the Sabbath, and saw that his mother was already up and about. He went down for a light meal, and then ventured out into the streets.   He hardly knew what to expect when he stepped out. Would all of Jesus' enemies recognize him and demand that he make an account of himself? Would they jeer at him for the loss of his brother? Would they call him the brother of the son of God? James was in an awkward position before those who would make fun of him: he would not disown his brother, but he also would not admit that his brother was the son of God. If pushed he would defend Jesus, but only to a point.

As it turned out, the outside world appeared to have forgotten his pain already, and did not go to the trouble to cause him any more. As he headed for the house of the high priest, he saw no one he recognized, and no one appeared to recognize him. This was a distinct relief to James. After first attempting to read the look on every passing face for signs of hostility, he finally gave over to the idea that his moment of fame had already passed, and that he would not be remembered.

On this approach to the house of Ananias, James had more time to survey the surroundings. He was struck by the small but luxurious garden in front of the house, and by the height and width of the vaguely Hellenic facade, even though the house was of only two stories. The stone facade was pierced by three windows on the upper level and two on the lower, with a huge, ornate wooden door in the middle. This being the Sabbath (or perhaps because it was the day after the crucifixion of the interloper) there was no longer a guard on the door.

James walked up and hit the door with the huge iron knocker for that purpose. A surly male servant answered the door.

"I would see Ananias, the priest of the temple," said James.

The servant regarded him - and his less than aristocratic appearance - with barely concealed disdain. "Who shall I say is calling?" he asked, after a brief delay while he favored James with his best stare of contempt.

"A friend." James answered. "From Nazareth."

"The priest has many friends of late," said the man, sarcastically. "What is it that you want?"

"To discuss the life and death of the man Jesus," James said.

"The priest cannot discuss this matter with everyone who comes to the door," the man said. "Is it not enough that the man was a blasphemer? What more do you disciples want? He put himself to death with his own words. Do not come here to blame the priest for that."

"I have not come here to blame the priest for anything, and I am not a disciple of the man Jesus. I am his brother. Tell Ananias that James is here. He will see me." The man raised his bushy black eyebrows ever so slightly at the mention of the fact that James was the brother of Jesus, and after a brief pause, withdrew and closed the door behind him. James waited for a few minutes, confident that he would be admitted. Soon the door opened again, this time at the hands of the man himself. Though he had apparently been aroused from bed by the servant, he was just slightly less ebullient than ever. It even appeared to James that Ananias made an effort to calm himself down when he opened the door.

"James, my dear friend, I am happy to see you and sad at the same time," said he, giving James his usual bear hug. "Come in. Let us eat and talk matters over." He led James to a huge sitting room, ornately decorated with tapestries hanging on the white stone walls, many cushions and low stools scattered about, a thick, colorful Persian rug on the stone floor, and unlit candles in gilded sticks mounted on the walls. As they entered from one door a female servant entered through another carrying a tray of drinks. Ananias took both and handed one to James, and then motioned to the cushions.

When both were comfortable, Ananias began, "I cannot tell you how it pains me to see your family suffer. I would have given anything to prevent this awful occurrence. But there was nothing to be done. When your brother claimed before the entire Sanhedrin to be the son of God, there was nothing left to do for him."

"What, exactly, happened?" asked James.

"It is simply told. There was a trial the night before the Passover. Your brother Jesus was questioned about many things, such as the miracles he was alleged to have performed, the nature of his mission, some aspects of his teaching and living, and other questions one might see asked of a preacher who gathers such a large following to himself."

"But why was there a trial at all? On what charges was he arrested?"

"He was reported by one of his own followers to be divergent from the law of Moses."

"One of his own followers you say?"

"A man by the name of Judas, I believe. He was one of the small band who followed your brother at all times. There were about twelve or fifteen together, I believe. But this man told us that Jesus was preaching in

106

contradiction to the Law, and the Sanhedrin decided to talk to him on the matter."

"In the middle of the night?" asked James.

"It was said that his teachings had become especially dangerous, and there were those on the Sanhedrin who wanted to have the matter dealt with before the arrival of Passover."

"Have what matter dealt with? It sounds as though the results of the trial were determined before it began, and that you merely wanted to be rid of him."

"Not I, my friend, not I!" protested Ananias vehemently. "His trial was by no means assured. But there were those who were afraid of your brother preaching in Jerusalem over the Passover, and this faction wanted him locked up until all of the pilgrims had left. In this way, they hoped, he would not stir the people up against the Romans."

"I have never heard of my brother inciting the people against the Romans. He has never expressed a political opinion as far as I know."

"That may be, James, but you know that the facts are not necessarily what people react to. There was some fear that he might disrupt the Passover, and because of this fear he was arrested. It is not necessarily fair, but it is the way of human nature."

"So he was turned in by one of his own? What happened at the trial then? Did he have any defenders in the Sanhedrin, or was he left to face them alone?"

"He had friends there," said Ananias. "He was given a vigorous defense, but at the end, when it came to blasphemy, there was nothing anyone can do. In fact it was difficult to defend him because he would say nothing in his own defense."

"Defend him against what? I still do not understand how it is that he deviated from the Law. I heard him speak only once, but it did not appear to me that he violated our teachings."

Ananias shifted on his cushion. "There were questions about what he has called his 'kingdom.' Many have heard him refer to it, but he is always unclear as to what kind of kingdom it will be. He admitted that his kingdom was not 'of this world', as he put it, but he would not make it clear where his kingdom would be, or how we might recognize it when it came to be. Others demanded to know how it was that he appeared to cure the sick or the blind, or how he could claim to be able to forgive sins. He made no answer to these accusations, and if he will make no answer there is little that his defenders can do for him."

James considered for a moment. "And yet you say that he was crucified on the charge of blasphemy, which, in your telling, he has not yet uttered. So none of these attacks had any effect on him."

"That is true," said Ananias. "There were witnesses brought on these various issues, but none of them appeared to sway the majority of the Sanhedrin. But near the end of the questioning about his kingdom he made a mistake. Caiaphas asked him in a loud voice if he were the son of God, and he replied 'I am.' There was a great outcry in the room, from both sides of the question, but it was clear what his fate must be."

"Could you do nothing for him? There have been others who have made wild claims who have not been crucified. Why did my brother have to suffer this gruesome fate?"

"Your brother has made some powerful enemies since he has been in Jerusalem. He has spoken very harshly of the Sanhedrin, the Pharisees, the Sadducees and the Scribes, just to name a few, in front of many people. His claim that he is the son of God was just what they were waiting to hear. You and I have talked before on this matter, and you endeavored to talk to him once at my urging. What I predicted has come to pass: some of his teachings, as well as his intemperate words in Jerusalem recently, left him with too few friends in high places. I am quite sure that there are those who were delighted to hear him make that claim, because it gave them an excuse to do what they have wanted to do all along."

"I do not find this hard to believe. The speed of the trial was unseemly. Why should they meet in the middle of the night, condemn him, and then rush him off to face the Romans before dawn? Your theory that they wished to deal with him in some way before the Passover has some weight, but why then did they wait until the night before the celebration? They could have had him arrested at any time since he arrived in Jerusalem."

"It was not until then that this Judas came forward with his information."

"What did he offer that was not already known by the Sanhedrin? My brother made no effort to hide his teaching."

"He offered them someone willing to turn Jesus over to them - someone who could be said to know his teachings."

"'Someone willing to turn Jesus over to them,'" James repeated slowly. "This suggests that they knew they wanted to arrest him, which in turn suggests that they planned to put him to death, and that all they were in need of was a pretext for the arrest."

"I think that it only means that they wanted to arrest him before the Passover so that he might not make trouble in the streets among the pilgrims."

"You know that my brother would not make trouble among the pilgrims. The last thing he would have wanted was trouble in the streets"

"I know that, but it is difficult to convince a roomful of the Sanhedrin, who do not know him as well, of this fact."

"No, I prefer my explanation, after all," said James, after a brief pause. "I believe that they were looking for an excuse to do away with him, preferably, I grant you, before the Passover, and that this disciple of his who turned him in was merely the tool they used. I would not be surprised to hear...." but James paused here, thinking to bring up the point later. "What was the nature of this man's testimony?"

"He did not testify."

"What?" demanded James, angry now. "You mean to tell me that the Sanhedrin, which absolutely needed this man to turn my brother in for his alleged crimes, did not then hear any testimony from him? How can that be? If he did not testify then there was no need for him to turn my brother in."

"James, James," began Ananias, "let us not be angry. Remember that we are talking about many people, not a single person, and that these are emotional times. The fact that this man turned your brother in was all that was necessary: this served the purpose of having a witness to name his crime."

"But I keep coming back to my original point: everything that my brother has said he said in public. Anyone could have acted as the witness to his crimes. Even I could have been that man: I have seen enough, from the sound of things, to have him convicted by the Sanhedrin. Why was this man not called, if he had necessary evidence?"

"It was felt that his testimony was supplemental to that which was already available."

"Available from what source? Who did the Sanhedrin drag out of their beds at that hour of the morning to testify against my brother? Or did the members of the Sanhedrin act as witnesses as well as judges?"

Ananias began to get angry. "Now you are being unfair. There are many among the Sanhedrin who have heard your brother preach many times, and who are well acquainted with his teachings. They are as capable of being witnesses as one of Jesus' own disciples."

"But you said that none of the witnesses were able to condemn my brother of anything," interrupted James. "You said that he might have escaped his fate if he had simply not declared himself the son of God. If that were true, why did the Sanhedrin not bring in this Judas to see if he could tempt my brother into an error?"

Ananias' voice continued to rise, and was now booming through the house. "Do not goad me, James. I have been your friend, and I was a friend to your brother as much as could be. Remember that in the end it mattered not how many witnesses we produced concerning his past. In front of the entire Sanhedrin he proclaimed himself the son of God. What need had we of more witnesses? We all heard it. There could be only one result: he was accused of blasphemy, and was given the punishment demanded by the law."

"Only one result? Then you too voted to condemn him. This is friendship?"

"I defended him as I could. I do not make it my habit to defend blasphemers. When he made this outrageous claim he passed out of my purview, and into that of God."

"So why could you not vote to let God judge him, and not other men. If it was as you say, and all the other members of the Sanhedrin voted to condemn him, you could hardly call yourself the loser. The Sanhedrin would still have gotten what it wanted, and you would have done what you could for a friend of the family."

"I do not defend blasphemers. They are the lowest kind of criminal, and not fit for the honest attentions of man."

"Well, I suppose there was much rejoicing among the Sanhedrin when it was all over. You had got your man, and in time to have him out of the way for Passover." James could not contain his anger. "And all you had to do was pay a disciple of his....what? Ten pieces of silver? Twenty? Don't lie to me. You say that this man was necessary to turn my brother in, and then he fails to testify. What am I to make of this? He was a tool for the Sanhedrin, and I believe that the Sanhedrin must have paid him for his infamous deed."

"Infamous? Do you believe that the trial and execution of a blasphemer is infamous?"

"He was not yet a blasphemer when you brought him in, even though by your own admission you have been watching him preach in the countryside for the last three years. He became a blasphemer under the pressure of the Sanhedrin, who were anxious to be rid of him. If he had been allowed to stay in a cell for a few days he might have been calm enough not to make such a rash statement. If I were on trial during the pre-dawn hours, I might be goaded into admissions that I did not believe."

Ananias leaped up from his cushion, and faced James, who immediately did the same. "Do not blame the Sanhedrin for the shortcomings of your brother. It is our responsibility to ensure that the laws of our nation are upheld by all, and your brother was a trouble maker who might have caused misery for many. That he blasphemed in the course of our investigation is his own fault, not that of the Sanhedrin. And he was rewarded properly for his blasphemy."

"Mercy might have prevailed," James yelled at Ananias. "You might have exercised mercy. His crime was not one that has never been committed before. It was not the kind of crime for which the trial cannot be held in the middle of the day or for which he cannot be punished in a few days time. You still have not given me an adequate answer: what need was there of the witness who had him arrested, but did not testify? Why was he tried in the middle of the night? So that his followers would not get word of the matter until it was too late? Why was he then dragged to the house of the governor and then out to Golgotha with hardly time for a breath? There can be no other explanation than that you intended to be rid of him, and the arrest and trial were a mere show case so that the Sanhedrin would not find its hands red with the blood of my brother."

"Leave this house James. I will not be the victim of this kind of talk from an old friend. The Sanhedrin acted in the best interests of the nation, and for that we have nothing to apologize for."

"So it is 'we' now, is it? I might have thought as much. I was wrong not to be more alarmed for my brother when I saw how much interest the Sanhedrin and other clerics from the city were showing his work. Twice I was sent to warn him, and both times it was I who underestimated the relentless approach of the Sanhedrin. I was an inadequate messenger to my own brother because I did not recognize the nature of the men who opposed him. And now my eyes are open, but it is too late." At this realization James had to fight back tears.

"Leave here James, before we do more damage to our friendship of many years. You are in no condition to talk of such matters, and I was in error for asking you to come by here and do so. My intentions were the best, but now let us part ways before we make it impossible ever to talk again."

James suddenly thought of the others of Jesus' followers who were in hiding somewhere in town. "Will you at least give me assurance that those others who were followers of Jesus will come to no harm?"

"It is not I who is the judge. They have nothing to fear so long as they obey the law, and so long as they fail to blaspheme. Let them heed the law, and let the memory of your brother die a peaceful death, and they will have no reason to fear anyone."

"Very well then, that is how it must be." With that James turned and stalked out of the house.

He walked about the city for a few minutes, still enraged over what he considered the revelation that the Sanhedrin had conspired with one of Jesus' followers to have him arrested on some pretext, and then had found a way to have him put to death. It occurred to him that he had only Ananias' word for it that Jesus had actually blasphemed, and that that was the reason for his crucifixion. He would need to see someone else who was at the trial - to attempt to find out the story of the proceedings from another party. He hoped that the account given him by Ananias was accurate for the most part. That would at least absolve his friend Ananias from most of the blame. But he knew no one else who might have been there. There was no one who might tell him of the proceedings. Suddenly he remembered Joseph of

Arimathea, who had buried Jesus in his own tomb. He appeared to be sympathetic - perhaps he would see James and tell him the truth.

He went back to the home of Mordecai to see his mother. She was sitting in a large airy room talking with the wife of Mordecai. He reported the gist of his interview with Ananias to the women, both of whom were shocked at the apparent callousness of the Sanhedrin. James told his mother of his plan to search out Joseph of Arimathea, and asked if she wanted to accompany him. Surprisingly, she declined. She rose from her chair and beckoned him to follow her, and they went into the small garden at the back of the house.

When she was sure that they were alone she said to him, "James, you are surprised that I do not wish to see this man about the trial of Jesus. But it is as simple as this: I have suffered enough. I did not think that I could live through such pain as I have suffered these past few days, and yet here I am. But what good would come of knowing the exact words that were spoken at the trial of Jesus? How would I, or you for that matter, be better off for knowing that this member of the Sanhedrin supported your brother, and that one did not? Suppose it turns out from your interview with this man that Jesus did not commit blasphemy at all - that it was a mere pretext to his crucifixion? There is nothing I can do to right that wrong. Your brother has been crucified, and now, more than you or I, lies at rest. It is enough for me to hear what you have told me concerning Ananias, because it confirms my own suspicions. I will not torture myself with the details, as you should not. In fact, your brother predicted this. It may have some higher purpose that we do not understand."

"You are still convinced that Jesus was a holy man of some sort, but I am not. In that respect only I agree with the Sanhedrin. But I want to know as much of the truth as can be found out, and I believe that this man will help me. There can be no question that my brother was murdered by the Sanhedrin because they were jealous of his followers, or afraid of his influence. It is true that there is nothing I can do with the knowledge, but I will at least know the truth. If for no other reason, I want to find out what role my old friend Ananias played in this travesty."

"It will only make you angry and bitter, James, and you are a young man yet. Do not throw your life away."

"Of course I am angry and bitter. You should be as well." James had hardly let these words escape before he was heartily sorry for them, and he stopped to apologize. "I did not mean that mother," said he, earnestly. "I am sorry. It is probably you who are right in this matter, and not I. Forgive me, I beg you." He fell to his knees in front of her, clutched the front of her cloak, and buried his face in it.

112

"There is nothing to forgive, James, my beloved son. I know that you are not malicious." She took hold of his hands and raised him to his feet. "You are feeling the pressure of these last few days. Do not apologize to me: I know what is in your heart. Go and see the man if you must, and when you return I will be interested to hear what he had to say. Go for us both, but promise me two things: try not to be angry - we do not know the will of God; and be careful - without you I would be utterly lost." As he departed the house James said a quick prayer of gratitude for his mother.

James had no idea where he might find the man, so he began by asking their hostess if she knew him. She did not, but suggested her brother, who lived near the temple, and was a trader with many from area villages. James went to the home of this man through the hot mid day sun, and was told that he was not at home, but was expected within the hour. James was granted permission to wait for him, and did so for nearly two hours. Upon the man's return, he told James that this Joseph was a prosperous businessman with many responsibilities to oversee, and that he had a house on the south side of Jerusalem that he used when he was in town, and might be found there. The man did not know if Joseph was in town at the moment, but he doubted it.

James knew that he was, but did not stop to explain to the man how he came to know this. He hastened to the other end of town and, when he believed he had reached the correct vicinity, began asking after the house. He was shown a large stone structure by the third person he asked, situated on a corner. It was a two story abode but had little or no land around it, befitting a man who spent only parts of his time there. James knocked at the front door, and was met by a servant.

"I would like to see Joseph of Arimathea, if he has the time," said James to the man.

"And whom should I introduce?" asked the man.

"Tell him it is...." James hesitated here for a moment, considering, and then said, "Tell him it is James, from Nazareth. Tell him that we met yesterday outside of town."

The man looked at James in some surprise, a reaction to which James was becoming accustomed, and then disappeared back inside. James waited for only a few moments before the servant appeared again and invited James inside. He left him in a large, airy sitting room stocked with small chairs and cushions and decorated with art and tapestries from around the world. It was luxury to which James was not accustomed, and he was still marveling at it all, and mentioning to himself that it was remarkably like the home of Ananias, when Joseph entered.

He was dressed spotlessly from head to toe in clean linen, and looked nothing like the tired man who had taken possession of the body of Jesus the day before, and had buried it. His eyes shown more brightly now, and his voice resonated as before. He approached James, hugged him, and said, "I am sorry for what you and your family have had to suffer. Please tell your mother of my sympathies." He then beckoned James to a very comfortable set of cushions. They sat down together and the man ordered some wine from one of the servants in attendance. "What is it that you seek?" asked the man. "Have you come to find out why I asked for the body of your brother?"

"I would be glad to know that, if you desire to tell me," James began, "but that is not the object of this visit. If you can do so without betraying any confidences, and without betraying your position, I would like to hear the details, to the extent that you can remember them, of my brother's trial before the Sanhedrin."

"I will be happy to relate them to you, but I have two questions first: why do you wish to know, and what do you intend to do with the information?"

James thought for a moment on how much truth he should apply to answering this question, but decided , based on the fact that the man had had the courage the day before to be publicly associated with Jesus, to trust him. "I am attempting to discover whether or not it was the intention of the Sanhedrin to punish my brother when they arrested him, no matter what was said at his trial, and I will do nothing with the information - there is nothing that I can do."

"Well then, is it every detail that you wish to know, or is there something specific that you are seeking?"

"I do not need all of the details, but there are certain areas that interest me. We can begin with the obvious, if you have no objection: how came you to claim the body of my brother?"

"I have spent much of my business life in the area around Capernaum, and I have heard your brother speak many times. I believe that he was a prophet, and that he was undeserving of the fate meted out to him yesterday. It was out of this feeling that I went to Pilate to claim the body. It is also true that at that time I did not know he had any family here."

"But you do not believe him to be the son of God?"

"No, that I cannot accept, but it is enough for me that he is a prophet, and a very great one, I am convinced."

"Did he make that claim at his trial? And was that claim the reason he was condemned to the cross?"

"He did make that claim, and it is the reason used for condemning him to such a fate."

"You sound as though there is some doubt that that was the real reason."

114

"I believe that things were as you appear to suspect, and that the purpose of the trial was to find some pretense for hanging Jesus." Even under the circumstances, and only a day later, James felt a strange feeling of relief at hearing this news.

"Who were his principal detractors?"

"Caiaphas was one, though it appeared to me that he hoped not to come to the fore during a trial. Another was Demetrius, and there was Cleopas, and Ananias, and....". Here James interrupted him.

"Ananias? Did you say that he was among the enemies of my brother?"

"Yes, he was among the most eager questioners, and among the first to call for his crucifixion." This news, stated matter-of-factly by Joseph, who could not know the pain they caused, startled James. Here was his friend of 20 years, who had claimed the opposite only that day, among those attempting to do away with James' harmless brother. Joseph noted the look on his face. "Does this surprise you? Do you know the man?"

"He has been my friend for 20 years, and only this morning he was telling me that he supported my brother until the time of his claim that he was the son of God."

Joseph gave a short laugh. "Well, if he did support Jesus he did it so quietly that no one would have noticed. And it would have been before the trial started because as soon as it started he fell in with those determined to be rid of Jesus. So you have talked to Ananias about the trial already?"

"I have. When I saw him on the day before Sabbath, he invited me around that we might talk about it, and we did so for a long while. Who, then, were on my brother's side?"

"I was, as was Nicodemus."

"That is all? There were no others?"

"That is all - two of us. It appears that you are unaware of how many powerful enemies your brother made for himself over the course of his ministry." James interrupted here to tell, briefly, of the two trips to Jesus to try to get him to come home. "That is interesting. I was not aware that there trips had been arranged for. At the request of the Sanhedrin, you say?" James nodded in affirmation. "That is extraordinary. I was not aware that there had been less dramatic attempts to talk Jesus out of his mission."

"Had this trial been planned, or was it suddenly concocted at the last minute?"

"Oh, it was concocted at the last minute at the behest of Cleopas. I was summoned to the home of Caiaphas after midnight, and was there until well past dawn."

"And what was the role of this man, Judas, who was the flame for the wrath of the Sanhedrin?"

"He was persuaded to turn your brother over to the Sanhedrin, for a few pieces of silver, I believe." Again James was startled.

"He was paid for turning my brother in? I suggested as much when I talked to Ananias, but did so half in jest, and really thought nothing of it. How much did it take to convince him of my brother's guilt?"

"I have heard that he was paid thirty pieces of silver, but I could not promise that this was true."

James could only sit in shocked silence for a moment. "Then what I have feared is true. My brother was convicted on trumped up charges, and it was the mission of the Sanhedrin to do away with him one way or the other. They were not concerned about what he was teaching - they simply wanted him out of their way - to restore their influence."

"There is no question in my mind that they wanted to do away with him, and quickly, else there would not have been so extraordinary a meeting at so unusual a time. It is also true that the original charges against your brother were created, and could not be made to stick to him. But it is also true that he claimed to be the son of God in front of the entire Sanhedrin. This cannot be ignored: this claim gave the Sanhedrin all the excuse it needed to have him crucified, and it was all they could have hoped for, and more."

"Was the vote for crucifixion unanimous?" James asked, hoping to test his new acquaintance in his truthfulness.

"No, Nicodemus and I voted against."

"Ananias said to me that the vote was unanimous - that it could be no other way."

"He is right, in his way. Nicodemus and I had no leg to stand on in our position of voting against crucifixion. The punishment demanded by the law is strict and harsh, and should not be made light of. Nicodemus and I were stepping outside the bounds of our faith by calling for mercy in this case, but we believed that your brother might have simply been so tired from all of the crying and arguing that he simply did not know what he said. By the strict terms of the law, the vote should have been unanimous."

"Then I thank you for your courage on behalf of my brother. I do not believe he should have been crucified either, though of course I am biased in the matter." Here James paused for a moment, to gather his thoughts, and Joseph sat quietly regarding him. After a moment James began again. "It was told to me by Ananias that this man who betrayed my brother was not called to testify. Is this true? Why not?"

"The man was merely an agent, sent by the Sanhedrin because he would be able to find your brother late at night so that the business could be done before the Passover. He was paid and went his way. I have heard, by the way, that he was found hanged from a tree outside the city early this morning."

"By his own hand?"

"By his own hand. There was no sign that he was forced. Apparently his conscience dragged him down." This brought some stunned satisfaction to James, though he attempted to hide this from Joseph.

But Joseph seconded his thoughts. "I cannot but believe that it was what he had coming." James nodded in stunned agreement. James sat in silence for a few moments, so Joseph began to sketch the facts for him. "I will not trouble you with all the details, but here is how it went: When your brother was called in, or rather dragged in, there was some disagreement in the room about what it was that we were trying to do. Not everyone agreed that we should have a trial at that time of the morning, and not everyone was present, due to the hasty nature of the meeting.

"Finally Caiaphas and his group prevailed, and it was agreed - no, not unanimously - that there would be a trial. A number of witnesses were called, principally from among the Sanhedrin, who testified as to the various perceived faults in your brother. But they could make nothing stick, and he refused to defend himself, so they resorted to name calling. There was a brief debate on the meaning of his 'kingdom' and where it would be made known to us all, but he said only that his kingdom is not of this world. Caiaphas was outraged at this kind of talk, and demanded to know whether your brother was the son of God. He said that he was, and there the trial ended. Caiaphas took an immediate vote, and, as I stated, all but two members voted to crucify."

"There is really nothing more I need know," said James, rising to leave. "You have been most kind with your time, and I am grateful for the information, though it is sad to find that a man with whom I have been friends for twenty years should have turned on my brother."

"You are speaking of Ananias? I venture to say that you have not seen him much of late? No? I thought not. He is not the same man he once was. He hungers to be high priest himself, though it is likely to be some time before Caiaphas yields the throne. Are you aware that his father was once high priest? You are? I did not know him, but I have heard it said that he had not the ambition of his son. I now value my place on the Sanhedrin, and if you attempt to attribute to me I will deny it most vehemently, but it is surely true that all dealings with Ananias must take into account the likely effect of the transaction on his succeeding to the position of high priest. He is amiable and generally well intentioned, and he is faithful to the law, but all this is tempered with ambition."

James shook his head ruefully, thanked Joseph once again, and departed the house into the bright sunshine. It was now approaching evening, and time, James decided, to report to his mother.

James had been walking somewhat absentmindedly thinking these thoughts, and it caused him to bump into a hooded man whose path he happened to cross. Their eyes met, and they recognized each other: it was the other James, carrying a basket of food.

"James," he said, softly, "I have just been to see your mother, who is well. She says that you have been to see Joseph of Arimathea. What had he to say?"

James related the gist of the conversation to the best of his ability.

"We - that is - the others and I suspected as much also, but there was nothing we could do about it. In fact, Jesus told us that it was for this purpose that he came into the world."

James said nothing at this, preferring to stay away from such a debate.

The other James continued: "Please let me show you where we are hidden. My brothers would like to meet you, I am sure."

"Your brothers would probably rather stay hidden," said James. And remember you told me earlier that I was not one of you."

"I can take you in so that you'll not be noticed. These are difficult times, and it is important for those of us who are like minded to stay close together." James protested further, but the other James would hear none of it, and took him through the city to the west side, and down a dark alley off of a small side street. There was no traffic in the alley, and the two climbed a narrow, outdoor staircase which led to a door on the upper story. On this the other James knocked three times in slow succession, and his reward was to hear the bolt on the far side pulled back and the door opened. They walked in, and James found himself in a small, bare room, approximately twenty feet by twenty feet with a low ceiling. There were a couple of small windows near the top of the room, which would have given it a cheery prospect were it not for the somber occupants. A quick glance told James that there were ten men in the room when they entered, and deduced that this must be the remnant of the twelve men who allegedly followed Jesus on his ministries through Galilee and Judea. One of the ten advanced on the two James's, and asked the other James who the stranger might be. Upon being introduced as the brother of the Lord, a moniker that he felt uncomfortable with, James noticed the tension in the room ease a bit. One by one they came by to make introductions.

The one who had accosted them on entering the room was known as Peter. James also recognized Andrew from the wedding at Cana, and he believed that he recognized one or two of the others from somewhere else, even though he could not recall all of the names immediately.

For all of the late afternoon sun shining in, it was dismal place. The men were morose, apparently over the crucifixion of their idol, and they had no where else to turn. They talked little and ate less, so that the ten of them did not even finish the basket of food brought by the other James. The other James told the group of James' meeting with Joseph of Arimathea and Ananias, which news they received enthusiastically. They bombarded James with questions about the trial, and were wholly satisfied that Ananias had been back of the whole affair, and that it had all been created as a pretense to trick Jesus into doing himself in.

After this enthusiastic intermission, the mood of the room settled back into the somber affair that it had been when James entered. It was apparent that the men had discussed the fate of Jesus until they could do so no more, for they rarely mentioned it, and gave off an aura of being tired of the subject. On the other hand it was apparent that they were greatly pained at his death, and James felt a strange sense of pride in this - that his brother could command such loyalty even in death. Nevertheless, he felt uncomfortable, and was about to take his leave when the one known as Peter spoke to him.

"What is your opinion, James, brother of Jesus? Was Jesus the son of God, or an impostor?"

"He was neither," James answered immediately and decisively, surprising himself. "He could not have been the son of God, for he was not divine. This we can see by the fact that he is now dead. But neither was he an impostor: he had many loyal followers, worked many wonders, and preached a good message."

"You see, brothers," said Peter, turning to the others scattered about the room eating, sitting in various positions on the floor as the light coming through the windows began to dim. "Here is another who agrees with some of you. I tell you, though, that Jesus was -is - the son of God, and that he will make his purpose known to us. He told us that he would die for the sins of many, and that he has done. God will work his will so that we may come to understand it."

"That is it exactly," said Andrew, the brother of Peter, if James had heard the introduction correctly, and the man that James had met at the marriage in Cana.

"You are both dreaming," said another, whose name James did not get. "We have been following a great man - we have seen his works. But it is also true that he is now dead, and no longer the leader of his own movement. James is correct that he was neither Messiah nor impostor."

"Why did he claim it then?" asked Peter.

"When did he claim to be the Messiah?"

"Did he not call himself the son of Man? Did he not say that he would be sacrificed for the sins of many? Did he not point out to us how the prophecies were fulfilled in him? Did he not refer to his 'Father in heaven'?"

"Any man who hoped to establish himself as a religious leader might make such a claim, to gain credibility. Besides, his 'Father in heaven' is the Father of us all, is he not?"

"This is how you treat the master the first day after he is gone, Thomas?" reproved Peter. "If he is merely another faker claiming credit with heaven for his own sake, then all of our efforts of the last three years have been for naught, and we are all fools for having followed another fool. And if he is a faker, how do you account for all the miracles? You yourself witnessed many, including the raising of Lazarus from the dead. This is not the act of a man who is not from God."

"I did not say he was a faker - I said the opposite: that I agree with his brother James that while he was not the Messiah, neither was he a faker. It is certainly true that he was a man of God, else he could not have raised Lazarus from the dead. But he was still a man, and a man is likely to say things that will enhance his credit with his fellow man. The fact that he was a man of God would not mean that he was incapable of making human error."

Andrew joined the fray. "If he was not the son of God, what was the meaning of the Passover meal? Did he not tell us that it was a symbol for a new covenant between God and ourselves? Who but the son of God could make such a claim?"

"Anyone who wished to enhance his status with those who would be his followers. I could make such a claim now, and there would be no way for you to know which of the two - mine or that of Jesus - was the more legitimate."

Another man, sitting in a corner eating, chimed in, "Allow me to differ with you there, Thomas. You did not raise Lazarus from the dead, or feed the crowds with a few loaves and fishes. I would have no trouble deciding which was the true covenant." There was some very mild laughter at this, and Thomas turned on his new tormentor.

"Simon, you joke at a bad time."

"So do you. Please do not compare yourself to the Master."

"I did nothing of the kind. Is there no one here who understands the point I am making? I love the Master as much as any of you, and I am prepared to carry on his work, but let us not glorify him more than he deserves."

"How do you intend to carry on his work, Thomas?" asked the other James. "Do you intend to go into the countryside and say to the people: 'Please follow the teachings of my now dead Master, who said that we should all love each other'? I doubt that you will find many takers for such a proposition. The only way to continue his work is to believe that he was the son of God, and that that is the reason people should follow him. The only message that you can bring to people is the healing power of the Messiah.

They will not seek redemption or change their lives for the sake of a dead prophet of whom they have never heard."

"That is exactly right," said Peter. "If the Master was not the son of God, then we have all wasted our time and there is no need to go on with his work. But if he was the son of God, then we are compelled to continue spreading his teaching. It can be no other way. We have seen too much for it not to be true."

"I wish that it were true, Peter," said Thomas. "It would make everything that is to come easier."

James had not spoken to this time, preferring to listen to the debate. But here he could not contain himself. "What is to come?"

Thomas regarded him for a moment, and then said, "The Master is dead, and yet you see us gathered in a quiet room a day after his death. We are all saddened, but it is my belief that we are all thinking of how we might carry on his work. We will find a way, but it will not be easy."

"We cannot do it without some agreement on who the Master was. If we cannot agree on this, we will be out in the world saying eleven different things," said Bartholomew.

"But what do we say?" asked another man sitting in the middle of the floor leaning on a post. "That people should follow us now? That they should follow our dead leader? What exactly will be the message? It is not even clear to me that we should be out in the world preaching. We are not the men the Master was. How is it that we are qualified to carry on with his work? We do not know the things that he knew, or have the power of God with us. We will seem like puny specimens to the people who hear us."

"We do not have all the answers yet. Perhaps they will be forthcoming in a short time, and perhaps not. But too much has happened for me to believe that we are now intended to return to our fishing and selling and tax collecting. We will pray and beg God for the answer to our questions, and he will provide it to us," said Peter. James was surprised to see that this simple assertion was enough to still the debate for the moment. They all bowed their heads and Peter prayed: "Father in heaven, we know not what is the meaning of these recent events, or how we should carry on the work of your....your servant Jesus. Give us this knowledge oh God, as you gave it to Jesus. Teach us to serve you. And now let us pray the prayer that Jesus taught us:" Here all of the men present, James excepted, began to intone, "Our Father, who art in heaven, hallowed be thy name; thy kingdom come, thy will be done on Earth as it is in heaven. Give us this day our daily bread, and forgive us our trespasses as we forgive those who trespass against us. And lead us not into temptation, but deliver us from evil. For thine is the kingdom and the power and the glory now and forever. Amen."

It was a moving moment for James, because it brought further proof that whatever other faults his brother may have had, he commanded great loyalty among his followers. Here was a group of his closest followers who were willing to devote the rest of their lives to his mission, if they could just figure out how to do it. The life of asceticism, of poverty, of wandering the world in search of lost souls appeared to be the call for one and all.

James began to feel uncomfortable in their close company because he felt like an outsider. While he was the brother of Jesus, he had not been there for any of his "miracles" and had heard only one sermon; he also had not wandered in the desert with him, or with them, observing the effect he had on people and attempting to absorb his message. He did not feel the kinship they felt for each other, and there was nothing he could do about it. He rose to make his apologies and go, and Peter came over to him.

"James," said he, "I hope we have not offended you arguing over the merits of your brother. We all loved him dearly, and would not have missed following him these three years for all the gold in the world." James mumbled in an embarrassed way that he had not taken offense, and Peter continued, "This is where we intend to stay for the time being, to gauge the mood of the city before venturing out. You are welcome to visit here any time you like, but please be careful to ensure that you are not followed."

James thanked him for the offer, and then ducked out the door and down to the street. It was now fully dark, and James hastened toward the home of Mordecai to impart the news of the day to his mother.

She was as shocked as he at the news concerning Ananias, for whom she had always felt a certain affection. Neither wanted to believe the testimony of Joseph of Arimathea where Ananias was concerned, but they could think of no reason why he would lie to them on the matter, since it could do him no good in their eyes. It was also true, as Joseph had said, that they did not see as much of Ananias as they once did, and it might be that he had become more ambitious. Without more information they decided to do and say nothing on the matter: there was nothing they could do.

After a pause Mary said to James, "Tomorrow I go with Mary Magdalene to the tomb to anoint the body of your brother. We will leave before light so as to be there when the sun rises."

"Who will roll the stone away for you? Awaken me, and I will accompany you."

"You are tired, and should not get up that early. I have rested all day, and am ready for the trip. Stay here and rest, I will see to the anointing. As for the stone, we will find someone to move it for us. There are always people about."

Though he felt somewhat guilty, James could not resist the urge to rest. He had had little sleep since that first night in Jerusalem and had suffered more in the last 48 hours than in the whole of his life to date. He would be glad of the opportunity to sleep late. He might then go for a walk outside the walls of the city in an attempt to clear his head, and then the next day it would be time for he and his mother to begin the three day return trip to Nazareth.

When James awoke the next morning he found that, as promised, his mother was already gone. It was a fine warm morning with an unseasonable, pleasant breeze blowing, the sun was just up and peeking over the walls of the city, and James felt a little more like his old self. He had not had the best sleep, but it was better than he had had for some time, and he felt more rested.

It was time for a walk – with nothing but his thoughts.

He went first to Golgotha, the site of the crucifixion of his brother. He could think of no reason why he should go there since it held nothing but painful memories for him, but he felt compelled to visit once again. The sun was shining on the spot this morning, and the breeze felt particularly pleasant at that small altitude. There was no one else there at that time of the morning, and because of the Sabbath no one else had occupied the local place of honor since Jesus two days before. Most of the evidence of the crime was now gone, though there were some blood stains on the ground that might have belonged to Jesus. James kicked at the dust and small stones around the hole in the ground where his cross had been propped up, and found a small fragment of wood that looked as though it might have been from Jesus' cross. He picked it up and examined it minutely, but could find no tell tale marks that would definitely place it at the back of Jesus. He was repelled by the memento, and threw it away.

The hill was peaceful now, and James felt it hard to believe that it was the scene of such violence as he had seen two days before. Worse yet, it was commonly the scene of such violence. The two men who were crucified with Jesus might have deserved their punishment, though James doubted this, given the fact that Jesus certainly did not. Could the other two have been political casualties like his brother, or were they murderers, or some in between sort of criminal? How many people like his brother had been punished for what amounted to irritating local officials? James looked to the spot where Jesus was buried, which was hidden on the far side of a rock face. He thought to walk over to see if his mother were still there, but decided he did not want to face his brother's tomb in the presence of others.

James looked around the area for a few moments. To the east and south he could see only the walls of the city, while to the north and west he could see the plains, small villages, and farms that fed the area. It was all too peaceful somehow; he wanted all those people to be in the same uproar as he - outraged over the crucifixion of an innocent man. He wanted them all to be up with him, pondering the mystery that was the soul of man, demanding to know why there should be such suffering, and why other innocent people should have to suffer such losses. When it was apparent that they would all ignore him, he then returned with a heavy heart to the road that skirted the edge of Jerusalem. He began walking to the south, thinking to round the city to the south and then enter by one of the southern gates when he tired. The sun was now high in the sky, and so even the road on the west side of the city was bathed in sunlight, and the walk a warm one.

The road was heavily traveled this morning, with some of the pilgrims who had come to the city for Passover departing, traders, merchants and mendicants coming to the city to conduct business, Roman soldiers out exercising and patrolling the wall of the city, though James could not think what for, and others of purpose to disparate for James to recognize. In this throng James could not walk and lose himself in his own thoughts - he was constantly bumping into other people, or being bumped by them, or being tripped by their children or their animals, so he decided to leave the main road and walk on a small path he knew of that led away from the city, and had been cut by travelers taking a short cut to the road heading south away from the town.

As he walked on this more lonely path he entered a small grove of loosely gathered trees - date and walnut among them - and James slowed to enjoy the occasional shade that they provided.

He wanted to get his mind off of the events of the last two days, if only for a few minutes. He had thought of nothing else, and it seemed as if he were no longer capable of addressing the subject in a remotely intelligent way. All he could do on the subject of his brother was entertain the same tiresome thoughts on the cruelty of man, the injustice of the punishment meted out to Jesus, and the shock of seeing his brother suffer so. It was not that these subjects did not interest him, but that he had thought of nothing else, and appeared to be out of fresh ideas on the. He began to look forward to departing for Nazareth the next day. Perhaps the distance and time would provide him with fresh perspective on the matter.

He tried to think of Esther. They had talked of marriage. The thought of marrying her was pleasing to him, though he tried not to feel too confident about the matter, and he longed for many children if the match could be made. But even here the death of his brother interfered: he kept wondering to himself how what he had seen the last two days would affect the two of them, and how the two of them might now be different since he had seen it and she had not. He wanted to believe that it would make no difference, since she was of a caring and sympathetic nature, and would probably be able to understand what he had been through.

He tried to think of his carpentry business, because surely it was now his. There had never been any hope that Jesus would come home and take

124

over for him, but while Jesus lived James had always felt that somehow he was doing work that Jesus ought to be doing, and so had never developed the proper enthusiasm for the craft. It was lucrative enough for he and his mother when he worked at it, but he frequently took time off to work with the poor and the downtrodden, and this had cut into the faith that some in the small town ought to have owed the only carpenter in the area. Now his brother was dead, and it was as if, in this area at least, a weight had been lifted from his shoulders. He was suddenly in the mood to be back at the tools in his workshop, to hear the rasp of the saw and smell the fresh sawdust at his feet. And he thought that he would have to work harder than he had done in the past, if he was to ensure that the citizens of Nazareth did not go to the trouble to import another carpenter. He would need the funds if he were to support a wife (he would not want to rely on whatever she might inherit), and there was still his mother to care for.

But wait! He had almost forgotten as all the painful memories piled on top of each other. What had Jesus said, hanging there on the cross? He had told one of his own followers to look after Mary their mother, and this with James, who had been looking after her for three years, standing right there. What was the meaning of this? Was he saying that James had not done the job properly? That he was not the right man for the job? Was he simply trying to buy the continued devotion of one of his followers? None of these answers made any sense to James. So many times in their lives Jesus had been a vexation to him, from the incident in the Temple when James was eleven until he had caused James to leave home and work twice to attempt to talk him out of the preaching that was to eventually cost him his life. And now, at the last moment of his life, he takes their mother away from James, and places her in the care of one of his followers. James would not have it. He respected Jesus as the eldest brother, but he had left home three years before, and that disqualified him to make decisions about how the family household was to be established. James would tell this John to pay no attention to this last command of Jesus, and that Mary would stay where she was.

James told himself to give up this line of thought because it poisoned his mind against his recently dead brother. He had wandered off of the path an in among the trees, hoping to absorb the cool of the shade. He found that it could not be done, and made his way back to the path. As he stepped on to the path he noticed a man sitting in the shade of a tree on the right side of the path ahead of him. Otherwise the grove was deserted. He was leaning on the trunk of tree facing the road, with his hooded head down, looking at the ground between his drawn up knees. James was trying to decide whether to pass the man on the road and risk being accosted when he did not want to be, or to take a route through the grove to miss him, when the man looked up and faced him. Too late now, he would have to continue on the path so as not to give the appearance of avoiding the man.

James could not see the face of the man because of the shadow cast by the hood he wore, but his build suggested he was about James' age, perhaps a little younger. James met his gaze, and said to him, "Good morning, stranger."

The man did not answer right away, but as James drew closer he could see more of the man's features. He could see the strong chin, the dark brown, curly beard, the clear, white teeth framed in a kindly smile - a smile that looked remarkably like that of....no, it could not be. As James stopped in front of the man the man looked up at him, and then stood in his place under the tree. This allowed more light to penetrate under the hood, and James felt his heart beating harder and faster than it ever had. He was suddenly short of breath, his eyes open wide, his lips dry, his chest feeling as if it would explode. He reached both hands up slowly, and placed them on both sides of the hood the man wore over his head, and slowly pushed it back to reveal....his brother Jesus. James' hands clutched at his chest, he gasped aloud, and involuntarily took a step back, not knowing what he did. He felt the world closing in on him, a creeping darkness began to envelope him, his breath and eyesight seemed to fail him at once, the tunnel through which he seemed to be looking began to spin around him, and for the first and only time in his life he fainted away.

As he opened his eyes he found himself sitting on the ground leaning against a tree. Though his eyes were open, it took a few moments for him to regain his senses. He looked around himself in that vacant way that the newly recovered have - he could see and hear, but he could not immediately account for his presence under the tree. He combed through his memory searching for the last thing he did, but could not come up with it until he looked just to his right and saw his brother Jesus sitting next to him.

Surprised again, he let out a cry and jumped sideways, pushing himself away with his hands and feet, as though he needed distance between himself and the specter at his side. Jesus smiled at him, but James could not find his voice. All he could do was stare, open mouthed and wide eyed. After a moment Jesus said to him, "Peace be with you, James."

But James did not find peace immediately. His breathing was labored, his heart pounding, and he feared that he would faint again. He wanted to speak, to ask questions, but all he could muster were high pitched croaks. Jesus continued to simply smile at him, and James struggled to control himself. His voice came to him, however croakingly and haltingly. "How can this be? I...I placed you in the tomb myself."

"All things are possible for my Father in heaven."

"Then it is you," James continued to croak, his throat dry, his eyes still wide open and now dry from his failure to blink. He sat upright, bracing himself with his hands, facing his brother. He forced himself to blink and swallow, but he could say nothing else. Everything he had ever believed, everything he had thought all his life, and particularly in the last three years, were now proven wrong. In his enforced silence, the implications of what he saw before him began to manifest themselves to him. Here was the brother he had buried only two days ago alive again. Just to make sure James glanced down at Jesus' wrists. Jesus seemed to know what James was looking for, because he stretched out his arms so that James could see the marks from the nails. The wrist was clean now, but there was a large scar where the nail had penetrated. Here then was Jesus, his brother, risen from the dead. There could only be one answer. None of the prophets had been able to raise themselves from the dead, and none had had the powers of raising others from the dead that had been attributed to Jesus. All of the miracles James had heard about must have been true. Even the changing of the water and wine at the wedding feast at Cana, at which James had scoffed, had been the doing of his brother. He was therefore more powerful than the prophets, and he had claimed to be the Son of God. It had to be true. There could be no other explanation. Surely, if he had the powers that he appeared to have, he would know for what purpose they had been given to him. His claims were true! He was the Son of God - the Messiah sent by God to restore Israel.

Such thoughts occupied only seconds, but they paralyzed James. He had been focused on his thoughts, and so while he continued to stare he really didn't see Jesus. For a moment his mind cleared and he focused again on the kindly, smiling face of his brother. He was suddenly gripped by fear, to be in the presence of such a figure, and with a cry of alarm he slid another two feet away on his behind using his hands and feet for power.

But, retreating into his thoughts once again, he wondered how this man, the offspring of a carpenter and his wife, could restore Israel. He had not the power and connections. But of course he had the power - that was obvious now. He could do anything he wanted. And yet he could have prevented his own crucifixion and did not. Why was he born poor, if he were the one to save Israel? The questions poured in so fast that James could not keep track of them, did not know which were the most important, and did not know which to ask, if any. Who was he to question such a figure?

Here was the Messiah, and yet he was also James' brother. What did that make James? How could it be that the mother of both of them should give birth to the Messiah? James focused on Jesus again, to force himself to speak, and to ask him how this could be.

"But...but....we are of the same mother and father..."

"We are of the same mother only James. I am born of woman and the Holy Spirit that I might take on the sins of the world, and reconcile all people to my Father in heaven."

This meant that James and Jesus were half brothers, apparently, if Jesus meant that he was not the son of Joseph of Nazareth. This made more sense if Jesus were the Messiah, and yet it was incomprehensible all the same. James could not get his thoughts organized to speak clearly.

"But...Israel...and the Romans? How...?

"My kingdom is not of this world. I have come to atone for the sins of the world - to restore the world to my Father." James did not understand the meaning of this - Jesus appeared to be claiming that he would not restore the glory of Israel, which would be contrary to all that the Jews understood about the Messiah. But who else would have the powers that his brother had? Who else could be sitting across from him this morning, after all that had happened?

Once more James focused on the face of Jesus for a moment, and a glance at his eyes convinced him, beyond his reason, that his brother was indeed the Messiah. Jesus said nothing, made no move, and yet James read in his eyes the answer to his basic question. He still did not know how they could both come from the same mother, or why Jesus would not restore the glory of Israel, but James did believe that he was who he said he was - the Messiah.

But the implications of this were not to be borne. Had not James, just that morning, criticized his brother for having told John to take care of Mary? How many times had he denied Jesus' claim to his face? He had taken two trips to Jesus to attempt to talk him out of the work that was given him by God. To everyone with whom he had discussed the matter he had denied Jesus' claim. He had criticized, denigrated, denied the existence of the Son of God, and he had done it to the Son of God. He had been living with or in close proximity to such a man for over thirty years; how many times had he been selfish, shortsighted, mean, and too many other things to Jesus? The realization of his shortcomings sank in, and James rose suddenly from his sitting position, still staring wild eyed at him, and began to berate himself.

"How abominably I have treated you! I have lived with the Son of God for these thirty years! I have teased you, cursed you, denied you to your face, to our friends, to everyone who asks! I have sinned a great sin not only in the sight of God, but to the face of his Son!" James said, in the last stages of desperation. He then fell to the ground and began to cry, but that did not seem like adequate punishment, and he began pounding at the ground with his fists in an attempt to relieve his frustration at himself. Even this did not seem to abase himself enough - he sought some other way to atone. He picked up handfuls of dirt and rubbed them in his face, and tore at his clothes, all the while crying plaintively, sometimes begging for forgiveness at the top of his lungs.

But even this rage and fear could not go on forever, and, tired from the exertion he rested a moment, lying on his stomach on the ground, his head resting on his hands. He then raised his head slowly to look up at Jesus, was once again overcome with fear and shame, and began to pound his forehead on the ground. Jesus rose and advanced to him, but James saw him coming, and jumped up himself.

"No!" he cried. "Do not come near me! I am not worthy that you should approach me! I have thought myself a man of faith, and I have denied the existence of the Son of God to his face! I have shared table with him! I have played and walked and talked with him, and still I did not see him! He told me who he was and I denied him! I was present at one of his signs to the world, and still I did not believe! I am unworthy of you! Do not come near me!" James backed up a several more steps, always while staring wild eyed at Jesus, his brother. His breathing was labored from the exertions on the ground, he was perspiring heavily, his cloak was torn and dirty, his face and arms were grimy with the dirt that he threw on himself, his forehead bloody from pounding it on the rocky path, and he was crying tears of rage and frustration.

Jesus took another step forward to comfort James, but James backed off again. "No! No! I am not worthy! Stay away! I have been within arms reach of the Son of God all my life, and all I have done is deny him!" At this James felt weak and stupid and inadequate, and fell to the ground again, and began pounding at it with his fists, and picking up the dirt to rub in his face. As he lay on the ground punishing himself he saw, out of the corner of his eye, Jesus begin to walk toward him again, and again he jumped up.

"No!" he screamed again. "There is no indignity I have not heaped upon you! No sin I have not committed in the eyes of God! I deserve to be punished! I have not been a worthy subject of God or his son! I have told the son to his face that he was not the son! He told me of his mission, and I sent him away!" James stood there staring wild eyed at Jesus, the energy generated by his frustration and rage almost dissipated.

Jesus replied simply, "And do you send him away now?"

This penetrated James like a shot, and he fell to his knees. He began to weep more loudly, and more uncontrollably, and from his knees he fell to his face. After a moment of crying, he raised himself weakly to his hands and knees, and crawled the few feet to where Jesus stood. There he raised himself to his knees again, and tried to look Jesus in the eye, but found that he could not. Still crying he clasped his hands together and said, staring at the ground, "I...I...do not know what to do. I am out of my depths," between sobs. "I have failed you too many times to count, though even one would be enough. Do what you will with me."

"James," said Jesus calmly, "peace be with you." James heard the words - in fact it was the second time Jesus had said them to him - but they had a calming effect on him this time, and he felt the sense of panic that had engulfed him lift, and for the first time he could think clearly. He attempted to get control of his emotions, while Jesus waited patiently. Gradually he succeeded, and finally slumped to the ground, holding his upraised knees with his arms and resting his head on them. Jesus sat next to him.

James pondered the situation for a moment, and then raised his head. "I do not understand," he said, in a tired, sorrowful voice. "I am prepared to believe that you are the Messiah, and yet you are not what was foretold to us."

"I am not what was imagined. I have come to fulfill the prophecies, not to change them."

"But, the Messiah a brother to a poor carpenter?"

"The Father in heaven does not need to work through kings. Who was Moses but the son of slaves?"

"How came you to be born of woman?"

"That I might share the humanity of my Father's chosen people."

"But you say that you are not the son of Joseph, the carpenter of Nazareth?"

"I am the son of Man, born of a virgin through the power of the Holy Spirit." None of this made sense to James, and he decided that he would not be able to understand at the moment, no matter how much he applied himself to the problem. He rested his head on his knees again.

After a few moments, James looked up at Jesus and said, "What would you have me do?"

"You will serve the same Father that I have served James, and thus will you serve me."

"Am I to follow you along with the others?"

"My work here is done. Those who believe in me will preach the good news to those who have not heard. My time here is short, and I have much to do."

"Can you not lead us? How will we know what to do, or what to say? And how will we know that what we tell those who will listen is your will? I have heard you teaching the crowds, and I am not capable of rising to such levels."

"James, do you believe in me? Then believe that you will carry on the work that I have begun."

"What would you have me do?" James asked again.

"In time all will be made plain to you." How often had James heard that, and yet, in general terms, there was much that was more clear to him now than formerly. For the first time, James was prepared to accept his brother's word that this would be true. "Give no thought to the time and place," Jesus continued, "but only believe that you will serve."

"I am at your command."

"Blessed are they who believe in me, for their reward will be great in heaven." James looked up once again, to see Jesus smiling at him. "Rest now, for the way for you will be long," continued Jesus. James put his head down again, for only a few seconds, but when he looked up again his brother was gone.

James leaped up immediately and looked around him, but there was no trace of Jesus. He began to run around the grove of trees in a desperate, panic stricken search for Jesus, but he was not to be found. At this realization James cried out as loud as he could, "Jesus! My brother! No, no! Not my brother, but the son of God! Hear me! Come back to me that I might understand!"

But there was no answer, and he ran all through the small grove and out into the open in search of Jesus, but he was nowhere there. He called out several more times, but got no answer. He gave up after a few minutes, and stood alone in the grove of trees, perspiring, dirty, clothes torn, hands and face bloody, and ragged, a sea of emotions over what had just happened to him. He suspected that it must be a dream, and that he had just woken. How could he ever be sure that he had seen his brother, and how could he convince others that he had? He could not leave it like this. He wanted it to be true, but he had to confirm it. He was seized by an idea and ran back to the tree where he had seen his brother. There he crouched down on his knees and began to look for evidence that Jesus had been there. He was not long in looking because there on the ground, in the loose dirt under the tree, he could see the marks that Jesus had left while sitting and walking. It had not been a dream! He had spoken to his brother who had been crucified only two days before, and that brother was the Messiah sent by God. James wanted to shout the news to the world, but he already knew from looking for Jesus that there was no one else in the grove to hear him.

But then the implications of the news occurred to him. He would be ridiculed by those who had contrived to put Jesus to death, possibly even by the followers of his brother with whom he had gathered the night before. And Jesus had said that his time here was short. This did not make it clear whether or not Jesus would appear to anyone else. James might be the only one to see his brother, and no one else would believe him. He would say nothing for the moment, and see what might happen.

But that would not do. Jesus did not ask him to serve only to keep such news to himself. He must mean for the message to be spread far and wide. But he had not said so. James could hardly run through the streets of the city proclaiming that a man recently crucified was now among the living. James would be sent away as an imbecile, and the message lost.

The tomb! That would prove that he had risen from the dead. If the body were not there, who could doubt? James set off at a run in the direction of Golgotha and the adjacent tomb.

He rushed through the crowds on the road, pushing people aside, sometimes swerving off the road to avoid a particularly large mass of travelers, and finally came to the tomb where Jesus had been lain. There were Roman soldiers on guard, which James did not understand, but, tired from his exertions he slowed to a walk and attempted to pass them. One stood up from his perch leaning on a date tree, and confronted him.

"Where would you go?"

"I would see the tomb of my brother, who is risen."

"You are the brother of the man Jesus? Then you must know what has become of his body. Where is it?"

"He has risen from the dead! I have just seen him."

"Are you crazy? Only a god could rise from the dead. Now what have you done with him?"

"I have done nothing with him. He is risen by the power of God! Is it not wonderful? And I was his brother!"

"He was a god, and you are the brother of a god!" sneered the soldier, to the delight of the other four soldiers assembled. "Well forgive me for not believing you. I believe that you stole his body, and that you are hiding it somewhere. You will tell me where it is," said the soldier, and then glancing up he added, "or you will tell them."

James turned to look where the soldier was looking, and saw that several members of the Sanhedrin were approaching accompanied by a centurion (the one who had been near the cross two days before) and one or two other Romans. The only one of the members of the Sanhedrin that he knew was Ananias.

As they approached the tomb, the leader of the group said to the guard, "There have been reports that the body of Jesus is missing. Is this true?"

"It is," replied the soldier.

"Who has taken it?"

"We do not know who has taken it. We have been here all night as ordered, and we have seen no one."

"Let us see the tomb." With that the entire group advanced up the short slope to the entrance of the tomb, and James followed along. Each took a turn looking in the entrance. When James looked he saw that the tomb was indeed empty. Not even the cloth that he had been wrapped in remained. There was no sign that the tomb had ever been occupied.

"Are you sure that this is the correct tomb? Are you so foolish that you may have posted a guard on the wrong tomb?" asked Ananias.

"This is the correct tomb because I was present when he was placed in it two days ago. There have also been some women here this morning looking for him, though he was already gone, and now this man comes to claim that he is risen from the dead."

With that all eyes turned to James. Ananias regarded him carefully, before finally recognizing him.

"James! What has happened to you? Have you been assaulted on the road this morning? What do you know of the disappearance of your brother's body?"

"I know nothing of it."

"But this guard claims that you said that he had risen from the dead."

"I do not know what has happened to him. He is not here, and there is no reason why anyone would come to steal the body, so I merely guessed at what may have happened."

The elder member of the Sanhedrin spoke. "In fact, there is ample reason to believe that one of his followers might have stolen the body. It is said that he predicted that he would be killed, and that he would rise again from the dead. They might have stolen the body to make it appear that this prediction has come true."

There was general agreement among the members of the Sanhedrin at this, but James said nothing. The elder spoke again. "Who did you say this man is?"

Ananias spoke up. "He is the brother of the man called Jesus. But I do not believe that he would steal a body from a tomb."

"And why do you not believe this? Is he not a follower of the blasphemer?"

"No, he is not. In fact he has undertaken missions on my behalf to attempt to talk Jesus out of his teaching."

"Has he? Well, that is interesting. Why are you in this disheveled condition?" the man asked James directly. James could not think of an answer. He hated to lie to the man, and hated to tell him the truth. Ananias came to his rescue.

"It is obvious that he is in mourning for his brother. I do not know what form his oblations took, but you must admit that even a blasphemer is still a brother to someone. If he had taken the body he would hardly be here asking after it."

This seemed to satisfy the others for the moment, though James could see holes in it: a clever grave robber might do just that to throw suspicion off the trail. But he said nothing.

There began an urgent discussion of what was to be done next. There could be no question that the body was gone, and it seemed unlikely that it would be recovered. That would surely, said the elder, spark Jesus' followers into claiming that he had risen from the dead. They must have a story ready to counteract such claims.

"You will tell those who ask," said the elder to the soldiers, "that his followers came in the night and stole his body while you were sleeping. This shall be your only story, and you shall tell it to all who ask."

"We were on guard," said one of the Romans. "You would have us go back and claim that we were sleeping on watch?"

"I shall see to it that you are paid handsomely for your trouble," said the elder. "I am going now to call a meeting of the Sanhedrin to discuss this matter, but I have no doubt that the result will be as I have laid out." With that the small group began to walk back toward the city. One of the guards asked if they should maintain their post. "Guard an empty tomb? I fail to see the use in it. As the word gets out people will come to see the site, and we must not appear to attach more importance to it than is necessary."

James lagged behind the others, and allowed them to outpace him, so that after a very few minutes he was once again alone.

The day was not far advanced when he recovered his composure after deciding that he would do something to make his views on the matter of what happened to his brother's body obvious. He did not yet know the form that his declaration would take, but he would make it soon.

He walked slowly, in part because he was afraid of the reception he might find there, and in part because he was tired. His disheveled appearance did cause some heads to turn, but he ignored them and continued on his way.

His first puzzle was where he ought to go first. He wanted to talk to his mother, but he also wanted to talk to the followers of Jesus. As he walked he heard one or two comments about his appearance that convinced him that his first order of business ought to be to return to the home of Mordecai and clean himself. There also he would find his mother.

It was obvious when he entered that his mother had only just returned. She appeared to have just sat down with the wife of Mordecai when James entered. When she saw him she leaped from her seat and ran to him, saying, "James! I have news...But what has happened to you? Were you beset by robbers?"

"No mother. I was beset by my brother."

"Then you have seen him also?"

"In a small stand of trees outside the walls of the city. I did not know him immediately, but when I recognized him, and realized what it meant, I was overcome with shame. I had been living with him all my life. He told me who he was and I denied it. You told me who he was and I denied it.

Each new memory of how I have treated him over the years brings me new pain. I was in the habit of blaming him for not taking up the tools of our...my... father Joseph." James could not help the rueful laugh at his expense. "Can you believe what I am saying? I told the son of God that he must be a carpenter so that I may go to Jerusalem to study the Scriptures." James did not know whether to laugh or cry at himself. "What is worse, I wanted to study under the very men who put him to death. There is no shame I have not heaped upon myself in my life. I am lucky that he spared me."

Here Mordecai's wife could contain herself no longer. "Are you saying that you have seen Jesus - the man who was crucified just two days ago?"

Mary and James answered simultaneously, "I have."

"You have seen him alive and walking? You believe that he has risen from the dead?"

"I believe it, but I also know it," said James, "for I have seen him."

"This cannot be. How is it that a man can raise himself up from the dead?"

"Man cannot raise himself up from the dead," answered James. "Such things are possible only with the power of God."

"And you called him the son of God just now, did you not?"

"There can be no other answer for the power which he possesses," answered James. "I have denied it all my life, but I now understand who he is, if not exactly how his plan will work, or even if there is a plan. When I saw him outside the city, I attempted to continue to doubt, but I could not. All the things that I have heard of over the years came back to me, and I realized, to my great shame, that somehow I was a brother to the anointed one, had been living with him most of my life, and all that time I denied his existence to all who would listen. I went twice and attempted to talk him out of his work." James laughed a small, sad laugh to himself. "It will torture me always."

Mary said, "Mary Magdalene and I went to the tomb to anoint the body, but when we arrived the stone had been rolled back and the tomb was empty. Standing without was a man dressed all in white who asked of us, 'Why do you look for the living amongst the dead? Jesus is not here.' We did not know what to make of this, but as we returned to the city in great confusion, he appeared to us, first as a stranger, and then scales fell from our eyes and we knew him. He spoke words of comfort to us, and then disappeared, we know not where."

"I want to believe you," said the wife of Mordecai, "but you are his family, and this is what I would expect you to want to believe. Perhaps when he has shown himself to his followers I shall see him."

135

"I do not believe that he will teach again in public," said James. "I believe it is his intention to be with us for a very short while."

"Then your claim will be difficult to prove," said the skeptical woman.

"You must have faith," said Mary to her.

"When I have seen him, I will believe." These words were painful to James because he was guilty of that same lack of faith: he had not believed until he had seen, and Jesus had gently chastised him for it.

James and Mary decided not to argue the matter with her, because they hadn't the persuasive power of others. Doubtless Jesus would appear to others, and James would bring one of these around to convince the woman. Mary looked James up and down again, and then looked into his eyes, prior to asking the obvious question, but James anticipated her.

"When I saw him all my sins against him came back to me; it was as if everything that I ever did to deny came rushing back on me at once, and I was shamed. I did not know how to react to the sight of him, or what the sight of him meant. I have done this to myself, and," he added ruefully, "I deserve much worse."

"Do you know where he is now?" Mary asked James.

"No. He bade me be seated to rest for a moment, and when I put my head down for a moment he disappeared. It would seem that there is some method to his comings and goings, but I confess I do not know what it is. However, from this day forth I will act as you act, and believe in him, no matter what happens."

"You will find that life is much easier to face, my son, if you believe in the power of God."

"I have always believed in the power of God. It is his son that I am still becoming accustomed to. As far as such faith making me happier, I do not know about that. I have already had occasion to render myself sad over him, and he is only just arisen." Here he related the story of the confrontation at the tomb only moments ago with particular emphasis on the story that the Sanhedrin would tell the soldiers to tell, and his own failure to claim in front of them that Jesus had risen from the dead.

"There is much pain to come mother, because those who do not believe will be adamant that the rest of us are fabricating our stories to give him credibility. And we will have no proof unless he appears to many sometime in the near future. What will happen to those who believe in him, but cannot offer proof that he rose from the dead? Are they to be harried and tried as well? How many will make the claim for him publicly, knowing that they might suffer the same fate? I have already proven that I haven't the courage." Here James told Mary of his plan to exculpate himself from this dilemma, and she was unswervingly against it.

136

"What purpose will it serve?" she asked him. "How will that set right what has already been done and cannot be undone? Do not go, and leave the matter rest for the moment. There will be other chances to serve Jesus."

"Jesus had just treated me kindly, telling me that I would serve him, and, I thought, forgiving me for the way I have treated him. Not even an hour later I refuse to acknowledge him to those who put him to death. Is this the proper action for one to take in the sight of God? No, no, it is better for me that I make amends the very first chance I get."

James and Mary argued back and forth on the matter for a few more minutes, but when Mary saw that she would not talk James out of the mission, she dropped the matter, and proposed to go to the far side of town and see the followers of Jesus. James was desperate to share his revelation with others who might be of like mind, and immediately assented. His emotional exchanges with his mother were satisfying, but he wanted to see the reactions of others when they heard the news.

Thus it was that they set off for the far side of town shortly after noon, after James had had a chance to wash himself and don fresh clothes. James led Mary to the room where he had met the disciples of Jesus - when had it been? only the day before? - but when he knocked on the door in the same manner that the other James had done the day before, there was no answer. He tried the latch and found the door unlocked, and they went in, only to find the room empty. They retreated to the street so that James could ensure that this was the same room he had come to before, and he decided it was. He asked the landowner what had become of the men who stayed in the room, but he did not know. They had left earlier that morning, and he did not know where they had gone. James speculated to himself that they were doubtless moving so that their whereabouts would not become known, and it may have been his visit of the night before that panicked them into moving.

James and Mary then walked back to the house of Mordecai, to find Mary Magdalene waiting there for them. The wife of Mordecai exclaimed that even if Jesus was not the son of God, and she was still not convinced, he was a powerful man indeed to inspire such loyalty in the people around him. Mary Magdalene had been telling her the story of how she and the mother of Jesus had happened on him in the road that morning, which was the second time she had heard it.

"At least you have got your stories straight, if you are telling lies," said she. "This Mary tells me the same story as that Mary."

"Who could forget or confuse the details?" exclaimed Mary Magdalene. "How often does one talk to the son of God after he has risen from the dead?" Mordecai's wife continued to deny this story, and Mary Magdalene vehemently engaged her in a debate over the matter. James and Mary watched for a moment, elated in their own knowledge of the truth, and feeling sympathetic to Mordecai's wife for the fact that she had not seen what they had seen. Mary Magdalene gave up the effort after a few minutes, but not without exerting the other woman to believe in what so many had seen ("There have been reports from only three people thus far, and two of them are of the man's family," she had replied.) and telling her that she was alive on the greatest day in the history of the world.

When she had done with the woman the three of them retreated out of doors to discuss matters sitting in the shade in the small garden. It was here that James wondered if Jesus had appeared to his twelve closest followers.

"He has not - or at least he had not when I saw them not long ago," said Mary Magdalene. "I went to tell them of the good news, and they did not believe me."

This revelation shocked James. "His own followers do not believe that he has risen?"

"They do not. I told them what we had seen, but they showed me out for being a silly woman. I told them that his mother had also seen, but they said that of course his mother would want to see such a thing. I hope that he appears to them, for, when he does, I will be sure to ask them who is the silly woman now: the one who saw and believed, or those who hid in their rooms and did not believe."

This led James to ask how she knew where they were, since they had moved since the previous evening. Mary Magdalene said that while on the way to the room that they formerly had, she had run into James in the street and he had taken her to their new rooms upon hearing the news she had to convey. They were huddled there like sheep hiding from the slaughter, she reported, and she did not know how long they planned to hide. "You see that I am in the open. I am not afraid of the people who have crucified my Lord."

"You were not among the closest people to him," James reminded her. "I can understand their being cautious for the moment, though of course it cannot last forever."

Mary Magdalene bristled. "How can they hide in their rooms when the son of God, the man they have followed these three years and who was crucified only two days ago is now out and about the streets? Let them give him homage by having the courage to own him." At this James smiled. It was the first time in so long he could not remember, though it had probably been only since their arrival in Jerusalem three days before. All since then had been pain, until this moment.

A short walk found him back at the house of Ananias, where all of this had begun three days before. In the face of Ananias that morning he had hidden the truth from his old friend, and now it was time to make up for that oversight, at least in the eyes of his brother. He felt some fear, given what had just happened to his brother two days before, but it was also something he felt obligated to do, given what had happened to his brother just that morning.

The door was opened for him by the same surly servant, but this time he was shown into the house without delay. Ananias made his appearance in very short order, though this time without his usual jaunty step and booming voice. In a subdued voice, apparently wondering what the cause of this visit could be, he asked after James and his mother. James replied that they were both fine, which appeared to surprise Ananias somewhat. It was apparent that Ananias was uncomfortable with the subject, since he had had a part in the recent events, but his manners overcame his reserve on the matter. James saw an opportunity and he took it.

"I have come to thank you for looking after me this morning when it appeared that the small crowd at my brother's tomb might think I had something to do with the disappearance of his body." At this Ananias' eyes lit up, perhaps thinking that the meeting might be harmless after all. "It was most solicitous of you, and I am grateful," James continued, "but I should not have put you in that position. The fact is that I know what happened to his body, as does my mother. That is why I am able to give you such a rosy report on our well being."

"Who took it?"

"No one has taken it."

"What do you mean? Of course someone has taken it, or it would still be in the tomb."

James paused for a moment for effect, and then said, "Ananias, he is risen."

Ananias paused for a moment, digesting this. "What? Do you mean to say that you believe him to have risen from the dead? Come now James," he said in a cajoling manner, "I have known you for many years, and you have always been a level headed man of affairs. I know that you don't believe such nonsense."

"But I do believe it."

"Where would you have gotten such an idea? You were not among the followers who hung on his every word, hoping for some sign from heaven. You and I have talked many times about where his preaching would end, and, sadly, it has come to that. You heard us talking at the tomb this morning that his believers would claim that he had risen, and that we should have a story to refute them with, but surely you have not abandoned reason so completely that you now believe along with the fanatics."

"In one way I have not abandoned reason, but in another I have. When I see my own brother crucified on one day, and help lay him in the tomb, and then see him alive two days, later, I reason that something extraordinary has happened. It is at that point that I abandon reason, and say to myself: 'He claimed to be the son of God, and now he is raised from the dead. His claim must therefore be true.'"

"You have gone over! You have become one of the followers of your brother!" said Ananias. "How can this be? Surely you must know that the son of God will not be the son of a carpenter, and end crucified outside the holy city. Your brother was just like all the others that have come before him: he claimed to be what he was not, and in accordance with the law, he was punished for it."

"Am I to be punished also, because I now believe it?"

"The law says that only those who make the claim for themselves are subject to the punishment. But it will not please the Sanhedrin to find that his followers have gone about town claiming that he has risen from the dead. But why do you believe it? What has changed your mind after all these years?"

"I tell you that I have seen him."

"Seen him where?"

"In a grove of trees outside the walls of the city. He appeared to me there as clearly as you stand before me. He spoke to me, told me that I would serve him, and then disappeared when I put my head down for only a moment. You saw my condition at the tomb - I was not set upon by robbers, nor had I been mourning over his death. I was mourning, but not for the reason you suspected: I mourned for myself, for my own shortsightedness and stupidity and lack of faith. I abused myself because I was overcome with anger and fear and shame that I had been living with, and had criticized, the son of God."

"This is nonsense. You may have seen a man who looked like your brother, but you could not have seen him! He is dead, James, dead. Perhaps your grieving mind was playing tricks on you, and allowing you to see him because you wanted to."

"Do I not know my own brother, Ananias? Did I not see the wounds in his wrists? It was he, and no other. I would not have believed it myself, were I not there to see it. That is why I fell into a faint at the sight of him."

Ananias switched tacks now. "James, my dear old friend," said he in his friendliest voice, "let us not have disagreements about this matter. What is possessing you to come here and tell me such things which you know cannot be true? Are you seeking to cause me pain? If you are then you have succeeded. I am saddened to see you like this, my brother."

"I am here because I feel compelled to be. I have been in the presence of the son of God, and it is my duty to say so. I am also ashamed, ashamed of the fact that when I saw you and the others at the empty tomb this morning, I had not the courage to tell what I know."

"But you had discretion. There is a mistake here somewhere: either your mind is playing tricks on you, or someone has made himself to look like your brother, or you are lying to me for some unknown reason, and we will figure out where it is, but if you and the others continue to make this claim there is likely to be more trouble. We cannot allow the followers of one itinerant preacher to undermine the Jewish faith with their false claims."

"There is nothing false about the claim. You should look to the fact that you consider me level-headed: would I make such a claim as this if there were no factual reason for doing so? If I were you I would be doing and saying he same things that you are doing and saying. I have seen my brother. He is alive at this moment, though I know not where." A sudden thought occurred to James. "He has also appeared to my mother and to Mary Magdalene."

"This proves nothing. The fact that your mother claims to see him merely suggests that both family members are suffering the same pangs of sorrow. I do not know a Mary Magdalene, but the claims of three people, two of whom are family, will not convince the masses that he is alive."

"I have no doubt that there will be others, and it is also possible that he may go back to teaching. There may be many who come to believe in him over time. The Sanhedrin will not succeed in killing them all."

Ananias bristled at this. "It is not the intention of the Sanhedrin to kill them all," he snarled. "We will not interfere with people who will keep the law and not claim to be the son of God."

"How will you treat those who claim to know the son of God, or claim that he is among us?"

"There is no law which prohibits a fool from saying that someone else is the son of God. If such types wish to go about the countryside making fools of themselves, we will not stand in the way." Ananias was angry now, and James was immediately sorry for it.

"Ananias, my old friend, I cannot claim to be happy with what has happened in Jerusalem this week, but I did not come here to antagonize you. This issue will finally be larger than the two of us, and I should not find fault with you. Nevertheless, I have seen my brother alive this morning, and I now believe him to be the one who is to come. I failed him at the tomb this morning, but I do not intend to do so again."

Ananias was mollified somewhat. "James, can you not see the absurdity of what you are telling me?" he asked in a plaintive voice. "How can the brother of my friend James be the Messiah? How can the one who is to come be born of a Nazarene?"

James could see where Ananias was heading with this line of questions, and he began to debate with himself over whether or not he should tell Ananias the story that Mary told him - that Jesus was not the son of

Joseph, but the product of some spiritual union between herself and God. It seemed fantastic to James, and he was now convinced that Jesus was who he said he was. How absurd would it sound to the likes of Ananias? He decided to compromise with himself on the matter.

"I do not pretend to understand all that has happened, or all that will happen. I know the stories that have surrounded Jesus concerning his miracles and cures, some of which were related to me by you, I have seen one myself, and now I have seen him arisen from the dead. It is all too much to be coincidence or the invention of man."

"You say that you have seen one of the miracles. What did you see?"

"At a marriage feast in Cana, before he became well known, Jesus turned six jars of water into wine."

"Bah! That is preposterous. No man could do that. How do you know that it was he who affected this miracle?"

"I watched as he sent the servants to fetch six jars of water. When they returned, he told the manservant to take a ladle from one of the jars and give it to the steward to taste. The man exclaimed that it was the best wine he had had that night. I then tasted it myself in disbelief, and it was excellent wine."

"This is too easy. It is obvious that the servants brought the jar back full of wine, rather than water."

"I questioned them thoroughly on the matter. I had them take me to where they fetched the water, and I tasted it."

"They lied, as part of some plot with your brother."

"As part of a plot with my brother, who could pay them nothing since he had nothing, they risked the wrath of the groom by hiding good wine on the premises and then pretending to run out? It is not credible, Ananias."

"There are other ways it could have been managed."

"What have you to say of the other tales - tales where there are many witnesses who know that he was not in league with others? What of the man Lazarus that he raised from the dead? What of the blind and lame whom he restored to health?"

"There may be explanations for these as well. The mere fact that there are witnesses does not prove that Jesus was not planning with some agents to fool the people. But let me grant you, for the sake of argument, that he might have performed some of these miracles. There have been others in the past, particularly the prophets, who have been able to do as much. God can provide such power if it suits him to do so. This fact did not make them sons of God, and it does not make Jesus son of God."

"I know of no man who was able to raise the dead from their tombs, to say nothing of coming back from the grave himself."

"Here we have only the word of three people that he came back to life, and they are not the most unbiased of witnesses."

"The raising of the man Lazarus was reportedly seen by many."

"The raising of the man Lazarus could have been faked. And it proves nothing."

"You know that my brother was not one to use a ruse. He had very little trickery in him even when we were boys."

"He disappeared into the city when he was only twelve, as I recall, without the permission of his parents, and presumed to teach the elders even then. This is how you and I met. He led people who followed him around in the desert, telling him that he was their savior, only to end on the cross himself. If this is not trickery, I do not know what is."

"If you were to see him, would you then believe?"

"Possibly, if you were to convince me that it is really he. It is not too much trouble to find someone who looks like him, and parade him around as the real item."

"Could they also fake the wounds of the cross on his wrists and feet, and the lance wound in his side?"

"You have seen these?"

"I have seen the marks on his body where the nails were driven in. I have not seen the wound in his side made by the lance. But I am sure that they are there."

"Like all else, these could be contrived."

"You don't want to believe. You are like I was, denying all for the sake of the faith that you already have, and unwilling to face the new reality."

"I face the reality that the self called son of God has been crucified, and now lies dead somewhere in the area," Ananias snarled again. "If he is the Messiah, where is the new kingdom that he was prophesied to establish? Why are the streets of Jerusalem still cluttered with Roman soldiers? Will you tell me that? Why is there still poverty and want in the capital city of our people?"

"I do not pretend to understand all such matters. I am told by one of his followers that he claimed that his kingdom would not be of this world. I do not know all such yet, but I cannot avoid the evidence of my own senses. He was dead, and now he is alive. No man is capable of this, therefore he must be the son of God."

Tempers were beginning to rise, and James decided to make his exit. "We will not solve the matter here, Ananias, so let us call a truce. We shall see in the coming days which of us was right." James knew that he was right, and did not expect anything to mar this simple fact. He could not prove it to Ananias, but then he was likely to be among the more difficult to convince.

He noticed that he felt a strange calm, and decided that it came from the fact that his questions about the Messiah were answered. All people had been wondering what was the truth on this matter, and now James knew. It gave him satisfaction and peace to know that he had seen aright, even if only under duress.

As he passed through a small marketplace, he happened to look up and see the other James walking on the far side, carrying a basket of food. James feared to hail him, but ran up to him and touched his arm. The other James was momentarily surprised, and jumped at being approached, but relaxed when he saw who accosted him.

"Have you seen him?" James asked.

"Seen who?"

"Why, Jesus, my brother. He is risen." The other James did not appear as startled as James hoped he would be.

"So we have been told by Mary Magdalene, who came to us early this morning. But none of the brethren are convinced. Come with me once again, and let us see what effect your report has on them." James willingly accompanied him, and they talked as they threaded their way through the crowded streets.

"Where did you see him?" asked the other James, apparently without mockery. James related the story of his sighting of his brother, and the other James listened with interest.

"Mary Magdalene came to us early this morning to tell us that he had risen, but it was too much for most. They could not believe."

"Do you mean to tell me that my brother's own followers do not believe the reports they have received?"

"Some are inclined to, but most are skeptical. But you may understand that: consider how hard it is to believe that a person has risen from the dead."

"But did not all his followers understand his nature, and his mission?"

"By no means. He has given many hints over the years, and has said that he is the son of man, and that his father is in heaven, and of course we have seen the miracles, but none of that explains completely who he is and what it is that he is doing here. And then to see him arrested, tried and crucified - well, there are those among us who fear that they were wrong to believe in him."

"If they could just see him, as I have done," said James, "there would no longer be any doubt. You know that I have never been a believer in my brother as other than a country teacher. I have made many efforts to ignore him, to shut him out of my life, and twice I attempted to talk him out of his life's work, at the behest of people on the Sanhedrin who feared him. I

144

resented the fact that he would not become a carpenter so that I might go to Jerusalem and study. Yet when I saw him this morning all the scales fell from my eyes and I saw who he really was. I do not understand it all, but I believe it. You and your brethren would as well."

"Perhaps."

"Perhaps? You might not believe in him if he were to appear to you this day? Did you not see him crucified? Did you not assist in laying him in the tomb? How could you be skeptical if you saw him today, as alive as he ever was?" demanded James.

"And yet those of us who followed him all these years are not the first to see him. If he were to appear, why would he not appear to us?"

"I no longer question the motives of God. I do not know why he should be born apparently the son of a carpenter, nor why he should teach so short a time, nor why he should die and rise again, unless it is to fulfill the prophets. But I have seen him, and I know that there is some purpose in all of it. We shall just have to wait to see what that purpose is. Today is only the first day of his rising."

The other James said nothing for the moment, and James pondered the odd situation that had him lecturing one of his brother's closest admirers on the divine properties of Jesus.

"Do you believe that he is risen?" asked James of the other James.

"I do not know what to believe. There are so many contradictions, so many odd twists to the entire tale that it is difficult to know what to believe, or whom." As he said this, James turned down an alley and once more ascended a staircase to the second story, though not the same one as last time, and knocked. There was a muffled voice which the other James answered with a word James had never heard before, the door was opened quickly and the pair admitted.

Much as the day before (which as James thought of it briefly, seemed like long ago) the followers of Jesus were hiding in a plain, unfurnished room. This one was even smaller than the last, and appeared to be cramped even while they were all awake. James wondered how they could all sleep there, but decided not to ask. If they had been following Jesus for three years and treated money the way he had done, they probably had little or nothing in the way of funds to show for all their labors. They welcomed him perfunctorily, until the other James told them the reason he had come.

"James, the brother of the Lord, has seen him today." At this some of the perked up, though there were others who did not comprehend what was meant.

"Seen who?" asked one of the crowd.

"Like Mary Magdalene, he has seen Jesus alive, today." Here the other James asked James to re-tell the tale, which he did. The reaction in the room was mixed. Some gathered around to demand more in the way of details, while others sat back down to discuss this revelation among themselves. One of the latter said to him:

"Have you and Mary taken it into your heads to be-devil us on this saddest of days? Why can you not leave us alone?"

"Let him be Thomas," said one of the others. "He believes that he has seen the Lord, so let him believe it. There is no harm done."

"I do not believe that I have seen him, I know that I have," corrected James.

"It may have been someone else who looked like him, or it may have been the result of your grief over his death. It is not likely that a man crucified two days ago is now up and about the town."

James bristled at this. "That is the same excuse provided me by a member of the Sanhedrin this afternoon, when I told him of my brother's rising." The mention of the Sanhedrin got their attention. There were cries of "To whom did you talk?" and "What did you tell him?" James recounted in brief his conversation with Ananias earlier in the day (and even that seemed long ago now), and, for the sake of the skeptics in the room, repeated more of his conversation with Jesus than he had previously done. All in the room were paying close attention now, some with wide eyes and open mouths, others looking skeptically out of the corner of their eyes, others simply staring ahead.

When he had finished, the one known as Peter stepped forward out of the crowd, and stared thoughtfully at James. "That is two reports we have heard of his rising, both in the same day. There must be something to it. But why did he not appear to us, that we might worship him, and carry on his work with him?" James made no attempt to answer this question. "It is my belief that he was no mere man, and yet why did he allow himself to be crucified, only to rise from the dead two days later?'"

"It is my belief that he is who he says he is, the son of God," responded James. "I never believed it before, and I have told other people that I did not believe it, but now that I have seen him, I believe. There could be no other answer. None but God has the power of life and death."

"How do you know that someone did not sneak into the tomb and remove his body?" asked another voice.

"I have seen his body," replied James. "I have seen the marks of the nails in his arms. I have no need of more proof. The blinders that have hidden the truth from me all my life fell away when I saw him, and I believed in his nature and his mission." There was no comment at this, and James began to wonder to himself what kind of followers his brother had gathered around him. Jesus was at the center of the most important event ever, and here were his hand-picked followers moping in a dark room with the door

146

locked, hoping not to be bothered by the rest of the city. It was almost enough to dampen James' faith. If Jesus did not go back to his teaching, he would be relying on the likes of this group to continue his work, and they did not appear to be up to the task. What then would be the meaning of it all?

Peter stepped forward. "I am prepared to believe that he has risen from the dead. With God anything is possible, and it is true that Jesus claimed to be the son of God. It may be that he is, and if so we are privileged to have followed him for these three years. The question we have to answer now is, what next? If he was the son of God, we cannot let things rest as they are - he must be proclaimed throughout the land. Let us hope that he comes to us and explains what it is that he wants us to do."

There was general, though unenthusiastic response to this, and the room fell silent. It was clear to James that the death of Jesus had been hard on his closest followers, and that they were suffering from more than physical fear.

The other James began to distribute the food he had brought from the marketplace, and some was offered to James, but he declined, seeing how little there was to go around, and departed. It was with a heavy heart that he made his way back to the home of Mordecai.

There he talked with his mother and the wife of Mordecai, who was still skeptical but less unconvinced than she had been in the morning. Mary expressed a desire to see Jesus' followers before she and James departed for Nazareth the next morning, and James agreed that he would take her there, provided they did not move again in fear of the townspeople.

For all that they had a short sleep, and it was well before mid-morning that they were up and packing their meager belongings for the return trip to Nazareth. James could not help but marvel at all that had happened since they had arrived only four days before, and could not but wonder what his brother's plans were. He was tempted to stay in town until his brother made another appearance, to see what would happen, but he and his mother were out of money, and they needed to return so that James could earn more. It was his goal this morning, while his mother was paying a call on Jesus' followers, to see if he might arrange to stay in touch with one of them, so that he would hear the news, if there were any.

They set out for the alley that James had been led to the day before, which he found on the second try leading away from the marketplace where he had met the other James. Walking up the steps to the second floor room James could sense a different atmosphere than the one that he had felt on those same stairs the day before. It was apparent that the men had not yet moved, because they could hear voices, all male, wafting down the stairs; this in itself was a surprise, since the men had been so cautious about being discovered that they had moved twice in the two days since the crucifixion of Jesus.

James attempted to knock on the door in the method that the other James had used the previous day, but this time it was opened without question, and he and Mary faced the animated other James. They were immediately invited in, and James could not believe that he was seeing the same people in the same room.

The men were laughing and talking over a simple meal, and there was none of the gloom that hovered over the place like a cloud the previous evening. He and Mary were welcomed heartily, and the other James explained to them: "You were right, James! He is risen! He came to us last evening soon after you left. Even though you had told us, we were so stunned that we could not find our tongues. I and some of the others wished that you were still here to see him again."

"What did he say to you?"

"He upbraided us for having little faith, as though he had been here when you and Mary Magdalene were here, and then told us to go out into the world and teach all people his message. You see that we are different men this morning than the morbid crew you saw last night."

"You are encouraged by this? It seems a very difficult undertaking to me. See how many people have heard him, seen his miracles, and still do not believe, and you will go out and teach those who have not seen? I don't envy you."

"He told us that we would suffer for him, but that he would be with us always. Is that not enough for those who know him to be the son of man? We are privileged to have followed him and seen his work, and we are privileged to be those sent by him to carry his message."

"Is he going to continue teaching himself?" asked James.

"He did not say, but he did say that he would not be with us much longer - that he 'goes to his Father.' We are so stunned that we do not know exactly what that means, but we believe that he will disappear some time again soon. That is why he is sending us out again."

"That is a very big responsibility for you, then. Not everyone must carry the message of the son of God to the whole world without the son of God present to prove that it is the true message."

"Do you think that we are not aware of this? We have been up all night discussing the matter - none of us has had any sleep, and yet you see us - and there are those among us who feel that we are not up to the challenge. We can but try."

This was astonishing language from a man who less than a day earlier was hiding in this same room for fear of the outside world. James looked around the room for signs that some among them did not feel the elation that the other James felt, but he could see no signs of fear on any of their faces. It was true that not all of them appeared to be afire to begin the mission, but none appeared reluctant or unwilling. As he and Mary walked around the room greeting and saying good-bye to the others, James asked some of them how much they looked forward to continuing their work for his brother.

To a man they were ready and willing to go, though there were those who wished that they could have had some easier task to undertake. Again to a man, they all said that they would go where Jesus sent them - that their own wishes in the matter could not be consulted. James wondered aloud to Peter if he, James, might have been included in the mission.

"He did not mention you by name," said Peter, "but then he did not mention us by name either. He talked to all who were here in the room. It may be that if you had stayed a little longer you might now be preparing to go with us into the wilderness, instead of returning to Nazareth to take up carpentry. It will finally be a much larger task than the twelve of us are capable of."

James and Mary talked with the men for a few moments, and then left for the house of Mordecai and the trip to Nazareth. They discussed the situation of the men who had followed Jesus, with Mary openly envying them, and James mentioned to her his supposition that he might have been among those called.

"If that be God's will, then so be it," said she, "though it would be hard for me to lie in bed at night in fear of losing another son."

"Losing another son?"

"You know very well that the mission these men undertake will be dangerous. They will be the sheep among wolves, unable to defend themselves if they are attacked, and they will be attacked. If the Sanhedrin have gone to the trouble to have Jesus crucified, you may be sure that they will not hesitate to stop those who would come after him preaching the same message."

"It is possible that no one will listen, and that these men will not gain any following. If that were to be the case, surely the Sanhedrin will not fear them."

Mary looked at him with patience, though James could see that she thought that he had missed something obvious. "Do you believe, my son, that all the events of the last few days have happened so that no people will get the message intended for them by Jesus? Surely there will be those who will hear and understand, just as there will be those who hear but do not understand. Jesus' followers will certainly have followers of their own, and the Sanhedrin will fear them. I do not know how the course will run, but you may be sure that it will be rocky. If you are called then you must go, but my heart will be heavy."

CHAPTER 8

The return trip to Nazareth took the usual time, and though Mary and James were full of the events that had so recently rocked their lives, it did not appear that any of the other travelers in their group knew of the events in Jerusalem, and James and Mary made no effort to tell them. James felt somewhat ashamed at this, knowing as he did that the followers of Jesus were about to venture out into the world to tell that very story to these very people, but he could think of no reason that he might broach the subject with them. It was also true that they were of all nationalities, and there were few Jews among them. James had heard what Peter said about teaching all nations, but it was unclear what was meant by that. If Jesus had meant that all were to be saved, he was departing radically from what Jews traditionally believed about the Messiah.

James wanted to believe in his brother, but the more he thought on the matter the more difficult it became. The more deeply the question of his identity and his missions were examined, the more it was apparent that there was much that was unknown.

How could the followers of Jesus approach the future with such calm? It would be they who would bear the brunt of the reaction to Jesus, if there was to be any. They would be stepping into an alien world and talking about a man that most had never heard of, and asking that they believe that he was the son of God. A son of God, moreover, who allows himself to be crucified by men.

And what, exactly, was the message they should be telling the people who would listen? Even if they were to believe that he was the son of God, what were they to do then? Give up their current religion to believe in Jesus? What were his laws that they should obey in place of those they would be forsaking? How should they live now? Were they all to become Jews? There had always been massive resistance to this idea, and it seemed unlikely that an unknown man from Nazareth would have the effect of making people wish to become Jewish.

But was that even what Jesus wanted? It appeared that he had charged his followers with teaching the whole world, and it was readily apparent that such a charge would not be popular with the Sanhedrin and others among the faithful. Had he meant to create a new church that would replace all of the old ones? He had not said so, but that was the implication. What exactly were his followers supposed to say to the people they met and talked to? James found that he could not answer this question, because he tried once of twice while traveling back to Nazareth, and he found that he could not even find a way to broach the subject with the others in the caravan.

As for his own future, he did not see any change. Jesus had chosen to call his own close followers to be his teachers, and not his own brother, so he would leave it at that. He considered it an honor that his brother appeared to him early on his first day back among the living, and drew some satisfaction from that. He also had to admit that he had not shown Jesus the same loyalty that his followers had, and so may have fallen in his estimation. The pangs of embarrassment and shame came flooding back to him at this thought. He had had a chance to be close to the son of God, and he had thrown it over out of a lack of faith.

There was also Esther to think of. He recovered his good spirits at the thought of his impending marriage to a woman whom he considered, as far as he was able to know her, his perfect mate. She was kind, thoughtful, intelligent, well respected in the town, from a good family, and willing to lower herself to marry a carpenter who could have no claim on her other than the fact that he loved her very much. All in all, he wanted to think, it had all worked out very well.

James left the house immediately after a simple meal to see Esther. He found her at home, wondering about when he would return. They sat down on cushions in the sitting room of her large house, with no chaperones now, and, after lover's greetings, James began the narration of his trip. No news of the doings in Jerusalem had yet reached her, so he found himself having to repeat all the unpleasant details from the trip to her. She was insatiably curious, and seemed to know when James was leaving out a detail that would be of interest, for she peppered him with questions about the Sanhedrin (little of which James could answer), about Jesus (which James could answer, at least for what happened after he and Mary arrived), about the crowds of people who formerly followed Jesus, and many other things.

While James hated the retelling, it was not particularly difficult until he came to the day after the Sabbath. Here the story became unbelievable to the average person, and James did not know whether or not Esther would accept his version of what had happened. More importantly, he did not know if she would accept his version of the reason for Jesus being able to rise from the dead. James described his meetings with Ananias and the eleven followers of Jesus on the Sabbath day, and then paused for a moment, giving brief consideration to not telling Esther the rest. He thought of his failure to tell the truth at the tomb, and plunged ahead with the story.

"I went for a walk outside the walls of the city on the morning after the Sabbath, but the roads were crowded near the town with pilgrims returning home and businessmen making up for the prior day's closing. So I veered from the beaten track, and followed a smaller trail away from the city. It led to a small grove of trees, and as I walked through it I saw, to one side of the path, a man sitting on the ground leaning on one of the trees. I thought nothing of him until I got closer and was about to speak. I had some feeling that I knew him from somewhere, even though his head was hooded. As I got closer he rose and looked at me, and I was astonished. I pushed his hood back from his head and saw my brother Jesus! I fainted immediately."

Esther looked at him quizzically. "It must have been the heat, James, or your grief, that made another man look like your brother, and cause you to faint."

"So I might have thought, but when I awoke I was sitting on the ground leaning on the same tree he had been leaning on, and he was squatting next to me. It was my brother Jesus!"

"James, do not talk this way. You know that this cannot be, unless what you have told me up to now about his being crucified was a lie."

James wanted her to believe, and went on breathlessly: "I know it is difficult for you to believe, but I was there, and I have seen it. He spoke to me, he showed me the wounds in his arms. I then went to his tomb, and saw that it was empty. My mother and a friend of hers have also seen him, as have his eleven closest followers! There are many witnesses, and there will be others!"

Esther said nothing for the moment, but James could see the incredulous look in her eyes. "This cannot be. Men do not rise from the dead. Why do you tell me such a story, and why would you involve your mother?"

James wanted to plead with her to believe, but he controlled himself, and attempted to win her over. "I would not involve my mother if I did not think that she would confirm my story. Do you think that I am such a fool as to name a witness that you may confront yourself if I did not know that that witness would agree with me?"

"James! Think what you are telling me! You are saying that a mortal man - your brother - rose from the dead! Can you explain that? How could he? Why could he of all the people in the world who have died?"

"I know that I am asking you to believe the impossible, but it is not true that I said that a mortal man had risen from the dead."

Esther waited, wanting to hear more, but James waited for this to sink in. As it did, her eyes widened, and expressions of fear and anger chased themselves across her face.

"James! Are you now saying that your brother was not mortal? Please don't say that! I don't want to think what I am thinking. If he is not mortal, then who is he?" She paused for a moment, waiting for an answer, but James made none, knowing that it would come to her. After a moment her eyes widened again, and she sat erect on the cushion. "No! No! Tell me that you do not believe it! We have talked about this, and you have told me that it could not be true!"

"We talked about it, and I said that it could not be true. And I believed that it could not. But now I have seen my brother crucified, I have helped to lay his body in the tomb, and two days later I saw him again on the road outside Jerusalem. No, no Esther, do not favor me with that look. It was he. And he was alive."

"No! It must have been your imagination. Perhaps you saw a specter because you were so aggrieved at the loss of your brother. Perhaps he was another man who looked like your brother. It may have been someone who made himself to look like your brother to take advantage of his fame in some way."

"You cannot believe that it was a specter, because you know that there are no specters. And if it were some strange man wanting to take advantage of my brother in his grave, how came he to have the marks of crucifixion on his arms and feet? And what happened to the body of my brother? I went to his tomb, and it was not there."

Esther could not answer any of these charges, but it was not because she did not want to. She knew that none of this could be true, and yet she could hardly believe that James of all people - steady, dependable, faithful James - could make it up.

"I see that you are struck dumb as I was. You may rest assured that I was not a calm and thoughtful man upon realizing that I was seeing my risen brother on the road outside Jerusalem. I abused myself awfully, so aware was I of all the sins I have committed against my brother. I could not bear to face him, knowing that I have denied him, and tried twice to talk him out of his mission. I could not talk coherently, I could not sit still, I could not stand, I was like a man possessed of demons."

"That was it then! You were not in control of your faculties! For some reason you lost control for a few moments, and believed that you saw Jesus risen from the dead."

"I was in perfect control until I saw him. I lost control for a few moments, both when I fainted and then when I realized the implications of what I was seeing. But when he spoke to me, and made me be at peace, the power of his words was overwhelming. The demons that haunted me for a moment left me, and I was able to sit and regard him. It was as though I were drained of all other strength but that required to listen."

Esther was more resigned now, if not to believe it herself, at least to understand that she would not talk James out of it. She sat quietly and with a tired expression on her face. "And what did he say to you?"

"He told me only that I should be at peace, that his work here among us is done, and that I should serve him."

"Serve him? Serve him how?"

"I do not know. He would not say, save telling me that I would serve, and that I should believe in him and be patient."

"What will you do?"

"I will wait until I am called. I do not know when that will be, or where. All I can do is wait."

"Then are we.....?"

"No! We shall be married, and we shall raise a family! I do not know how my brother will call me, or what he will ask of me. Until that is known, I will go about the only life I know, and marry the woman that I love."

Esther perked up at this, and said, "Yes, we will not let this come between us. We are still the same. Even if what you say is true, you can serve your brother as you have always served him, by helping the poor and destitute here in Nazareth! We will be together, and that will be the most important thing." She came to his cushion and sat next to him, putting her arms around him and resting her head on his chest. James held her with both arms, but wondered at his own words. There was no question that he was not the same, and the more he thought of going back to his carpentry the more he realized that it would be impossible.

They sat quietly for a time, neither wanting to disturb the quiet that enveloped them. Finally Esther raised her head and looked him in the eye. Her eyes were red from crying, James realized, but otherwise she was the same beautiful woman that he wanted to marry. She recovered her spirits as best she could and said, "I can assure you that Nazareth has not been as exciting as Jerusalem." She then brought him up to date on one or two small doings in the time that he had been gone, and then sat quietly again.

"I told some friends that we are to be married, and they are glad for me, as I said they would be. Already they are teasing me, and asking how long it will take me to learn carpentry." James laughed weakly with her, but said nothing. "And my family rejoices, as I told you they would. You were afraid for your status James, but my family knows that you are a good man. That is what matters, and not status."

"There are families in which that is not true. I am fortunate that the woman I want to marry comes from a family that is not consumed by wealth, and not worried that the marriage of their eldest daughter will net them nothing."

"We will be happy, will we not, James? We were made for each other, I am sure. I could not be happier than when I am with you, save possibly when I imagine how it will be when we are married."

"I do not know why it took me so long to realize that you are a treasure to be grasped tightly, and never allowed to escape. It is no reflection on you, but on my own stupidity and shortsightedness that we are not married already." Esther smiled and held him tighter.

Upon inspection he found that his shop was intact, and that it had not been robbed in his absence. He rolled up the canvas walls and opened the hot and musty interior to the outside air. One or two of his neighbors greeted him, including the old woman across a small alley who always came for James when she had some chore that she could not do herself.

"There have been many people seeking after you, James," she said to him. "I always told them that you had important business in the city, and that you would be back. I hope you are prepared to work, because if they have not taken their work elsewhere, they have much to give you."

"There is no one else here for them to go to, fortunately for lazy types such as myself. I will be glad to see them when they return."

"I must tell you, James, that I have seen some people nosing around your shop at some odd hours. I chased them away though, when I thought that they might do you harm."

"And how does such a small woman as yourself chase away bad men?"

"Oh, some were more like boys, and they ran at the sight of another person. Others refused to go, but you know that I have a huge dog. They all pay attention to him."

James laughed merrily at the good will of the old woman, the first light-hearted laugh that he could remember for some time. As he set about rescuing his tools from the house and setting them up in their accustomed places, he tried to look with a glad heart on the future before him. The people who needed work from him somehow heard that he was back, and they began showing themselves, and their projects, to him. There was a demand for a small chair, another for a low table that might be used for eating, another wanted a new ladder with which to reach the roof of his house. They were all projects easily within James' capabilities, and they would all be profitable. That would be important, because he and Mary had spent a large sum in Jerusalem, and he would need to replenish their finances.

Among the visitors were the poor as well, who had become accustomed to James' efforts on their behalf, and who wondered where he had been. He explained that he had had to go to Jerusalem on business but that now that he was back he would do what he could for them. But not right at that moment. Some would not go away easily, and James went into the house to see what food he could find them, but there was nothing since he and Mary had been away so long. When James had returned home Mary was out, and James guessed that she went to the market, and it happened that she returned at just the moment there were two families of poor - four adults and seven children - asking James for help. Mary had bought the food for James and herself, but as James took the baskets and packages from her they looked each other in the eye only briefly, and then gave all of the food to the families. When they were gone, Mary said to James, "Well, then I shall try again," and off she went to the market. James offered to come with her, but she insisted that he stay and catch up on his work.

He had thought that he had it all worked out at last, after years of railing at Jesus for having abandoned the craft that should have been his. (He could not remind himself of this without feeling once again that overwhelming sense of remorse and stupidity which had enveloped him in the grove on the morning that he saw Jesus alive.) Soon thereafter he had become engaged to Esther, an event that had rendered him happier than at any time of his life. He could at last look forward to the future with some degree of delight, rather than dread.

But all that had changed now. He was in his shop on only his first afternoon back from the momentous events in Jerusalem, and already the old doubts were back, and they loomed many times larger than before. Whereas before he had only desired to immerse himself in the study of scripture, and was pestered by the abdication of his brother, he was now convinced of the divine nature of his brother, pestered by his own failure to believe, and convinced that his former desire to lurk about the temple in study a selfish waste of time.

"You are troubled, James," said Mary, as they sat down to eat some bread and dried fish that Mary had brought home from the market on her second trip the night before.

He said nothing for a moment, attempting to decide whether he should raise the subject with her just yet. He weighed the options in his mind carefully, and then, as he would do only with his mother, threw caution to the wind. "I no longer believe that this is where I belong. Too much has happened to allow me to go back to my old habits. I am a brother of sorts to the most important man ever to walk the face of the earth, and it does not seem right that I should come from that realization back to my old home to build with wood."

"What will you do?"

"I have no idea. There are not many options open to me."

"There are only two that I can see: you can either stay where you are and do what you are doing, or you can choose to follow Jesus, in whatever way he might command."

"I see those as my choices also, but there is the additional complication of my impending marriage to Esther. If I were to follow Jesus, should I take her with me? She has already made it clear that she does not believe in my meeting with him, and it is possible that she would refuse. There is always hope for conversion, but if it did not come we could make each other miserable. I would not cause her pain for any sum in the world; in fact there is nothing other than Jesus which could cause me to reconsider the future at all." He paused for a moment. "Only ten days ago I considered the future secure, and I was happy with the direction it would apparently take. Now all that has changed, and it is becoming virtually certain that I cannot continue as a carpenter, but also certain that I do not know where else to turn. I can only hope that my brother makes his wishes known to me soon."

Mary sighed deeply. "It is apparent to all who follow him that they must do so, and yet it is very difficult to do so. One would think that such certainty would render the remainder of life's small problems invisible, but it does not. One follows the path that must be followed, but it never becomes straight, or cleared of stones and thorns."

This was beginning to dawn on James. He had had the most important revelation that any human could hope for, and it had so far done nothing but cause him misery: he had occasional doubts about whether or not it actually happened, he had doubts about how he should react to what he saw, and now he had doubts about whether or how he should allow it to interfere with his marriage plans.

It was by no means certain that Esther would not interfere with his marriage plans. The chances of her following where ever he might lead were slim, if following meant following Jesus. James did not feel himself to be under any illusion as to why Esther might be so happy to have him for a mate: she regarded him as sensible and practical, and she believed that he would be able to provide for her far into the future. There may have been other, more romantic reasons as well, but these had to be the principal ones. But deciding to leave his life behind to follow Jesus, if that were what was required of him, would hardly be in keeping with this reputation, and it was entirely possible that Esther might wish to throw him over.

James went back to work after eating, but he could gather no momentum, and could not clear his mind of the distracting thoughts that had been plaguing him. To further complicate matters, he was surprised late in the afternoon by a visit from Esther.

After a quick, out of sight greeting behind James' house, Esther said, "I was concerned about you, James. You appeared to be in some doubt about our future when you left my house yesterday."

"I was not concerned about our future," he lied, somewhat. "There is nothing that would make me happier than to take you as my wife. I was merely thinking what effect what I had seen might have on me over time."

"You have not yet convinced yourself that it was a dream, and that you saw nothing?"

"No, I am convinced that I saw my brother risen from the dead. I admit that I sometimes wonder if it might have been a dream, but when I reconsider the events, I am sure that it was not."

"What do you think it might do to you?" she asked him, in a wary voice.

"I do not know what it might do. It might do nothing, and it might change me forever in ways that would no longer appeal to you."

"That could never be. I will always love you. You are a good man, James. You know what is important in the world, and you will adhere to those proper things."

"Let us hope you are right."

After a pause, "So you still want to marry me?"

"More than anything. You see that I am still at work, attempting to prepare for the future." Esther smiled at him in the way that charmed him most - a girlish, too-happy-for-words smile - and, after a quick glance in the street to see that no one was looking, she put her arms around his neck quickly and kissed him, and then she was off.

When she was out of sight, James threw his tools down in disgust and sat down on the floor of his shop, where he would be out of sight behind the work table and clutter, and cursed himself. Once again, when confronted with an opportunity to tell the truth about his brother, he had passed it up in favor of a convenient lie. It was still true that he wished to marry Esther, but it was less true that he did not think that his encounter with his brother would have no effect on their future together. The effects were already being felt: James no longer wanted to work in the shop, but he did not know what else to do. His decision would have a lot to do with whether or not he and Esther would marry, and, if they did, how successful the marriage would be.

Then he realized that he had been back in the shop less than two days, and that it was unfair to judge based on so short an exposure. He would give the matter some months before making a final decision about what he would do. This decision made life somewhat easier for him, because it gave him a deadline to work with that was not in the next couple of days.

The next morning, while busy in the shop, he was haled from the street by a male voice. Looking up, he saw himself being approached by Simon and Andrew, the followers of Jesus that James had met at the wedding feast at Cana.

"Hello, James," called the two men simultaneously. "We are on our way to the northern regions," continued Simon, and we thought that we might stop by for some companionship and refreshment."

"Welcome, welcome," cried James, glad to see them both. "You are very welcome to come in and have what you like. Mother," he called, turning to face the house, "see who is here."

Mary came out and greeted the two men warmly and then went back in to fetch refreshment. James and the other two men followed, and settled themselves on cushions within the main room in the house.

"Has anyone seen him again?" asked James.

"Yes! We have!" they answered at the same time. "You know that he appeared to us in our room the day of his rising, but one of our number, Thomas, was not there. When we told him of what we had seen he did not believe, and we could not convince him. But eight days later he appeared to us in the same room, and this time Thomas was with us. He saw the Master, and saw the wounds in his hands and feet and side, and was overcome with grief at having doubted. The Master told us to go and preach to all nations, and that he would be with us, so you see us on the road. To our knowledge he has not appeared to anyone else."

"Have you proof that he was with you, that you may use in the presence of others?"

"None. There is nothing that would serve, save for his appearing to larger crowds. But he was not specter. He showed Thomas his wounds, and he dined with us, and broke bread as he did on the night that he was arrested."

In answer to James' question, Andrew said "We are going to Syria, to preach the message of Jesus to the Syrians."

"So you have increased your expectations," said James. "You are no longer content to teach the Jews about my brother." James felt a certain amount of pride when he said that, and was immediately sorry for it.

"It is not up to us. We have been instructed by Jesus to teach the message to all people in the world. He has promised to be with us, and so we are going."

"We have divided up the area among the eleven of us, and Syria fell to Andrew and myself," interjected Philip. "We are scattering to the four winds in pairs, as we have done once before, to bring the good news to all people."

"You will have a difficult time teaching the Syrians," said James. "I am not aware that my brother ever went there, so they will have heard nothing of him. You will be preaching to virgin ears."

"That is so," agreed Andrew, "which is why James and I agreed to begin there."

"You volunteered for the most difficult assignment?" laughed James.

"We volunteered for a difficult assignment," answered Simon. "None of us have an easy chore before us, but there is nothing that can be done."

"Why not?"

"Because we have been sent by the master to carry his word to all nations. It is not for us to refuse, even if we were inclined to do so."

Here was real faith, thought James. But before he could carry the thought further, he was interrupted by Andrew.

"The master has given us explicit instructions as to how to carry out our mission. You see that we have nothing with us save these small bags of bread and dried meat. We also carry no money. The master told us that we should rely on him for all our wants, and that is what we will do. We are to take sustenance only from the members of the community that we talk to, and accept no payment or scrip of any kind."

These two men, and presumably the others, were walking out into the world to teach the message of Jesus, a complete stranger to the people they would be talking to, and without so much as a penny between them. They would be utterly powerless, without connections, without wealth, without the means of resisting the machinations of those who would surely be aligned against them. But, of course, that was the situation his brother had been in, and see where it had gotten him.

"My brother told me, as I mentioned to you in Jerusalem, that I would serve him as well, but it is not yet clear to me what he wants me to do."

"There can be little doubt, James, that if he means for you to serve him, he means for you to follow him as we are doing. What else is there to do?"

"I do not know. It may be as you say. He told me not to worry about the time or the place, only that I would serve him."

"Then you have placed your faith in him, and that is all that is necessary," said Simon. "In the past we were frightful - afraid of what would happen if this event or that were to overtake us. But all of us, I believe, are now convinced that he is with us always, and that we have nothing to fear. He told us this when he was alive, but we have not come to realize it until his death and resurrection."

"But there are things to fear. It seems to me very likely that you will suffer greatly preaching among the heathens."

"But what is that to us, compared to the charge we have been given, and the person who has given it to us? It is a rare honor not to be taken lightly, and you may rest assured that we do not. If we are treated as he was treated, we will suffer of course, but then we will be with him again. And we will not have done anything that he did not do himself."

Mary entered at that point with some food and drink, and the conversation between her and the two followers of her son continued, but James' mind drifted away from the others in the room.

James had been laboring over what to do with his life in the wake of his meeting with his brother Jesus, wondering about his marriage, his shop, his mother, and myriad other things, all while waiting to be called by his brother. But Andrew and James were right: there could be only one thing that

Jesus would want of him now, and that would be to continue preaching his message to those who would hear. There was no other function to be carried out. His waiting for a call from his brother was simply stalling on his part, in hopes that some other answer might present itself, and allow him to slip away from his dilemma.

But there would be no slipping, because he could see that others had already answered the call in his place, and they were heading out to teach the Syrians, among others, without money and with little or no food to sustain them. They were relying completely on Jesus to take care of them. James was embarrassed at what he considered to be his inadequate faith in the wake of seeing his brother. He had dithered and stalled while they made preparations to go out into the world. Once again he was shamed and humiliated by his brother. He made up his mind in that instant to go to Jerusalem to see what could be done there, and to attempt to join with the others.

This brought his mind back to the conversation at hand, wherein Andrew was saying that they, apparently meaning the eleven, had not seen him since that night the previous week. James interjected, "What have you done with your families as you go out into the world?"

"None of us have any families," said Andrew. "The master told us to follow him before any of us, except Peter, had any families, and now we have none to worry about, except each other. Peter? He had a wife and children, but the Lord called him anyway, and he came. They now live with his father. He does not see them, and of course he has no income to give them."

This was painful news indeed. No wonder these men could go off into the wilderness so quickly, and without a care in the world. It was one thing to set off on such a journey with only a small bag of bread for yourself and your friend, but quite another to do so when one has a family to care for. How could Peter have left his loved ones to follow a man who at time was a stranger? How his family must have cursed him when he left.

None of Jesus' followers, then, was caring for a family. If James were to go with them, he would be setting a precedent. "How is it that none of my brother's closest followers have married?" he asked. "It is not surprising that one or a few would not have married, but highly unlikely that all would have foregone so natural a step."

"He called us when we were young, so that we had not done so yet. And of course there is little chance for that traveling all the time as we do. But more important is the fact that the master told us not to do so. Yes, he told us that the true follower must give up all of his worldly possessions and leave behind his family, if he is to follow the Lord."

"My bride-to-be will take comfort in the fact that he gave me no such admonition," laughed James. The other Philip and Andrew smiled, and said nothing. James had half hoped for some kind of comfort from them on this matter, but they offered none.

They ate for a moment, while James considered what they were about to do. "What will you say," he asked, "when you walk into a town, and are ready to teach? It will be difficult to stand in front of the crowd and tell them of a man of whom they have never heard who will lead them to heaven."

"We do not know," answered Andrew.

There was a pause, while James allowed this to sink in and waited for the rest of the answer.

"What do you mean, 'we do not know'? Do you mean to say that you embark on this mission without a clear idea of what to tell them about Jesus?"

"He told us that we should not concern ourselves with that, when he sent us out the first time, and he has just reminded us that he will be with us."

Here was ample faith indeed - they were relying on the help of a man recently dead, yet come back to life, and whom they had all seen only twice since his resurrection.

"He sent us out in pairs two years ago, and gave us power over sickness and disease and demons, and we found that we could achieve some of the same miracles that he achieved. He will be with us," he concluded with some finality, as though there were no more to be said on the subject.

"But what is it that you will ask them to do? Become Jews? In this you would not even have the backing of the Jewish hierarchy, I am afraid, since they have recently crucified the man. Or are you attempting to start a new church with my brother at the center? Here you will have difficulty with those who believe that we are the chosen people."

"We are going to call them to Jesus, tell them that he is the son of God, and pass on his teaching to them. If they come to him through the Jewish faith, we believe that he will be happy to see them."

"Are you telling the people you teach that the son of God has overthrown the Jewish faith with his arrival, or are you telling them that he is fulfilling all that the Jews have hoped for?"

"We are going to repeat the message that he left us with. Remember that we will not be talking to Jews in Syria. We will be talking to heathens who have never heard of the one, true God."

"But they will ask what you are, and you will say 'Jews', and they will want to know if Jesus was a Jew, and you will say 'yes', and then they will ask if what you want is for them to become Jews, and you will have a difficult time from there. And there are others among you, I presume, who will be speaking to Jews. What will they say?"

"Jesus told us that he did not come to break the law, but to fulfill it. He also gave us a new law: that you will love your enemy as yourself. Most importantly, he told us that no one could get to the Father except through him. This will be our message."

"It is not clear to me how you will answer the questions that arise about which church it is that you are asking them to join. Is it to Judaism that you want them to come, or to some other way?"

"James," said Simon, "you lack the faith that God will be with us. We do not claim to be perfectly in communion with the mind of the Father, nor do we claim to know in all ways how Jesus meant that we should carry on his mission. We believe he will tell us when the time comes, and that we will understand the answer that he gives us."

"How are the others answering this question?"

"We are of various minds, at the moment. We will compare notes when next we meet, but at the moment there are those who believe that we have seen the birth of a new faith, and others who believe that Jesus only meant to revive the Jewish faith - to point out the error of their ways in expecting a savior who would lead them in war against the Romans. The central point is the same: no one can go to the Father except through the son."

"This may serve to leave more questions than it answers."

"We accept that the answers will be forthcoming. The Father and the Son will lead us down the right path. You see that we are unclear only about the proper label to attach to our lesson. We all agree that Jesus is the son of God, that he gave us new laws that must be obeyed if we are to see the Father, and that the old understanding of a warlike Messiah come to lead us in battle against our oppressors is a failure of the human imagination. The kingdom of God is within us, and it matters not what cloak it wears, or what it calls itself, so long as it is faithful to the Son, and through him to the Father." This short soliloquy by Andrew earned nods of agreement from the Philip, and left James to ponder the question on his own.

"Do not think that it is easy for us to trod the unknown path, James," said Philip. "We followed Jesus for three years, and yet we lacked the faith to believe in him. It was not until he rose from the dead that we finally understood all that he had told us, and saw through the parables that he preached. You may believe that we have each been in our own private hell these last days, berating ourselves for our failure of spirit."

"I understand," James replied. "I was his brother; I lived with him in the same house for thirty years. He told me his mission, and, near the end, who he was, and I denied him. You at least may comfort yourselves that you had enough faith to follow him, and learn at his knee. I twice attempted to talk him out of his mission by citing the danger of running afoul of the Sanhedrin. Consider! I attempted to tell the son of God that he should not tell people what he was telling them. I told him that his message was not the correct one, and that he should leave off teaching it. I, a carpenter with pretensions to study with the Sanhedrin, telling the Messiah that he should cease his teaching and return home. When he appeared to me after his resurrection, and I finally understood who he was, there was no way that I could chastise myself properly - no way to punish myself as I deserve. How I have thought on that this last few days! How I have punished myself again and again for not having seen who he was! Each new memory of our lives together brings me some painful event, some churlish comment that I made to the son of God. And not once did he reproach me, or correct me, or hold my conduct against me. Each time I consider it, it wells up inside me, and I have the urge to throw myself off of the nearest cliff as a sign of my apology."

There was silence for a few moments while they ate, and it appeared to James that all of the men must have thought the same thing at the same time: for, as a man, they all lifted their heads from their food and gazed at her. She hesitated a moment, and then anticipated their question.

"I had the advantage of you. I was told by a messenger of God that I would conceive the son of God, though I did not know man. All else has been left for me to understand, and it has not always been plain to me how his mission would end, or what it would mean. No one has ever suffered as I suffered when he hung on the cross, and yet I had to keep faith that it was all the will of God. I do not know the answers to the questions that you pose, yet they will have to be answered in time. It is for you all to do the will of God, knowing that he will be with you and that he will give you the words to speak."

Philip and Andrew nodded in agreement at this, and James could only stare at his mother. They continued eating in silence.

When they had finished and put away the food, James asked, "Will we see him again?"

"No one knows," the two men said together. "We have all hoped for it, but he does not appear," continued Andrew. "We cannot even say how long he will stay with us, or what he will do while he is here. We do not even know where he is staying, or what he is doing. We were with him always before he was crucified, but now we see him only twice, and he goes his own way."

"He told me that his time here was short," said James, "and I do not believe that he will teach again, though that would make the task of reaching out to other people of the world much easier."

"How?"

"It was known to many that he was crucified. If those same people were to see him alive again, as we have done, it would remove all doubt about his nature."

"It would remove doubt for those who saw him, but there would always be those who choose not to believe him. I do not imagine that the

Sanhedrin would accept him, even if he were to appear in their midst," said Andrew.

"How would they explain his presence?" James asked.

"They would find a way. They might claim that he is a rare actor, or that he is a twin, or they might just crucify him again, to be rid of him."

"It has been the way of God since the beginning - to seek the love of his people, and not to demand it. Thus only a few men have ever felt his presence directly, when he had some message for the people. For the rest, they had to believe what they were taught, or go hungry in search of him," said Philip.

There was a general nodding of heads at this, and it seemed to put conversation to an end for the moment. It was obvious that many questions attended the men who would spread the word of Jesus, and that they would not be answered any time soon. It was also true that his followers would spread the message anyway, whether the details were worked out or not.

James and Mary asked the two men to stay the night, which they readily assented to do. After a breakfast in the morning they were on their way, promising James that they would stop by on their return trip to tell James of their success or failure.

James brooded over these matters for the next few days. Indeed he found that he could think of little else. This was in part because Esther made daily visits to his shop to talk and to discuss the details of the marriage ceremony, particularly with regard to setting a date on which it might take place. James entered into all these discussions with her, but without the enthusiasm he would have felt only days earlier. He covered himself as well as he could, and, he believed, managed to deceive Esther about his true state of mind. He even agreed to a date that was only four weeks away, thinking that he should go ahead if nothing is decided by then.

One afternoon Mary came into the shop because she had not heard his tools for sometime. She found him sitting on the floor behind his principal table, knees drawn up and held in place with his elbows, staring into the air in front of him, and utterly unaware that she had entered.

"You have not worked for sometime, my son," she said to James.

"I have no joy in the work. I cannot get my mind off of my brother and his followers, and I cannot help but think that I should be with them."

"Perhaps, while you sit in your shop and wait, you have already been called," said Mary, gently, while looking him in the eye.

This struck him like a pail of cold water, and he sat up straighter. "It is true that I have dithered while others have worked. Perhaps my brother is testing me, to see whether I have the mettle to follow him. But I have held on tightly to my shop and my dreams even while acknowledging publicly that I have no choice but to follow him. But would Esther go with me?" He still could not bring himself to throw over everything he had known.

"You have said that she did not believe what you told her of Jesus. If that is so, why would she?" After a moment's pause Mary added, "And should you?" James looked at her after hearing this remark, but he said nothing. Mary could see by the look on his face that he was thinking the matter over. "Perhaps that is not what is expected of you."

"Perhaps not."

"No one would be happier than I to see you happily wed to Esther, or look forward to the coming children with more delight. But we are in the midst of extraordinary events, and we must follow where we are led." She paused briefly here, gathering her thoughts. "I want my beloved son to be happy," she continued, "but it is more important that we obey the will of God." Mary said no more, but she could see by the look in his eyes that James had made his decision.

"You may be right, mother, but if this is to be the way, my brother will find it difficult to find apostles among future generations," said James, ruefully.

Mary smiled. "You have already found, in only a few short days, that it is not easy to believe that Jesus is the son of God. There are many demands upon the believer. This is why it will be difficult to find his followers among the Jews. For so long have they looked for the warrior king who would make all right with this world, and Jesus offers them only peace in the next."

With that Mary went back into the house, leaving James alone with his thoughts.

There she worked for several hours, wondering what James was thinking but making no more effort to influence him or even to see what he was doing. She knew he did not return to work because she heard no more noise the rest of the afternoon. In the evening, when it was nearly dark, James finally came in the house, and, without washing himself as usual, sat down to talk to Mary.

"I have considered the matter every way that it can be considered," said he, "and there is no way around the correct answer: I must go to Jerusalem."

Mary's answer was to smile, which surprised James somewhat. Then she said, "I thought that you must."

"But as you have said, it is not to be easy," added James. "There is much to be seen to, and most important among these is your welfare."

Without hesitation Mary said, "You will remember that your brother instructed John to look after me as he was dying on the cross, and it is to him that I will go."

James had not thought on that for some time, so crowded had his mind been with other concerns, but she was right. He had been insulted at the time, and it had continued to irritate him, but here at last he could see the purpose of it. The thought only made him wonder how much else there was that he should see but that he did not.

"But it would seem," said he, "that John will join the others on the road. It also appears that he has very little. What will happen to you?"

"God has always provided."

James wanted to be more sure than that, but he realized that there was nothing he could say that would talk his mother out of her plan. It was as she said: Jesus had commanded it, there was little else in the way of alternatives - but wait. There were his own two siblings in Jerusalem, Joses and Judah. He was out of contact with them now - so much so that he had not seen them when there recently, and he had not heard of them looking after the welfare of their brother - but Mary had word from them periodically, and she might go there.

"I will not. It is not that I don't love my sons, because I do, but that I have been commanded to go elsewhere." And there the suggestion died, because James knew better than to push the matter.

After a pause he began again: "There is also the matter of selling the shop and the house. I have no doubt this can be done quickly, since I would ask a price that would guarantee such an outcome, but that would leave you with comparatively less."

"I want nothing," said Mary. "I have no need of any belonging."

"But it is good to be prepared against any threat."

"I will have God and his son at my back, and that will suffice. If something is to happen to me, will that not be the will of God? My consolation would be that I would be reunited with Jesus, and that is the greatest comfort of all."

"What do you propose to take with you then?"

"You see that I have been mending those of our clothes that were in need of attention." She motioned to the pile of clothes beside her, to which James had paid little attention until that moment. "These we will take for our own comfort, and beyond that we will follow the example of your brother and live as God would have us."

James had thought that he was coming in to make a momentous announcement to his mother, but it was plain that she had already anticipated what his decision would be and had begun to act on it.

"If you do not want the money that will come from the sale of the house and shop, what shall we do with it?" he asked Mary.

"It is possible that it would be of great service to those of Jesus' followers who are still in Jerusalem. Perhaps it can be used to buy food and pay for shelter as long as they shall need it."

They talked over the details for a few more moments, but it was a very simple transaction that they proposed to undertake, and there was little to plan for. In foregoing the profit motive in the sale, they were foregoing many of the pains that go with selling property. They resolved to accept the first offer that came along, and that James would take the money to Jerusalem to share with Jesus' followers.

The next morning he went to see Esther. He found her at home and pleasantly surprised at his visit, but she could tell from his countenance that all was not right. They settled once more on the same cushions they had settled on his first day back from Jerusalem, but this time he did not let her get so close.

"What is wrong?" she asked. "I can see the cloud over your brow."

"We must talk about the marriage," said he, simply.

"Why? Do you wish to postpone it?"

He hated to cause the pain that was coming, but he decided to be blunt, and make it pass as quickly as possible. "It cannot take place. Ever."

She sat up straight at this. "Why?"

"I have decided that I must go to Jerusalem to follow in the footsteps of my brother. It would not be fair to ask you to accompany me there: I am likely to have little money, there will be no way of earning any, and it is likely to become dangerous."

"You mean that you intend to wander the countryside preaching to the down and out? For what earthly purpose?"

"Those are the people who need the comfort that he can give them."

"But why you? Did he not have followers that can serve this purpose? And, for that matter, he can no longer give them comfort because he is not here."

"He has followers for the purpose, and many of them are on the road already, teaching. But those will not be enough. There are too many people to reach, and too short a time to reach them."

"You still believe that he is risen from the dead, and that he is the son of God, don't you?"

"Yes, I do believe it, or I would not be undertaking this effort. I would not go to the trouble I am about to go to for the sake of a man, even my brother, who might be a false prophet. But I can do no less for the son of God."

"Did this come to you in a dream? Why have you suddenly come to me this morning to say that you are leaving?"

"My brother told me on the morning that he rose from the dead that I would serve him, but that I should not worry about the time or place. I would know when the time and place would be right. I have agonized over this ever since, particularly since I began to work in my comfortable shop and met two of his companions off to spread his word. What I was doing seemed trivial by comparison, and I could not restore my former joy in it. I now believe that I have already been called, and that I have simply been delaying my departure."

"What of your mother? Does she approve of this?"

"She is going with me, and will assist me in the sale of our belongings so that we may approach the task unencumbered."

"How will she live? Who will take care of her, if you are to have little money?"

"My brother commanded that one of his followers look after her from that day forward, and she will go to him. It is her will and she will not be denied."

"You brother, on the cross, commanded, and three adults, two of them his own family, will accede to his wishes," said Esther sarcastically.

"Who are we to deny the will of God?"

"If you are not more careful in Jerusalem than you have been with me, you may join him on the cross."

"I have considered that, but I repeat the question: who are we to deny the will of God? My brother told me that I would serve, and this I go to do. I can hardly refuse a direct request from such a person."

"No," said Esther, defiantly, "I suppose that you cannot, if you are willing to believe that he is the Messiah." But for all her tone, tears were beginning to well up in her eyes, and James' mission became that much more difficult. He worked hard to avoid crying himself.

"I cannot make it clear enough that I am going because I feel that I have been called to go, not because I no longer love you or do not wish to marry you," he said pleadingly. "I have never in my life been more sad than I am at this moment - not even when my brother was hanging on the cross. I have wanted to marry you for some time, and I looked forward to that day, but I cannot say to my God that I am sorry, but he will have to choose someone else!"

"Why could I not go with you?"

"It will be no life for you. I do not even know what I will be doing - but it is likely that I will travel like my brother and his followers. What would you do then? And what would be our source of income? It will be difficult enough for me to support myself - I will not even be able to take care of my mother. No, you deserve better than that. I do not want to see a woman such as you dressed in rags and starving because of some misplaced loyalty to me."

"It is not misplaced," she cried. "I am loyal to you because I love you and want to be with you."

"But there will be no life for you. I repeat that I do not know what I will be doing, or where I will end up. I will be building nothing that will have any appeal to this world. That cannot be what you want. I know that you want children - in fact, so do I - but there will be no way to take care of them. They will end like those children we saw among the poor - in rags, with no food and no future."

"You tell me what a horrible life you will be leading, and that it is not fit for me or for marriage, and yet you go to lead it. What was your brother that you should do this for him?"

"My brother was - is - the son of God. He was crucified and yet he rose from the dead, and his followers tell me that he predicted such a thing in advance. I denied him all my life, but after seeing him that day outside of Jerusalem I need no more proof. He told me that I would serve him, and I believe that this is what he meant. It is not my choice, but his. What would you have me do?"

"Find some other way to serve. There must be something you can do that does not require wandering about the countryside teaching."

"What? What else is there at this stage? There is no church to speak of, no organization to manage. There is nothing else to do but tell people that my brother was here, and hope that they believe."

"And what if they do? What will you do then?"

James had to think on this for a moment, but the fact was that he did not know what would be done then. If the people believed in Jesus and lived according to his teachings, that would be all that he could expect. "I will go on teaching until I can do so no longer, I suppose. All I can do is tell people the truth, and hope that they hear me. There is nothing I can do to force them, and if they do believe then they will not need me any longer."

"And what if they don't believe? You know that there will be many who will not only not believe, but will be hostile to the fact that you are trying to teach them."

"I do not know what will happen then. I may end up as my brother for all I know now, but what choice do I have?"

"You can stay here where you belong, and leave such teaching to others. There were many who followed Jesus when he was alive - let them teach."

"They are not enough, and they will not live forever. There must be others to help spread the word. There is no more important mission than this. All men wonder why they are here and what it is that they are supposed to be doing, and now I know the answer, with only a few others. Is it not my duty to spread what I know?"

"But you have no way of knowing that you know the answer. There are others who claim to know all that there is to know, and to have seen God. How will you compete with them?"

"My brother has appeared to many people, and he performed many miracles, two of which I have seen myself. There can be no question that he is the son of the one true God."

"You can prove none of this. No one that you will be teaching saw any of there miracles or saw him alive two days after he was crucified."

"You have not seen Moses or the commandments or the Ark of the Covenant, and yet you believe. All such things are based on faith, and not on the physical senses. This is why I berated myself so when I saw my brother. I recognized that I did not possess the necessary faith that is demanded of me. I did not believe until I had seen. I will not make that mistake again: my brother has called me, and I must go."

Esther seemed beaten down now, and that was fortunate for James because he had nothing else to add. It was a simple issue, really: he was going because he felt compelled to. It was required of him by the son of God, and such a request cannot be refused. But Esther was a strong woman, and she kept her composure. She did not break down and cry, though it was a mighty struggle not to, and she did not slump on her cushion, as though beaten by the world. She sat erect, looking down at her lap, and now and again up at James, who could hardly bear to look her in the eye. Finally after a long pause she said, "I will wait for you."

"NO!" James almost shouted. "You will not wait for me because I will not be back. What is there to wait for? I will serve my brother until I can do so no more, and then I will die. There is too much for you to look forward to - too much else to do - to sit around the house pining for me. Live! Find another man who will care for you properly and give you the life you deserve."

Esther looked up at James suddenly, and he was moderately alarmed. "James," she said, "how is it that you will go to teach the barbarians but you will not teach me?"

"What do you mean? I have tried to teach you, and you do not believe. Perhaps it is because you knew my brother just well enough to think that he could not be the one."

"You tell me to stay here and live the life that I deserve. If your brother is who you say he is, do I not I deserve to live the life he would dictate to me, as you are about to do?"

"I do not understand."

"You say that you are going to live the life that befits a man who has seen the son of God, and yet you say that I should stay here and live the life that you and I planned together with some other man." This thought pained James. "Only one of those two lives can be the proper one. Is it yours, with your traveling and teaching that is the proper way to serve God, or is it the one that you would save me for?"

"Not all those who believe must travel and teach. There will always be those who must raise families. I must do otherwise because I was specifically called by my brother, but also because I have so much to atone for."

"You say that not all of those who believe must travel and teach, and you say that there is little else to do. Which is it? And if it is to traveling and teaching, why cannot you be one of those who procreates? Leave the teaching to someone else."

"I must teach because I was so close to him - mine is a story that must be heard. The fact that I knew him for so long might give credence to my story, and thereby win more converts. Because of who I am, I must do more than stay home."

It was by now clear that neither or the two would persuade the other. Esther would not believe that Jesus really was the son of God, and James would not allow that she could be happy following him to where ever he might go. They seemed to sense this at the same time, for Esther began to cry quietly, almost beneath her breath, and James slumped sadly on his cushion.

"There is nothing more to say, then," said Esther. "We must part ways - each, it would appear to me, unhappily to go about their business. I do not want to live without you, and yet it appears that I must. You must follow your brother, even if it means leaving me behind. For some reason, though I do not know why, I believe that you are unhappy at this parting, perhaps as much as I. And yet you go. Do you realize, James, that you have yet to live your own life?"

"What do you mean?"

"Everything that has happened to you since you were a young man has happened in deference to Jesus. He did not want to be a carpenter because he would rather teach, and your family allowed him to go. You then, out of a sense of obligation to your father, became the carpenter when you would rather have gone to Jerusalem to study. You had just accustomed yourself to that fate, and undertaken to establish your own life, with me, when your brother was crucified, and now you are off again to do what your brother requires. Is there to be no time in your life when you do that which pleases you?"

"What I am about to do is not unpleasant to me. It is my duty, and I am happy to do my duty. It is much more important to show people the

173

correct way than to laze around Jerusalem studying the law in an abstract manner. I would have been studying at the feet of the men who crucified my brother; men who are more power hungry than they are spiritually hungry. They have distorted the faith, and it is the mission of my brother, and now of myself, to set it right. I am unhappy to leave you, but I cannot but be satisfied to go where I know that I am wanted and needed."

"You are wanted and needed here," said Esther, in a dejected voice that was clearly meant as a last gasp measure.

"Do not force me to say things that you and I both know you will misunderstand. It is enough to say that all other wants must come after those of God."

With that the conversation seemed to end, and James and Esther both felt that it had.

"I would not cause you pain for all the riches in the world," James told her, "yet I know that I have hurt you this morning. I will put an end to it by leaving now." He rose to go, and she rose with him.

"Let me hold you one more time," she said to him. "It does not seem as if we were ever as close as we ought to have been. I have looked forward to our wedding night, and to holding you close to me for the rest of my life, and now I find that this is to be the last time. There are no words to describe the emptiness I feel."

James did not want to hold her one more time, not because she was less desirable, but because she was more so. Holding her one more time would only make the parting worse, and it was bad enough as it was. Nevertheless they embraced once again, as tight as ever, and James lingered in that embrace, feeling, in the only way possible, all of his senses heightened at once, and none of them satisfied. He could not hold her tight enough, or pull her close enough to him, nor, did it feel, could she to him. It was sweet and peaceful to hold her, to know that she wanted to be held in this manner by him and no one else. She appealed to him in every way that it was possible for a woman to appeal to a man and James, who had not considered the matter in romantic terms until now, sensed what he was about to lose.

It crossed his mind just for a moment that maybe he would stay and wait for another call, or maybe she could come with him, but he could not sustain himself. He felt, believed that now was the time he was wanted, and he could not tell the messenger 'no'. As tenderly as he could he freed himself from the captivating embrace, and ran from the house, fighting back tears. He ran outside of the town to be alone for a time in a small clump of trees that he knew of from his boyhood, and stayed there, out of sight of others, until well past midday. There he cried loud and long for the loss he was about to suffer. At no time in his life had he ever felt more dejected.

When the sun was hot in the afternoon sky he returned to his home and dejectedly made a sign announcing the sale of the property and all its belongings, and then went to the local market to spread the word. When he returned home there were already some people gathered talking to Mary about the sale, and asking after some of the items in the house, if not the house itself. Neighbors wandered over, and asked the inevitable question: "Why?"

"We are moving to Jerusalem," said Mary, to those who asked.

"Why? Is there not enough carpentry work here to keep James occupied?" asked one wag.

"Why would you go to the city that crucified your son and brother?" asked another.

"We go there to follow him," said Mary. "We will help spread his teachings."

"To whom? Who is there that will care for the teaching of a man who was crucified as a blasphemer?"

"He had many followers throughout the land, and we will reach out to them."

"That should not take long. But in the meantime, how much do you want for this saw?"

And so the banter went all day. There were those who flatly did not believe that they were going for the stated reason, and others who believed them but thought them crazy for making the effort. At the end of the day, when they had sold most of their possessions, not including the house, and almost always for less than they were worth, James remarked to Mary, "It is going to be difficult for us to follow in the footsteps of Jesus as we have been saying. We have told people that we will reach out to his followers so that they may believe, but even here, in our own town, we have not imparted the piece of information that will attract more followers, and we have not done so out of fear. We have mentioned to no one that he is risen from the dead, and it is because we are afraid. How much more afraid will we be when we are out of the safety of Nazareth?"

It took two more days to dispose of most of their belongings, including the house, all of which they sold for prices that they knew were below the true value of the items. But they were interested in speed more than profit, so the sale continued. At the end of three days there were still some sundry items left that would be difficult to sell, so James took them to the marketplace and some of the haunts that he used to frequent when giving to the poor, and gave them away. The local tax collector got wind of the sale and so appeared on the final day looking for his share of the proceeds. Mary and James gave it to him, though grudgingly, and James was careful to make sure that he did so in the presence of a small crowd that could hear his admonitions to the tax collector to seek the forgiveness of God by sharing with those less fortunate than himself. With that James and Mary packed what they intended to keep and set out for Jerusalem by themselves.

Three Sabbaths had passed since Jesus was crucified, and when James and Mary re-entered the city they found it quiet, and heard no mention of Jesus in the streets or the markets. They had not really expected to find him still talked of, and they had to remind themselves that his death had been a larger event in their lives than in the lives of the people of Jerusalem. What was more, most of the people of Jerusalem were unaware that he had risen from the dead. James and Mary could hardly doubt that word had gotten around, but it was easy to dismiss such stories with claims that the body had been stolen by Jesus' admirers.

They went directly to the alley where the room that the eleven had been occupying before was located, and knocked. The door was opened by the other James, this time after a quiet and careful inquiry as to who was knocking. He welcomed James and Mary effusively.

"Yes," he said, in answer to James' question, "times have become more tense in Jerusalem since you departed. We have made some efforts to tell the story of Jesus to the people of the city, but we find that they are not receptive. There is a small community of people who are believers, and these we know, but we have had no success at getting others to believe. The things that we thought we might use to convince them - such as the fact that he rose from the dead - they are prepared against: they have been told by the Sanhedrin that his body was stolen by us to make it appear that his predictions have come true. No amount of protesting that this is not the case will answer. I believe it was you who told us that they would say this."

"That is the story that was dreamed of that morning at the tomb, and it would appear that they did not go to the trouble to seek another. I see there are only five of you left," said James, looking around the rooms as he put his and Mary's bags down and greeted the others present.

"The others have gone out into the provinces to teach, to see if we might have more success there."

"We were visited by Simon and Andrew on their way to the north. Have you had any reports?"

"None - they have not been gone long enough for the news to have come back to us. At the moment we are only hoping that they will come back to us safely."

"We know that you have enough burdens, but if you are forgiving we have come to add to them," said James. "After being shown by my brother, I finally have the faith that you have had all along. My mother and I have come to join you."

"We are glad to have you, of course," said James, looking around the room for approval, and getting it from all the others present. "But we have to warn you that we do not have an easy lot. You will find that here in Jerusalem you do not have much freedom to move about as you are accustomed to, unless you do not mind the unfriendly stares of those who know who you are and what you stand for."

"We have come prepared for that. You see that we have brought nothing and want nothing, other than to be able to serve my brother."

"What have you done with your business?" asked Bartholomew, sitting nearby on the floor.

"We have sold all that we owned that others would have, and given the rest away. In fact," said James, "here are the proceeds from the sale. We have brought them to give to the community for its support."

This brought a round of appreciation from the room, with all of the men rising to thank them for their generosity.

"This will carry us far, if we conserve it wisely," said James. "And what faith! When we were called by Jesus, most of us had little to give up. You have given up everything."

"You do not know all that he has given up," said Mary.

The other James looked uncomprehendingly at her, and then asked, "What will you do? That is to say, how do you feel best qualified to contribute? Please do not mistake my meaning - I do not intend to give you an entrance test. It is just that we are having difficulty among ourselves discovering how best to carry out the instructions of the Lord."

"I take no offense. I do not know how I will contribute. I have not followed my brother these three years, so I do not feel qualified to teach others about him. I have much to learn myself. I can only say that I will find a way to earn my keep."

"Of course, of course," said the other James. "If nothing else you will be the symbol of faith in our Lord. You, his own brother, denied him, but you saw him risen from the dead, and have surrendered everything to serve him. It is a tale that I will tell many times. It is unfortunate that you may have to begin the process alone, for we have divided ourselves up and are about to embark on tours to teach. Within the next two days we will all be gone, and there is no way to know when we will come back, or if we will come back."

"Perhaps, then, if two days is enough, you will take me about the city and introduce my mother and I to those who are members of the community. While you are gone we will visit them and attempt to keep their spirits up."

This met with great enthusiasm with all in the room, particularly the ebullient Matthias. There were handshakes, hugs, and claps on the back for James, and respectful bows to Mary, who readily agreed to James' scheme.

"That we will do," said the other James, "and you may believe that there is plenty of time to introduce you to the faithful because at present they are a very small group here in the city. But for the moment we must give you food and rest, for it is apparent that you have come directly from the road."

That evening James and Mary were led about the city by the other James, who appeared to be the only one with the courage to frequent the world outside the room on a regular basis. But it was apparent to James why he and the others felt some fear: there were occasionally people on the street who recognized the other James - or thought they did - and pointed and stared. They made the rounds of various small houses in the city, none of which spoke well of the economic powers of the owners, and James said that this was typical: Jesus did not attract a large contingent of the rich, possibly because he made it difficult for them to follow him by insisting that they give up their wealth.

Two days after that the other James and the rest of the eleven were all gone from the city, scattered throughout Judea and Samaria to teach. James suddenly felt very alone. He did not have any responsibility since there was nothing that had to be done, yet he felt obligated to do something for his brother in the absence of the others, and he was at something of a loss as to what to do. He did not know how often the community of believers in Jesus met, or if they met, but if they did they would have questions about Jesus that James would not be qualified to answer. Other than having heard the sermon on the side of the mountain, having seen the miracle at the wedding feast, and having learned what he could from talking to the five over the last few days, he knew little of the scope of Jesus' teaching. He had heard that Jesus liked to teach using parables, but he had heard only a few of these and he could not tell what was meant by all of them. For that matter, since he was listening for his own entertainment at the time, he could not remember much of the sermon that he had heard.

For inspiration he looked to the eleven, who were on the road attempting to bring the message to strangers who might never have heard of Jesus or his miracles, and doing so little better equipped than he. They knew more of his teaching, but there was still much that they did not know, and what they did not know, as they had already discerned, would be the area where the most questions would be asked. They did not know what his teachings meant for their relations with their current faith, if they were Jews, and they did not know whether such people, convinced of the nature of Jesus, should become Jews or join some other faith that was about to begin.

And yet they persevered, based on nothing more than their faith in the man who told them to go and teach. James would have to do the same, though he still felt he could not teach just yet. He began by revisiting the houses that he had been to with James, and, during the conversation, asking if

178

they knew of any other faithful that he might contact. As anticipated, many of the questions that were asked of James were questions that he could not answer. His standard response was that he did not have all the answers that they might like, and that he had many questions himself, but that he would rely on the goodness of God and his son to look after and guide them.

Other than asking questions that he could not answer, the other common request of the people he met was that the entire community meet somewhere so that they would know each other. They all knew some others in the group, but when James mentioned names that he knew to others, he often was greeted with a blank stare. The idea of the group meeting together was somewhat worrisome for James, because he still feared the wrath of the Sanhedrin, and a group meeting of this kind was just the vehicle that might frighten them into taking some sort of action.

But first he would meet the people whose names were given him by those he already knew. He obtained rough directions and then began his rounds. He was greeted with some suspicion at first, since he was calling without warning and since these people were also aware of the climate in the city, but upon mentioning the name of the people from whom he had obtained their names, he was always admitted.

Once in the door the meetings went well. James found that the population which followed Jesus was very diverse, including all age groups, sexes, and incomes, though for the most part they were from among the lower classes of the city. They all hungered for news of Jesus, were delighted to meet his brother and mother (when Mary went with him, which was not always), and badgered him for stories of Jesus' youth.

James told them what he could of Jesus' youth, but he could tell them next to nothing of his ministry. He did tell of the sermon and the wedding feast, and of course the rising from the dead and James' own conversion. They frequently listened wide eyed to such tales, and questioned him endlessly on the details, as though they could not know enough. Strangely, James never tired of telling the same stories, and enjoyed the fact that he appeared to be an inspiration for the people with whom he met. They uniformly stated their pleasure at the fact that someone would stay behind while the eleven were out teaching, and appeared glad of the fact that there might be some organization of them before too long. James promised nothing, but they all looked to the future and drew the conclusions which suited them.

James considered the matter, and decided that it might be useful to get all of the new believers that he could find together. He therefore passed the word around that there would be a meeting in the room where the eleven had gathered, provided directions, and named a time on the following Sabbath. As he considered what they could hope to achieve at this meeting, he wondered what the other eleven would think of his initiative. He also wondered what the Sanhedrin would say if they were to find out what was to take place.

But the crowd came on the Sabbath as asked, and came altogether to about 75 people. James was pleased at the size of the crowd, and in fact some of the people there were unknown to him, even though he had attempted, for safety reasons, to invite only those he knew. He had no way of knowing if they were truly faithful or if they were infiltrators from the Sanhedrin. He decided to trust them for the moment, assuming that the Sanhedrin would not be on to them as yet, or fearful of them in such small numbers.

CHAPTER 9

As it turned out, all of the eleven were back in Jerusalem within the week, and none had any more success to report than did Philip and Andrew. All were disappointed at the results, but James was surprised to note that none showed any sign of quitting the effort. The question was not whether or not to continue, but how.

"We are off to a slow start," said Peter to the gathering the first evening after they were all back in the fold. All of the eleven were there, with James and Mary, and they settled on the cushions over a meager meal of bread and dried meat. "This is not to say that we will not succeed, but it will be more difficult than we thought to add people to the movement. We have each added a few people, and it is possible that all we will ever be able to do is add a few people at a time. We have not the abilities that the master had. We will never have crowds following us, hanging on our every word. We must prepare ourselves to be content with this."

"So are we to continue to sally out among the surrounding territories, teaching a few people at a time?"

"We will have to keep teaching a few people at a time, but we must also develop an organization so that the people who join us have somewhere to turn when we are not there. I have been pleased to hear what James has accomplished here in Jerusalem. His meetings have been an important tool in bringing the local faithful together. I have talked to many who are glad that they have met the others of the number, and I believe that we have the groundwork for an organization here in Jerusalem. It is obvious that we of the eleven cannot be everywhere, and that we must set up a church that will survive us."

"So we must have deputies?" asked Bartholomew, to general laughter.

"Yes, that is it exactly. You do not see the Sanhedrin attempting to minister to their flocks with only one person per city. There are many of them, and they are organized and well funded. We will not be able to compete with them, and we do not want to. In addition we will have the Sanhedrin opposing us. But we must start slowly with a small organization that will attract and keep new members to us and which will survive us."

"Perhaps James could tell us what he has done here in Jerusalem to organize the locals," suggested Matthias.

"I wish I could tell you all the answer to the question of how to organize, but I do not know the answer. We had meetings because I thought that all of members might like to know each other for mutual support. But there is a fundamental question that must be answered before we can begin to organize, and that is: what is it exactly that we are? Are we a new movement that will break off from the Jews? Are we another branch of the faith of our fathers? Or are we simply Jews who know something that the others do not? We cannot organize without answering this question. For my part, I believe that, with the difficulties we will already have telling people about the risen Jesus, we do not need the active opposition of the Sanhedrin, which we will surely have if we attempt to establish another church."

"It is too late for that," said Peter. "We are already another church whether we like it or not. There is no way to cooperate with our brethren who do not believe that Jesus is the son of God. It is too fundamental a distance between them and us. This is not to say that we should antagonize them, but let us not fool ourselves that we can be with them. For us to get along with them, we would have to deny the nature of Jesus, and this none of us can do."

There was some agreement with this around the room, but also some dissension. "You are asking much from us, Peter. We are life long Jews. Would you have us throw that over?"

"It is not I who ask it, but Jesus. It is he who chose us, it is he who is the son of God, it is he whom we follow. What would you have me do? Compromise with the son of God so that we may remain Jewish?"

"The Jewish faith has a body of law that the people may adhere to, that guides them in their daily lives, that provides them with an organization. We have nothing of that sort. How are we to tie the people that we talk to together?" asked Matthew.

"We have got a body of teaching left us by the Master," said Peter. "We must write down that body of teaching to preserve it and to tie us together. It will not be as extensive as that which the Jews have built up over the years, but it need not be. Jesus did not give us many rules to live by, and it is not for us to create them. That record, preferably written by one of us, will serve as the basis for the church we create. We will help the scribe write it down, and then we will all teach from it so that we are all telling the new faithful the same thing."

"Who will be the scribe be?" asked Andrew.

"I will do it," volunteered Matthew.

"That was easier than I thought it would be," said Peter, to general laughter. "Very well Matthew. You are among the most qualified candidates anyway - I was thinking of you."

"This is all very well," said James, "and it is a good idea to write the life of my brother down, but you must realize that we are courting open warfare with the Sanhedrin if we attempt to establish another church."

"It will not be us courting warfare," said Peter. "We will endeavor to cooperate in every way possible, save for the issue of the identity and nature of the Messiah. It appears to me that we will have to strike out on our own because of this issue, but we will not attempt to dispute with the Sanhedrin on the matter. We will attempt to go our way, and allow them to go theirs."

"No matter how willing we are to let them go their way, I do not believe that they will let us go ours. If they have no compunction about crucifying the leader of our movement, I doubt that they will have any scruples doing the same to the rest of us."

"There is little that we can do about that, except that we might focus our teaching outside the city of Jerusalem for the moment. This will delay or ameliorate their wrath for the time being. They did not take action against Jesus until he came to their city."

"That is not to say that they were not watching him. In the days before I was a believer, I was sent twice by members of the Sanhedrin to attempt to talk Jesus out of his ministry, and this was before his entrance to Jerusalem. It was apparent that they were watching him very closely, as they will do to us."

"That is likely true, James," said Peter, "but there is little that we can do. We will focus our conversion efforts outside the city for the moment, but beyond that we will have to deal with the Sanhedrin. Jesus did not tell us that it would be easy, and he paid the ultimate price himself. Can we do any less?" There was a general, but unenthusiastic shaking of heads about the room, indicating that the others could see the truth of what Peter said, even if they could not do so heartily.

"If we are to be a separate church, then," said James, "it is even more important that we organize. It will be one thing to tell people that we want them to understand the nature and identity of Jesus, and quite another to tell them that they must surrender the faith of their fathers to do so. They will need a net of people around them that they can turn to in times of trouble. This organization must be able to sustain them in their faith by understanding the message of Jesus, but it must also be able to name its own priests since none of you will be able to remain in any one place for very long."

There were general nods of agreement at this.

"We must begin, then, by agreeing as to what the basic teachings of Jesus are, so that we will be giving the same message to all who hear us," said Peter.

Everyone seemed to agree to this, thought James, yet no one offered to begin the process.

"Very well, then," laughed Peter, "I will begin. First, I believe it impossible to see the kingdom of God without believing in Jesus, his son. We have been told this too many times to doubt it. And it is not enough to believe what Jesus taught; one must also believe that he is the son of God, placed here by God to save us from ourselves. Any disagreement so far?" There was none, and there was some nodding of heads in agreement.

"Secondly, Jesus did not throw over the law of Moses. He said specifically that that was not his purpose. Therefore we are bound by the law as given us by Moses." Again there were nods of agreement about the room

"But it is also clear that strict obedience of the law is not enough. Jesus may have caused his own crucifixion by condemning the Scribes and Pharisees for obeying the letter of the law and not the spirit." There were fewer nods this time, as Peter ventured onto ground that the others were less sure of.

"He also gave it to us that there are two commandments that are more important than the others: that we love God, and that we love others as we love ourselves." Peter paused here for effect. There were nods again, since they had all heard Jesus make this claim.

"Thus it follows that some aspects of the law of Moses are more important than others. These would be those which dictate how we treat God, and how we treat those around us." Peter thought he detected some dissension here, so he paused to make the point. "Of course it must follow: we were told which are the two most important commandments, were we not? Are we to assume that these count for no more than the prohibition against eating seafood which has no scales?" There were some murmurs that this made sense, but James, and apparently Peter, could detect some doubt.

"Brethren, what else could have been the meaning of the last supper that we shared with him? Did he not tell us that it was a new covenant that he made with us, symbolized by the breaking of the bread and the sharing of the wine, which he called his body and blood? All the prophecies of scripture point to the coming of the Messiah, as promised by God to our ancestors. We believe that Jesus was the fulfillment of that promise, and that his word shall supplant the scripture."

There were protests at this, including James, who did not want to see the new movement break away from the traditional faith, and others who did not share Peter's interpretation of what Jesus meant. They argued back and forth across the room for a few minutes, each one taking his turn making his point before the others. James watched them in the faint glow of the torches mounted on the walls, and could not help but think that God worked in mysterious ways, sending his son to work among such humble men as these, as well as James himself.

Peter let them vent their frustrations for a few minutes, then raised his hands for silence. "Brethren, I understand your concern for the law, and I am not throwing it over. Clearly each of the ten commandments given to Moses on Mount Sinai are still in effect - they tell us how to believe in God and how to treat our neighbor. But did not Jesus tell us that it is the spirit of the law that matters? Did he not illustrate for us that simply obeying by rote some habitual formulae is not enough? Remember the parable of the two men praying in the church: the one goes to the front to pray so that the others may see him doing it, while the other stays at the back and is more sincere in his prayer. I am not saying that the old law is no longer valid: it is not sinful to refrain from eating the meat of pigs, but doing so is also not enough to obtain everlasting life. We have all agreed already that for this one must believe in Jesus as the son of God and love one's neighbor as oneself. When we teach the people about Jesus, we will not emphasize those laws which do not affect the way we live. We will emphasize the ten commandments and the teaching of Jesus, who told us how to live, and what to believe. We do not know why God does what he does, or why Jesus has given us this new covenant, but we must obey. If we do not, we are not being faithful to the most important man ever to live in the world."

There was still some disagreement about the room, but less so than before. James wanted to protest, but he could not find the words to do so. He could not vouch for the sayings that Peter gave Jesus credit for, but none of the others seemed to doubt him, and, if they were as Peter quoted them and not taken out of context for some reason of Peter's, then Peter made a persuasive case. It all depended on believing that Jesus was the son of God. If one accepted that, then one could believe that there was a new covenant given to them. If Jesus were just a magician or a prophet, then his pronouncements on the subject of the law meant nothing. James was convinced that Jesus was who he said he was, but he was not familiar enough with his teachings to be able to enter the current debate.

Peter began again. "Brethren, I submit to you that Jesus gave us a new covenant, and that as a result of that covenant we are the first members of a new church, dedicated to the worship of God and his son Jesus. Those who continue to obey the old law are not wrong in doing so, but unless they also embrace the teachings of Jesus, the son of God, they will not see the kingdom of God." This much James could agree with, and he did so by nodding his head, as many of the others did.

"Jesus told us," continued Peter, "that not one part of the law would pass away until all had been fulfilled. I believe that it has all been fulfilled, in the person of Jesus. We have a new law to teach, and it is that law that we must agree on." James looked around the room for dissent, but there was none. He did not expect to see the point carried so easily, yet it was. Eleven men were willing to give up the faith of their ancestors for that of his brother - or rather half brother - the ostensible son of a carpenter from Nazareth.

"Remember, brethren, that this will only be a problem when we talk to our own people. For those we talk to outside, we will be asking them to throw over a religion that is foreign to God and his son. There will be no conflict between the old and the new." This point brought some relief to the room. There were murmurs of "That is true" and "Then let us teach those outside the city", and Peter heard them.

"It would be easier to ignore the problem by not teaching the Jews the meaning of Jesus, but we cannot avoid it. Jesus told us to teach the whole world, and we cannot ignore his wishes. If nothing else, we are still based here in Jerusalem and we are certain to come into contact with them as we begin to spread out and as we bring in more believers." Peter paused here for a moment, and then continued again. "Here then is what we will teach. Some things I have already mentioned: Jesus is the savior promised us by God, and it is through him that we will see the kingdom of God. He has fulfilled the prophecies of the scriptures, and so has given us a new covenant between his father and us. That covenant dictates that we keep faith with him and his father and that we love our neighbors. What else does that covenant mean to us, and to those we will be teaching?" Peter paused here for a moment, but it was apparent to James and the others that he was not waiting for an answer, and no one spoke.

"The spirit of the law is more important than its forms. It is not enough to claim that one believes in Jesus and his Father if one does not live according to his teaching. It is therefore the duty of all to carry Jesus, the Christ, to the rest of the world. We do this with charity, with service to others, and with public acknowledgment that we are disciples of the risen Lord. We must pray the prayer that he taught us to pray, and teach others to pray it. That which we faithfully ask for in prayer will be given us, save that we must not ask for those things which will be greedy in us. We must obey the ten commandments handed down to Moses. We must repent our sins, and constantly make straight the paths of the Lord, as John would have us do. We must be prepared at all times for the end of the world and the second coming of Jesus, when he will separate the wheat from the chaff, and send the one to eternal damnation, and the others to his Father in heaven. This must be the basis of our teaching, brethren. There will be questions about how a situation shall be handled, and whether or not the questioner can do this or that, and I cannot attempt to anticipate all of those questions. We will have to answer them in light of what Jesus has taught us, and place our faith in him."

There was silence in the room when Peter finished. So much they could all agree on, it would seem; the only real contention between them was over the question of whether or not they were establishing a new church or attempting to reform Judaism. Peter believed they were establishing a new church, and James was beginning to believe this as well: this issue of the nature of Jesus was too important to gloss over in the name of peace.

The room was dark now, save for the faint light of the three torches on the walls. The food was cleared away, and what little remains there were stored for the next day. The thirteen men and Mary looked at Peter expectantly, waiting to see if he had anything else to say. Despite the fact that the door to the room was locked, James suddenly felt the presence of another in the room, and looked around himself to see if he were dreaming. But the others were confused as well, because James could see that they looked uneasy. There was a sudden breath of fresh air in the room, as though someone had opened the door, but James could see that the door was locked and bolted on the inside. Suddenly, there was a man standing amidst them, in the middle of the room, next to where Peter sat. When James could focus on his face in the meager light, he could see that it was Jesus.

He started up, and then thought better of it, and instead knelt down - all so quickly and naturally that he hardly felt himself do it. The others did the same.

"Peace be to you," Jesus said, in the voice familiar to them all. There was no answer, and James himself could not find his voice to speak to his own brother. The meeting on the morning of his rising from the dead now seemed like a long time ago, and in the interim all of the talk and speculation about the meaning of his life seemed to have removed him from the human world. James could not think of him as a man standing in their midst, though that was what he was, but as the son of God. Thus he was far removed from James now, as though James really should not have been in the room with him. All of his disrespect to his brother suddenly overwhelmed him again, in less time than he could actually think of it all, and he fell face down on the floor.

"Peace be to you," said the familiar voice again. As with the morning of the rising, this second greeting had more of an effect on James, and he permitted himself to raise his head. Jesus' arms were spread from his sides slightly, and he bid them all approach him. This they did slowly, without a word, and without taking their eyes off of him. James could see why: one did not want to waste even a second of time by looking away from the son of God. He wanted to soak it all up, to take in every sight and sound, to be fully alert to every spoken word and nuance, and to every gesture and movement.

They seated themselves around him, though, James thought, like penitents afraid of the master. Only a moment ago they had been talking about how they would spread the word of Jesus, and suddenly here was the man - and God - himself with them. James felt small and inadequate, and hoped in the back of his mind that Jesus had not heard what they had been saying.

Jesus smiled at them, and asked, "Is there any food?"

Two or three scrambled up to fetch the remains of the bread and fish that they had had so recently, and Jesus sat down amidst them and began to eat. No one said a word while he did so.

When he had finished, he said, "I will be with you only a little while longer. The work for which I called you, and of which you have had only a small taste, is about to begin. But do not leave Jerusalem until you have been told to by my Father. John baptized with water, but you will be baptized with the Holy Spirit and with fire, that you may know that my father is with you, and that you may make yourselves known to all men. You will be reviled and cursed and spat upon in my name, but know that I am with you, even to the end of time."

He rose as though he would go, and everyone in the room rose with him.

"Lord," asked Peter, how are we to continue your work? Are we to invite those we teach into the faith of Abraham, or are we to start anew?" There was a pause after Peter finished speaking, and the room was deathly silent.

"Invite all men to follow me. I am the way, the truth, and the light. He who does not believe in me will not see my Father. Force no man to join, and turn no man away. Do not take judgement into your own hands - those who will not join will have their reward."

With that he was gone from their midst, as suddenly as he had come. No one saw him disappear, and no one saw him walk out of the room, but he was gone nonetheless. All of them stood about for a moment in a stupefied silence, as if they did not dare disturb what they had just seen. Peter was the first to sit, and slowly, one by one, they all followed suit.

The other James laughed quietly to himself, but said aloud, "I spent three years with this man, I see him crucified and rise again from the dead, and I have come to believe that he is the Messiah. Now, in his presence, I cannot utter a sound." There was a general nodding of heads and murmuring of agreement at this.

"This is understandable. There can be no lingering doubt that he is the son of God. Who knows how to act or what to say in such a presence? It seems to me," continued Peter, "that we have our answer. We are the first of a new faith, dedicated to the worship of Jesus and his Father, the one true God. We have been told to invite all men to worship him, and that those who will not believe will not join him in the kingdom of heaven. You see that he is with us at all times: his appearance here tonight could not have been better timed for us: in the midst of our debate on what to do, he provided us with the answer we had been seeking."

"He said that he would not be with us long. What does that mean? That is the same thing he said before he was crucified," asked Matthew, sitting near Peter.

"I do not know what it means," Peter answered. "I do not believe he is threatened by the authorities again. There would be no need for him to suffer once more. We will simply have to wait and see."

"It will not be easy finding new followers. You heard him say that we would be hated and scorned for his sake," said the other James.

"He has said that before, and we tended not to believe him, or to believe that he would spare us. But I have already had a small taste of it in only the short time that I have been out teaching, and it is easy to believe that it will get worse." This was not news to the others, but they could do little about it, and all appeared to accept it as best they could. Before the arrival of Jesus they had been showing signs of being tired of the discussion over how and what they would teach, but this visit renewed their energies, and they talked far into the night.

Even with the eleven back in town, James continued his visits among the faithful in Jerusalem. He enjoyed his visits with them, and he found that he had the ability to raise their spirits now and then, at least in part because he had been so close to Jesus, and had seen him arisen. They could not hear enough stories about his appearances since his crucifixion, and were particularly intrigued to learn that he was still about the area.

James spent most of every day out with the people, and took many of his meals with them. So that he might not appear to be taking advantage of them, he was careful to change his eating habits so that he ate very lightly, and never more than twice a day. In this manner he was able to spread his eating around among those he visited, and to lighten the burden on the other eleven and his mother.

He was in the midst of just such a meeting with an elderly couple when they were suddenly interrupted. There was a banging on the door, and then two men burst in upon them. James did not know either of them, but they were large, powerfully built, and young, and James immediately thought that they might be henchmen for someone else.

"What are you doing here?" asked the taller of the two, a man about James' height, but with coal black hair and thick beard.

"We are simply talking," said the old man. "Who are you?"

"Are you talking of the blasphemer Jesus, who was crucified for his crimes?"

"What if we were? Is that a crime also?"

"Do not grieve me, old man, or I will do more than warn you. Were you talking of the man Jesus?"

"We were," James interposed. "But so have many people. He became famous throughout the land. Surely it is not against the law to talk of him."

"It is against the law to admire him, or adhere to his beliefs. He was a blasphemer. We know that he has followers in the city, and we will not permit them to pollute the city with his blasphemy."

"What would you have us do?"

"Who lives here? Then you," he said to James, "must leave, and do not come here again. We will be watching this house to see that it does not become a haven for followers of the man Jesus." James began to argue with them, but they seized him and threw him out into the street. He rose carefully and slowly, brushed himself off in a slow, determined way, all the while eyeing the two men, and then walked away.

He wandered around the town for two hours to make sure that he was not followed, and then very cautiously headed back to the room he and the others had been keeping. It was evening when he returned, and the others were on hand. He repeated the scene for them.

"So it has begun, even here in the holy city," said Peter. "Who did they say they represent?"

"They did not say because they did not give us a chance to ask. But there can be only one answer: they came from the Sanhedrin. Who else would go to the trouble to break up a meeting of three people?"

"This is likely," agreed the other James. "But you see what it means: we are either being watched, or followed, or the people of the city are reporting our movements, or it could be all three. Were you followed here?" he asked of James.

"I do not believe so. I wandered about the city for over two hours so that they might get bored following me, and go about other business." This brought gentle laughter from the others, and a hug from his mother.

"We will have to begin looking for other quarters again," said Peter, "because it will only be a matter of time before they find us here."

"Why should we fear them?" asked Matthew. ""We are not blaspheming, so there is little that they can do to us."

"We do not believe we are blaspheming, but it may be convenient for them to believe it, particularly if it is their intention to see that we are not allowed to find other followers of Jesus. You see how implacably they brought Jesus to his end - or at least what they thought was his end - and there can be little doubt that they will not suffer us to take up where he left off."

"James," said Judah, one of the quietest of the eleven, "it might be best for you to stay out of sight for a while."

"I have considered that, and rejected it. It has not been long since Jesus told us that we would suffer for him, and it would not be right for me to go into hiding at the first sign of trouble. I will not go back to that same house for a time, if for no other reason than to keep that family out of trouble, but I will continue my rounds. Of course, I will be more careful of being watched."

"Just so," said Peter. "We must be careful not to invite the authorities down on other followers, but it is not fitting for us to go into hiding. On the other hand it is not fitting that we flaunt our belief to the authorities, since if we were to all be disposed of at once, there would be no one left to carry on the movement. Let us continue to preach the message then, but let us do so carefully. If it becomes apparent that Jerusalem will not hold both the Sanhedrin and us, then we will go elsewhere. There is a wide world of people who need to hear the news that we have to offer. Jesus has said that we are not to leave Jerusalem for the moment, but he also said that we would be told when we should leave. Let us wait for that time, and minister cautiously in the meantime."

Thereafter James went about his rounds more carefully, and was solicitous about explaining to the people he visited why he came less often. He also asked them to refrain from visiting the room where the meetings were formerly held, since that might lead the Sanhedrin to them. In addition, he told them, the apostles of Jesus would be moving again soon, and he did not want the faithful to think that they had simply decamped and left them with no ministers.

Despite all his cautions James was burst in on twice more while talking with others of the faithful, including once in the house of a fanatically faithful man by the name of Stephen, and another in the home of a physically strong but simple minded fuller, though for the most part by different messengers. The fourth time it happened, however, one of the two was the same taller one who had broken in on the first couple. He recognized James immediately, and demanded to know who he was, since he did not heed the previous warning. He told the man that he was James of Nazareth, and no more, and the man went away with that information.

No more meetings of the faithful were held in the apostles' room, since it would be easy for such watchful people to find them out. James was given the task of canvassing the city in search of other accommodations, and he quietly scared up two or three other places that might suit them, and made the rounds looking at them all. He selected an upper level room in the southern end of the city that was much like the room they had now: bare, little in the way of ventilation, but inexpensive and off the main street. One had to know to turn down two different alleys to get to it, and more than one of the number got lost attempting to find their way there for the first time. They all heartily approved of his choice.

From there he continued his rounds, meeting with people in their homes, encouraging them to introduce others to him who might like to hear the story of Jesus, and telling them that the move had taken place, though not telling them where they had moved to. He wanted to ensure that the new room would not be found out, but also to reassure the people that neither he nor any of the rest of the apostles were about to decamp. He told them of the most recent visitation by Jesus, and his words to them, but assured them that someone would stay behind in the city when the others left.

It was upon his return from these rounds one afternoon that he found his mother and the eleven all sitting in the room at once - an unusual occurrence. James could not read the mood of those present, but stood inside with the door closed behind him, wondering what was up. His eyes moved about the room, looking for some hint, but they all looked back at him - he thought - somewhat sullenly. He finally fixed his gaze on Peter, who explained.

"The Master has been taken to his Father," he said, "and while we should be happy that this is so, and that we were there to see it, we cannot but feel alone."

"What do you mean, 'taken to his Father'?" asked James.

"The Master appeared while you were out, and before any of the rest of us had left, and invited us out to pray. We followed him to Mount Olivet, where he chastised us for not having enough faith in him. He then told us that we are to go out to preach to the whole world, though we should remain in Jerusalem until we have been given the word from the Father, and that we would be able to cast out demons and speak with all manner of tongues. He said that the Holy Ghost would be upon us so that we would not fear and be able to carry on his work. Then, as we watched, he was lifted into heaven, and disappeared into a cloud - the only cloud in the sky, and one which we believe had not been there only moments before. At first we were overjoyed at this manifestation of his power, but we now recognize that it will be difficult to go on without him. We have not understood until now what his role would be, and have always harbored the hope that he might rejoin us, but now we know that this will not happen." Peter paused here, as though he were finished.

"Peter has not related all that happened," added the other James. "The Master also gave us the power to forgive sins, and placed Peter at the head of the church."

James stood silently for a moment, contemplating what he had just heard. It was not difficult to believe the story - he no longer doubted where his brother was concerned, but he was vexed that he had not been there to see it. And to think that he would have been there, had it not been for the fact that he was out early meeting with the few faithful in the city. Had he been less diligent, he might have been there for what was obviously another very important event in the history of the world. He said nothing, and sat down in a corner of the room, away from the others.

Peter and Mary instantly arose and joined him, though for a few moments they said nothing. Peter broke the silence.

"It is not for us to judge God, or his son Jesus. We cannot know his reasons, and we must believe that they are just. Consider that you have known him all your life, which is more than any of the rest of us can say, and that you are born of same mother. This is a treasured place."

James considered his words for a moment, and brightened considerably. It was true that he had known Jesus the longest, though much of that had been wasted in disbelief. And perhaps, he had to admit, this was his punishment for all those years of disbelief.

"My brother continues to vex me," said he. "My entire life has been built around him. I was a carpenter because he would not be one; I was a traveler and I was robbed because he would not listen to those who suggested that he stop, and I was called to make the case. I saw him crucified, I saw him raised from the dead, I have given up carpentry and marriage that I might follow him, and then I am absent at his final departure. It is hard to bear. But you are right that I must not judge. He is the son, and I am not."

"You must have a special place in his heart, because he has seen fit to bring you into the fold of the faithful," said Mary. "Only think how few people have seen the risen Christ! How many would love to have changed places that morning with you only a few weeks ago?" James nodded at the justice of her comments, and resolved to himself to be less selfish, and even thought to chastise himself for corrupting himself with thoughts of personal glory. He said nothing but smiled at Peter and Mary.

James looked about the room to see the effect of the recent events on the others, and they appeared to be brighter than when he walked into the room. It was only then that he noticed a stranger in their midst. He was a smallish man in his 20's, with thick black hair and beard utterly uninterrupted with gray. Despite his small stature James thought he looked a tad imperial, until they had both stood and James had the chance to study his eyes up close. They were the kindest, most open he had even seen (excepting his brother). The other James saw this, and rose to make introductions.

"Here is a man you might not have met," said the other James. "Matthias," he said to the newcomer, summoning him over with a flick of the wrist, "this is James, the brother of Jesus. This is Matthias, whom we have voted to add to our number to restore it to the original twelve as desired by our Lord."

James would have greeted the man, but he was not given the chance. Matthias hugged him both and beamed up at him, saying, "It is an honor to meet you. How much you will have to tell me that I must know!"

"It is possible that my mother can help you, but I am afraid that I will be almost useless to you."

"But there is so much that I would know about his youth, about his young manhood."

"My mother will be able to tell you about those things, but, sadly, I will be able to add little. I did not believe the true identity of my brother until I saw him risen from the dead. So many times he tried to tell me, but I refused to listen. Unlike all of you, I lacked the faith that I should have had. I am here now in part to make up for that shortcoming."

"Believe it or not, considering what has happened, but we thought to wait for you when we voted on Matthias," said the other James, but we decided that it was a decision that we should make - we who were of the original twelve."

"I understand perfectly," said James, secretly glad that he had had the last few moments to prepare for what amounted to personal disappointments such as this. "How could I know who is worthy to join, and who not? I do have one question: how is it that I have not met him in my travels about the city?"

"He is a Gallilean like us, and has been to see his family these few weeks. He also witnessed the resurrection of the Lord," said Peter.

CHAPTER 10

Despite the two recent visits by Jesus, there was still much that the apostles, now including Matthias, had to discuss. There were still some, such as James, who though not one of the twelve was always included in their counsels, believed that they should not break away from the faith of their fathers. Jesus had come to fulfill the prophecies of that faith, not to overthrow them. His one alteration to the assumptions of the Jews was that it was clear that all would be welcome to join, not just the Jews. James recognized that this would be difficult for many Jews to accept, but it need not cause a breech between them.

Peter and most of the others were of the opinion that they were to begin a new church. They had the words of Jesus, telling them that he would build his church on the rock that was Peter, and placing Peter at the head of that church. Further, they could not see how they could reconcile themselves with the Jews, who would not accept that Jesus was the Messiah. How, they constantly asked, could Jews and the followers of Jesus be members of the same church?

They had this discussion over and over, until it seemed to James that they could talk it over no more. Yet they kept coming back to it because it was fundamental to their efforts. It even became something of a joke among the brethren, because every time they fell silent over a meal or immediately before bed in the evening, James would bring up the subject for discussion. They laughed every time he did so, but always ended in a serious debate on the matter.

"Do you mean to say," asked James one evening, when going over the issue once again, "that God has thrown over his chosen people? After all these years?"

"No, He has not thrown them over," answered Peter, "He is merely telling them that the prophecies have been fulfilled, and that they must accept that the Savior has been sent. Jesus himself made no changes to the laws of Moses - all that we have had passed down to us by our fathers is still true, and still may be observed by the faithful. The only difference is that they must be faithful to a new reality: Jesus is the Messiah. There will be no restoration of the Jewish state, no reincarnation of David to restore Jerusalem to its place in the ring of nations. The purpose of the Savior is to bring men to God, and nothing more."

"But if we are to accept all that Jesus said, and I do, then can we not say that there is no longer any reason to obey the laws of Moses, since they have been supplanted by those of Jesus?" asked James.

"Supplanted in what way?"

"He asked which are the greatest of the commandments, and answered that one must love God, and that one must love one's neighbor as oneself. If these are the core of Jesus' message, what meaning is there in continuing not to eat the meat of a pig? As for those whom we would hope to add to the church from outside of our own faith, it will be difficult to convince them to take up the law of Moses when we tell them that Jesus left them with two commandments only. If we are to assume that one cannot see the Father after eating the flesh of a pig, then many of those whom we would convert are already doomed, for they have been doing it all their lives."

"Jesus did not say that the laws of Moses are invalid, only that it is not necessary to obey them to see the Father. Those Jews who join us may still obey such laws if they wish, and those who join us who are not Jews will not have to obey them. We are at a new beginning, and this new church will have few laws to obey that are mere formula. Jesus placed his emphasis on faith and works, so we will waste little time deciding what people should eat and drink."

"Why then did God give such laws to Moses, if He did not mean for them to be observed?"

"I am not the one to judge God. He has His reasons. Perhaps he has tired of sending prophets to the Jewish people telling them to repent. But it is even wrong of me to suggest that much. There can be no question that He meant for the laws of Moses to be observed, but it is equally clear that Jesus has given us a new direction. And why would that be hard to believe? Would you not expect that the arrival of the Messiah would result in upheaval? Why would God send his son to us if nothing were to change as a result?"

"But those laws," returned James, "are what kept us together as a people, supported us in the desert, in exile, and in the face of invasions from every direction. They are the physical soul of the nation."

"All very true, but Jesus is not calling us as a nation. Have you not noticed that, in contrast to the Scriptures, where the prophets recalled the Jewish nation to God, Jesus calls individuals to him? He is not seeking to rescue nations, but people, and there is no need for people seeking God to be held together in any way other than their faith." Here Peter rose from the floor on which he had been lying, preparing for sleep, and addressed the room. "Let there be no mistake brethren: we are the privileged few who have seen the Messiah, and come to know his purpose in the world. One wants to fall on one's knees in humility at the thought. But we have been given a difficult task, and that is to convert our fellow man to belief in Jesus as the Messiah, and convince them that He is the one true way to everlasting life.

"When we go out into the world, or even into Jerusalem, it will not be to convert governments or nations, but people. There will be those who make the same claim against us that was made against Jesus: that he was here to overthrow the government, and replace it with a kingdom of his own. It was for this reason (or, should I say this 'excuse') that he was crucified. We must make it clear that we are not for the purpose of competing with government, because Jesus has made it clear that the form of government one lives under makes no difference to him. We are seeking after souls, not nations."

Peter sat down after this, and was about to lie down again, when an afterthought occurred to him. He sat up on his elbow again and said, "Of course, that is not to say that we will not take them if they come." There was general laughter at this, and the room settled down for the night.

The next morning James was off early on his rounds again, and again he ran into the strongarms sent by the Sanhedrin. It was at the same home of the elderly couple where he met them before, and one of the men was the same as the previous meeting, and recognized James.

"I have warned you off once already," said the unpleasant force, "but it seems that I did not do so strongly enough. What is your name?"

"My name is of no concern to you. I do not answer to strangers who put themselves above the law."

"I have been sent here by the highest authority there is," said the man.

"I doubt that," rejoined James.

"It is true, and if you know what is good for you you will take my word for it," said the man, as menacingly as he could, leaning into James face.

"I believe my authority is better than yours."

"If you mean this crucified Jesus, you are sadly mistaken. I can tell you that my authority has power over him. And I come to tell you to stop spreading lies about him in the city."

"Your authority has not power over him, except that granted them for his purposes. He has risen from the death visited on him by your authorities, and thereby triumphed over them."

"I did not say who my authority is, but it doesn't matter. Jesus is dead. You or others like you have stolen his body and hidden it to give credence to your lies. But it will do you no good. Wise people will avoid the likes of you, and his memory will die with you."

"His memory will never die."

At this the man lost his temper and, grabbing the front of James' clothing with both hands, pushed him against the opposite wall, nearly knocking the breath out of him. While James was not large, all of his years of carpentry work made him strong, and he broke the man's grip on his cloak and pushed him away. Then both men set upon him, and threw him into the street once again.

"Every time you come to this house you end in the street. You should tire of this soon. Now what is your name? If you do not want to tell us I am sure that we can convince this couple to do so."

"I am James of Nazareth."

"That is better. I believe that name has been given to us once before. The San...that is, those who sent us will be curious to see it again." With this the two men walked off, warning James once again not to go into the house. When they were out of sight he went back in to comfort the people who lived there, told them that he would devise some other strategy for meeting so that they could not be watched so effectively, and departed.

He stayed at his rounds all day without seeing the two men again, or any others like them. When he returned to the room, it was late in the evening, and he once again noticed that all of the twelve were there with his mother. He had the same feeling that he had had before: something had happened to alter their mood. This time, rather than somber they appeared to be lighthearted, talking joyously among themselves, eating, and apparently planning for the future.

As before, he stood just inside the door surveying the scene, and asked, "What has happened now?"

"We have been visited again," said the ebullient other James, "but not this time by the risen Lord. It is as though he sent his spirit to touch us, to give us strength for what is to come."

"We were sitting here as you see us," said Peter, with the room nearly dark, when we were buffeted by a strong wind, even though we were indoors. It was as though the storm had found its way through locked doors to trouble only us. The room was full of wind and noise. Then, while still wondering at this, we were bathed by the brightest, whitest light that could be. We knew that wind and light such as this were not the work of man, but we have seen the Lord taken up into heaven, and we knew not what to think. I, though I am supposed to be faithful, was afraid." Peter paused here for a moment, which was all the opening that the other James needed.

"Then there appeared among us a ball of fire that would have burned us all, we feared, but it separated into tongues, and we were each of us visited by tongues of fire." James paused just for a moment to catch his breath, and that was all the opening Matthias needed.

"But they did not touch us, nor harm us, nor even cause us to fear. Instead we felt calm, as though all of the burdens of the world had been lifted from our shoulders. And we found that we could speak in all the tongues of the world, and understand each other, no matter which tongue we spoke!" Here Peter reclaimed the floor.

"It is the sign from God that was foretold to us by the risen Lord when he told us to stay in Jerusalem until we should be told to leave. He has given us the ability to make all men understand us, so that there is now no one who cannot be told of the power of God." All of the apostles began to speak among themselves at this, and several continued to tell the story to James - all at the same time - but he hardly heard them. He would not have been able to anyway, for the noise of all of them talking at once, but he was distracted: once again he had been absent for what was obviously an important event.

"I have sinned greatly against my brother by not believing in him, and now he is exacting his punishment on me," he said, to no one in particular.

Peter seemed to hear him above the confusion, and came over to where he was still standing. "I have no comfort to offer," he said, "save the thought that you have come to see his true nature in time, and so will not be left out of the kingdom of heaven. Do not lose faith. There is surely some higher purpose that we do not know." But James could say nothing. He had put the first incident - the ascension of Jesus into heaven - behind him, though he felt left out even then. This second omission was too much for him. He felt as though he were being singled out for exclusion from among the brethren. He knew that he had sinned, and acknowledged it to be a great sin, but how much would he have to suffer to make up for it? Had he not given up everything to follow Jesus? What more could be wanted of him? He sat down in a darkened corner of the room and wept silently to himself. His mother Mary came to sit by him, but she said nothing.

After the tumult died down, and after James recomposed himself somewhat, he remembered that he had not told the others of the second attack by the henchmen of the Sanhedrin. He got the attention of the room and then related the story briefly, focusing on the fact that at least that one house was being watched for the believers in Jesus. This fact alarmed them all to some extent, though James noticed that the threat of intimidation did not seem to phase them as it had before.

"It is not that we have to fear the Sanhedrin," Peter said to them, "but that we must make more converts for the risen Lord before we allow ourselves to fall into the hands of murderous priests. But if they are to be murderous, let them do so of their own accord. Let us not provoke them into attack. Brother James," he said, turning to James, "we must all follow the example of the Lord and not offer resistance to those who would persecute us. He did not do it, and neither should we. What good would come of it? You would be arrested all the same and have bumps and bruises to show for it. Let them have their way, knowing that in the end it is Jesus who will triumph." They then sat down to divide the surrounding areas among them, and did so quickly.

"There only remains the question of who shall shepherd the flock here in Jerusalem, where it is at present the most dangerous place to be." said

Peter. "Someone will have to stay when we disperse again, and be leader for those who are here, and attempt, quietly perhaps, to gain more. I know of no better person for this difficult job than James, who has already given so much to the church here." This motion was unanimously carried, and James, who without having uttered a word had been elected the first bishop of the first church, felt the gravity of the honor, and accepted with alacrity.

One evening in these early days before the apostles departed again, they sat down to a modest dinner, but Peter was not yet returned to share with them. They sent out into the city for word of him but could hear nothing. He finally came into the room near midnight, when all were asleep.

"Such a day I have had, brethren, but it is all for the glory of God," he said, when the candles had been lit and all the room roused from their sleep. "As I entered the temple this morning by the gate called Beautiful there was there the lame man who has begged for alms these many years." There were nods of understanding from the gathering, since they had all seen him. "Inspired at that moment by the Holy Spirit, I prayed over the man and bid him walk, and he did! Now there was a great tumult in the temple when the word spread of the event, and many people flocked to me. I taught them of the life and death of Jesus, and they appeared to hear me, for I converted many - my companion John thought there to be 3,000 people in the area who heard and believed. But of course the Sanhedrin got word of what had happened, and sent henchmen to capture me and bring me to them. There I was grilled for many hours, the lame man was brought in so that the Sanhedrin might see him, and other witnesses called. They all confirmed that the man who had been lame could now walk, though the Sanhedrin could see that for themselves. Finally I was sent away while, I suppose, the Sanhedrin counseled among themselves. No, I was not released, or I would have gone back to the temple gate to teach; they kept me in a locked room with a guard posted at the door. But finally they summoned me back, and said that they could not deny that the man was now walking, which I did not expect that they would do, but they also said that his ability to walk was a gift from God, and that I was not to take credit for it unto myself. Of course, I had never done so: I told all who would listen that it was God, answering the prayers raised to him through his son Jesus, who cured the man.

"But they told me that I was not to invoke the name of Jesus any more in the temple precincts, or in the city. They said that such talk of a blasphemous criminal would stir up the city needlessly, and that they would not permit it to continue. On pain of such threats I was allowed to leave late tonight, too late to begin teaching immediately on the steps of the temple, which I will do tomorrow."

Thus did the apostles receive notice of the harassment that was to come. James feared for the people in the city who had converted to Jesus, and hoped that it would be the teachers that the Sanhedrin would focus on.

James hoped, in an off hand sort of way, that there would be no more miracles to confuse the company. He considered the miracles and the resurrection of Jesus as the two events most likely to convince converts that Jesus was the Messiah. If Peter or the others were also able to do miracles it would confuse those who might listen to what the apostles were teaching: how were they to distinguish between the apostles' miracles and those of Jesus? But events were not to cooperate with him.

As part of the agreement of the community of followers of Jesus that they would own all things in common, members of the community would occasionally bring the proceeds of some sale or some other business transaction to the apostles to be shared with the others according to their needs. In this way a man named Ananias, but another man, not the member of the Sanhedrin, came to the apostles one evening and, with great joy, placed a sack of money on the floor of the room and announced that it was for the brethren to share.

There were claps on the back and hugs of congratulation from the assembled company, and questions about how he came into the money.

"I have sold my land outside the city, brethren, since I have no use of it, and brought the proceeds for the poor and unfortunate."

There were cries of "Admirable!" and "Well done!" throughout the room, and someone asked how much was there. Ananias mentioned a figure which somewhat surprised James, since he did not think that land would be that dear outside the city. The other apostles appeared to be suitably impressed in the same way, and there were more cries of "Well done!" and "Your generosity becomes you." Peter had said nothing, but only gazed at the man as he stood talking to the apostles gathered around him. Finally, above the general din of conversation Peter said, "Ananias, why has Satan tempted your heart, and convinced you to lie to the Holy Spirit and, by fraud, keep part of the price of the land?"

There was a stunned silence in the room, and not even the breathing of the men could be heard. James looked at Peter in an awkward way, hoping to warn him against finding fault with such a handsome gift. The others only stared at Peter and Ananias, hoping to see the answer and not knowing who to believe.

"While it remained, did it not remain to you?" asked Peter. "And after it was sold, was it not still in your power? Why have you conceived this thing in your heart? You have lied not to men, but to God."

The other apostles could only stare, not knowing what to think. James stood with his mouth open, wondering whether he ought to take the lead in chastising Peter for his lack of faith, when Ananias, who had been standing stiff and wide eyed in the midst of the apostles during this short speech by Peter, suddenly put his hands to his chest, and collapsed in a heap on the floor of the room. Matthias and the other James rushed to kneel over him, but they looked up almost immediately.

"He is dead," announced the other James. The other apostles could say nothing, so stunned were they by this development. James was as tongue tied as the others. They simply stood around the man on the floor in a dumbfounded silence, not knowing what to do next.

After a short pause, an obviously shaken Peter said, "It is the judgement of the Lord. I have done nothing but point out his sin to him."

"But how did you know?" asked Andrew.

"The Holy Spirit came upon me, and I could see into his heart for only a moment. But you see that I was right: he has collapsed under the weight of his own iniquity."

No one knew what to do, or what to make of the situation. James thought for a moment to be afraid of the power that Peter possessed, but such thoughts were overcome by the necessity of deciding what to do about the body on the floor of the room. They haggled back and forth for a time, and finally decided to bury the man since he had neither kith nor kin to notify, save his wife.

"But what will we tell his wife," asked Bartholomew. "We must go and give her the news. Are we to say that it was an act of God that killed her husband, or that it was Peter, the leader of the followers of Jesus?"

"Say nothing to her. She will be here seeking after him, and we shall confront her," said Peter, eyes wide and staring straight ahead, to the still shocked group. "Bartholomew, Andrew, James, James and John bury him, and then return."

The five men picked up the suddenly lifeless body and carried it out of the room, down the stairs, and halted in the alley below. Fortunately for them, it was dark, and there was no one about. Bartholomew asked them to stop for a moment, and they put the body down.

"We cannot simply bury a man who has died on our floor," said he. "There is the matter of his wife, his estate, and the authorities, who will want to know what has become of him."

"Nor can we leave him here," the other James pointed out.

"We will have to bury him in a temporary grave until we can decide what is to be done with him. We will have to notify the authorities tomorrow," said Andrew.

"We will never be able to notify the authorities," said James. This was met with questioning glances.

"How can we avoid notifying them of what has happened?"

"Think of the tension that already exists between the followers of Jesus and the Sanhedrin. Will not the authorities look with glee on the fact of a man being found dead on our very hearth? They would be able to use such information for any purpose they pleased, including having all of us arrested or put to death. Where would our movement be then?"

"But Jesus said that we must be willing to suffer for him," said Bartholomew.

"Yes, and so we must, but going to jail for a crime that we know did not happen would not be suffering for the sake of Jesus. It is likely that this man's heart quit, and that the fact of his talking to Peter when it happened is pure coincidence. How would being arrested by the Sanhedrin over such an incident be in the service of the Messiah? That would be a political death, and I do not believe that such an end is what my brother had in mind. We must somehow convince this man's wife that this is so...."

"But we are men of God!" insisted Andrew. "We cannot be in the business of carrying bodies out into the night and secretly burying them!"

"That is not a business that any of us want to be in," said James, "but it is also true that we do not want the work of Jesus to end here with only a few followers in the Holy City. We have done nothing wrong - we did not cause the death of this man, and we will have to trust to God that he will not punish us for putting his church above the administrative requirements of the civil authorities. We will give him all of the rites associated with burial that are due him, and trust to God and his Son for the rest."

This did not satisfy the others, though the other James appeared to understand what James was attempting to tell them, and they argued, in hushed tones, over the matter for some time. Finally Andrew said, "There will be no solving it here. We must do something with the body for the moment, and then discuss the matter with the rest of the brethren to see what is to be done." They then haggled over what to do with the man for the moment, but could think of nothing immediately. James scoured his brain in search of someplace where they could bury the man for the moment, and finally hit upon a small plot behind the home of one of the faithful that had been dug up recently as part of a construction project. They then wrapped the man thoroughly in his own cloak and put the body in the back of a cart that they could push, and set off through the city in search of the home mentioned by James.

It was late during the night and there were few people about, so they ran into no one who might ask them questions. On the way they debated waking the home owner and telling him of what they were about, but decided it would be better for the man and his wife if they knew nothing of what transpired.

They had brought with them a spade, and made short work of digging up ground that was already disturbed from the construction on the house behind. They dug as deep as they could and lowered the man respectfully into his resting place, and then covered him over carefully to ensure that the ground did not look any more orderly than it did when they came upon the scene. After what they hoped was a reverential prayer, they hastened back to the room.

Upon their return to the alley beneath the room where they stayed they deposited the cart and the spade back where they got them and then ascended the steps to the room.

James went first, and when he opened the door they were met with an astounding sight. Peter was standing, with the other of the twelve who were not with James around him, facing Sapphira, the wife of the man that they had just buried. James knew the couple from his rounds in the city, and had always thought them to be pious. As he opened the door he advanced, in surprise, only far enough into the room so that the others behind him could see what was happening. As he stopped, the woman looked around at him and the others, apparently noted their soiled clothing, was overcome with an astonished and frightened look, and immediately fell in a heap to the floor. Everyone in the room was wide eyed with astonishment, and there was a deathly silence. For a moment no one moved to help the woman, and then they all did so at once. Matthias, who had been standing near Peter, was the first to reach her, and he looked at her carefully before announcing to the room that she too was dead.

"This is too much," said James to the assembled. "How can this be twice in one night? From whence comes this power, Peter?"

"It comes from the Lord in heaven. I have done nothing to this woman save confront her with the deviousness of her husband and her."

"But Peter," said Matthias, "you did tell her that the men who had just buried her husband were returning, and that they would put her away as well." All eyes focused on Peter, waiting for his answer to this.

"I do not know how I knew that this might happen. I did not intend that it should be so, but as I was talking to her I had a vision of her being buried with her husband. But I only meant to threaten her - to convince her to tell the truth about the sale of the land and the proceeds therefrom. I did not will that she fall over this way, and I would have preferred that she not do so."

"These are mysterious powers that you possess," said Andrew. "I have not seen the like, even from the Lord. He did not cause people to collapse and die in front of him."

This angered Peter, and he shouted at Andrew, "I do not have this power, I tell you. What has happened here is between her heart and her conscience, as it was for her husband before her. This is a lesson from the Lord God, not from me."

There was a long silence while they considered the implications of what had happened, each in his own way. The hot tempered Peter was not to be dealt with for the moment, and none dared challenge him again on the subject. James looked around the room and saw the mixture of fear and awe on the faces of the twelve and his mother. He finally broke the silence.

"It has been said that we must notify the authorities of what has happened, but I do not believe that we can notify them. The story that a man and his wife both collapsed on the floor of our room over guilt from a small debt is too incredible to be believed. I have seen it happen, and I am not sure that I believe it. The authorities will have a weapon to use against us, if they are inclined to do so. They used much less evidence to crucify our Lord."

There was general nodding about the room, but as before Andrew raised his concerns.

"It is not proper for men of God to defy the authorities in this way. How can the followers of Jesus be skulking about the alleys of the Holy City with bodies to be buried secretly in the night?"

"What talk is this?" asked Peter.

"James does not think that we should notify the authorities of the deaths of these two people," said Andrew. "He is afraid that the authorities will use their deaths against us."

Peter looked at James without saying a word.

"It is entirely possible that the Sanhedrin, if they are in the mood to do us mischief, will decide that we are responsible for their deaths, and use this decision against us. Consider the problem, and the story that we would have to tell: two members of our own community come to us in the night, and both die here on our own floor. Who would believe such a story, particularly if they discover that there is money at the back of it?"

"But Andrew is right," said Peter. "We are men of God. We cannot be sneaking about the city hiding bodies. Perhaps this is one of those times when we shall be forced to suffer for the Lord."

"This is not what he meant. We all know that we are innocent of these peoples' deaths; hiding them from the authorities is a civil violation, not a moral one. What would it profit us or the new church if we are all sent to jail over such a relatively minor matter? Why provide our political enemies with such ammunition against us? If we had somehow killed the man and his wife, that would of course be different. But we have done nothing wrong, and there can be no harm in the sight of God in burying them, with all the rites due them according to the law, and saying nothing to those who would use the facts against us."

"This is not for men in our position," said Andrew, and the entire room erupted in argument over what to do about the man and his wife. There were cries of "Shame!" and "We are not meant to be body stealers!" and others of "We are innocent - do not give the Sanhedrin power over us!" Peter listened to what he could of the debate, which was precious little since all of the participants were talking at once, and then held up a hand for silence.

"James is right that this can be used against us. Andrew is also correct that we cannot be skulking about the city with dead bodies that we do not know what to do with. James, I appreciate your point about putting ourselves into the hands of the Sanhedrin, but this is one of those times when we will have to trust in the Lord. We are men of God, and it is not for us to be making political decisions of this nature. As faithful men who knew Jesus, the Christ, the Messiah, we must do what is right and trust to the protection of heaven for the rest. Ananias and Sapphira must be buried properly, and the authorities notified."

James could understand Peter's concern over the appearance of the matter - it also made him squeamish to carry dead bodies about the city in hopes of finding a place to secretly bury them. But he could not help but think that in doing the right thing they would be incapacitating themselves before the Sanhedrin.

The apostles then fell into a discussion on what to do with the bodies. Some were for digging the man up and bringing him back to lie beside his wife and then calling for the authorities, while others were for burying the woman next to the man until the next day when they could understand better what had happened. James, miffed at having lost the argument over notification, took no part in the discussion over what to do next. It was finally decided by Peter that they would bury the woman next to the man for the moment, and then notify the authorities later the same day, since it was well after midnight.

Thus the burial detail found itself on the road again, with cart, shovel and body, and headed back to the same spot where they had buried the man. They dug up the hole again, laid her beside her husband, and then covered it over, once again being careful not to make the ground look too neat.

The next morning Andrew volunteered to go to the authorities with the incredible tale that would have to be told, joking as he left that if they did not see him again, he would have joined Ananias and Sapphira, wherever they were. The other James retorted that if Andrew were sent there, so would the rest of them be. They had decided that they would go to the Roman authorities in hopes that they would be so hungry for the tax revenue from the estate that they would not concern themselves with the details.

Andrew did not return until early in the afternoon, and it was apparent that he was tired. His story was soon told to those who were there:

"It was probably a good idea that we should go to the Roman authorities, because they proved to be as greedy as we suspected they might be. But this did not mean that they did not ask questions: 'Where did they die? How did they die? How can we be sure that you did not kill them? How much is their estate worth?' are some of the questions they asked me, and they asked more than once. They would have first insisted that I go to the Sanhedrin, but when I mentioned that there would be an estate to be divided they were much more cooperative. In fact we went to the house first to see what was there, and the petty officials were pleased enough. They stayed with the house while sending me with two soldiers out to find the bodies. These were dug up with no ceremony and carted away. We took them to the cemetery outside the city and buried them, and of course I did most of the work. The two soldiers with me supervised my efforts. I would have come back then, but the soldiers sent me back to the home of Ananias and Sapphira, where I was asked to sign a paper saying that the couple had died with no heirs. I thought of resisting this request, just to keep the authorities on their toes, because the house was already empty: in the short time we were gone to dig up the bodies and rebury them outside the city the officials had emptied the house of everything. It was a small house, so it did not appear that the Romans would keep it also, but they took everything inside. But I thought of our predicament, and signed. It would appear that we are to be bothered no more, at least officially, by the untimely deaths of Ananias and Sapphira."

This did not ease their consciences, however, and James could tell that the others were as bothered by the incident as he was. There was much to bother them: there was the matter of the cause of the deaths and whether or not Peter had anything to do with it; there was the matter of what was to be done with the bodies; there was the issue of which authorities to notify; and there was the continuing issue of the signs that kept appearing among the followers of Jesus - the healings, the speaking of various languages and other items - that left them wondering what their place was.

CHAPTER 11

Not long thereafter James was suddenly stopped on the street by two men whom he did not know. They insisted that he accompany them to the Sanhedrin. He would have resisted, but it appeared that they were ready to use force if necessary, so he went with them.

They led him, surprisingly, to the home of Ananias, whom he had not seen since the day months before when Jesus was crucified. There could be little doubt of the reason for his being brought here, however: they were about to argue over Jesus, and whether or not his followers ought to be allowed to teach in the city.

His guards led him into the house without knocking for admittance, and left him in the same room where he had waited once before. He reflected on all that had happened since, and the changes that had come over his life since he had last seen Ananias: he had seen his brother risen from the dead, had come to believe that his brother - half brother - was the Messiah promised by God for so many years, thrown over all of his past life, including the prospect of a happy marriage, to follow Jesus, and was now the unofficial head of the new church in Jerusalem. It was likely that little had changed for Ananias, save for the fact that he and his brethren had removed a troublesome preacher from the midst of the people. James felt as though he had traveled a great distance, and felt it likely that Ananias had not traveled at all.

This did not mean that Ananias was not prepared to be pleasant, as was usually his way. He entered the room a few minutes later as jovial and jaunty as ever, booming voice welcoming James to his home and apologizing for the inconvenience of the way in which he was brought.

"There are, you see," said he, after the usual hug and kiss on the cheek, "forces at work that must be appeased. As you know I am still a relatively junior member of the Sanhedrin, and I must make it look as though I am handling affairs in the prescribed manner. You know, James, that I would never send for my old friend in this manner if left to my own devices."

"I know that you would not have in the old days, but these are new days, and it can be difficult to know who one's friends are," said James, evenly.

"There is no reason why you and I should not be friends always, James. What is there that can come between us?"

"There is much that can come between two men. But let us not dwell on that unless there is a need. What force are you bowing to by having me brought here today?"

"Always to the point, is my James. I will put it to you simply: there appears to be an active enclave of former supporters of your brother Jesus in the city, and this is distressing to some in the Sanhedrin. Sadly, it has become

208

my lot to keep track of such people to see if they sow the seeds of dissent among the people, or if they still claim, as your brother did, that he was the son of God. Now you know that I am not the vindictive kind, and that I will go to great lengths to avoid conflict. Thus I have been casting about for some way to warn those of your brother's former supporters that if they do not cease their activity on behalf of your brother, they risk the enmity of the Sanhedrin. I have approached you before on similar missions, and I am risking my good reputation with you by asking you again: will you tell them of the nature of the Sanhedrin's displeasure, and see if you can have any influence with them?"

"I wonder you would ask me, Ananias, since my two previous missions to my brother were utterly fruitless. You see that I am not of a persuasive nature."

"Your brother was singularly....uh, stubborn, if you don't mind my saying so. I think you and I have agreed on this in the past. It may be that in the emotional aftermath of the death of your brother his former supporters are simply carrying on the game for the sake of form, and that they can be persuaded not to do so, preferably, or at least to do it elsewhere."

"This is unlike you, Ananias. You are usually the very soul of forthrightness. Yet you bring me here to talk around me. The fact that I am here tells me that you know that I have been involved with the 'former supporters' of my brother, as you call them, and that it is to me that you are talking, not to them."

"As I said, always to the point. You are quite right: I am aware that you have been involved with these people, and I have called you here, as I have said, partly to assuage the anger of the remainder of the Sanhedrin, and partly to talk to you face to face, to see what it is that you are doing, and what you hope to achieve. As for the members of the Sanhedrin, their sole duty and hope is for peace among all our people. We hope there will not be any religious uprisings over the teaching of a man now dead, a man who was an acknowledged blasphemer."

"Then we are in agreement on this, for we also want no trouble with the authorities. But...."

"We?" interrupted Ananias. "Does this mean that you now count yourself among the followers of your brother? I thought perhaps that you simply were providing them with the support that they need in their hour of affliction - it would not be unlike you. Surely this is not the case! You and I have talked this matter over many times, and we have agreed that while your brother was an effective teacher, he held no special wisdom fit for the ages."

"That is the nature of our former agreement on the subject, but there is something that you do not know: I saw my brother risen from the dead on the third day after his crucifixion."

Ananias could only stare at James for the moment, too shocked to speak. When he recovered he began thus: "There have been tales spread about the city and the countryside that your brother had risen from the dead, as he apparently predicted he would do, and it would be useless to deny that his body is missing, but these are easily explained as the rantings and acts of people desperate to believe in a man who ultimately failed them. I confess that this is the first I have heard the tale told by a person I know to be reliable and sensible. Come, come, my old friend, why fall back on such a story as this? Why can you not admit that Jesus was a good teacher, but that he had no other powers to speak of? Why invent something that cannot possibly be true to bolster his reputation?"

"You may call it what you like, but it does not alter the fact that I saw him in the grove of trees on the west side of the city on the day after the Sabbath on which he was crucified. He spoke to me, I touched him, I saw the wounds in his hands and feet. It was he, and he was alive."

"Men cannot rise from the dead, James, you know this. Your brother was crucified for having blasphemed that he was the son of God. You know this to be the result of the law, and it was an unavoidable sentence. You saw him dead on the cross, and I believe you helped to bury him. How can you now tell me that this man has risen from the dead?" Ananias paused to hear James' answer, but James only waited to see if the implications of what he had just said would sink into Ananias without James having to spell them out for him. After a short pause, the priest's eyes slowly widened, and his stare at James became more fixed. "Do you mean to say that you now believe your brother to be the son of God?"

James hesitated for a moment, once again afraid to make the admission in public, but he remembered the words of his brother and said: "That is exactly what I believe. What else could I believe, after he appeared to me on the day of his resurrection? Who else can he be?"

"James, James, I wish that I had not heard you. I wish that you had said anything else in the world but that. God's son is not here - he has never been here. Jesus was born of a woman and a carpenter, not from the loins of God. How is it that this man could be the son of God?"

"Tell me who else he could be if he is able to raise himself from the dead?"

"It is possible that his teaching may have gained favor with God, and that God might have raised him up, but this is not likely to be the case. Surely you will agree that the chances are that his body was stolen by his supporters, and that they have hidden it somewhere to give his story credibility."

"Yes, I will agree that that is what the chances are" - here Ananias brightened temporarily - "but that is not what happened. I was among his closest supporters that morning, and they knew nothing of the matter. Some even denied that it happened, as you are now doing. No, Ananias, you cannot talk me out of what I saw."

"And the mere belief that you saw this...this event....is enough to make you believe that you have seen the son of God? To make you take leave of all your senses, all the history of our people, even of the lessons that your father would have taught you at his knee? You are abandoning everything to follow a dead brother who claims to be the son of God? James, it is not credible."

"Here then we will always part ways: it is credible because I have seen it. I only wish that I had the faith of his followers who believed in him before they had the physical proof that I have had. You cannot know how it has pained me to be guilty of denying him all these years; I have only the consolation that he is punishing me for it now."

"He is? How?"

"That is between he and I."

"Well, if your brother is risen from the dead, bring him here that I might believe also."

"I cannot. He has been taken up into heaven. His closest followers were witnesses to the event."

"Taken up into heaven," said Ananias sarcastically. "That is certainly convenient is it not? You are now spared the embarrassment of producing the man lately returned from the dead so that others might believe." He paused for a moment, collecting himself, and then he returned to his old self to begin again, plaintively: "Can you not see how such a story plays into the hands of your enemies? You claim that he has risen from the dead, but you cannot produce him. Those who would oppose you will say that your story fits the situation as you find it: you claim that he is risen, but you conveniently do not know where he is."

"I grant all of that, and I grant this as well: if we felt the need to make up a story about him, we would certainly have done better than this. We see what our critics will say, but it is out of our power to make up a better story because this one is the truth."

"Very well. It is obvious that we will get nowhere debating the theology of the matter. But there are practical concerns as well. You know that I have been attentive to the needs of your family in the past, when I warned you of the attitude in the Sanhedrin against your brother, and you see that their awful designs were carried out. I am here to try again: the Sanhedrin will not take kindly to former supporters of your brother carrying on for him. They will not view it with kindness. You must tell me what it is that you are attempting to achieve, so that I will know how to act to keep the peace."

James studied this offer for a moment. He had never decided to what extent Ananias warnings about the danger to Jesus had been self fulfilling, if at all, and he preferred to believe that his old friend was sincere in his desire to protect James and his family from the Sanhedrin. But the truth was that he could not feel confident on that score. He had had a report that Ananias had become ambitious since his appointment to the Sanhedrin, and it certainly appeared that he had done little to look after Jesus in the last days before his death, as Ananias had promised to do. Now here he was again, making all of the old assertions about being the peacemaker between the followers of Jesus and the Sanhedrin, with his usual good nature and bluff assurances and sincere expression. Should James follow his lead a third time? Had he been duped either of the first two times? Impossible to know.

"We make no claim on the authority of the Sanhedrin, nor do we wish to have any disagreements with the Romans or any other official body. All we ask is that we be allowed to pursue the meaning of my brother's teachings in our own way. We believe as my brother taught that his kingdom is not of this world, and therefore we are no threat to anyone whose kingdom does belong to this world."

"But you can see what the Sanhedrin response will be: what do you mean when you say 'pursue his teachings in your own way'? This could well mean many different things to different people."

"I do not think so. We care nothing for the powers of this world. We live under them, but otherwise we leave them alone. We do not want power in the sense that you mean it: all we ask is that we be allowed to worship as we see fit. We do not know why this should be a problem. There are others in the city who do not practice the faith of Abraham, and yet you do not persecute them. Why do you single us out for attention?"

"Because you are with us. You are the sons of Abraham, as we are. But you follow the teachings of a man who claimed to be the son of God. And you would lure other faithful Jews to follow you. It is not in the best interests of the city or the Jewish faith to allow the spread of a sect of followers of a blasphemer."

"Are not all those who come and go the followers of blasphemers, since they proclaim allegiance to the wrong God?"

"They are pagans, and there is little we can do about them. They are outside the attention of our faith because they have not even grasped the one true God to themselves. But you would split the believers in the one true God into camps that would believe different things about the Messiah, and that would be the end of the harmony between us."

"There are those who would say that that harmony is already gone, when they see that certain houses in the city are watched for signs of the followers of Jesus, and that one of the followers of Jesus is forcibly hauled before one of the members of the Sanhedrin to explain himself."

"But it could be worse. There is a chance that the battle will escalate as each side becomes more committed to its cause."

"We are not fighting a battle, and we have no intention of taking up arms against anyone. If you mean the battle of the ideas, then there is no cause for concern, because that battle is already engaged."

"How so?"

"The Sanhedrin, the keepers of the flame for the faithful in Jerusalem, has reduced itself to pushing innocent people about the streets of Jerusalem. This sounds to me like the actions of an army that has already lost the battle of the mind, and is counting on ultimate victory won by ridding itself of the other side. Whenever I see one side begin to threaten and harass the other, I believe that the intellectual battle is already won by the latter."

There was a pause here while the two men looked at each other across the floor. They had not sat down since Ananias entered the room, and he now felt the loss. Ananias pointed to a cushion for James and took another himself, and both sat and considered the situation for a moment.

"If it is any consolation to you," James began, "we are well aware of the probability of splitting off from the faith of Abraham, and have spent much time discussing the matter between us. Unfortunately I have no progress to report."

"What is there to discuss?" answered Ananias. "If you believe that Jesus of Nazareth - a man you have called your own brother in my presence - is the son of God, then we are already split. There is no way to reconcile such distinct differences between faiths."

"That is what some of my brethren have been telling me, but I have told them, and I tell you now, that there is no reason why we cannot part ways, if we must part ways, peaceably. It is a wide world, and there is room for more than one answer to the eternal questions."

"You know very well that there is only one answer to the eternal questions."

"Yes, and I believe that I have found it. Nevertheless, if we are to insist that everyone find the same answer, we will have constant warfare till the end of time."

"And it is the position of some in the Sanhedrin that that warfare will begin now if the followers of Jesus do not allow him to rest. Remember that there are many things to consider when one considers the peace in Jerusalem: in addition to the Sanhedrin there are the Romans who must be assured that we have no designs on their sovereignty."

"And so we do not. Why would the Romans care for a small group like the followers of my brother?"

"They care for all groups which threaten their power and their revenues."

"We are fortunate, then, because we do neither of these."

"Do not be so glib, my friend. A nervous procurator may be convinced of many things if his primary goal is to keep his seat and his head."

"Convinced by whom?"

"There are many who want the ear of the procurator for many different reasons."

"I can think of none that would care to whisper in his ear about a small sect that does nothing but meet now and then to talk over the teachings of their departed Master."

"There is more to it than that, you may be sure. There are reports that your number is growing, and that some of Jesus' earliest followers are out of the city attempting to bring others into the fold. How do you think that will sound to the Romans?"

"They will not care a bit when they find that all of these new converts continue to pay their taxes and obey the Roman laws. In fact they may be glad for the fact that we are not revolutionaries out to rid ourselves of them, but peaceable people who simply want to worship. But even if the Romans do not care, there are others who will, I am sure."

"Is this a reference to the Sanhedrin?" asked Ananias, his eyes narrowing.

"Of course, and such a reference is already justified, for here I am, summoned against my will to the home of an old friend who would have me give up what I believe and cause others to do the same."

It looked for a moment as though Ananias would lose his composure, but he recovered quickly. "I have told you, my good, good friend, that your summons was purely for the sake of show. I am sure that we will be able to work out our minor differences, but in the meantime we must allow it to appear that we are confronting each other on the subject. Believe me, it is for the best." James said nothing.

"But I think that enough has been said for now, so let us part ways still friends, shall we?" asked Ananias, extending his hand, preparatory to the usual bear hug. "I have been friends with you longer than anyone else I am still in contact with, James, and I would hate to see us split over such matters as these. Let us talk to each other constantly, in the interests of peace between ourselves and the Romans." James agreed to this, at least on the surface, and then went his way.

James reported his day to the only person there to hear them - his mother - and she agreed with him: it would be wise to accept the olive branch if it were offered sincerely, and that a sharp eye should be kept to discover whether or not it was. No information would pass from James to Ananias.

214

He, or someone, already had spies and thugs deployed - let them do the reporting.

One morning within the next two weeks, when all of the apostles were at their meager morning meal, they heard the sound of approaching marching feet. This was not uncommon, and so they paid little attention to it, but they stopped in the street below, and this caused them to prick up their ears and listen. Within moments the formation broke and there was the sound of heavy footfall on the stairs leading up to the room. Within seconds the door was forced open and the room quickly filled with Roman soldiers.

Peter and one or two of the others demanded to know what was up, but they got no answer. All, save Mary, were forced out of the room and down to the street where they were marched away by the soldiers.

They found themselves taken to the common jail in the center of the city, and thrown in. It was in the lower level of the Roman administration building - the better to keep the prisoners secure by not providing them with tempting windows - and as they descended from the street level it became darker and darker. On the lowest level there was no light save that provided by torches mounted on the walls of the passageway outside the cells and it was difficult for James and the others to see, since they had just come in from bright sunlight. They were then divided into groups of three or four and thrust into cells and the doors shut behind them. No word had been spoken to them.

James found himself in a cell with Andrew, the other James and Matthias. The room was no larger than six feet on a side so there was little they could do but sit and await developments. What little light there was in the passageway outside filtered in through a small window in the door, but it was still so dark that the apostles could only make out each others' vague shapes. The floor was of stone, but moisture seeped in from the surrounding earth, so that the floor was damp at all times. The ceiling was so low that they could not stand up straight. They felt, but did not see, the presence of rats. They found themselves in that cell all that day and into the night. They discussed the possibility that they were being served as Jesus had been, but they could come to no conclusion

They could not know that it was night, since they had no idea how much time passed or whether the sun was still up, but they finally tired of waiting and attempted to sit down and sleep. None dared lay down for fear of the rats.

When their conversation stopped it was easier to hear the rats skittering across the damp stones of their cell, and James found it difficult to relax. He had never been arrested before, as some of the others had, and was not accustomed to the discomforts of the jail cell. What was worse was not knowing their fate, or even why they had been arrested. He wanted to believe that it was somehow tied to the deaths of Ananias and his wife Sapphira, but he could not figure out why they were arrested now, unless it was that the higher Roman officials had got word of the deal and wanted their cut.

But sometime during the night, amidst his dosing off for a few moments here and there, he suddenly heard the door of the cell being tampered with, and was awake soon enough to see it swing open. All four of them were on their feet, to the extent that it was possible under the cramped circumstances, and saw the head of a man lean into the cell and beckon them to come out. They followed him into the passageway and saw that some of the other apostles were already standing there, though they had heard nothing. The man who summoned them out went down the passageway to other doors and brought out the rest of the apostles, though he did not appear to have a key to the doors. It was also apparent to James, who was trying, like the others, to understand who this man was, that the two guards in the passageway just stood and watched the man without lifting a finger to either help or hinder.

When they were all free he lead them up the deserted stairs, through the hallways they had come down earlier, and out into the courtyard outside the building. It was dark out, obviously sometime deep in the middle of the night. There was no moon but the stars shone brightly and there was faint light in the courtyard provided by torches on the walls. They saw no one else.

For the first time there was enough time to examine the man who had freed them. He was dressed all in white, and it appeared to be white of a fine linen though it was but a simple cloak. He wore sandals on his feet, and they too appeared to be expensive. His hair and beard were of a lighter color than James was accustomed to seeing in the area, and this, combined with the quality of his clothing, suggested to James that he might have been a Roman official. He must have been a well placed one to free them all without so much as a peep of protest from the guards on the inside or on the outside of the jail.

They all began to ask the man who he was and what it all meant, but he said to them, "Go to the temple and teach the people there - tell them all the words of this life." With that he began to walk away from them, and quickly disappeared into the darkness.

They all looked after him, but it was clear that he would not be back, and Peter said, loud enough for all to hear: "It is God who has brought us out of our prison. Let us do as we have been told do." They returned to their room for the rest of the night to get some sleep. On their way they discussed the matter of their release, and all agreed that it must be the work of God: there was no reason to be arrested only to be turned out like this in the middle of the night. The man who freed them was obviously known to the Romans since they did nothing to stop him, but that would irritate the Sanhedrin the more, since it was the opinion of all that they had been arrested at the behest of the Sanhedrin, who had now been foiled. They were sure they had not heard the end of this matter.

After a brief silence, Andrew asked no one in particular: "What if it was the Lord who rescued us?" None of the others believed that it had been Jesus, because he did not look like the Lord as they remembered him.

But Peter added: "It was not the Lord himself, but an agent of the Lord. This is why the Romans allowed us to leave - they were powerless to stop us. It is a pity that we did not see the man who was reported to us to have been in the Lord's tomb on the day that he rose from the dead. This might have been the same man."

All thirteen reported to the temple the next morning after eating a huge meal - they had not been fed at all the day before - and began to teach there as they had been instructed to do. They gathered a large and attentive crowd about them, and talked of Jesus, his life, his suffering and death and resurrection. There were some hecklers amongst the throng, but for the most part they listened attentively. But about mid morning, while still teaching, they again heard the sound of marching feet, and knew instinctively that it was for them. They were approached by Roman soldiers again, and again marched away. Instead of going to jail, however, they were marched inside the temple to the council chambers of the Sanhedrin.

There they found the Sanhedrin already in session, and the rows of benches filled with observers. The high priest Caiaphas sat in the only chair in the room, and the apostles and James were marched to the middle of the open area in the center of the room. They were addressed by Caiaphas.

"You were arrested yesterday. How came you to be out of the jail overnight?"

"We were released by a man dressed all in white," answered Peter, who was obviously choosing his words carefully.

"Was this man a Roman official?"

"We do not know who he was. He came to us in the night and released us, and then bade us teach this morning in the temple."

"He bade you to teach in the temple?" asked the high priest sarcastically. "Do you mean to tell me that the man who released you from jail is one of your own followers?"

"We have no followers - we are all disciples of the Lord Jesus," answered Peter. "We do not know the identity of the man, except that we believe that he was an agent of the Lord, sent to free us that we might go on with our teaching."

There were catcalls from among the assembly at this, and Caiaphas answered, again sarcastically, "Now it was not a Roman, or even one of your followers, but God himself who freed you? You have powerful allies indeed." There was laughter at this from among the throng.

"It was not God himself who freed us, but an agent of the Lord. And yes, we do have a powerful ally." Again there were catcalls and hooting from the assembly, but Caiaphas silenced them with a raised hand. He looked them over for a moment.

"I am accustomed to seeing and hearing of twelve of you since the time of Jesus. Yet I see thirteen here today. That must mean that I am in the presence of the brother of Jesus, who gave up everything, including an advantageous marriage, to join his followers. Which of you is that brother?"

James stepped forward, out of the middle of the group, and said, "I am James, a half brother of the Lord Jesus." James was nervous, though he tried to hide that fact when he spoke. Most of the others had been arrested before in their travels, and this was not new to them.

"You are a half brother, now? I had not heard this. How is it that you are a half brother?"

"We were conceived of the same mother, but not the same father."

"Who were your fathers?"

"My father was Joseph, of Nazareth, and Jesus' father is God." There was an immediate and powerful uproar at this, and the entire room was in tumult. There were cries of "Blasphemy!" and "Jail him!" and "Jail them all!" James looked around the room and it appeared that all of the people there were against him. Even Joseph of Arimathea sat quietly, as did Ananias, both on side benches. Behind him sat another man sitting quietly, and he proved to be Nicodemus. Caiaphas allowed the crowd to rage for a moment, and then silenced them with a raised hand.

"You know that your brother was crucified for just such a statement. Is this what you are hoping for as well? I am told that you were on the hill the day your brother died. You saw how he suffered. Is that what you want for yourself?"

"My brother told me that I would serve him, and if I must serve him by dying as he died, then I will do so." There were whispered words immediately behind him from the apostles: "Well said!" and "Let him have that for his next meal," and one or two hands clapping him on the back and shoulders. Caiaphas regarded him benignly.

"I see that you stay together. Very well, that is what I should do as well, if I were attempting to build my life around calling a condemned blasphemer the son of God, and convincing others to do the same." There was laughter around the room at this. "You are a stiff necked, willful bunch, and yet we on the Sanhedrin have no desire to repeat the sentence given to Jesus. We are willing to be tolerant..." (James was not so sure of this, looking around the room and seeing the angry faces.) "...but we are not willing to see you spread revolt and disobedience among the citizens of Jerusalem. You have been told before, Peter, as the leader of this group of....this group, that you are no longer to teach the doctrine of this Jesus. Why do you persist?"

"We have been bidden by God to teach the word of his son Jesus. We must obey the word of God before we obey that of men." There was another uproar in the room at this, and James was somewhat afraid that some of the people would storm down off of the benches. Peter and the others seemed unperturbed, and James tried to be also. Caiaphas looked at them malevolently, and let the crowd rage on.

Out of the corner of his eye, and from the left of Caiaphas, James saw a man moving down from the benches and toward the floor. He walked out on the floor toward where the apostles and James stood, but he walked slowly and calmly, and did not appear to be a menace. He stopped between the apostles and Caiaphas and raised his hands. Caiaphas did the same, and the noise gradually stopped.

"I would speak with my brethren on the Sanhedrin without these men present," he said. Caiaphas wanted him to talk to the entire assemblage, including the apostles, but the man refused. Finally Caiaphas summoned the soldiers again and bade them remove the apostles, which they did. When they were out of the room they began to discuss among themselves who the man might be, but their guards would not let them talk. They had time to discover only that none of them knew who the man was. They waited in the anteroom for perhaps ten minutes, and then the door opened and they were brought back in.

"Our brother Gamaliel has made some excellent points where you are concerned," said Caiaphas, and we will abide by his suggestions. Hear me: you are again reminded that you are not to teach the doctrine of this Jesus in the city again. There will be dire consequences if the Sanhedrin hears that you continue to teach and to convert others." He turned to the Roman soldier who was the head of the detail guarding them and said, "Take them away and give them twelve lashes each, and then let them go." With that they were surrounded again by their guards and led away.

James felt an odd sensation in his stomach when he heard Caiaphas pronounce that they would be scourged. He immediately felt fear - he had never had any such punishment administered to him before. But he looked at the others as they were led out of the room, and it did not appear to him that they were as bothered by the sentence as he was. They appeared calm and confident to him, and it even appeared that one or two of them enjoyed the prospect. He knew this must be wrong, and chided himself for not being able to properly read their feelings even after having been with them for so long.

They were led out into the streets of the city and off to the Roman administration building where they had been in jail the night before, and thence to an inner courtyard. In the grassy center of this courtyard there were three thick wooden poles planted in the ground, each having a height of about seven feet. On two sides of each pole near the top there were metal rings, and hanging from these rings were short lengths of rope. James realized with a sinking feeling what they were for: he and the others would be tied to these poles while they were whipped.

The apostles were forced to stand in a line near the poles while the leader of the detail disappeared inside the building. He came out carrying three short whips, each with a small handle and many strands of leather with which to beat the victim. They picked Peter first, stripped him of his garments, and tied him to one of the poles. They then took Andrew and Matthias, stripped them, and tied them to the other two poles. The whips were given to three of the guards, and the leader told them to begin, and he would count the strokes.

All three guards laid to with a will immediately, so that they first three blows fell almost simultaneously. First there was a loud whish as the whips cut through the air, and then a sharp crack as they landed on the backs of the three men. All three cried out in pain, blood began to flow from the wounds almost immediately, and James and the others started involuntarily at the sounds of the whips landing and the cries of the men. James feared for a moment that he would be sick. Again the whips whistled home, again they cracked on the backs of the men, and again they all cried out. James started again, and nearly fainted from fear and rage. Ten more times did the blows land, but none of the men stayed conscious that long. At the end of twelve blows they were all untied and allowed to fall to the ground, lying in pools of their own blood. Others soldiers pulled them out of the way to make room for the next group of three.

James was among the third group to be selected, and so had to watch the punishment once more. When he was selected for the next group he nearly fainted again, so great was his fear.

The guards supported him up to the pole and stripped his cloak off of him, leaving him naked as the others had been. This was humiliating, in addition to the indignities to come. They then stretched his hands over his head and tied them to the rings on either side of the center pole - so high that he had to stand on his toes to support his weight. James looked to his right and left in fear, and saw that he was being punished with Bartholomew and John. He found it hard to breathe and hard to support his own weight on his legs, so great was his trepidation.

Once he was securely tied - so secure that the ropes threatened to cut off the circulation in his hands - the guards stepped back. At a word from the leader James heard the whish of the whip through the air, and felt the crack on his back. It was a cutting, slicing pain, rather than a dull, throbbing one.

The impact felt as though many knives had suddenly been applied to his back and then dragged across his skin. The impact took his breath completely away, so that he could not even cry out. In the interim between the lashes the wounds on his back burned as though they were on fire. There was only a brief pause, however, before he once again heard the whish of the whip and felt the crack on the lower part of his back. He had been about to recover his breath when this latest assault took it away again. Now his entire back burned, and he could feel the blood oozing down his back, over his buttocks, and down the back of his legs. Another brief pause, another whish, and another crack on his back. With each application of the whip his body involuntarily jumped, and he attempted to free himself from his bonds. The jailers were expert at their work, however, and he could not move his hands. He wanted to squirm around to the other side of the pole, but he could not move in any direction.

Another pause, another whish, another crack on the back, and James at last found his voice, crying out in agony. Had it only been four lashes thus far? Had he eight more to go? How would he endure this torture eight more times? At that moment, for the first time in the ordeal, he thought of God and of Jesus, and cried out to them: "Oh my God, my Lord Jesus, spare me!"

But nothing changed. Another whish, another crack on the back, and more blood dribbling down his back, twirling around his legs, and running on to the ground at his feet. He cried out again: "Father in heaven! Have mercy on me!" In the brief interlude between his prayer and the next landing of the whip he could hear his compatriots crying out also, though he could not understand what they were saying.

His back was completely open now - there was no new spot for the whip to fall. Thus each blow landed where another had already been, cutting deeper where his flesh had once been, ravaging the nerves that had once been under his skin. He kept trying to squirm this way and that, hoping that one of the blows might land elsewhere on his body, but he had no room to move.

James had occasionally injured himself in the carpentry shop, but he had never know pain like this. He could not think clearly, he could not ignore the pain, he could do nothing, it seemed, but feel every separate line on the whip as it landed on his back. What was worse, as the ordeal continued, the blows seemed to come further apart, increasing that moment of anticipation when James knew that the next blow was due, but not knowing exactly when it would come or where on his bloody, open back it would land.

Each blow landed where the others had been, and the guards were thorough in the way they spread the torture all over his back, so that there was nowhere that was not stripped of skin and bleeding profusely. James guard was apparently playful, and was careful to land at least two blows on his bare buttocks, causing James to scream the louder. Another blow near the top of his back allowed one of the lines on the whip to reach his right ear, cutting it like a knife and increasing the agony.

James finally lost count of the blows, but his prayers were answered when he passed from consciousness before the ordeal was over.

He awoke to find himself lying on his stomach in the grass near the poles, but far enough away to be out of the way. Three of his brethren were tied to the poles now and receiving the same treatment he had received, but he could not even pull himself together enough to see who they were. He was immediately conscious of his back - it stung and throbbed and ached all at once, and there was nothing he could do about it. He seemed to be on fire between his buttocks and his ears. He could hear those on the poles at the moment screaming and praying, he could hear the whish and the crack of the whip as the blows were struck.

He felt sticky and wet, and raised himself enough to see that he was lying in a pool of blood, though it was apparently not all his own. For the first time he noticed that he was lying close to the others of his brethren who had already been whipped. None had risen or managed to dress themselves in their cloaks, which were lying on the ground near them. There were low pitched moans among them, including those emitted by James himself, and he could hear one or two of the men praying. This brought him to his senses enough to mumble: "Oh my God, you have spared your servant. My brother Jesus, forgive my weakness."

It was at this moment that, for the first time, it occurred to James that this was the same treatment that Jesus had received before he was crucified, and he had apparently received more than twelve lashes. There had been some who claimed that Jesus had been scourged twice - once by Pilate and once by Herod. He had then been forced to carry his own cross through the city to the hill where he was finally hung on it. James did not know how he had endured the punishment that he had just suffered. How had Jesus managed to survive his punishment, never mind carry his burden to the hill and then hang on the cross for nine hours? James suddenly felt weak and embarrassed, and now had this inner pain to add to that of his body.

He did not know how long he had been unconscious, but finally he whish and crack stopped, and out of the corner of his eye he could see the last group of men being untied and allowed to fall to the ground, apparently as unconscious as he had been. He sensed that people were walking around him - probably the guards putting their equipment away - and he could still hear the low moaning of some of his friends. He wondered if they were through - the high priest had said to scourge them and then let them go - but he could not raise himself enough to attempt to dress and leave, to say nothing of helping the apostles.

He seemed to hear a gate opening followed by the sound of running feet, and presently he felt the presence of other people around him, and thought that he could hear voices soothing the afflicted. No one came to him immediately, but he soon heard a female voice cry "James!" and felt a woman's hand on his head. He turned his head enough to see his mother looking down at him in alarm, and he felt her push his head back to the ground.

"Oh my son!" she said to him, "What have they done to you? Is there no end to the suffering of my children?" James could not answer, but he could feel warm water washing over his back, apparently being applied with a rag of some sort. It made the pain no worse, but it did not help either.

He lay there quietly, allowing Mary to cleanse his back while he regained his senses. As he did so gradually, he became aware that there were now many people in the courtyard tending to himself and the apostles. He could not at first see who they were, but he began to hear familiar voices, and one or two faces that he caught a glimpse of were known to him to be among the faithful of the city, including the ever present fuller. When he regained the ability to speak he lifted his head and asked his mother, "How came you to be here?"

"When I heard that you had all been arrested at the temple I immediately contacted some members of the church that I knew would help, and we went to Herod's palace to see what would happen. You were not there, but we asked another member of the faithful who works there where you might have been taken, and he told us to come here. We have waited outside to hear of your fate, and someone just this moment has opened the gate to allow us in. We brought water for you to drink - we did not think that we would have to use it to cleanse your wounds. I knew your cry among the others - how it pained me to hear you suffer!"

James lay there for some time, allowing his mother to look after his wounds as best she could, and trying to regain his strength. After a time one of the Romans came out of the building and told them that they had to move on - they could not stay any longer. With that the others who had come with Mary began to help the victims to sit up and dress.

Sitting upright for the first time, James looked about him. The other apostles were in various stages of undress and posture on the grass, each with several people looking after them. There were men and women that James knew to be members of the church from the city; in fact, the longer he looked the more of the people he recognized. They were bathing various backs with great care, covering the same backs with clean cloths or, in cases where there were none, putting on the same cloaks the men wore in.

For the first time two men joined Mary in helping James dress himself and rise. At first he would not let them cover his back for fear of the pain, but his mother convinced him that he needed to do so to keep the insects off. When he finally consented he immediately wished he had not - the pain was exquisite. But they let the cloak down on his back as easily as could be done, and helped him to his feet. He was exceedingly weak from pain and loss of blood, and the two men put his arms over their shoulders and supported him out of the gate and into the road beyond.

When they finally reached the room all any of them had the strength to do was fall on the floor, on their stomachs, to rest. Those of the faithful who had helped them home stayed for some time to help them dress - that is to say, undress - more comfortably. Peter raised his head in a moment of relative quiet and said to no one in particular: "We are truly blessed brethren." He evidently thought there might be a reply to this, but there was none. James thought that possibly he had been affected by the heat, but he said nothing. When it was apparent that there would be no reply, Peter added: "We have been punished as the Lord was punished, though not as badly, and in his name. Did he not tell us that those who suffered for his name would be blessed in heaven? If so, then we have made a step on that path to eternal life." James could not deny that this appeared to be so, and he had heard that there was to be credit for suffering in the name of his brother, but he had always hoped to avoid the possibility. He could not tell what effect Peter's pronouncement had on those listening who were not of the twelve. After a time all of the other helpers were forced to leave by the heat and the crowding. There was simply no room for all those people to stay in that small room. Mary was left to tend them all by herself.

As James lay there he had nothing else to do but consider Peter's remark, and as he considered it gave him more and more comfort. He had survived the ordeal without renouncing anything, and as the pain began to subside somewhat he felt more ambivalent about the experience. He would not want to go through it again, but he had at least done it once, and it was true that he had done it in the name of his brother. He had been told by the apostles many times that Jesus had said that those who suffered for him would be blessed, and this thought gave James a feeling of elation that he would not have expected to come to him at that moment, so soon after the event.

As the others began to perk up, they discussed the matter in more detail, and James found that, to a man, they all felt the same small glow of satisfaction at having some shared suffering with the Master, and at having done so in his name.

"Brethren," said Peter, "I see that we are all the stronger for having been scourged by the Sanhedrin, and that, after the fact has begun to wear off, we are all glad for it. Think what this means to the future of the church: how can we fail if such pain only makes us more devoted to the cause of the Lord

Jesus? What odds can we not overcome if we are rewarded for our pain with such a feeling of triumph? Only think: the battle is won! The church of Jesus will triumph because it will thrive where the opposition is the most intense. We have converts from much of the world already, thanks to the efforts of various people, and no doubt those people will grow in faith. But here, in the holy city, we have ourselves suffered from direct opposition to the message of the Lord, and it has only made us the more determined, and stronger in our faith. We cannot fail!"

James thought that perhaps some reply was called for here, though he could only agree. He had been thinking the same thing, though in not so organized a manner that would have allowed him to put it into words. There were murmurs of agreement from the others, and James noticed that the mood of the room picked up immediately. Within minutes they were all sitting up, though none were leaning on the walls or the posts that supported the roof as they would normally have done, and talking and joking as if nothing had happened. Peter led them in a prayer of thanksgiving, and then in the prayer they had been taught by Jesus, and then they fell to a meal of meat and bread with a will.

CHAPTER 12

It would not have done to try to gather the entire group together under the current clouds, so James moved the meetings around, always holding them for small groups, sometimes outside the walls of the city, sometimes in the marketplace so that they could watch the watchers, sometimes in stables in and around the city. It was quite a juggling feat - to keep the meetings happening on a regular basis, at different locations, and in such a manner that the right people would always hear about them. But James managed to stay ahead of most of it, and was rewarded by the appreciation his small flock showed by attending most of the time. They seemed to look up to him as a leader, something he had not experienced before, no doubt because he was the brother of Jesus, and not because of his teaching ability. He could still not teach on the level that the twelve, even including Matthias, could teach, and doubted if he would ever be able to reach that level.

He encouraged the others to invite likely candidates to join them, even though he recognized the risk that they might invite a spy into their midst. There were some protests over this, since others feared the same thing, but James reminded them that they were being watched anyway, and it was doubtful that they were getting away with anything that the Sanhedrin was not letting them get away with. He told them, if they invited someone else, to inform the outsider that they were being watched, and the price for attending a meeting about Jesus of Nazareth would likely be that they would end with their name on some list kept by city authorities.

For all that some few did trickle in, mostly people who had heard of Jesus and had been wondering what had happened to him. Their interest was piqued by the stories they had heard when he was alive, but then lapsed when they heard of his being crucified. Their interest was revived upon learning that he had risen from the dead and had been seen by many, that his followers still met, and that his brother was the leader of the local group.

They were always self conscious upon their first appearance, but they listened with rapt attention to the stories that James could tell about Jesus, early life, including being lost in the temple, which now took on new meaning to James, and the stories of his ministry told them by the other apostles; the miracle of the marriage feast at Cana, which James used as a self deprecating story against himself - running out to test the water where the men said that they drew it; the crowds who followed him about the countryside; the sermon on the mountain outside Capernaum; his crucifixion and resurrection from the dead. They took it all in, but were especially amazed at his rising from the dead. Most would not have believed it were it not for the fact that James claimed to have witnessed it, and now and again produced his mother or one of the other apostles to verify his story. Unlike the credulous Ananias, who would not believe precisely because it was James and Mary who were telling the story, and who were likely to lie over the matter to give their son and sibling more credit than he was due, these simpler people tended to believe for just that reason, and pledged to join the group.

What exactly it was that they were joining was still a matter of some debate, however. Most were willing enough to believe that Jesus was a great man who deserved a hearing, but some were skeptical of the claim that he was the son of God - the promised Messiah that Israel had been waiting for. Like Ananias, they looked around themselves for the restored glory of the Jewish state, and wondered what had been his purpose, if not that. James had a standard speech for that purpose: he pointed out to them that God had no interest in the state of Israel - he was interested in the people themselves. He had picked Abraham when he was but a shepherd with a small family living the life of a nomad. Had he wanted grandeur he could have chosen the Egyptians. Lastly, and most tellingly, he showed them that no one else could have performed all of the miracles attributed to Jesus, including the raising of Lazarus and himself from the dead, unless he had the power of God. None of the great prophets could claim such feats as these.

This was enough for many, and they accepted him, while others remained skeptical. It was at this point in the discussion that someone would always bring up the question of the relationship between the followers of Jesus and the established faith. This was a ticklish issue for James, as it had been for all of the twelve and all of the followers, but he approached it head on. He told them that they were still free to obey the law of Moses, but that Jesus had been the fulfillment of the prophecies of the scripture, and that he had given them new laws to live by. He further pointed out that Jesus had called all men to God, not just the Jews, and that Jesus had greatly simplified the rules for the faithful into two paramount commandments. This frequently had the desired effect, particularly for those who might have smarted under the heavy hand of the Sanhedrin. But others were turned away to learn that this new group considered itself a new church and did not intend to follow the law of Moses as their forefathers had done. For all that there was a net gain in membership, and, James was pleased to note, no losses from among the original crowd.

For those that remained there now appeared the next question: if they were indeed joining a new church, what was the symbol of their conversion? There were no rites to solemnize the event, no habit that could be called on to validate the conversion. There was some talk of a baptism of some kind, perhaps, someone suggested, as John used to do. Nothing was agreed on, and James was left with the uncomfortable alternative of telling the new people that he would address the matter with the twelve, but that for now they should simply consider themselves members of the faithful.

James believed that the twelve would want to baptize in the manner of John, since that was the first rite associated with Jesus and his movement and since it was also the Jewish way. But James was timid about making such decisions by himself, since he felt somewhat inferior to the longtime followers of Jesus. Peter was now acknowledged by all to be the Earthly head of the new church - let him decide what was to be done. As it turned out, the twelve, lead by Peter, opted for a simple baptism in water, signifying the cleansing of the soul of its sins. This ritual washing would be accompanied by a public repentance for all sins, and acceptance of Jesus as the Messiah and son of God.

Many of those who came to Jesus in the early days were desperately poor, and it occurred to James to attempt to minister to them in the same way that he had done in Nazareth. The twelve agreed that something needed to be done, but that there were simply too many, given the successes of the apostles, for one man to minister to. It was also true that some of the Hellenist people among the converts believed that their families were being neglected by the Hebrew members of the faith, and they protested to the twelve that they did not get their share of the common goods. The twelve did not want to give up their preaching to fill this office, so they decided to elect from among the faithful seven deacons who would take the matter in hand. This was done, and so great was the spirit of the people that all seven accepted the offered post as someone else might accept a large fortune.

Over the next few weeks the persecution of the followers of Jesus was stepped up, and James found himself unable to speak to Ananias about the matter. He went several times to the priest's house, but was never able to find him home. As before, he found himself largely spared the ignominy of being treated like a second class citizen, barring being followed here and there, but the other known members of the community suddenly found their lives hard.

This was because the former policy of harassment had apparently been replaced by one of active resistance. Members of the community who were known to the Sanhedrin found their homes broken into and looted, businesses and shops destroyed, and were set upon by ruffians who beat them and left them to bleed in the alley or street.

One evening there was a knock on the door of the room where the thirteen men and Mary lived and James opened it cautiously to find Tobias, a member of the faithful in the city and a man whom James had met many times. He insisted on entering with the most horrible news.

"Stephen is dead!" said the man, in the saddest, most depressed tone. "He has been stoned by the mob at the gate to the city."

"What? Stephen the deacon? For what reason?"

"He would not deny the Lord. You know that he has been providing aid to those members of the group that are in need, and preaching to them. Something that he said caused him to be arrested and brought before the Sanhedrin. There they enraged at him, but to no avail. They brought false witnesses against him, just as they did against the Lord, but they could not stand up to Stephen. Finally, as with the Lord, he was accused of blasphemy, and taken to the gate where they stoned him to death!" Tobias was now weeping openly.

"How come you to know of all this?" asked James.

"I was with him when he was arrested, but since he has been a teacher and not I, they had no interest in me. I was not allowed into the trial before the Sanhedrin, but I was told of it by a witness. I followed the crowd to the gate, but I was powerless to help him. At the last he prayed to our Lord for those who killed him, just as our Lord did."

"You say that the Sanhedrin simply turned him over to a mob and allowed them to stone him? What manner of law is this?"

"It may be that they did not wish another spectacle like that when Jesus was crucified, and that to avoid such a scene they simply allowed the mob to take Stephen, all the while pretending that the Sanhedrin wanted to obey the law but were prevented by the crowds."

"This is likely, but it is no excuse. If Stephen has been put to death for his belief in the Lord, then we are all vulnerable. Stephen has not done or said anything that the rest of us have not been saying as well. Are we now to have a bloodbath? Have you anything more to tell me? Very well, then. Go and spread the word to those who have not yet heard, that they may be cautious. I will go and see my old friend the priest Ananias, who seems to have so little influence in the Sanhedrin."

He found Ananias at home this time, and as slippery as ever on the subject. He would not tell James who in the Sanhedrin was behind the persecution, if it was not Ananias himself, nor would he explain why the pressure had been stepped up. Predictably, he stuck to the story that Tobias had concocted - that the mob had been so enraged by the behavior of Stephen that it had seized him from the Sanhedrin and taken him to the city wall for stoning against the wishes of the Sanhedrin. It was all the work of the others, he continued to maintain, he - Ananias - was simply too young and to lacking in influence to alter events. At James's departure Ananias renewed his usual plea that they should continue to talk, and James reminded him that he had not been available much lately for talking, and that the talking seemed to do no good - the pressure only increased.

It was only three days later that James once again found himself the center of attention of the Sanhedrin. He was accosted on the street by two ruffians whom he recognized from past meetings who hauled him to the temple meeting room of the Sanhedrin. There he was left alone, with the strong suggestion that he should not try to leave. He stood by himself for only a moment, until he was joined by a medium sized man about his own age, with a black beard and short black hair. He had never seen the man before, but he guessed just by the fire in his dark brown eyes that he might be at the back of the recent persecutions.

The man stared at James for a few seconds, and then said: "You are James, of Nazareth, brother of Jesus of the same town, who was recently deservedly crucified for blasphemy. That is not really what is important, however. What matters is that you are now a leader of the group of people who believe that this Jesus was some kind of deity; that he was the Messiah foretold to us by the prophets."

"All of this is true," said James. "But I did not hear what you said your name was."

"This is because I have not said - it is really no concern of yours. However, I have no objection to your knowing me, since we may meet often. I am Saul, of Tarsus, and I have been given the power to rid the city of the blight that is the group that calls itself followers of Jesus."

"Blight, are we?" asked James. "This is news to me. I have been in conversation with one of the members of the Sanhedrin, and according to him there is nothing wrong with us that will not be cured by our simply allowing ourselves to quietly die out."

"I do not share that opinion, but there is something to be said for the usefulness of you and others like you to allow yourselves to die out. However, we hear that this is not what you are doing. I have been told that you are actively recruiting so that your numbers might increase, and that you have had some success. This must halt immediately. We cannot allow such a disease to spread within the body of the Hebrew nation. There is only one God, and we are still waiting for him to send us the Messiah."

"I am really beginning to tire of having this discussion with authorities who happen to be against the existence of my brother and those people who are still loyal to him. I will state the case one more time, however, since I have not yet talked to you. My brother, who was crucified by the Sanhedrin and the Romans, has risen from the dead. From this fact, I and others like me believe that he was sent by God to bring us a new law. My brother did not tell us to tear down the old law, or to ignore it, but in addition to it to obey these two commandments: love God with your whole being, and love your neighbor as yourself. We are attempting to love our neighbors, though some of them make it difficult to do, what with breaking into homes and looting them, beatings in the street, and mortal attacks on elderly men."

"How do you know that your brother is risen from the dead?"

"I have seen him, my mother has seen him, all of his twelve followers have seen him, as have other people."

"All of the people who might be interested in the myth of keeping him alive have seen him alive."

"Yes, that is true. If you wish to believe that we went to the trouble to steal his body from his tomb, under the noses of the Roman guard placed there to guard against that sort of thing, and then spread stories about his being risen from the dead, all so that we may suffer persecution at the hands of the Sanhedrin, then please do so. It is a strange sort of loyalty, do you not agree, that would cause such people to suffer harassment and death for the sake of a man whose body is lying in some hidden grave somewhere?"

"Do not take this tone with me. You are an ugly growth on the body of the people, and you cannot be allowed to prevail. There is no way for the Hebrew nation to survive this occupation by the Romans without its being cleared of such divisive types as yourself. Such can only be the will of God."

"You know the will of God? Is it your clear vision of the will of God that allowed you to stone Stephen, a very charitable and kind man, to death outside the city?"

"I am as aware of the will of God as you are, with your dead son who comes back to life but who is seen by no witness who might verify his existence. And yes, I had a hand in the death of Stephen, and I make no apology for that. Perhaps if he had more regard for the law this might not have happened to him. But there is a lesson there for the rest of the followers of Jesus. I have the law of Moses behind me, and the years of faith that is the Hebrew people, over against the teachings of an itinerant who thinks that he is the son of God, and who wrote not a single word that I am aware of. As for the man Stephen, he blasphemed in such an outrageous manner that the Sanhedrin had no choice but to condemn him. But it was not the Sanhedrin that carried out the sentence, but the people of Jerusalem, who tire of these preachers telling them to break the law of Moses. Take heed that you do not follow his footsteps. But I tire of this discussion......."

"So do I."

"The fact remains that you are in contravention of the teachings of the law of Moses and the Sanhedrin, and you are to be silenced."

"The Sanhedrin will be kept busy if it intends to exterminate every person who does not agree with it on the subject of God. I believe they would have to exterminate most of the world."

"The world outside the Hebrew nation is not the concern of the Sanhedrin. It is the concern of the Sanhedrin to see that Jews do not stray from the law of Moses. But speaking of which," said Saul, suddenly adopting a more conversational tone, which put James on his guard immediately, "I understand that the twelve original followers of Jesus, of which group you are not a member, are in the provinces spreading the message of the blasphemer. My compliments: you are quite the aggressive fringe group, to think that the wide world is ready for your message so soon. But then I suppose you would need to make haste - the body will begin to stink anytime now."

"If there were a body the stench would be powerful already. And you are right that I am not a member of the original twelve, though that is through my own shortsightedness. You are also correct in saying that the original twelve (eleven actually - the twelfth is a substitute for the man who condemned Jesus to the Sanhedrin) are in the provinces spreading the good news. But you have said that this is not the concern of the Sanhedrin."

"It is the concern of the Sanhedrin insofar as such liars are able to spread their lies among the Jewish community. You have no doubt surmised that I have been behind the recent attacks on the followers of Jesus here in Jerusalem. It so happens that alarming reports of the success of some of your liars have reached the ears of the Sanhedrin, and I am being sent to Damascus to answer them. I will not be here to watch over you, but I will be replaced in the city, possibly by the priest Ananias. So, fear not: even though I will be gone from the city, you and the others like you will be in good hands."

This last was directed at James with a sneer, but it was likely that Saul did not realize how interesting the piece of information was. It would appear, as James had suspected for some time, that Ananias was involved in the persecution of the followers of Jesus, and the fact that he might replace Saul led one to believe that Ananias might be among the ringleaders, and not a too-junior-to-have-any-influence priest that he would like James to believe that he was.

"I am sure that we are grateful for the attention of the Sanhedrin," replied James sarcastically.

"You are free to go, but if you want to live in peace, you and your followers must renounce your claims to the blasphemer, and come back to the law of Moses."

"They are not my followers," said James, as he turned to go, "but the followers of Jesus. I have no control over them, and want none. They can no more turn their backs on my brother than I can, or than you can turn yours on the law of Moses."

It was apparent that Saul had no intention of turning his back on the law of Moses, because the harassment did not stop. There were no more fatalities, but the action of the Sanhedrin had the desired effect: the small community of believers ceased to function for a time as a group. James thought it best that they lie low for the moment, to see if the immediate danger might pass. He also recommended that those who could move out of Jerusalem and re-establish themselves elsewhere, to be out of the grasp of the local authorities. Some did so over the next few weeks, but most were tied to the city for one reason or another - usually the necessity of earning their daily bread.

James spent a good deal of his time walking about the city in hopes that he would meet members of the community, and he succeeded on several occasions. When he was certain that he was no longer being followed, which was the case after about six weeks, he told those he met to spread the word to others that he could be found in the streets of the city most days, and that if they wanted to talk to him they should find him there.

About six weeks after his meeting with Saul, he received a letter from Judas, a member of the faithful living in Damascus but unknown to James. It read thusly:

"James and those in Jerusalem,

Greetings. Received your warning about the coming of Saul of Tarsus, and was glad for it. He has indeed come, but you will be startled to hear how it came about. As I sat at dinner with my family one evening, two men came to the door bearing a third who claimed to be blind. I did not know him or the men who left him, but they would not take him away, and I, mindful of the admonitions of the Lord, took him in. Imagine my surprise to hear him tell me that his name was Saul of Tarsus. I was struck cold with fear, and motioned to my family standing round about to say nothing of our belief in the Lord. This Saul we laid down on cushions and made comfortable, and soon confirmed that he had lost the sight of his eyes. I asked him how he came to this condition, and he said that he had been struck blind by a light on the road to Damascus, and that he had heard the voice of Jesus telling him to go to Damascus that he might serve the Lord. I feared that this might be a trick, and so said nothing. He lay with us three days, and upon the third a young man came to my door named Ananias (not the priest), who asked if the man Saul was with us. I said that he was, but that he had been struck blind. Ananias said that he knew this from a vision he had received from the Lord in a dream, and that he had come to heel the man. I was afraid at this, thinking that Saul might rise up and have us carried away, but the man Ananias insisted. He laid his hands on Saul and said, "Saul, the Lord Jesus whom you persecuted, and who struck you blind on the road to Damascus has sent me that you might be full of the Holy Spirit and be made well." And at that moment the light returned to the man's eyes and he could see. He immediately fell to his knees praising God and Jesus, and begging forgiveness for all his sins. He then rose and asked us if we were members of the faithful community. We were afraid to answer, but he said "I see that you are. God has given me sight that I might see the truth, and teach it to all." From that moment on he spent his time in prayer and supplication to the Lord and, and, at the end of four days, ventured out into the city to teach. He struck fear into all those of the community who had heard of him, not believing that he had been converted. He caused an uproar among the Jews of Damascus who expected that he would come to drive us from their midst, and they threatened to kill him. We contrived to lower him from an opening in the city wall so that he might escape, and he accompanies this letter to you. We believe that he has been converted because he has spoken in public that the Lord is the son of God, and because he has allowed himself to fall in danger to the Jews of Damascus."

James hardly knew what to make of this missive, and looked up again at the well dressed bearer, somewhat alarmed by the reference to the fact that Saul was accompanying it. But the man was not Saul, but said that he was hidden elsewhere in the city, and seeking an audience with the apostles.

"Who are you?" asked James of the man.

"I am Barnabas, of Cyprus."

"And what is your connection to this man Saul?"

"I heard the word of Jesus from others of the faithful at Antioch, and in one of my journeys to Damascus I met Saul at the home of this man Judas, also a member of the faithful. I had been considering coming to Jerusalem for another purpose, and it suited Saul, the others members of the community and myself that I should bring Saul here to rescue him from the clutches of the Jews at Tarsus."

James considered this for a moment. "Are you convinced that his conversion is true?"

"I am."

"On what basis?"

"I heard the talk in Damascus of his conversion among those who would have been his allies in the persecution of the faithful, and I saw the efforts that the faithful went to hide him. I do not believe that it all could have been contrived. Beyond that, I trust my senses and my feelings on the subject, because he appears to be a truly penitent man."

"I hope you will understand if I hesitate, because this man has been a terror to us here in Jerusalem, and I have been arrested for the sole purpose of being harangued by him myself. During that session I was informed by him that it was his intention to erase all trace of Jesus from any area that he could reach. But how come you to know of this room and the method for gaining entry?"

"I was told of both by Judas of Tarsus. I do not know how he came to know."

"Forgive my doubts, but this is all so sudden and unexpected that I hardly know what to make of it all. Do you know who I am?"

"Yes!" said Barnabas, animatedly. "You are James, the brother of the Lord, said by all to be the most pious and just of men. I am told that you did not believe in Jesus while he was alive, but that he appeared to you after his resurrection, and that you are now among the most fervent of believers."

"This is all true, though I cannot think how you came by it. I have much to make up for, where my brother is concerned. I suppose I should stop calling him that, since at best he is my half brother. But let us get back to the subject at hand. What was your other purpose for coming to Jerusalem?"

"I was a wealthy man on my home island, but I have decided to give over my old life in service to the Lord. Therefore I have sold all my belongings and it is my desire that the proceeds should be shared by the original followers of Jesus. When I made this pact with myself I did not know of you. Of course you are welcome to a share."

With this he pulled from under his cloak a heavy bag of coins that James had assumed was simply the man's girth. He handed the bag to James and said, "This is for the church in Jerusalem and the leaders of it. There is more that I will bring later, but I could not carry it all at once."

He dropped the bag on the floor and it fell open, revealing many coins of varying values from many countries. James was open mouthed with astonishment. When he could recover himself he said, "You mean to hand over all this to the apostles of Jesus?"

"And to yourself."

"But it is so much."

"It is nothing compared to the joy I have found in faith in the Lord. I hope it will sustain the church here for the immediate future."

"It will do that and more. I also surrendered the proceeds of my worldly life to the apostles, but we lived through that in about two weeks. My contribution was nothing compared to this. Are you sure that this is what you want?"

"Beyond doubt."

"It is most generous. On behalf of the others I thank you. I am sure that it will be put to the best use - it is difficult for us to sustain a church here under the present conditions, and you can be sure that little of it will be spent on our persons."

"I am sure of that. I have no fear on that score."

"But you are confident that Saul is now one of us?"

"I am."

James hesitated for a moment, not sure what to do about the man. This surely was one of those moments that Jesus had spoken about when he said that they would be tested in their service to him. He decided to meet the man, but in some spot away from the room, and out of sight of the authorities. He therefore instructed Barnabas to have Saul meet him on a certain street that James knew to be quiet after dark. The man left, leaving James to ponder the problem.

He could decide nothing other than that he had to meet the man to size him up. Thus he set off for the named street after dark had fallen. Upon arriving at the south end of the short street, James saw no one save a beggar on the corner. He walked to the far end of the street and, seeing no one, returned to his starting point. It was here that the beggar accosted him.

"Alms for the poor? Alms for the poor?" James walked over to the man and fished a small coin from his cloak and bent to put it in the man's cup. Suddenly the beggar's voice changed, and he whispered, "James, it is I, Saul of Tarsus." James looked under the hood covering the man's head and recognized the dark hair and beard, and the bright eyes. This time it did not seem as though the eyes were as menacing as before. They were alert and quick witted, but they had a peaceful gaze about them, as though the man had not a care in the world.

"Why do you approach me in such secrecy?"

"I have made many enemies among my former allies in a very short time, and I do not know if the Sanhedrin is searching for me here."

"Keep your hood up, then, and let us walk." So James and his former tormentor Saul rose and began to walk the quiet surrounding streets.

"You are wondering at my conversion - whether or not I have done all this to trick you," said Saul.

"I am."

"I assure you that I am not. On the road to Damascus I was struck blind by a light from God, and I heard the voice of Jesus saying that from that day forward I should serve him and him alone. If I were to trick you, I would not have contrived to have the Jewish population of Damascus searching every inch of the city for me."

"This appears to be true. Why have you come here, if what you desire is to be hidden?"

"I know from experience that there is no better place to hide than in the midst of many people. I have also come to meet the apostles of Jesus, so that they will know that I am one of them."

"They might be difficult to convince of this."

"But you must help me to achieve this. I am to dedicate the rest of my life teaching of the Lord, and spreading his message. Am I to do this without the support and knowledge of his closest friends?"

"If I can convince myself that your conversion is real, then I will be happy to prevail upon the others to believe in you as well."

"What will convince you of my sincerity?"

"I do not know. No, I take that back. I will believe in you, and I will introduce you to the others." James was suddenly overcome with the belief that Saul was telling the truth, though he had no idea why he was suddenly so confident. "I will take you to them. Do you know any of them by sight?" Saul did not. "Very well then. Have Barnabas bring you to the room tomorrow night at this time, and we will see what happens. I can guarantee nothing about their reception."

James fretted over the matter all the next day because he could see where the others might not accept the story of Saul as he had done. There were sure to be recriminations from those who refused to believe. Perhaps the testimony of Barnabas and the letter from Damascus might carry some weight, but it would be a near thing.

As the appointed hour approached all of the men and Mary were gathered in the room, as was customary, for their evening meal. James had told them of the appearance of Barnabas and his gift, partly because it concerned them all, and partly because it might give the story of Saul some credibility when they heard it for the first time. They were eating their usual fare, in keeping with Peter's admonition that they should not spend the money on themselves, and when it appeared to James that they were all satisfied and comfortable, he broached the subject.

"I am expecting a guest tonight - a new member of the faithful."

"He must be a special member to be invited here. This is not something that we can do often, since there is not room to invite all of them," said Peter.

"Perhaps he has a gift for us too?" asked the other James, to general laughter.

"I could not hope to be the bearer of such good tidings twice in one lifetime, to say nothing of twice in two days." James' plan was to introduce the man slowly by allowing the brethren to read the letter, but there now came the telltale knock on the door, and James rose to answer it. On being assured as to who was there, he opened it and allowed them to enter. The light in the room was dim, coming only from three torches on the walls, but the two newcomers, Barnabas and Saul, had to blink for a moment to adjust. It was clear that none of the others knew either of these two by sight, because no objection was raised immediately.

"Brethren," said James, indicating Barnabas, "this is Barnabas of Cyprus, of whom I told you." All of the apostles rose to greet him, to shake his hand, to hug him, and to thank him for his generosity. There were slaps on the back, smiles and laughter as they joked about what good clothes and servants they would be able to purchase with it. For his part, Barnabas seemed overwhelmed by the company he was suddenly in, for he stared at each of the apostles wide eyed, clasped them to himself, and was virtually speechless, except for saying that he was humbled. It was clear that he had heard many stories of Jesus and the apostles already, for at the mention of each name that was introduced to him, he repeated it, as though to cement the face that went with it to the stories that he had heard. When the tumult died down somewhat, Barnabas cast a glance at James that James immediately understood the nature of, and shook his head in answer.

When he could see that they were anticipating the second introduction, he said simply, "And this is Saul of Tarsus." There was a moment of silence while they absorbed this unexpected piece of information, since Saul of Tarsus was known to them by name, if not by appearance. Some expected that it was a joke, or that they had misunderstood, but when James made no move to clarify the outrage set in, and it was worse than James had anticipated.

There were cries of "What is he doing here?" and "Who has done this?" and "Are we betrayed?" Some demanded that Saul be seized immediately, others that he be shown the door immediately, and others turned on James, demanding to know why he would bring such a man to them. James tried to quiet the storm so that he could explain, but Saul himself became the engine of peace.

In a commanding voice he called to them, "Brothers, let me be heard!" This brought cries of "How dare he call us brothers!" and renewed demands that he be seized and thrown out. But Saul would have his way. "Listen to me!" he said above the din. "I am here and there is nothing that can be done about that. Surely you desire to know how I came to be here, and what is the purpose of my coming?"

This quieted them somewhat, though it didn't settle their minds, and Saul continued, "If I were still the tormentor that you take me to be, I would not need this act to get to you. This room is no secret to the authorities, no matter how hard you have tried to hide it. I am here among you because I am not the man I was. While on the road to Damascus some weeks ago, on the orders of the Sanhedrin to seek out the followers of Jesus, I was struck blind and off my horse by a light. While on the ground I heard the voice of a man asking why I persecuted him. I asked who it was that spoke to me, and he told me that he was Jesus. He told me that I should cease to persecute, and that I should follow him. My attendants carried me to the house of Judas in the city of Damascus, and I was not healed of my blindness until the man named Ananias laid his hands on me. Both of these men are followers of Jesus like yourselves, and they had the same doubts that you have. I recovered for some time in the house of Judas, to regain my bearings and contemplate what my new role would be. I, Saul, the tormenter of the followers of Jesus, then began to teach in the city about Jesus, and urge those that heard me to come to him. This many did, but the elders of the city, seeing who I was and what I was achieving, set their forces against me, and I was forced into hiding. I was smuggled out of the city by others of the faith, and I made my way here that I might meet you. James has a letter from the very worthy Judas of Damascus that will recount the story to you, and my friend Barnabas here can attest to it."

James then produced the letter from Judas and read it to the company, which listened in the same stony silence that it listened to Saul's own story. When he finished the silence continued until it was broken by Peter.

"This is a most interesting story, yet I think that you can understand why we might be skeptical. We are prepared to make sacrifices for the Lord, but we like to think that it is not time yet. A man like you in our midst could learn much that could be used to damage what the Master has built thus far. What can you say that will convince us that you are not a spy, planted here to learn what you can before turning on us?"

"There is nothing I can say that will convince you of that, if you do not believe the letter from Judas and the testimony of Barnabas. I have already been teaching in the city of Damascus, with some success, though not with the knowledge and insight that each of you possesses. I also intend to teach here in Jerusalem, in spite of the animosity that will cause among those who know me and sent me to Damascus, if there are no objections from anyone here. What more testament do you need than the fact that I am willing to antagonize those for whom I used to work?"

"I am not sure that antagonism is what it needed at this moment, even if we are convinced that your conversion was real. We are an infant church, struggling to achieve a foundation on which to build. It would not do to give the Sanhedrin cause to purge us from the city."

"But you are teaching in the city daily, are you not? You are already taking that risk. All I ask is that I be allowed to share it with you."

Peter hesitated and looked around the room at the other faces present, possibly in search of inspiration, but there was none to be had. "Your conversion," he began, "if it is such," - here Saul groaned - "would be like throwing fat into a fire: it would inflame the already tense relations between the Sanhedrin and us. What would they not have to fear, if even the dreaded Saul of Tarsus is become a follower of Jesus? I fear that it will spark them to action that they have not yet taken, assuming as they apparently do that we will die out soon."

"That is what they assume," said Saul, "but never underestimate the distrust of the Sanhedrin. They greatly fear movements such as this, and will do what they can to see that it does not grow. Nevertheless, I am willing to take that risk, if you are willing to have me. Even if you are not willing to have me, I will still be a loyal servant of Jesus for the rest of my life."

There was silence in the room. The apostles looked at Saul and each other, clearly at a loss as to what to do. They preferred not to trust Saul,

James believed, yet they had seen enough over the last few weeks to believe that anything could be possible. Saul seemed to sense this.

"I can see that you still do not trust me, and I understand this, for the moment. But consider: if you do not tell me otherwise, I will be in front of the temple teaching tomorrow morning, exhorting all who will hear to come to Jesus as I have done. I will tell them who I am and what I have done, and dare them to follow the path that I have chosen. For if even I should come to believe in Jesus, a man who persecuted his followers and was involved in the death of one, who are they to doubt? If I can be saved by the Lord, then so should they all be."

"For the moment," said Peter, "I ask that you not teach. We need time to decide what is to be done, and how best to carry on the work of the Lord without calling down the immediate wrath of the Sanhedrin on our heads. I now believe what you are saying, though I cannot say why I believe. You are welcome to stay here with us."

Saul glanced around the room to see how this would be taken, and it appeared to meet with the general approbation of the room - there were nods here and there, and a comment of "That will do for the moment", so Saul accepted with alacrity.

"I do not mean to be troublesome on my first evening among you - an evening that I hope will be the first of many - but it is wise to consider my case quickly. I am sure that the Sanhedrin have by now heard of my escape from Damascus, and it is not unlikely that they will begin to look for me here. Naturally, given all that has happened, they will look among you first."

There were cries of "He will lead them to us!" and "He is a spy after all!", but Peter raised his hands to quiet them. "There may be mischief in all this, but I do not believe it likely. If he wanted to be done with us, he could have contrived a better, easier method than this. James: you are the only one among us who has seen him before his conversion and after. What do you say?"

After a slight hesitation, James said, "I have seen him both before and after his conversion, and I can say only that I believe that the fire in his eyes has changed. He is not the same man he was: when I was summoned before him he burned with the fires of hatred for us and all that we stand for, but now he burns with love of my brother. I was skeptical as you upon first hearing his story in the letter, but I now believe him to be a genuine convert to the cause." He paused here for another moment, and then continued, "It pains me to be the one to say this, given the grievous lack of faith on my own part, but let us remember to have faith in my brother. See what a powerful tool Saul would be for those of the faith: who better to show that all can be saved, if they will just turn to Jesus?"

This brought a hush to the room, and James could not help but be pleased at the effect that his short speech appeared to have had on the company. He habitually said little in such debates, preferring to defer to those he considered more knowledgeable than he, but it did not appear that the others were offended by his forwardness or his admonition to be faithful. He looked specifically for his mother, and found her smiling at him.

There was a short period of silence, and then Peter said, "We will consider the matter in the morning. It is late. You are welcome to stay here, as I have said." The others turned to settle themselves for the night, and accommodated Saul in his search for space on the floor. James felt that a great battle for the hearts and minds of the people had just been won: Saul would be an important ally.

CHAPTER 13

The night was a short one, however. James awoke after having slept some little while because he heard a noise outside the only door to the room, near which he had been sleeping. He was instantly awake, as a person will be when that odd sixth sense tells them that something is amiss. His first inclination, as he lay there straining to hear more, was that Saul had indeed betrayed them. But Saul had claimed that the authorities knew of the room; they could have come at any time. Why would it be now? Perhaps so that Saul could be there to see the arrest of so many of the leaders? Before he could speculate more, he heard the familiar coded knock on the door, though it was so low that for a moment he believed he must not have really heard it. He listened again and heard it again, only a little louder than previously. As he got up to see who might be there, he started to note that Saul, who had bedded down next to him, was also awake. Had he anticipated this visit? Saul grabbed James' forearm as he rose, which James found somewhat comforting.

"Who is there?" he called softly at the door.

"Tobias. Open quickly, I have news from the Sanhedrin."

As James opened the door the others in the room awoke, and James could hear muttering that they had been betrayed by Saul. But Tobias, one of the faithful in the city, quickly dispelled that.

"A fellow believer who works in the temple has told me that a messenger has arrived from Damascus looking for Saul of Tarsus, who it is claimed is converted to us. They are sending soldiers here this moment to search for him. I know he is not here, but what can it mean?"

"He is here," said James.

"Saul of Tarsus? Here? Then he has converted?"

"So it would appear," interrupted Peter. "James, take Saul to the home of one of the other faithful and hide him there for the moment. Is there anywhere you can go that is not known to them?"

"There are some new members that are not known to them yet, and they will help. But it is not wise that I go, for I will be missed, and that will arouse suspicion. Let Tobias take him."

"Very well then. Quickly Saul, take all of your belongings, and leave nothing that would tell them you have been here." As Saul gathered what little he had, mostly clothes, Peter said to James, "You are right that you would be missed. For their purposes you are one of us."

"I am to escort Saul of Tarsus through the streets of Jerusalem to the home of another member of the faithful?" asked Tobias. "It is well that I have seen so much already, or I would say that you all are taken by satan."

"You are no more surprised and confused than we," said the other James.

"We have spent the last evening debating whether we should accept him or throw him out the window," added Matthias.

"I believe that we know the answer now," said Peter. Saul was ready and came to the door. "James, tell Tobias where to take him, but do not let us hear. The fewer people who know where he is, the better for him and for us all."

James walked out on the small landing with Saul and Tobias, and mentioned the name of a person known to Tobias in his ear, and sent them on their way. Saul would not go without leaning quickly back into the room and calling, "Thank you, thank you," to the apostles. James then re-entered.

"Let us all go quickly back to bed so as to appear to be asleep when they come," he said, and all of the apostles laid down again.

They had not long to wait. Within the next five minutes they heard heavy footfall in the approaching in the street and then climbing the stairs to the room. The door was bolted but the intruders simply applied two shoulders to the problem and broke it down without attempting to rouse the sleepers.

There were three Roman soldiers in the room, all holding torches, when James and the others had adjusted themselves to the light enough to see what was going on. They were led by one of the brutes who had accosted James in the street.

"Where is Saul of Tarsus?" the man demanded.

"This ought to be the last place that you would look for Saul of Tarsus," replied Peter.

The brute glared at him for a moment, obviously trying to decide whether or not he was being toyed with.

"If he is in the city he has been here," the man finally said.

"That may be true, but if he had been here we would not be here now. You would likely find us in the jail."

"Do not tell me that you have not heard that he has gone over to your side," the man said, menacingly.

"We would be glad to hear that he has come to us, though we do not consider ourselves to be a 'side'. But the only reason he would come to our 'side' is to arrest a larger group of us at once, rather than the usual two or three. Why would a man who is responsible for the murder of one of our number come to us?"

"That is something that I cannot answer, since I do not know why anyone would come to you. Nevertheless that is what he has done while in Damascus. He was sent there to control the problem of believers in Jesus, and he became one himself. He escaped from the authorities there, but he will not escape here." Turning to the soldiers he said "Search the room!"

"'Search the room?'" asked Peter. "What need is there to search? It is a single room and you can see all that there is to see. There is no one here but us, and we know nothing of Saul of Tarsus."

"Better for you if you do not," said the man. "Anyone who hides him will be guilty of his own crimes, and will suffer the same punishment."

"What crimes has he committed?" asked Peter.

"He is a traitor to the nation, since he has given up his position to take sides with the opposition."

"Does that not make each of us traitors as well?" asked Peter.

"In my mind you are all traitors, and if it were up to me I would have cast you into jail long ago. But it is not mine to say." As he spoke the soldiers overturned the simple bedding that lay on the floor, tore all of the clothes they could find, threw all of the leftover food onto the floor where they proceeded to walk on it, and destroyed everything that could be destroyed. There was little question that Saul was not there, and no need for the destructive rampage that the soldiers went on. This was harassment and nothing less.

As the man and the soldiers were leaving he turned to Peter and said, "You will tell Saul of Tarsus that we are looking for him, won't you? And tell him that the faster we find him the less often this will happen."

When they were gone James and the others were left in the dark, since they had not had time to light their own torches. They opted to push the mess aside and leave it for the morning, since there had been no fresh food anyway, and to try to go back to sleep.

Their inventory in the morning was a painful one. None had any clothes left but those on their backs, there was no food left that was edible, and there were no blankets remaining with which to cover themselves at night.

"We will have to replace much of this," said Matthias, ever good naturedly, "but it might be useful not to spend much money to replace all of it. I have a feeling that we will have to face this again."

"No doubt of it," said Peter. "When they return, let them find nothing but the meanest rags to destroy. I see no reason to store food at all: it will only be wasted. James, how far may we impose on the flock here in Jerusalem for food?"

"They will support us willingly, but by asking them to do so we risk bringing the wrath of the Sanhedrin down on them. I suggest a daily trip to the market for our needs until this crisis has passed."

"Very well then. We will take turns buying food every day until they have stopped harassing us. Is there any one here who must have an immediate replacement for what was lost last night?"

All of the apostles had been living frugally since they began following Jesus, and so really lost little in the ransacking of the room. Since they had not had the clothes taken off of their backs, none had any immediate need for replacements. The two James were dispatched to purchase the day's food with funds that had been safely deposited with Joseph of Arimathea, whom the authorities would not dare to interfere with. They walked about the town for some time to ensure that they were not being followed, and then went to Joseph's house where they were provided with some of their funds by an agent. They did not see Joseph because he was not in town at the moment.

Their precaution was well founded, because they were raided each of the next three nights, ostensibly in search of Saul of Tarsus. They knew, however, that the room was being watched, and that the authorities knew very well that Saul was not there. In the meantime, through a series of messengers they kept Saul moving about the city, never staying in one place for more than two days. He moved about at night, and never left his hideaway during the day, even to relieve himself. James did not see him after he was spirited out of the room that first night, but he heard amusing stories about the aghast faithful whom Saul stayed with when they first heard who their charge would be.

But it quickly became apparent that the city would not cool down for Saul. The apostles hoped to wait the storm out, thinking that the authorities might give up the search, or, better yet, get over their anger, but they could see no cooling of the ardor which drove them to search him out. The daily searches of the apostles' room continued, and gradually spread to the homes of other members of the faithful. The crowds that the apostles managed to gather when teaching were frequently dispersed by soldiers or ruffians apparently sent by the Sanhedrin. Something would have to be done. A parley was held in the room with all of the apostles present, along with James and Mary, and with one of the faithful keeping watch on the stairs so that the meeting might not be overheard.

"There can hardly be any doubt that Saul is a convert to the faith," began Peter, when they had all settled down. "The Sanhedrin would not go to this much trouble to find him merely in the interests of finding us out. It is also true that we need no smoking out, since they appear to know where we are every moment of the day. We welcome him to the number, but we cannot allow him to stay in Jerusalem: as much as we are all prepared to suffer for the cause, there is no need for our suffering to take the shape of hiding Saul from the authorities. We must see to it that he is taken from the city and sent somewhere that will allow him to live a normal life."

"It is difficult to know where to send him, since it appears to be the goal of the Sanhedrin to hunt him down. If they pursued him in Damascus and Jerusalem, where is there that they will not pursue him?" asked Andrew.

"We must send him out of the reach of the Sanhedrin, possibly back to his own city of Tarsus," said Peter. "He will not be safe in Judea or Galilee, nor, I fear, in Samaria. It seems a shame to send him away when he so clearly wished to be among us, yet there is no choice. Who will tell him? I suppose it must be you, James, since you are the only one who knows where he is."

"Even I do not know where he is at the moment," said James, "though I can probably find out and send a message to him. But what are we to do? Arrange a caravan for him? Put him on a ship?"

"We will have to see what is leaving the city next that we can smuggle him on to. If there is a caravan in the next few days, so much the better. Whatever we arrange, we must not be seen to be arranging it. James, you must have some contacts among the faithful that will look into the matter for us."

"I have, though it will take time to see that it is done without appearing to be done. But never fear: I will look into the matter, and use all of my experience at smuggling people out of the city to see that it is done properly." This brought laughter from the group.

"Here we all thought that we were special since we were the chosen of the Lord, and we come to find that while we still live we are outdone in the eyes of the authorities by one of their own number," said the other James. "Oh well, the Lord said that we would suffer for him." Again there was laughter around the room, with James joining in.

Without waiting for the meeting to adjourn, James left to talk to some people that he knew about the situation. He saw that he was followed, and was careful to walk around the city for some time, in hopes of losing his pursuers in the crowd. They would not be lost, however, so James went to the marketplace to speak to one of the stall keepers there.

James walked up to the stall and began to inspect the fruit on sale there, and kept an eye on his watchers out of the corner of his eye. When he saw that they would not advance within hearing distance, he told the man of the problem in a low voice, and was relieved that the man believed him concerning the object of the search, and did not have to have proof of what James was saying. James told him quickly that transportation out of the city was needed as soon as possible, and that he should talk to some of the others about getting Saul in a caravan that would take him to the coast where he could catch a ship. He also asked the man to pass the word on to Saul, since James did not know where he was and did not want to be seen with him anyway. James would stop by again the next day to see if there was any progress. With that he purchased twelve apples and went on his way.

Next day the man told James, again out of earshot of his followers, that there was a caravan forming that would leave the next day for the coast, and that it would be possible to arrange to have Saul in it. He would need money and food for the journey, and the caravan leader would have to be paid off to cover for Saul if he were stopped. James raised his eyebrows at the figure mentioned, but agreed that it would have to be paid. James confirmed that word had got to Saul and that he was ready to go, and that he understood that he was not being sent away by the apostles simply because they did not want him around. With that James purchased some apples and apricots, and went on his way again.

James reported the results to the apostles, and they considered what to do.

"Can this be done without any of us appearing?" asked Peter, after James finished explaining what was about to happen.

"It is possible," said James, "but it may not be desirable. We would not want Saul to leave here with the impression that we are cowards hiding from the authorities, afraid to show our faces most times. At least one or two of us ought to make the effort to see him one more time." There was general nodding of heads about the room, and Peter agreed.

"Who will go? Perhaps you James, since you have been the instrument of all this, and since you were the first to believe. I will go also, as will Matthias and Andrew. For the rest, we will have to be content sending greetings to our new brother who has brought us so much attention. For us all to leave at once would be folly. But James, are the authorities likely to be watching this caravan for just such an attempt?"

"They may be, but it is also possible that they will assume that Saul would not leave the city since he came here to be with us."

"All precautions will have to be taken nonetheless. When next you see your contact, ask him how this is to be handled." James felt somewhat embarrassed that he had not considered all the angles, but he was not experienced in skullduggery. "The four of us who would see him must not even leave the room together, but must go separately to some meeting point, if one can be arranged. I assume that this indulgence on the part of the caravan leader will not come free, unless he is a member of the faith." James mentioned the sum, and heard Peter and some of the others suck in their breath. "Well, well, brother Saul is an expensive convert to the faith. This will have us back eating with the faithful some time sooner than we planned. Of course, Saul has helped to pay his own way. When will you deliver the money? In the morning. I see. Obtain the exact arrangements from your contact so that we may contrive to speak to Saul once before he leaves us."

James discovered the next morning that the stall keeper had arranged to have Saul join the caravan outside the gates of the city, that he would have his face colored to look like a Libyan, and that he would be given the appropriate clothes to look the part. This would make it difficult for the any of the brethren to speak to Saul, unless they were somehow able to do so before he left the home of the stall keeper. James said that he and some of the others would attempt to be there before time, but not to delay if they were not.

The stall keeper was someone who might have some items to ship now and then. A large crate coming from his house would attract less attention than it would from most others because he did use caravans now and then to distribute his wares, and Saul the new Libyan would be one of the two men who would carry it outside the walls of the city. It was decided that the apostles who were to see Saul would do so one at a time, in hopes of arousing less suspicion than they might all converging on the house at once. Some thought was given to their leaving the room at different times and going circuitous ways to the house, but it was decided that there were no circumstances under which they could risk arriving at the house at the same time. Peter left immediately upon getting directions, and was to be followed by Andrew, Matthias, and James.

When James arrived at the house he found that Saul was already in costume for his trip to the city gate, and James had only a few moments to pass with him.

"James!" Saul called out when he saw him enter the back room of the house. If he had not done so, James would not have recognized him. "I was afraid that they would come between us at the last." The two men shook hands like long lost brothers, though they had actually exchanged very few words.

"Do you think it will work?" he asked.

"There is no way to know until we have tried it, but it is certainly true that we are counting on any sentries being the most stupid people in the world," said the stall keeper.

"Have there been sentries?"

"There are sentries all the time, but it is not all the time that they are looking for this man," said the stall keeper. "It is very likely that they will be watching this caravan for just such a trick as this. We are hoping that they will focus on the crate and not on the men carrying it."

"Well, then, may God be with you," said James.

"And his son Jesus, I hope," replied Saul. "Thank you for all that you have done for me. I will never forget it."

"I have not done very much, and I feel guilty that we are spiriting you out of the city you worked so hard to come to. But we see little choice in the matter."

"That is what you have all said, and I understand. I will be better starting elsewhere under less pressure than here. In fact, it is not likely that I would ever start here. As soon as the authorities find me they will put an end to me."

"Where will you go?"

"I will attempt to take ship for my home country, and find my way back to Tarsus. I know that there are no followers of the Lord there, and I will begin to convert them."

"Are you ready to teach?" James asked. It sounded as though this were what Saul intended, but he had had even less contact with the twelve than James. It was hard to see how he felt so comfortable with the message that Jesus would have taught. James did not feel well versed enough yet to teach on his own: his missions among the people of the city amounted to surrogate teaching for the twelve, and when there was some question he could not answer he always referred it to them.

"Strangely, I do. I do not know why, though the Lord must have given me the will. I have been contemplating the matter these two weeks, and I feel that I have figured out what it is that Jesus meant by his mission. I will write to you and to the others upon my settling somewhere and lay the matter out so that you may instruct me if I have erred. Always remember, James, that faith will prevail. See what it has done to me: I have been converted in the road to Damascus, been thrown over by the people I formerly called my friends and accepted by those I persecuted, and in the two weeks I have lain here my faith in Jesus has only gotten stronger. Every time I consider it I am more convinced that Jesus is the way and the truth. How wonderful that I have been called!" Saul was giddy with the elation that came with the thought, and James said nothing for a moment so as not to interrupt.

"It is time we were off. We do not want to appear to be rushing at the last," said the stall keeper.

"You will hear from me James, and I hope that I will hear from you. Do not fret for me; the Lord will provide." The two men shook hands again, hugged quickly, and Saul took up his burden with the other man and headed out the door for the city gates. James wanted to go there to see that all was well, but he decided that he might arouse suspicion, and returned to the room.

"There is much promise in Saul," he said to the others when he returned. "We are smuggling him out of the city because we fear for his life, and at the end it is he who cheers us."

The apostles and James went about their business that afternoon as normally as they could, all the while wondering if Saul made it out of the town. James had asked that one of the faithful watch the doings at the city gate and report back when he saw Saul safely out of the town. Toward dinner this man came.

"It was a narrow thing," he said in a high pitched, squeaky voice when the introductions had been made. "All was well until they came to the gate of the city, and there they were stopped by Roman guards who insisted on seeing what was inside the crate. Of course they opened it, to show the fruit and vegetables put there for the purpose of throwing such men off track. One of the guards drew his sword to stick in the crate to ensure that no one hid there, but the stall keeper insisted that he not do so, since it would damage the food. This made the guard suspicious," said the little man, increasingly breathless with the retelling of the tale, "and he made them put the crate down so that he could look in. When he could see nothing he told them to unload it so that he could see all the way to the bottom. The stall keeper whined and complained at this, and that made the Romans that much more anxious to do it. Saul and the other carrier kept their tongues.

"When they put the crate down they began to empty it, with the stall keeper demanding, after the unloading of every piece of fruit, to know if they had yet seen enough. He irritated them so that one of the guards finally pulled his dirk and threatened the man if he did not be silent. Saul and the other man both wore hoods and kept their heads down as though they were afraid to look at the guards, and this ruse appeared to work. Saul looked like the proper Libyan in his coloring, and the guard took no note of him.

"When the man could finally see to the bottom of the crate - and he made them empty every piece of fruit from it, probably to spite the stall keeper - they reloaded it and went outside the walls of the city. But the caravan was alive with the men of the temple, and it was a near thing that they were not caught because they all knew Saul. All of the temple men came to look at the crate, one at a time of course, and they were forced to empty it twice more. The stall keeper was furious, though I do not know whether it was true anger or part of an act to deceive the temple men. He stomped and cursed and demanded to be taken to the man in charge of the 'farce', as he called it, and swore that he would never tithe again. I thought that perhaps he might call too much attention to the little group with his carrying on. But perhaps he figured it correctly because no one every paid any attention to the two Libyan porters who accompanied him.

"That is to say that only one man paid attention, and he not for long. He looked under the hoods of both men and he might have noticed that one of the Libyans did not look much like the other, but at that moment Saul pulled his hood back - yes, he did it himself - to reveal that he was drooling from the mouth and looked like nothing so much as a rabid animal. This scared the man off as though he had seen a spirit, and Saul recovered his head and was not bothered again.

"But he could not relax yet because the caravan did not leave at the appointed time. No one knew why it delayed. All of the porters were sitting on the ground talking, owners and traders were stamping and cursing to be on their way, the animals got noisy and testy, and the mood was generally ugly for a time. Finally another group of men came from town to walk through the caravan, and it was obvious to me that they were looking for Saul. They walked by each of the groups looking at all the men, all of the equipment and containers for signs of a stowaway. How it must have tortured Saul to sit there and wait to be looked over by men who were looking for him! This time he kept his hood on....yes, thank you, I would appreciate a drink - I am dry from talking....and when the men finally made their way to him he simply looked up at them with the most foul grin that you ever saw - all drool and foam at the mouth - and I could see the temple men shudder and look away. Me? I was standing very close by in case I could be of assistance. The priest asked me what I was doing there since he knows that I am a member of the temple, but I told him that I had been sent there by my master to see that his shipment got off. No, they do not know that I am among the faithful - I have converted only recently. If they had known that they might have been more suspicious of the people around me. As they were walking on I heard the priest say to the stall keeper that he ought to watch that one (meaning Saul the Libyan) because he had an evil look about him. No, I do not know how he contrived the drool and the foam, but it was a brilliant touch. Once this second group of men from the temple had completed their rounds there were some discussions with the leader of the caravan, and moments after that they were permitted to start on their way. I watched until they had passed out of sight beyond the nearest hills, and then came here to report to you all that I have seen."

James could not completely suppress a chuckle at this conclusion to a long winded story, and noticed that some of the others were having the same problem. But they thanked the man profusely, seeing that he had done his duty so zealously and courageously, and he went on his way joyful to have been of service.

When he had gone Peter said, "He was a worthy aid to the cause, but we are lucky that he did not give the game away standing so close to Saul. How Saul must have suffered to see the man standing there and not be able to tell him to be gone! Well, well, it all appears to have worked out for the best, and we will not hold this man's indiscretion against him."

James and the others spent the next few weeks explaining to the members of the faithful, most of whom appeared to have heard of the renegade persecutor's conversion, that it was real and that he had had to be spirited out of the city for the safety of all. There was great wonder in all this to the faithful since they had all thought that Saul was an implacable enemy, and many saw the hand of Jesus in the matter, just as Saul had done.

Saul dropped out of the collective consciousness of the apostles, James and Mary after a time, other than occasional idle speculation on how he had fared, until a letter arrived from him, hand carried by a traveling member of the faithful, several months later. It read:

"To Peter, James and the brethren,

Greetings. Much has happened since I was spirited out of the city like a traitor, which it would appear that I am, since I have left one camp for the other and will not hesitate to share my knowledge of the opposing forces.

To all those who assisted in my exit from the city: my gratitude and my prayers. There are many whom I did not talk to as I should have done because they simply flashed before my eyes in the press of leaving, but I trust that you will extend my heartfelt thanks to them.

Once the caravan was free of the city I could relax for the first time, and I was certainly in need given the presence of the faithful man who stood near me while the caravan was forming and the Sanhedrin making their rounds looking for me. I was afraid that in his zeal to watch over me he might give me away, but God looked after me.

I took the first ship in Caesarea that I could book passage on, and it took me to the coast of my native land, and I set off immediately for Tarsus. All could not have been better. I am told that there is an active community in Antioch, and thither I may go, if I can be of some help.

I am not the first follower of our Lord Jesus in Tarsus. I have found a small community of a few people who have either heard the Master speak while traveling in Judea and Galilee, or have been converted by those who have.

The community here was aware that our Lord Jesus had risen from the dead, as a result of a traveler passing through the area, though it is not long since the event. How wonderfully the Lord looks after those who are faithful to him!

While the community in this area is small, it is growing rapidly. We are able to teach in the streets and work among those who are most in need of our message, and we have been able to convert both Jew and Gentile.

I have commissioned some of the brethren to act as deacons for me, as you have done in Jerusalem. While they help spread the word they also look after those most in need, and there are many.

Brethren, you do not know the joy of being able to teach in the streets without fear of being interfered with by the authorities. We have not yet converted any high ranking officials, but neither have we been chased into hiding by them. It would seem that the Sanhedrin is a more implacable enemy than pagan Gentiles. Here we are safely out of reach." He signed the letter "Paul".

James sat down to compose an answer to Saul, now calling himself Paul, and then began to search for an opportunity to send it to him.

CHAPTER 14

And so the church grew and prospered, to the extent that it was allowed to by the local authorities. But what the apostles found, which disturbed them somewhat, was that the church seemed to grow faster among the gentiles than among the Jews. In fact, many of the believers in Jesus fled the city of Jerusalem after the stoning of Stephen for fear of their own lives. There had been a certain amount of fear among the faithful during the early days, but the mob action that saw Stephen dragged outside the walls of the city and stoned scared many of the new faithful off. If they hoped to stay out of sight of the Jewish officials, they could not hope to escape the justice of the mob if it came down on them.

Thus it seemed to James and the twelve that as soon as they found more converts to the cause, those converts would immediately decamp at the first sign of tension with local authorities. This is not to say that they were not pleased with the converts they found, though they had no more days like that of Peter when he converted 3,000 on one day and 5,000 on a single day a short time later. There were also stories that circulated about signs that the twelve were able to perform, such as curing the sick and the instance of Peter raising Tabitha from the dead, but these, while they might have the effect of bringing more people into the church, could not keep them in the city when they began to fear for their lives.

The raising of Tabitha from the dead brought on another disagreement among the twelve and James, because they did not know how to interpret the sign.

"That cannot be!" insisted Andrew when word of the deed reached the others of the twelve who were still in Jerusalem. "We have decided that Jesus is the Christ because he has power over death, which no one else can have. How is it that Peter can now raise the dead?"

"He did not raise the dead himself," said Hezer, the messenger who brought the news to the city. "He prayed to Jesus and to God His Father, and then told the woman to rise. Peter says that he only carried out the will of God, and that his prayers were answered."

"I believe in the Lord," said Matthias, "but I do not believe that he will give me power over life and death. Does Peter believe that if I also pray I will be able to raise the person of my choice?"

Hezer had no answer, being only the messenger sent from the city of Joppa to relay the news.

"Why can there not be a sign of this nature sent to the world through one of us?" asked the other James.

"Because it cannot be that both the son of God and his followers have the power of life and death. How many are there in this room who doubted what the life of Jesus meant until he rose from the dead? Nearly all, I wager. It was his rising from the dead that finally convinced us that he was the Messiah. Now we find that another man, like us exactly, can also raise the dead? It cannot be!" answered Andrew.

"This is true," added Matthias. "Peter is a man like us. It makes no sense that he should be able to raise the dead as Jesus did for Lazarus and for himself. How many Messiahs are we to proclaim to the people? What will happen to us when word of this reaches the faithful? They will then demand to know what was so special about Jesus, if Peter can do the same thing. And what will happen when word reaches the Sanhedrin? We have enough trouble with them as it is, without there being additional claims that one of us is also a Messiah."

"I cannot believe that Peter will claim to be the Messiah," said James. "He is the most humble of men, and loves the Lord. There is not a day that goes by that he does not torture himself for denying the Lord on the night of his trial."

"It does not take Peter to make the claim," rejoined Andrew. "Others will make it for him. Those who hunger for some respite from the world will flock to him hoping that there is something he can do for them. They will want him to be the Messiah because they want the Messiah to be close at hand. We all do. Were not there many of the faithful who began to doubt Jesus when he died? Have we not found that it is difficult to recapture those who formerly followed him, only to give up hope when they learned that he had been crucified? We tell them that he is risen from the dead, but they do not believe. They think that he is another false prophet who only lined his purse, even though they admit that they never saw him take any money. Now to replace the prophet they have lost comes another who claims to be able to raise the dead. Will they not flock to him, hoping that he is the one?"

"They will not when Peter tells them that he is not the one, and that Jesus was," said James. "For a man who has done this to then deny that he has any power will support the power of the Lord. There are few men who could accomplish this feat and then deny that they had any part in the matter, but that is exactly what Peter will say. Will this not impress the faithful with the power of faith?"

There was a short silence while the group considered this matter, and James used that moment to congratulate himself on the power of his oratory.

"I still think it better if word of this matter does not reach too many ears, though I admit that I do not know how to stop it," said Andrew.

"I think that your predictions are too dire, Andrew," said the other James. "We will use this miracle to show the faithful, and those we would gather to us, that there is nothing that is impossible with the Lord - that he works through all those who believe in him."

"And what are we to say when one of the faithful returns to his house, fully confident in his faith, and cannot raise his daughter from the dead?"

"First, that we are not to judge God. We do not know his motives. Second that this miracle is a sign for the faithful that God is with them, and that He hears their prayers. If he does not give them all power of life and death in this life, he gives it to them in the next: he has made it possible for them to have everlasting life with him."

There was a sullen silence for the moment, when Andrew turned to the messenger and said, "Who is this woman Tabitha, anyway, that Peter should show her such favor? Surely he does not plan to go about the country raising people from the dead."

"She was a woman of faith who has lived in the city all her life. She believed in Jesus as the son of God when first she heard about him, and dedicated her life to his message. She was known throughout Joppa for her almsgiving to the poor, and was known to live poorly herself though she had considerable wealth at one time."

"I thought that Peter had gone to Lydda. How came he to Joppa?"

"Upon the death of Tabitha, some of her friends and other widows sent for him that he might ease their pain."

"I suppose then, that they must have been delighted with the results of his mission to them," said Andrew with a bite to his voice.

"Oh yes, I am sure that they were," said the man, not catching the tone in Andrew's reply. There was some laughter around the room at Andrew's sally. "I am certain that they could not have expected this," added the man helpfully.

The apostles and James haggled over the matter a while longer without coming to any conclusion that could satisfy them all, at which time they gave up the effort. James could understand the arguments of Andrew, though he did not agree that this single example of power would confuse the faithful. He did not think that Andrew really believed that Peter had divine power, and Andrew claimed not to believe such, but James was afraid of the consequences of a schism among the hand-picked faithful of his brother. How could the movement hope to succeed in the long run if, in the first few years after Jesus' death, his immediate followers could not agree on the meaning of his message? Much would depend on the return of Peter.

When Peter did return from his journey, the raising of Tabitha from the dead was among the first topics of discussion. Andrew repeated his fear that some among the faithful might mistake Peter for yet another Messiah, or might claim that he was the real savior and not Jesus. Both James's iterated their position that while there would be some who might make this mistake, the event could only be used by them as a sign from on high that Jesus was still with them. They met in the usual room one evening when all had heard that Peter was back. They ate first and without discussion of the matter in keeping with their habit of eating in peace, no matter what else might happen. When they were done and the food removed, Peter listened to the various positions on the matter, and all of the men present had one, though they were divided into only two camps, and then he rose to speak himself.

"Brethren, I had no idea that my visit to Lydda would cause this much trouble. If I had known that I might cause a schism among the followers of Jesus by the mere act of leaving town, you may be sure that I would never have gone. But it is a simple matter really, and there is nothing to discuss. You all know that I am Peter, a fisherman from the sea of Galilee summoned by the man we knew at the time as Jesus to follow him. I do not know to this day why I did so - it would have been so much easier, and more sensible at the time, to stay in my fishing boat and let him go his way. But I did not. I followed him as he bid me do, and for that I shall always be thankful. We all learned over time that he was not a man named Jesus - or at least he was not only that - but the son of God sent to us to call us back to the Father. But even with this knowledge, on the night of his trial, which I did not understand at the time, I denied knowing him three times, as he told me I would do. There is no end to the torment this has caused me - it gets between me and my sleep. Would I, therefore, be the man among us who would claim the title of Messiah for himself? I dare not - my sins against him are too many already.

"Some of you claim that we came to know that Jesus is the Messiah after seeing that he rose from the dead, and this is true. Others say that the truth came to them when Lazarus was raised from the dead, and this is also true. Others point to his miracles as signs that he is divine, and this is also true.

"But then you claim that because a sign has been enacted through me, others might doubt him. Once again, there is some truth to this, but only in that some might draw the wrong conclusions. There is no truth in the claim that I have any power outside those given me by God through his son Jesus. I am a man as you are: I eat, drink, waste, sleep and work as you do. But some of you worry that the fact that a sign has come through me, in the form of raising Tabitha from the dead, will cause others to believe that I am capable of the same signs as our Lord.

"But consider these points: I have committed only one sign, while our Lord committed hundreds that we saw and know of, and maybe others as well. What is my paltry little effort compared to that? You might say that my sign was an important one, since I raised someone from the dead, but I would say that it is still only a single sign, and not one that I can do again. You know that our Lord had the power to work miracles whenever he chose, and you know that I cannot do them at all. My miracle was to have my prayers answered on behalf of the woman, and to have her raised up through my hands. I believe that it was a sign from the Lord that he is still with us, even though we are hounded and persecuted all across the land.

"But if the people persist, remind them that God does not need to perform signs to convince them that he is the one true God, and that Jesus is his son sent to redeem us. Ask them if it is Peter who spoke to them in parables. Ask them if it is Peter who gave them the sermon on the mount outside Capernaum. They will know that I did not, because they have heard me speak and they know that I cannot do it. Do not allow the people to focus on the physical signs that God is with us, but on his teachings through his son Jesus. Who but the son of man could fill their ears with such wonders?"

"Many of those we talk to have not heard the sermon on the mount, nor have they heard the parables or seen the miracles," said Andrew. "We are talking to new people who will have heard that Jesus raised Lazarus from the dead, then raised himself, and now they will hear of Peter, a follower of Jesus, who has also raised a person from the dead. What are they to think? If this continues we will all have to raise someone from the dead before they will believe."

There was some laughter in the room at Andrew's remarks, James and Peter among them, until Peter raised his hands to speak.

"You are a witty one, Andrew. If a sharp tongue could bring in converts we would have too many to deal with. We will have to risk that some people will misunderstand this sign from heaven, and hope that most see it for what it is. Jesus never claimed to be other than what we was, and neither will I. I will tell those who ask that I have no power except that given me by the Father in heaven. We will avoid confusion by pointing out that Jesus and I agree on this matter: he said that he was the son of God, and that God worked through him, and on this we will agree. I will say that I am a follower of the son of God, and that in this one instance God has chosen to work through me. I will not compete with Jesus for attention; perhaps in that the people will see that there is only one God and one savior and son, and that son is Jesus."

This did not settle the matter for all of the group, but they agreed to leave it in that state for the moment. There was no real solution to the problem, since they could not know how Peter came by the power he apparently possessed for the one instant. It came to matter little over time because they continued to successfully bring new members into the church. They all stayed for a time in Jerusalem teaching the Jews and the Gentiles who would listen, but there came a time when they believed that they could no longer make sufficient headway in the Holy City, and they began to drift away to teach in other areas.

Their problems in Jerusalem were two-fold: they continued to meet resistance from the Jewish authorities, and it appeared as though they had reached all of the people they were going to reach.

They were seldom arrested by the Sanhedrin or the Romans, but it was also apparent that they would not be left alone by them. They were harassed constantly, their room invaded periodically, their followers alternately heckled and ostracized. The city, after giving the Master a tumultuous welcome, had stood sullenly by while he was crucified a short time later. Many of those converted by the apostles left the city after their conversion, afraid to fight a pitched battle with the authorities. Of those who remained, the fledgling church was left with a small core of diehards who remained loyal to the church and were willing to overlook the treatment they received at the hands of the Sanhedrin. For the rest of the people it was apparent to the apostles that they could not be reached.

Thus Philip left for Antioch after a few months, and met with great success there. It was Philip who told them, in a message sent with a follower, that the members of the church there were being referred to as "Christians." Peter journeyed to various areas to teach, and would finally end his days in Rome, and the others went to various other cities to teach. James was the only one to stay in Jerusalem the entire time to attend to the flock there.

James could not bear the thought of the members of his flock being persecuted by the local authorities, and he endeavored to keep the peace between his group and the Jews. He would counsel his followers of Jesus to obey the Jewish laws handed down from Moses, and to go out of their way to minimize the differences between them. His real hope was that the two groups would simply stay away from each other since there was little way that contact among them would come to anything good.

It was inevitable that people who knew each other, and might even be related, would come to discuss the only difference between them - their religions. And there was no way that any such discussion could end other than a disagreement over the meaning of Jesus and the nature of the true Messiah. The Christians would insist that Jesus was the Messiah, and the Jews would claim that they were still waiting for him. James found that much of his time was spent mediating just such arguments among the people of the city.

His other principal headache during those years was that the success of the apostles in converting people in other cities and areas had brought the problem of obeying the Jewish laws to the fore. James had always believed that the new Christians ought to obey all of the old laws because nothing had happened to negate them. He even had the apostles' word for it that Jesus had said that the law would not pass away until all had been fulfilled. There were those in the group who thought that Jesus' coming provided that fulfillment, and James could not disagree with that assessment, but he was also concerned about the additional friction that would exist between the Jews and the Christians if the Christians did not obey all of the Jewish laws.

There were also concerns with the Christian church concerning the Jewish laws because, notwithstanding the debate among the church followers, those converts who had been Jews had continued to obey the Jewish laws, but many of the Gentiles who had been converted to the Christian faith could never hope to obey all of them, particularly those regarding diet and circumcision. Naturally this caused some friction, particularly among the Jews, since they believed that the Gentiles should not be allowed to enter the church unless they agreed to obey all the laws.

Among the first offenders was Paul, who developed a reputation for dealing loosely with Gentile converts, and baptized them into the church without insisting that they follow Jewish tradition. Thus there was growing up in the northern areas a church where none of the members obeyed Jewish traditional law, and this alarmed some of the converts and some of the apostles in Jerusalem.

Letters were exchanged among the church leaders on the subject, and it was an inevitable topic of conversation when any number of them got together. James, by nature an accommodationist, hated to see the church split over such a matter, concerned as he was that it was too small and weak to be able to withstand any storms from within or without.

He expressed these feelings to Peter periodically, and Peter urged him to continue in his quest for accommodation while realizing that he would not always be able to obtain it. James insisted often that for disputes to be solved finally the teachings of Jesus would have to be set down in writing for posterity. Peter agreed that this was so, and mentioned that several of the brethren were already at work on letters which would explain the life of Jesus in ways that would illustrate his position as son of God most clearly, and he mentioned that Saul, now calling himself Paul, was proving to be an apt letter writer who would put his thoughts on the matter down.

"But this cannot be," said James. "Paul is a good and holy man, but he did not know Jesus, and did not hear him teach. He knows nothing that will be useful in settling disputes in the future. He is no more qualified to write down the teachings of the Lord than I am."

"That is quite correct, James, and he is no less qualified, either. I believe that you also should put down your thoughts on the meaning of Jesus in ways that will be helpful to future members of the faith."

"But I heard him teach only once, and I remember little of that. It is not enough that I put down what I think. What must be put down is what is known, directly and exactly, about his life and teaching. The writing must be exact so there can be no question of how Jesus would stand on any issue that may face the church in the coming years. If I am qualified to put down my thoughts, then so are all of those who come into the church, and we shall have no discipline at all."

"It is not true that you are like the others - you are the brother of the Lord. You knew him longer and better than any of us."

"But it did me no good because I denied who he was until he was dead. I tell you that he knew the twelve of you and others of his followers better than he knew me."

"And we will write what we know, but you may rest assured that there is nothing that can be written down that will prevent all disagreements in the future. See how many disagreements there are now among the Jews. All we can do is tell what we know, and hope that future generations will see it rightly. But you are among us now, and have been for the eight years since the death and resurrection of the Lord, you are still the brother of the Lord, and you have been responsible for bringing many people into the church. Do not look at yourself so forlornly. Remember also that Jesus is still with us, and that he will guide your hand if you will let him."

James and Peter discussed the matter several times, and James could not get Peter to let go of the notion that James should write a letter to the faithful explaining who he was and what it was important for those faithful to know about Jesus. James had never done any writing of more than a few necessary words at a time, and was loathe to undertake such a task, particularly when there were other people who appeared to be more qualified than he for the task. Peter would not let go, however, and there was nothing for James to do but to begin. He began to make mental notes on the subject, but his progress was glacial.

CHAPTER 15

"We have been through this so many times, and yet it is not solved!" cried Peter. "How many times must this discussion take place? How can it be, I ask you once again, that Jesus should call only the Hebrews to his father? Did he not illustrate, with the parable of the good Samaritan, that all are called, and that it is possible for others to be holier than Hebrews, if they obey the spirit of the law?"

"But it is also the law of God that all men shall be circumcised, and none of the Gentiles have had this rite done to them. How can we commune with them, if they do not observe this basic law? They also eat foods which are unclean in the sight of God. How are we to sit at table with them?" asked Andrew, who was seconded by James, who nodded his head in agreement.

Peter could only roll his eyes and then shake his head. "Brethren, I feel as though I continue to cross the same bridge time after time, and each time I get to the end I must turn back and walk it again. Did not Jesus give us a new commandment, that he told us was the most important of all?"

"But did he also not say that not one jot of the law would pass away until all were fulfilled?"

"He was the fulfillment!" Peter almost shouted. "What are we doing here if he was not? All of the scriptures point to the relationship between God and the Hebrews, and after the fall he promised that he would send his son to bring his people back to him. This has been done: Jesus was that son! Or, at least that is what we have been telling people for the past six years since he died and then rose again. Do you tell me now that he was not? If he was not, then we are wasting our time teaching people that he was! And if he was the son, how can he not be the fulfillment of everything that was promised by the prophets?"

"But this centurion that you have brought into our midst - what was his name? Cornelius? - he is further removed from us than even the other Gentiles. He eats meat that has been strangled, he is uncircumcised, he is not clean enough that he should be with us. This is clear according to the law."

"The law has been fulfilled," Peter said, almost resignedly, "and we have new commandments to live with. But even if what you say were true, Cornelius has come willingly into the fold. What am I to do? Tell him that his faith is not adequate? That I am able to read the mind of God and that I know that he cannot be as well loved by God as I am because he is uncircumcised?

"Remember that I did not seek Cornelius out. He sent for me because he had a vision where he was told to find me out. He is a man of God, and he believes that Jesus is the son of God. The fact that he is not circumcised does not change that. The fact that he will eat meat that has been strangled does not change that. What else did the Master ask for? Only that we believe in him, and seek to see the Father through him, and that we love our neighbor. Are you telling me that Cornelius can do none of these things? Has the God of all the world, the Creator of all, created people that will not be allowed to love Him simply because they did not hear of him early enough in life, and so were polluted with pagan ways? And if they are ready to renounce those pagan ways, why would not God allow them to renounce them, and accept them into the brotherhood?"

There was a silence for a moment or two while the others absorbed this speech. James could see the point that Peter made, but he was afraid that the new church would be splintered on this issue, and did not want to see that happen. It would be very difficult to bring more Jews into the church if it were discovered that Gentiles were also allowed in without cleansing them of their habits.

Peter began again. "And what of the work of Paul and Barnabas in the north? You have all seen his letters and congratulated him on his success at bringing more people into the church. Are we now to write to him and inform him that henceforth we will accept no more Gentiles, no matter how true their faith appears to be? You have all been on the road teaching the good news. Did each of you scan the crowds that you would talk to make sure that all of your hearers were Hebrew before you could begin? If the church is for the Hebrews only, then we can spare ourselves much work in the future, because we have already reached most of the Hebrew people that can be reached. Yet you have all seen that there are many willing Gentiles who have seen that their pagan gods do not answer their questions or give them comfort, and they are willing to look at the God of Abraham, Isaac and Jacob. Would that God turn them away? It is easy to see that He might turn them away if they hear of him and then turn their backs on Him and continue in their old ways. But if they hear his word and believe, and live according to the word of Jesus, will God turn them away? I think not. It cannot be, brethren, and as long as I am alive I will not permit it."

There was a pause after this speech, and it only served to give Peter another idea.

"Why is there so much resistance to the idea of Gentiles joining us in the church? Whether they eat strangled meat or are circumcised is hardly a problem for those who are so. What is it to me if I sit at table with a man who is not circumcised? That is between he an God, not between he and me. And if he were to eat strangled meat, I merely have to refuse when it is passed to me. I hope that the Master has not left behind him a group of elitists who will not join him in eating with those who are shunned by the rest of society." There were some crestfallen looks at this, but again nothing was said.

Peter said nothing else himself, and there the matter was allowed to rest, but it was apparent to James that it had not been solved. It would boil to the surface again.

James continued his rounds among the faithful in the city, and their numbers continued to grow. Far from being able to see all of the faithful in a matter of hours - or even days - as he had done in the first year after the death of Jesus, he now had no hope of seeing them all at any time, and contented himself with seeing those he knew to be home bound or otherwise in need of the attention. He was flattered that many of the faithful referred to him as "James the Just", though at the same time it could be embarrassing to be called such in front of strangers who were not yet members of the faithful and had no idea of James' past.

It wasn't as if the days were peaceful for the faithful in Jerusalem. The harassment by the Sanhedrin continued, now and then abating but never straying far from the surface. There were occasional arrests of the faithful, robberies, mobs gathered here and there when it was known that the faithful would be there in strength, and frequent attempts to prevent the apostles from teaching and converting new members to the church. For all that, James was pleased and encouraged to see that the harassment had no effect on the ability of the apostles to bring in new members, and it had no effect on the faithfulness of those who had been in the church since the beginning. This had the effect of increasing James' own faith, because he came to believe that his brother and Savior really could overcome all opposition.

This greater faith caused James to go to the temple more often to pray - so much so that he developed calluses on his knees from the effort. It was on one of these daily trips to the temple, as he entered the temple courtyard, that he heard someone behind him calling his name. He paused for a moment in the traffic to see who it might have been, and found himself staring into the still lustrous eyes of Esther.

It had now been eight years since he had seen her, but she was as lovely as ever. She still looked young - her hair still shone, her eyes were the same shining brown that they had been, her frame still as attractive as that of a maiden. Her smile, while somewhat tentative on this occasion, was still warm and inviting. James found that he wanted to take her into his arms as he had always done. It was all he could do to resist. He was speechless for a moment.

"Are you not glad to see me, James, after all these years?"

"I am, I am - more than I can say. It is just that I did not expect to see you here."

"I confess that I did not expect to look up and see James ahead of me, and yet I thought there would be some chance that I might find you here in the city."

"What brings you here? Are you still living in Nazareth?"

"I am. Much has happened in the years since you parted from me, James." This hurt James deeply. "You may not know that my brother died of the fever, and that, since there was no one for the estate to pass to, it came to me. Yes, I am a wealthy woman on my own. I also married, but my husband did not live long, dying of the fever as well only a year into our marriage. So I am now more than thirty years old, without a husband or children, and my time for both passing quickly."

This made James feel guilty, as if it had been he who had deprived her of all this. He was glad to hear that she had married, for it relieved him of the burden of thinking that she was single because of him, but the fact that she was now a widow hung heavily on him. He realized that he had been pondering the matter when she broke in on his reverie.

"And what of you James? Are you still in the service of your brother? I hear more and more of his followers, and I am told that there are more of you every day. This must gladden your heart to think that your brother could have this much influence with people even after his death."

"Yes, yes. I am still, and mean to stay. I am the leader of the Jerusalem church, selected by the followers of my brother," said James, who could not understand why he should be nervous in the presence of this woman.

"That is it? After almost marrying eight years ago, and not seeing each other since, that is all that you can think to tell me? What else is there? Have you married?"

"No, no I cannot," James stumbled. "I am too busy tending to the needs of the faithful to do justice to a family of my own." After a pause he added, "If I were to marry I would have married you." James thought he detected a look of hope in her eye as he said this, but he could not be sure.

James had stopped when she called out to him in a well traveled part of the courtyard, and the constant stream of people forced them to move on. James indicated another spot off to one side of the courtyard where it did not look as if they would be jostled, and they turned to walk there. Esther was a step in front of James, and James could not but consider her as they made their way slowly through the crowd. She was as beautiful and graceful as ever - and, what was worse - still enticing to James after eight years of hardly giving a thought to women. When they reached the appointed spot she turned to look at him, and he nearly grabbed her in his arms to kiss her. It took all of his concentration and will power not to touch her.

"Surely your brother has not been as demanding as that. Are none of the other faithful married and with family?"

"Most of the members are, of course, but only Peter of the apostles is, and he does not see his wife. There is too much to do and too many people to reach to make such a commitment possible." James felt tongue tied, as though he were talking to the Emperor rather than to a woman he had almost married. He could not make conversation with her - he could think of nothing to say that might not be taken wrong by her, and the last thing he wanted to do was offend her. There was an awkward silence.

"James, it was not like this with us before - we talked as if we had known each other all our lives. What has happened that that is no longer possible?"

"Much has changed over the years, Esther, though you are still as radiant as ever." That had slipped out - James had been thinking it, but he hadn't meant to mention it to Esther. It appeared to please her, but James was still sorry for the slip. "I now have responsibilities, people are counting on me for certain things, I have no money and no belongings in the world. You have been married, you have inherited the wealth and comfort that is rightfully yours, you talk as if you are near the grave, but there is plenty of time for you to marry again and have children. Neither of us is the same person we were eight years ago."

"That is not true. Appearances have changed, but we are the same people we were. I can see that you are still the kind, gentle, hardworking man you were when I knew you. And as for money, when we planned to marry neither of us had much, and it never bothered us, though it is true," she said smiling, "that you could use some new clothes." James looked down in some embarrassment at the cloak he was wearing - it was ragged and torn in many places, and, while clean, had seen much better days.

He was embarrassed for a moment, but then he considered where Esther's comments were leading, and he began to fear. He looked her in the eyes, and thought that he could see the feeling that had once been there. It could not be - they had only been talking for five minutes. And yet he had to admit that he could see how it happened, because he felt the same way about her. Without paying any attention to the crowd he took her in his arms and kissed her more passionately, more deeply than he ever had, even more than the night that he had taken her in the alley when she had agreed to be his wife.

He did not know what to expect when he did it, but she responded in the way that he hoped she might. She kissed him back, and held him tighter than he held her. It was a long kiss, and when they finally parted they were both short of breath and drained. James did not know what to think of this: it was wonderful to be with her again, but he could not see where it would lead. He had nothing, he wanted nothing, he did not want to be bothered in his ministry to the people of Jerusalem. And yet, this was Esther - the only woman he had ever loved, and she was as sweet and kind and beautiful as he remembered her.

"James," she began after a moment, quietly and somewhat breathlessly, "you do not know how I have missed you. When you left there was nothing for me, and there has been nothing since. I would have married you because you were the best man in the world, and I wanted nothing more than to be with you. When I did marry it was out of necessity, because I must have my own family, and I did not think to ever see you again. But all those years there was no man for me, none that I loved as I loved you, none that I cared for above you. I loved my husband as best I could, and took care of him, but he was not my James." She was now speaking passionately, as though acting on a stage, but James believed every word of it to be true. "I have been so lonely these few years," she continued, "but there was nobody out in the world that I wanted. And now that I have seen you again, there is still nobody else that I want. I don't care if you have any money or property: I have all that we could ever want. Oh, let us be happy again as we once were!"

James could say nothing for the moment. He could not compete with her in stories about how he had wanted her all these years, because he had not - at least not to the degree that she appeared to have thought of him. He had probably been busier than she, and in contact with more people, and so it had been easier for him to forget the happiness that he had once looked forward to. That was not to say that he forgot her - not a day went by that he did not think of her - but he had managed to conquer the regret that he had felt at not being able to marry her eight years before. But at the sight of her all those old feelings came flooding back, and all his years of concentrating on his work, in part to serve his brother and in part to forget Esther, were as vanished as the wind. It was as though he had achieved nothing in all those years of concentration: one look at her, one sound from her voice, and his attempts to put her behind him were all for naught.

"I cannot tell you how I have missed you," he began finally, "or how I have worked to put you out of my mind. There has not been a day that I did not think of you and wonder what you were doing and if you were happy, and not a day that I did not think myself guilty for ruining your happiness. But it is all for nothing: now that I have seen you it is all as it once was, and I feel that same as I did the last time I saw you. I have tortured myself all these years for nothing."

"It is not for nothing James - there is still time for the two of us! Thank God that we have found each other again, and that we can take up where we left off. See how we are: we have not been together ten minutes, and already we cannot resist each other. See how quickly we fell into each other's arms! With all that has passed over the years, we still feel the same for each other!"

That was true - James could not deny it. "But there is one other thing that has not changed," he said to her, "and that is that I am in the service of my brother, and I must stay. There is no leaving. My faith is stronger now than even it was when I left you. I cannot turn back now, and I would not want to." They had been standing in the same spot for this entire conversation, but James suddenly began to fear that they might be noticed, and he did not want to have to explain himself to any of the faithful or to one of the apostles, even though he had no idea what they might say or even if they would object. So he took her hand gently and led her behind one of the columns nearer a wall where there would be less chance of their being observed.

"We are a small but growing group, and there are people in the city who have come to count on me over the years, and I would not disappoint them."

"But there are others James - no one is indispensable. Surely there is some one else who can be the leader - or whatever you are - of the people in Jerusalem."

"Of course someone else could do it, but I would not want them to. It is my duty - I was chosen by the original followers of my brother, and I consider it an honor. As for the rest of the faithful, how would it look to them to see the brother of the man they worship as the son of God leaving his duty to his brother and to them for the sake of a woman? You are a desirable woman, Esther, and if I were to leave it would be for you, but it cannot be. My brother told me that I would serve him, and I cannot disobey."

"I have heard of your brother over the years of course, and there is even a small group of believers in Nazareth now, though they are much despised." At this James could only smile ruefully. "It is remarkable that a man who was hanged on the cross should command so much attention so long after his death. He must have been a more remarkable man than I knew," said Esther, thoughtfully. "I admit that I have hated him all these years for what he did to us!" she added, angrily. "We should have been married almost nine years now, and have been blessed with many children. Instead I am a widow with wealth I care little for and no children, and you are a penniless preacher tending to penniless flocks, and without a wife and children." She paused for a moment, as if realizing that this sort of angry talk would not be best calculated to win James over again, and calmed herself down.

"I am sorry, so sorry," she said. "I cannot help myself when I consider all that has been lost."

"You must consider what has been gained: many people have found God through his son, and are now at peace with themselves because they know the source for everlasting life. I have come to realize what a special gift

I have been given - to have been so well acquainted with the son of God, even if I were so thickheaded as to deny him in his lifetime. We are slowly growing - think of the promise for the world if all of its people can be converted to Jesus!"

"I am not convinced that your brother was any more than a preacher who was not quite correct about Jewish law. But no matter: you know very well that the entire world will not be converted - such a thing could never happen. In the meantime there are good people like yourself spending their lives to make such a thing happen, when you know that it cannot."

"It was dream talk, I know, but it is not really our concern either: all we can do is serve the Lord while we have the ability to do so, and leave the success or failure of the mission to him."

"Let us talk of this no more," she said, suddenly coming close to him and putting her hands on his shoulders. He wanted so badly to embrace her again: he could smell the perfume on her body and feel the softness of her skin, but he resisted. He dared not get any more entangled than he already was. She continued, "Where there is love all can be overcome, including the wall between us placed there by your brother. Let us find a way that we can be together!"

"You have no idea how much I want you, or any idea how wrong it would be. How would any children be brought up? You would not want them to be followers of my brother, and I would not want them to be anything else. How would we live with such an impasse?"

"We can find a way James! Do not dispute such details now. The worst that could happen is that we would have no children, and so grow old together."

"But you have just expressed a desire for children. You cannot have it both ways."

"I want children, as all women do. But if the only way to have my James is to do without, then I will do without." James looked at her carefully, there in the shade of the temple column. She wore a bright blue cloak, and a white veil which had at first covered her hair and now lay behind her head on her neck, and her brown hair shown even out of the sunlight. Her eyes were still the same bright lights which they had always been, her full lips as inviting. It seemed to James that there was not an imperfection anywhere on her or in her. He put his arms around her and pulled her close. She embraced him in the same way and they indulged themselves in another passionate kiss that left them breathless.

As they parted lips but not arms, James saw a troubled look come over her face. She rubbed her hands on his back, though still outside his cloak, and James guessed what she had noticed.

"James! What is the matter? Have you had some disease? What is it that troubles your back?"

"I have had no disease other than the jealousy of the Sanhedrin and the Romans. What you feel is the result of Roman whips applied to my back at the instigation of the Sanhedrin. You would find the same marks on the backs of the original twelve."

Esther insisted on seeing his back, and James lowered his cloak somewhat, just enough for her to be able to see the upper half of his back, and after glancing about to see that they had not been noticed by passersby. She let out a gasp of astonishment when she saw it.

"But...but...why was this done? What did you do to deserve such treatment?" James recounted the story to her briefly.

"So you see, it would not be as easy as all that for us to continue together. You see how you may be served yourself."

"But why do you put up with such treatment? Is your dead brother worth such punishment? I cannot imagine how you did not all go away from such an experience damning his very name."

"So far were we from damning him, we actually praised his name in thanksgiving."

"What?" Esther demanded in astonishment.

"We gave thanks to God that we had been allowed to suffer something of the same treatment that our Lord endured for us. It made us feel closer to him."

"I love you, James, and I would do almost anything for you, but I wonder if I would be tying myself to a madman."

"It is clear that you do not grasp the nature of my brother. I should not even call him my brother - he is a half brother at best. We were born of the same mother, but not the same father. He was sent here by our Father in heaven to call us back to the Father, and to suffer that our sins might be forgiven...."

"Yes you have told me. I still remember our parting conversation eight years ago. You do not know how I was hurt. You told me that he had died on the cross and then risen from the dead for our sake, and that you believe him to have been the son of God," interrupted Esther, somewhat testily.

"You speak of the past tense, as though he had come and gone. He is risen, and he is with us still. Not in body, but in spirit. I feel him everyday that I am out with the faithful, teaching to the poor extent that I am able. I find peace of mind when I pray to him, asking for his help and his guidance, and when I am finally able to put real faith in him."

"James, James, it is only a few moments since I have seen you, and all of the old feelings have come flooding back to me. Do not talk of these matters now - let us enjoy one another for the moment, and come back to this later."

"You know that this is impossible. If we do not settle such matters we can never be together...." James was surprised to hear himself talk in this manner, but it was out before he knew it... "unless we are of one mind on this matter. Otherwise we will cause each other nothing but pain." In response she glanced quickly around them, apparently to see if anyone was looking, and once again embraced him and kissed him. This time, after a moment, James pulled away.

"No, I will not go through this again. We must agree on the issue that pulled us apart before, or there will be only misery." Esther embraced him again, and would not be pushed away, and James could not resist her. How wonderful it was to hold her after all these years. It did not even feel as though it had been years, but only moments since he had been leaving her house after telling her that he must go to serve Jesus. He had been around women in the interim, but none like Esther, and none that appealed to him as she did. He embraced her and they kissed once more.

They said nothing else but stood there in the shadow of the column, oblivious to the rest of the world. James did not know how long they stood in this manner, but he said nothing to her and allowed himself to revel in the moment.

"We cannot stand here all day, James, as pleasant as it would be. Where can we meet in the future?"

"We must meet here for the moment, and do so out of the shadow of the columns, so that we do not risk this sort of closeness again." Esther looked up at him, wondering what he meant. "We have not settled the basic issue, and we cannot allow ourselves to get caught up in each other until we do so." Come here tomorrow at the same time, and we will talk then - in public where we can be seen, and we will talk of serious matters. They cannot be put off." Esther kissed him quickly again, and then melted away into the crowd.

James watched her disappear among the worshippers and the traders and moneychangers, and then simply sat down in the spot where he had been standing, leaning his back against the wall and placing his feet against the column. His face he buried in his hands.

He had actually begun to think, and to talk, as though he and Esther had some future together. For brief moments he had contemplated what it would be like to have her around all the time, and what life together might be like. But then he remembered that none of the other apostles had a spouse at the moment, and some, like Peter, had left their families to serve Jesus. Could he, not even a member of the original twelve, do any less? Was he not as obligated as they to devote himself to the cause they all served? How could he bring personal pleasure into the midst of their austere surroundings?

And what would the others think, when they were already sharing what little they all had, if he were to bring in another mouth to feed?

The presence of a woman under the circumstances would serve to drive a wedge between the men in the group. Currently Mary was the only woman constantly with them, and her status among them did not allow them to think of her in terms which they might apply to other women. The presence of Esther, even if they all agreed that she might stay, would be apt to cause jealousy among them - not that they would all want her, but that they might all want someone like her, and their efforts would be diluted by the fact that they would suddenly have more personal concerns to tend to.

James could not think how he would tend to the faithful in the city, if Esther were on the back of his mind at all times, and she certainly would be. And for that matter, what would the faithful think if he were the first of the inner circle to take a wife? Would they look askance at the latecomer who now undertakes to spoil himself? Would they wonder if he were now less dedicated to the church, since he had provided himself with a source of personal pleasure?

More importantly, what would Jesus think? He had not taken a wife himself, though it was easy to rationalize that, since he was the son of God with a very specific mission to fulfill, he simply hadn't the time. But perhaps he expected his immediate followers to emulate him in this matter too, just as he expected them to love each other and the Father just as he did. It would not be easy to know what exactly about Jesus' life should be copied and which not. Which path that Jesus chose would lead to salvation, and which not? It could not be that he meant for all to be without a spouse and children - that would be the end of the people that God had created to love and serve Him. It was easy to see, however, that he might have meant for his immediate priesthood to copy him by serving the church with as few personal distractions as possible.

And yet, how could he live without Esther? It had been bad enough to leave her the first time, and here she was back in his arms again. How could he bear to part with her? How sweet it would be to see her last before he went to sleep at night, and first when he woke in the morning.

But where would that be? Would she live in that room with the other apostles? Clearly that would be impossible. Where else would they live? He had no money, and wanted none - it was liberating to stop thinking about the question of making a living, and he did not want to take it up again - and that would leave them living off of her money, possibly in her home in Nazareth, or in one she might purchase in Jerusalem. Neither of those alternatives would do either: James could not allow himself to be separated from Jesus' followers. He did not want to remove himself from the inner circle of the church that they were all creating, and did not want to put anything between himself and the faithful to whom he ministered in the city.

In this vein he agonized for several hours, before realizing that it was getting late in the afternoon and he still had not made it into the temple to pray. He rose stiffly from his long time seat, entered the temple to pray, and then walked back to the room.

Upon entering he saw that there was no one there but his mother. She came toward him when he entered, stopped when she had a clear look at his face, and then said, matter-of-factly, "You have seen Esther."

"It is that obvious?"

"It is. I know that she is in the city because I happened to see her in the market this morning, and I can tell from the look on your face that you have talked to her, and all of the old doubts have surfaced."

"What did she say to you?"

"I made sure that she did not see me. I knew that if the two of you got together there would be pain - at least for someone - and I made up my mind that I would let God decide whether the two of you should meet."

James sat down on the floor on one of the few cushions in the room and took the water that his mother offered. He considered for a moment and then said, "It should not be difficult. I am the half brother of the man I believe to be the son of God. I have seen him perform miracles, including raising himself from the dead. How is it that I can be tempted out of his service by a woman? There should be no temptation for me. I know what most others can only hope to know, and have seen what they would die to see, and my head is still turned by a woman." He could only shake his head, and wonder if he was weak.

"Why does it have to be one or the other?"

"There are many reasons, and I have been going over them in my mind all day rather than doing my duties: she does not believe that Jesus is the son of God; she is accustomed to wealth and comfort; she wants a family; all of the others are devoting themselves to Jesus without any family; there is no place for her to stay here, and I do not wish to leave; and what would the others think of me?" James ticked off all of his objections on his fingers as he talked, and actually began to feel better about the situation because he dwelled only on the negative aspects.

"She loves you James, and I am sure that she would adjust to life among the chosen. She would probably come to believe in Jesus over time, when she sees the signs that we have seen, and see how the faithful believe in him. And as for taking a wife, the fact that the twelve do not have wives does not mean that none of his followers ever will."

"Are you trying to talk me into it, mother? And how do you know that she loves me? It has been eight years since we have seen each other."

"There are some things that a woman knows James, that men never will. She loved you before with a true love that will never die, no matter what happens between the two of you." James could only roll his eyes - he believed in the intuition of his mother, and therefore believed that she was right about this, and that fact made it all the harder. When he had left her before it was in the hope and belief that she would forget him in a matter of months, and that had sustained him over the years. Now his mother was saying that she would never forget him, no matter what. "And no," she continued, "I am not trying to talk you into anything. I do not know what Jesus would have wanted you to do, and I do not want you to talk yourself out of anything before you have thought the matter through and talked with the others."

James shot her a withering look. "Do not mention this to the others. I do not want them to know anything of this. I will solve it on my own."

"Oh, come James, they are wise and discreet men, and they are learned in the teachings of Jesus. They will be able to help you, if you will let them."

"I will not let them, and that is the last word on the subject. I do not want them to think me weak or that my faith is lagging. I will solve the problem on my own." Mary laughed gently at him, but did not force the issue any further. When the others began to filter in that evening James worked very hard to look as though he hadn't a care in the world.

James took special care to clean himself the next morning and to put on the best cloak that he could find, but he was still dissatisfied with the result when he departed for the temple in the late morning. He resolved not to think too much of his appearance since Esther was well aware that he had no money, but this resolve deserted him when he first caught sight of Esther standing behind the same pillar as the day before.

She was radiant - dressed all in white with gold trim, her dark brown hair uncovered and wavering ever so slightly in the breeze. James had never seen her look so beautiful; in fact, James had never seen anyone look so beautiful, and suddenly all those longings that he had managed to steer clear of for eight years in the service of his brother came flooding back to him. He advanced on her and, without saying a word, took her in his arms and kissed her. She responded in kind, in exactly the way that he, with his blood up, hoped that she would.

When they released, after what seemed a long time, James said to her, "I have never seen a sight as lovely as you, and I have seen every woman in the city many times."

"Thank you," said she. "I would not tease your patience by speaking of your appearance, but appearance is nothing: you are the man that I want. You are the same good James that you were when we nearly married, and I will not let you escape again." This comment brought James back to reality, and while they continued to hold each other, he hung his head.

"I have heard all of your talk of your brother, but there is no reason that he should stand in our way. Either I will stay with you, or you will come with me, but one way or the other we will have each other." James could only shake his head, and Esther saw him do it.

"What can be the matter? How can you object? I have said that if need be I will stay with you. What more sacrifice can I make for us?"

"I fear that we will never be easy so long as you fail to understand who he is and what I and the others have committed to him. My brother is the son of God, and there is nothing that will stand in his way."

"I have not asked for anything to stand in his way. I have said that I will come to you, if you will not come to me."

"But none of the others have a wife or children....yes, I know we talked of this yesterday, but it must be talked of until it is settled. I cannot do less than those others who are committed to him."

"Why can you not? If he did not say that you cannot marry, then you may. Surely you are not suggesting to me that all of those who choose to follow your brother will never be able to marry. It would be a short lived movement." James could only shake his head again, and say nothing.

They discussed the matter for another hour, but there was nothing to be resolved because James could not make up his mind about how to proceed. Everytime he looked at Esther he wanted her the more, but just as he made up his mind that he would find a way to be with her, he inevitably began to tote up the difficulties, and they were many, and they always began with the reaction that he would get from the original apostles. He could not stand the thought that he might be less committed than they, or that he might do less than what Jesus wanted of him.

There were the other difficulties as well, such as how they would live if she attempted to stay with him while he worked. He had no money, and while the community was generous it was by no means clear that it would welcome another mouth to feed. Esther would have to find some way to earn her keep among the faithful, and this she could not do because she was not one of the faithful.

So it dragged on for a number of days, with Esther ever more insistent that James make up his mind one way or the other, and it was clear that she wanted him to go to Nazareth to live with her. She might not insist that he give up service to his brother, and she might even agree to stay in Jerusalem to be with James, but it was obvious to him that she preferred to go home. They met periodically in different parts of the city to discuss the matter, but never to any end. James insisted on varying the meeting places to ensure that they were not seen by one of the apostles or one of the faithful, but it came to naught.

Several days after Esther's first appearance in town, those apostles who were in town gathered in the room as usual. The group included, for the moment only, Peter and the other James, as well as Matthias and Andrew. When they had finished eating and there was a short lull in the conversation, Andrew suddenly started and said to James, "Say, who was the woman I saw you talking with today, James? You seemed very close to her." He said this with a broad smile and a twinkle in his eye, and the others immediately joined in the ribbing, but James remembered that, as usual, they had embraced each other the entire time that they had been talking.

"She is the woman I was to marry before the resurrection of my brother changed my life, and she has suddenly reappeared."

"I saw you as I passed the market this afternoon. From the look of things she must still be close to you." He said this with the same twinkle and wide smile, but he had the attention of all the others now, and there was no way that James could head off the conversation. There were cries of "Yes, James tell us all about her" and "A bride, James? You? The man who's knees are callused from the praying that he does in the temple?" and "When will we all meet her?" James was as mortified as he had been when such a subject had been broached when he was a boy.

"I was engaged to be married to this woman immediately before the death of my brother, but when I saw him risen from the dead and heard him tell me that I would serve him, it was clear to me that I could not marry, and that I should not. I told her as much when we briefly returned home to Nazareth, which telling broke both our hearts, and then I returned here where I have been with you since."

There was a brief silence while Andrew thought of more deviltry. "It did not appear to me that you have been apart at all." This brought more catcalls and teasing from the others, and James could see that his mother laughed along with them. He could feel his face turn red with embarrassment.

"It did not feel to me as though we had, either," he returned, to gales of laughter. There was another moment of silence, and James sensed that they all had the same question on their minds: what would he do now? James tried to formulate an answer, but before he could do so, Peter spoke.

"I know that you will not leave us, James, your faith is too strong. The only question remaining then, is will she stay with us?"

James wished he were as sure of the future as Peter believed that he was. James was not certain that he would stay with the others: he could see where his duty lay, and he could see what he wanted to do, and the two were not the same. James did not detect any hostility on the part of Peter or the others towards having Esther stay with them, but it was apparent that they assumed that she was among the faithful. Oh well, why not air that now, since everything else was being discussed?

"If we were to both stay, I suppose that she would stay with us. That would be the best influence on her."

"Why would she need influence so badly?"

"She does not believe that Jesus is the son of God." There was a moment of silence while this was absorbed by the room and then Peter spoke.

"You are correct then, that she has the best hope of coming to the truth amongst us. But can we be certain that she is not hostile to us, and would not work against us?"

"She believes that we are all out of our minds, but she would not do anything active to stop us."

"How can you be sure, James?" asked Matthias. "You say that you have not seen her since the Master's death, and that has been eight years. Perhaps the desire to do us in is the reason that she has suddenly turned up after all these years." There was a general nodding of heads at this, and murmurs that this could be the answer.

"I cannot be sure, but I trust her. You must accept my word for it that the emotions are the same, if not warmer now, than they were eight years ago." Nothing was said immediately, but James could see that he had not satisfied the group.

After an uncomfortable silence, Matthias said, "I want to believe you James, but it is odd that a woman should appear after an eight year absence and want to begin as though nothing had happened."

"Things have happened," said James defensively. "She has lost her brother and inherited her family fortune, and been married and widowed in the interim, leaving her middle aged and without children. Surely this much would explain her presence even if there were nothing else that would do so. But I also believe that we met by accident, and that she did not come to the city seeking me. If the look on her face when we met was an act, then she is the greatest actress that ever lived."

"I want to believe you, James....." began Matthias, before he was seconded by the others. They were all interrupted by Peter.

"If James believes that she is innocent of any designs against us, then we should believe it as well. He has been amongst us these eight years, and we know that he has opened his heart to Jesus. It is within his power to see clearly in such matters." This silenced the others. "But what do you mean, 'if you both stay'?"

"I do not know what I will do. She would have me go back to Nazareth with her, but she has also said that, if necessary, she would forgo all and stay here."

"How can you consider going back to Nazareth? It is true that the church there could use a man of your talents, but it is really so small that it must be beneath what you are accustomed to. Here you are the head of the first church in the holiest city in the world, and you have many people who rely on you." Peter paused for only a moment, and James could see a suspicious look come over him. "Or does she mean that you should give up the service of the Lord to pursue some other?"

"She does not care what I do, so long as we are together." Again a short silence while the group, but especially Peter, digested this.

"Now I am the suspicious one," said Peter. "It will be difficult for her, a non-believer, to tolerate the nature of what you do for the Lord, particularly since it knows no hours or holidays. The question is this: would you lure her to faith in the Lord first, or would she lure you away from him?"

James was intensely embarrassed by the question, because he had never heard the like in the company before. It appeared to him that he was the first ever to be weak enough to face this problem. Peter had effectively left his family to serve Jesus, and James thought that one or two others had broken off engagements such as his, but none, once they had begun their ministry for Jesus, had given any thought to quitting. He did not know how to answer, and felt as though the eyes of each member of the group were boring through him looking for the answer. Strangely, it occurred to him to be thankful that all of the group were not there.

Peter continued, when it was apparent that James would say nothing, "Consider what you are doing, James, and how any other task would compare to it. You are bringing souls to the one, true God; all else pales. Even if she were to stay with you, you would not be able to devote yourself to your work as you have done in the past. Consider what effect that would have on those in the city who depend on you."

"But think of the implications of what you are saying, Peter," offered Andrew. "It may be true that we must act differently from those who come after us because we have been so near the Lord, but by your reasoning no follower of Jesus could ever marry or have a family. We would then be a short-lived church."

"I did not claim that no follower of Jesus should ever be married. There are obviously many people in the new church who are married and with children, and this is necessary. But it may also be true that the priests of the church should not marry, the better to devote themselves to the service of the Lord."

"Such a policy will lessen the number of men who will serve. That is possible, but it might also increase the number of those who serve by separating them from the rest of the flock."

"We have no need of such elitists," said Matthias.

"It is not a matter of elitism. It is a matter of differentiating between those who are faithful to the Lord but live their own lives, and those who have devoted their all to his service."

"It has been somewhat easy for us to serve because we were called by the Lord himself. How will such a policy bring in those who have not known the Lord? What will we tell them? That they should give up every hope of domestic happiness for the right to live a life of poverty and pain in service to God?"

"That is exactly what we will be telling them, though it may not be in those words exactly. Only those who are fully dedicated to the Lord, and to nothing else, can serve as priests. If we exact a high price from them, it is to ensure that they understand the level of dedication that will be required. What good will it do for us to bring men into the priesthood, allow them to marry, and then see the marriages fall apart because the man cannot devote the amount of time that his family needs? And how is a priest in the service of the Lord to support a family? Look around. Look at this spare room. How are a wife and children to fit into such an atmosphere? All will be in misery, and there will be nothing that can be done about it."

"But has it been decided that it will always be this way? Is it necessary for all who come after us to live as we do?"

"They need not live as we do, but they must dedicate themselves to service, and that means that they will not have the time to devote to a family. How can a man tend to the needs of his flock if he has the cares of his own family to tend to?"

James felt this last remark intensely, and knew that it was directed at him as much as at future generations. But he had to admit that Peter was right: he was not married to Esther yet, and already he had done little for the people of the church for the last two days while he considered his own problem. How much worse would it be when he had married her and they had children to tend to?

He could not marry her, that was clear. As his mind raced on it wandered, as minds will tend to do, over to what he would tell her if he decided against marrying her. For the first time it occurred to him that his keeping her at arms length over the last few days would make the second break up as difficult as the first. He had allowed her - and himself - to hope once more, and now, if he carried through with his latest plan, he would be disappointing her again.

And it was a big if, because he could not convince himself that he did not want to marry Esther and move back to Nazareth. He had little physical to show for his efforts in Jerusalem: most of the converts had been brought into the church by the other apostles, and growth had been slow of late; he was poorer than he had ever been in his life; he had a back full of scars to remind him of the high regard in which he was held by both Jewish and Roman authorities; and he had not seen any of the reappearances of Jesus after he had risen from the dead save the appearance in the grove of trees that morning.

Against this he could look forward to a lifetime of happiness with a woman who, though no longer young, was still incredibly beautiful and who appealed to him more now than she did when he last knew her eight years before. They had never had a cross word, never a disagreement (save when he had informed her that he would not marry her, and that had not been as angry as it might have been) and he had every reason to expect that their marriage would be a happy one, and that they would produce many fine children.

Moreover, he lacked the enthusiasm for the missionary work that the others seemed to have. James did it because he wanted to, and enjoyed doing it, and felt that he was serving a useful purpose in the world, but he could not escape the fact that in his mind it was still a duty.

This thought did not seem to trouble the others. They approached every day of their plain and often painful lives with the same enthusiasm with which a child will approach a new toy. They could not wait to begin their teaching in the morning, and hated to come home from it at night. Those who left the city to teach, and this was all of them save James, did so with the same attitude that a tourist might begin a long awaited trip. They bore the abuse, both verbal and physical that was heaped on them with gratitude, never failing to praise God for having treated them in the same way that his son was treated.

While the others reveled in the lives they had found themselves living, James endured it. He wanted nothing else to do, he wanted no money or fame, and he was pleased that he had the opportunity to serve God in a way that he thought would please his half brother, Jesus.

James had not given the matter much thought over the years, but it had come home to him when Esther appeared. He was suddenly tempted in ways that he thought the others would never be tempted, and he was embarrassed to be the first in the group to have to discuss the possibility of leaving for the love of a woman. He felt weak compared to the others, and felt weak in the eyes of God. He could not believe that God would tolerate such weakness on his part.

What troubled him most was that, notwithstanding the fact that he was half brother to the son of God, and that he had been called by the son of God to his present work, both of which ought to have been enough motivation for any man, he was still tempted to give it all up. He could not understand why his temptations had not been completely conquered that morning in the grove of trees outside the city. No one, save the original twelve, had received a higher calling than he. How could he even think of leaving? What kind of man was he who could compare a calling from God and the lure of domestic life with a good woman?

Little more was said of the matter that night, and James continued to see Esther over the next few days. They tried to talk around the subject, but found that they could not. Every conversation led to the future, and the future could not be discussed with first settling their respective places in it. Finally, one day three weeks after she had first stumbled on James in the courtyard outside the temple, Esther told him that she could take no more.

"I do not know what else can be done. I have offered to sacrifice everything for you, and have asked for nothing in return. I would give up my home, my wealth, everything that is important to most people just to be with you, but still you hesitate. You say that you do not know how to take care of me, or what I would do here amongst your brethren, but I am not concerned for that. All I care for is that you and I are together. There is no reason I can see that we should not be, and yet you put me off. I know that you love me still - I can see it in your eyes and feel it in your kiss. I do not know any other man who could have everything in life that he wants, including service to his God, and will deny himself part of it."

"It is not easy to know what my brother wants exactly, or which example we are to follow. I know only what he told me, how he lived, and how he bid his apostles to live. I find it difficult to do less than they. I know that we cannot all be without wives and families, but it is possible that Jesus meant that his priests should be, that they may better dedicate themselves to his service."

"We have been all through this James, and neither of us is making any progress with the other. I have stayed in Jerusalem two weeks longer than I intended because I hoped to either take you back with me or stay here with you. But at the moment I find that I can do neither. There is nothing left but for you to make up your mind - though perhaps you already have and do not wish to tell me the same news again that you told me eight years ago. Therefore, since I am staying here to no purpose, I will return home to Nazareth, where you know that you can reach me if you desire to do so. A letter or a message will bring me back to you at the first instant, but even as I crawl before you in this manner, I tell you that I can stay here no longer. It is torture to consider the future every day and make no progress at deciding what is to be done about it, and to have no influence over the people and events that can make one happy. I am better, if you are still considering the matter, to let you consider it on your own while I go back to my home in Nazareth. At least there I will not suffer this sort of pain every day."

James could think of nothing to say. He could not urge her to stay or back her going. On this day they had walked outside the city to talk because Esther suggested she had something of importance to say. She had dropped her news as they walked outside the west wall of the city, within sight of the grove of trees where James had last seen Jesus. After walking in silence for a moment, he finally said, "I can think of nothing to say."

"You have said all that you need to say. You neither want me to leave nor want me to stay. You see before you a woman who loves you as no other woman ever has or ever will, and you cannot make up your mind about whether you want her to stay with you. I need nothing further from you."

"It is not that I don't want you to stay; I do not know how we would be happy living on so little, and under the pressure of the Romans and the Sanhedrin. Then there is my work: there is no end to it, and it does not know any hours. We would be together little."

"I think that you are afraid to break with the others - they do not have wives, and you do not want do act other than they would act."

"They do not have wives because Jesus did not take one, and they do not want to break with him. It is the same for me. But as close as I have been to the son of God and to his immediate followers, and knowing what I know of the demands of following him, and considering how personally I was called by him, I am still tempted to give it all up for the love of a woman. But I do not think there could be any greater lapse. I have been called, and I must stay. It is possible for you to stay with me, but impossible for me to go with you."

Esther looked at him hopefully for a moment, as they continued to stroll slowly, but James could see her face cloud over and the doubts return.

"No, I can see that it is impossible for me to stay with you. There are too many questions in your mind, and if they are not resolved to your liking, you will always blame me."

Again James was speechless. The next time they passed the gate they went into the city and proceeded to where Esther had been staying for the last three weeks. She and her servants would join with a caravan that was leaving the next day for the north, and she would be home in three days. Her hearing of the caravan was what prompted her to give James the final ultimatum: if he could not make up his mind, she would be able to leave the city and thus ease the pain.

James came the next morning to her apartment to see off, and helped the servants carry her baggage to the city wall. The scene looked much as it had when he had helped smuggle Paul out of the city: there were various kinds of animals, both for carrying goods and being transported for sale, and all of the attendant odors; there were merchants of every stripe attempting to con one last coin out of those departing; there were woman and children like Esther using the caravan as a means to a safe journey; there were boxes and rolls and bags full of every description of item to be sold in the next city or the one after that. There were hundreds of people waiting to depart already, though the sun was barely up. James and Esther walked off to one side to speak quietly one last time.

"It is possible that I may see you again, James, when I come back to the city, but I will try not to. I will somehow manage to survive such a parting as this two times, but I could never do it a third time. Twice...." she began, and then hesitated, before going on, "I was about to say that twice I have loved you and twice lost you, but that is not true. I have always loved you, even as I prepared for my wedding and lived with my worthy husband. He treated me like a queen James, and yet it is you, who forsakes me to follow your own brother, whom I love above all others. There is no justice in this, either for myself, for you, or for my husband. Perhaps you will ask your brother to explain it to you. No, I am sorry. That was mean. I did not mean to....." She stopped here for a moment, and attempted to choke back tears.

James pulled her close to him and embraced her, and was once again tempted to leave with her, but it was only fleeting. He could not bring himself to leave the life that he felt he had been called to by Jesus. He was in as much pain as he had ever been in his life, much more so than the first time he had left her. At that time he had just seen Jesus raised from the dead and was still under the spell of such a momentous event and all that it might mean.

Now, eight years later he was still dedicated to the calling, but he had seen the excitement wear off, and he frequently did his work out of a sense of duty as much as a sense of exultation. He had had eight years to consider all that he had missed by not marrying Esther, and now she had suddenly happened back into his life - the one woman in the world who could tempt him.

He feared that his own weakness would let him down, and that he would leave with Esther, were it not for the example of the apostles and his own private calling from Jesus. This embarrassed and puzzled him.

Esther and James stayed together that whole morning, even after the caravan began to leave. It was a long time between the instant when the first groups departed and when the last would join them, and Esther delayed her departure until near the end. James noted this, but also noted that neither of them said anything - they simply stood or sat on the ground holding each other. Both knew that a final parting had come, neither was happy at that fact, and there was no small talk that would cover the disappointment that they both felt.

Finally as the morning grew late Esther rose, arranged her clothes, and said to James, "Such sorrow. I did not think that I would ever feel this way again. It is worse this time than the last."

"It is. Much worse."

"I will always love you James....no, let me finish....and nothing will ever change that. But I will not see you again unless you send for me, because I cannot go through this again. If I do hear from you I will drop everything and run to you, but I do not expect that. I know that this is the end."

"As much as I hate it, I too know that it is."

Esther took a deep breath, paused, and then asked, "Is not your brother a cruel task master?"

James was shocked at the cavalier tone of her voice, and wanted to remonstrate with her, as he had done so many times, over the true nature of Jesus and the need for respect, but he could not. "He is not a task master at all - he is the son of God. I am fortunate to be called to serve him, however painful it may be at times."

"But you see the pain that such service causes. We could have been happy together for eight years now, with many children playing around the house, were it not for your brother and this call of his."

"This is true, but the call happened, and there is nothing that either of us can do now, or anything we should want to do. There is no higher calling, and I cannot give it up, no matter how I am tempted."

As if to punish themselves one last time, they embraced tightly and kissed passionately and long before Esther, in tears, tore herself away and ran into the crowd ahead of her servants. James, also in tears, watched until he could no longer see her and then turned sadly to walk back into the city.

He fought back the tears as best he could, as he walked aimlessly about the narrow streets, hardly knowing where he was or the time of day. He was greeted periodically by people who seemed to know him, but while he answered them he did not know to whom he was speaking, or what was said. He felt more alone than at any time in his life, including when he and Esther had separated the first time. He could think of nothing that could give him solace, or anything to look forward to that would put Esther out of his mind. He could see only many more days and nights of ministering to the same people he ministered to all the time, and that was a prospect which did not appeal to him at the moment. He wanted neither food nor drink nor sleep - all he wanted was to be left alone to wallow in his misery.

What pained him most was that he had not made the decision that he knew he ought to have made, which was to tell Esther that he could not marry her because he was serving the Lord. He had allowed himself to be tempted, and then had been so weak that he could not tell her what he knew she ought to hear. She had made the decision for him by tiring of his indecisiveness and leaving town. She had left the door open to a reunion, to be sure, but James knew that that could not happen. He had stalled in making a decision even though he knew the correct one to make, and was not left with the haunting suspicion that he was diminished in the eyes of God.

How could he not be? Had he not been tempted to throw over his service for a woman? Had he not been unable to sort out his priorities enough to tell her the truth? How could God excuse the way he had nearly given in to his temptation - and might have done had not Esther made the decision for them both? He felt small and weak and inadequate to the tasks ahead of him, notwithstanding the fact that he had been up to them for eight years. How much he loved Esther, and how he regretted the day she walked back into his life.

He walked with his head down apparently intently studying the ground in front of him when in fact he saw nothing. After a long time he suddenly lifted himself from his reverie, and noted that it was dark and that he was in the southern end of the city, far from the room he shared with the apostles. He did not know how long he had walked or whom he had met. He immediately began the walk back to the room, buoyed only slightly by the fact that he had, with some help from Esther, kept faith with the others.

CHAPTER 16

In spite of the difficulties James did manage to re-adjust to the life he had chosen, though he was known to take extended walks outside the city to the grove of trees where he had seen Jesus. It was some time before his enthusiasm returned, and many of those to whom he ministered noticed that he was not himself for a number of days, and asked after his health. He placated them by reporting that he suffered from a weak heart now and then, and that he would recover.

But upon his recovery from this first-of-its-kind malady, he threw himself into the work as never before. He was everywhere about the city talking to those who had been in the church for some time, meeting those who had just joined, attempting to keep the new church and the traditional Jewish religion apart, and attempting to see to the many needs of the people who knew him. He was thus aware of the currents in the city, since the new Christians (so called now after having been given this moniker by the people of Antioch while Paul and Barnabas were teaching there, and faithfully reported back to Jerusalem by Paul in one of his many letters) came from all walks of life and from all economic strata, and he could feel the increased tension between the Christians and the Jews, even though there was no outward sign of it.

One night, fully ten years after the death and rising of Jesus, James and four or five of the apostles were gathered in the shared room for the evening meal. It was only the third room they had occupied in all that time. As they ate Matthias burst into the room so out of breath that he could not talk, and the others had to calm him with wine before he could tell them his story.

"James!" he finally began, still before he was ready. "James!"

"Yes, yes, I am here."

"No, the brother of John! He has been arrested by Herod!"

"When did this happen?" demanded James.

"Only just now. I ran here as fast as I could. Someone said that he is to be tried tonight."

"Tried for what?"

"I do not know." At this there was a general uproar among the apostles. Some wanted to go to the jail and demand his release, and others were for waiting to see what would happen, insisting that Herod would not listen to any entreaties from them.

"Let us go and see what is happening, if we can find out, brethren," said Peter, recently back in town. "There may be nothing that we can do, but we must at least make the effort. Even if there is nothing we can do we should post a sentry to attempt to find out what is happening."

To this they all assented, and headed immediately for the center of the city and the jail used by the Idumean kings. It was a low stone structure standing next to the palace. There was a single door entering it, and a single window next to the door. To this door the apostles made their way, and Peter asked the guard if the prisoner James was being held within.

"The prisoner James is not allowed visitors," said the guard, without a trace of concern one way or the other. "He will be tried tomorrow for sedition, and likely hanged." To this news there was another uproar among the apostles, who demanded to see some authority who could authorize them to see their friend. But the guard became nasty and summoned two more of his number from inside the building, and the apostles were forced to back off. They retreated across the street where they would be out of the hearing of the guards to consider what to do. It was a short meeting because there was little they could do. They decided to post a sentry across the street from the jail so that nothing could happen without their knowledge, and James volunteered for this duty. The rest went back to the room, promising to return at sunrise.

James took his outer cloak off, folded it carefully, and then placed it on the ground near the wall of the building across the street from the jail, where it could serve as a cushion. He made himself as comfortable as possible and then settled down to wait. It was the first chance he had had to think since Matthias had stormed into their room with the news.

The other James was by far his closest friend among the original apostles. It was the other James who had introduced him to them after the death of Jesus, and who had supported his bid to join them after the resurrection. They had remained close over the years, notwithstanding the other James' frequent forays into the countryside to teach. He was a mild mannered man, but he was an ardent believer in Jesus, and he preached a fiery sermon that was not calculated to spare the feelings of those who did not believe. Without knowing exactly what was said, James could imagine that the other James had made the wrong statement about the power of the Romans or of Herod in front of the wrong people, and so found himself in jail and facing trial.

James had sensed tensions building between the Christians and the Jews and Romans over the last few months, but there had been no open battles. What puzzled James in the present circumstance was that James had been making the same hot blooded sermons for ten years and had never before been arrested, save the time they had all been arrested and scourged. He had either found some new way to incite the authorities, or they had become less tolerant of his beliefs. Either way it appeared to be trouble for the community.

James stayed awake as long as he could, but he found that he could not last the entire night. He spent a restless night attempting to sleep in different positions, including leaning on the wall and lying down flat out on the street corner.

The first footfall of morning traffic roused him, and he rose and donned his cloak again. He had a difficult time clearing the morning fog from his head, and took a moment to remember why he was sleeping on the ground in front of the jail. He had not recovered himself long when he saw the remainder of the brethren coming down the street toward him. Peter led the way, followed by Matthias, Andrew, Bartholomew, Simon, and Mary. None of the others were not in the city at the moment, and that number included John, the brother of James.

James had nothing to report, and a request of the guard for information saw them dismissed peremptorily. They had little alternative but to lurk about the street corner until they saw activity in either the jail or the palace. It was mid morning before they saw any such thing, and what they saw was the other James being half walked, half dragged from the front of the jail toward the palace. They immediately called to him and ran in his direction, but were rebuffed by the guards. The other James heard them and turned to look at them, and it was clear to James that he recognized them, but he was quickly pulled inside. None of the apostles were allowed to follow.

They milled about in the street wondering what they could do next. Before long they were pushed away from the low gate leading into the palace grounds by a contingent of bodyguards, and then by a delegation of the Sanhedrin. James did not know any of them personally, and was glad to see that neither Ananias nor Joseph of Arimathea was among them. None of the Sanhedrin would answer any questions from any of the apostles, and the apostles were left to speculate that they had come for the trial of the other James.

They attempted to settle themselves in for an extended wait, but they had no sooner done so than a guard came out of the palace to the gate and demanded that they all follow him. This they readily did.

They were led in through the same side entrance that had been used first by the other James and his guard and then the Sanhedrin. They followed a series of narrow, dark corridors until they suddenly emerged into a large, well lit room. At one end there was a throne, and on this was perched a well dressed, relatively young man whom they took to be Herod. He was surrounded by courtiers of various kinds, including those whose only purpose was to keep him supplied with wine and food. In front of him stood the bedraggled but proud figure of James, standing straight and tall though his hands were tied behind his back. Around the walls of the room stood what appeared to be members of the king's court, spectators and one or two Roman officials, and near the throne on one side stood the four members of the Sanhedrin the apostles had seen enter earlier. The apostles were led through the crowd standing against the back wall of the room and stopped fifteen feet behind the other James, who turned to look at them as they entered. In fact all eyes in the room were on them, as it appeared that the proceedings had stopped while they were being fetched. There were murmurings as they were placed at the head of the group that stood behind the other James, but James could not make them out.

Herod, brown haired and clean shaven after the fashion of the Romans, asked, once quiet had been restored, "Are these your friends?"

"They are," said the other James, without looking around again.

"It appears to be a small group that you are part of. I hardly think it sufficient to bring the kingdom of God to Jerusalem. Why, only a few of my guards would be enough to prevent whatever plans you may have." There was laughter around the room which the other James allowed to subside before he began.

"These are only the brethren who are here at the moment. The others are spreading the word of the risen Christ throughout the world, from Rome even to Syria. In this group of brethren I count only those who knew the man Jesus before he was crucified. There are many thousands of others who have joined the church since. But it is also true that they do not quarrel with the power of Rome. The power of Rome is nothing to the power of God. All of us wait for the kingdom of God, and we know that it will not be of this earth."

Herod only raised his eyebrows a little, and this caused those close enough to see the gesture to laugh once again. After a pause he continued, "So many, and yet you say that they have no ambition. How thoughtful of them." Laughter once again. "Do these thousands include women and children who can be counted on not to raise the sword against Rome?"

"All of them can be counted on not to raise the sword against Rome. It is not our way."

"But there are those who swear that you have told your followers that they should submit themselves to the power of God and his son Jesus"...here Herod smiled, once again pleasing the gallery with the exception of the apostles..."over all else, including Rome. Is that not an incitement to riot?"

"It is not. There can be no power higher than God - even the Romans would acknowledge this. They believe in false gods, but they will admit that their gods are their highest authority." James stole a glance at the members of the Sanhedrin to see how they took this statement, but they were impassive. "Submitting to one's god does not mean that one is snubbing the state."

"But the emperor is god," said Herod, still pressing the point, "at least according to the Romans. If you are telling your followers that they should follow your God rather than the god of the Romans, you are inciting them to disobey Caesar when it is convenient for them to do so."

"Our God does not put us in conflict with the state. His son Jesus"....here there was laughter again, which the other James ignored..." told us that we should give to Caesar what is Caesar's and to God what is God's."

"Should not the subjects of Caesar worship Caesar if he orders them to do so?"

"The fact that he claims to be a god does not make him one...."

"It appears to have worked for Jesus of Nazareth!" rejoined Herod, to the laughter of the room, once again with the exception of the apostles.

"Caesar has not raised another man or himself from the dead, or performed the other miracles that came from the hand of Jesus. Nor can he soothe the spirit of thousands with a sermon on a mountainside. We pay Caesar's taxes and obey his laws - he should not concern himself with our worship."

"You are the confident prisoner, telling the court what Caesar should and should not be involved in!" said Herod, playing to the crowd and looking for approval from them.

"I tell Caesar nothing - that is my point. When I am teaching people in the street I say nothing to them of Caesar or anything that matters to Caesar - I tell them only what matters to God."

Herod stood regarding his prisoner for a moment, apparently amused at what he had wrought. Murmuring began in the background until Herod raised his hand for silence. "Is there no one here to speak for you? It is a small and disloyal church indeed that will not provide support for one of its teachers."

"We are here to speak for him," said Peter, very loudly to ensure that all those in the room heard him. "We have waited all this night to speak to our brother, and have been denied. Now we are hear to speak for him, to tell you that he does not preach against the Romans or any other government. It is not our way." The other apostles and Mary all nodded their heads in assent at this, and there were added comments to the effect that "We do not preach about government" and "He is innocent of speaking against Rome" but it all appeared to have little effect on the crowd.

"This is a very small mob that you have gathered on your behalf," said Herod to the other James.

"It is all the crowd that will gather when an innocent man is arrested late in the evening and then bound over for trial early the next morning," said Peter. This appeared to perturb Herod, who suddenly sat up straight on the throne.

"Swift justice is the Roman way," said he to Peter.

"Then set James free, and it will be done," replied Peter.

"What is your name?"

"I am Simon, known as Peter."

"I am Herod, known as king," said Herod to laughter. "Do not try to match wits with me - you will come up short. What have you to say in defense of this man?"

"Only that he is like all of us: we do not teach against Caesar any more than we teach against the wind or the sea. While they affect our lives we live with them and cope. But they do not affect our worship and so we do not teach about them at all."

"Then how is it that you are always before the authorities? It began with this man Jesus who was crucified, and there was another man stoned outside the gates of the city, and you were all arrested and scourged. Yes, you see that I have studied the problem, and know what you have been doing. Now here we find this man, accused of treason against Caesar. If you are so innocent, why are you all here again?"

"We are here because there are those who would not let us worship or bring new members to the church. It is not because we teach against Caesar or curse the Sanhedrin. We would leave them be, just as we would like to be left alone, but they do not return the favor."

"Perhaps it is because they think that you are crazy. Is it not true that you call a man who was crucified outside the gates of this city the son of God?"

"Yes it is true that we call him that, and we call him the son of God because that is what he is."

Herod sat there saying nothing, but with a bemused smile on his face. After a moment the crowd broke into laughter once again.

"I understand there is one among you who claims to be the brother of the man Jesus," said Herod, emphasizing the word man.

James was surprised by the reference to himself, but after a moment the shock wore off and he stepped out from behind Peter. "I am the brother of Jesus," said he.

"You do not look like the brother of a god," said Herod, once again to the laughter of the spectators.

"I am only half brother to him, and I am not worthy to shift the sand that his feet have walked on. I did not believe in him until the third day after he was crucified, when I saw him risen from the dead. But when I saw him I knew who he must be. What I look like does not matter: what matters is that one believe in him as the son of God."

Herod was about to reply when one of the Sanhedrin motioned to him. He leaned over and listened to the member for a moment, and then straightened up again. "I have heard that your cult stole the man's body so that you may claim that he rose from the dead, and now I have it confirmed in my own hearing."

"I make no such claim. We had no reason to steal his body because his body was not there when our women went to anoint it. We have all seen him since that day, as have hundreds of others."

Herod stared at James for a moment, and then turned to Mary. "Who is this woman who is with you?"

"She is called Mary, and she is the mother of Jesus," said Peter.

"Well we are indeed honored today! We have with us not only the brother of the son of God, but his mother as well," said Herod, still playing to the crowd and being well received for it. There were laughter and catcalls throughout the large room. "Tell us, mother of the son of God, how did you and God conceive this child?" This brought uproarious laughter from the throng, which Mary gracefully ignored while she patiently waited for it to stop.

"The child was given me by God. I do not pretend to know how God can do such a thing, any more than I understand how his son can raise himself up from the dead. I accepted that the child was God's will, because at that time I did not know man."

"But it would appear that you have known him since," said Herod, once again setting the crowd off.

"I have five sons and two daughters, and all of my sons now teach the good news of Jesus."

"But not your daughters? Shocking, mother of the son of God, shocking!" said Herod, mockingly. James wanted to rush the throne where Herod sat, but he was restrained by the other apostles.

"So the brother of the son of God is angry now, and would come to hurt me? Well, well, let him come, and see if the son of God will save him from the swords of the soldiers of Caesar. I see that you will not try. Very well, hold your tongue until you are spoken to." James calmed himself after a moment, and the others released him.

"I begin to tire of this exercise," said Herod when calm had been restored. "Let us get back to the offenses of the prisoner James."

"Your friends do nothing more than tell me what you have already told me. I find that you have preached against Caesar by telling the people of your god and his son whose brother is among us." There were murmurs of approval from the crowd. "I sentence you to die by the sword as soon as may be." At this there were loud calls of agreement from among the crowd, and those nearest the apostles and Mary began to ride them, saying that they should receive the same punishment. It was apparent that, other than the apostles and Mary, there were no other friends of James in the throng.

The other James was immediately ushered out of the room by another door while Peter called to Herod and demanded to be heard. "This man is innocent of any crime, and he does not deserve to die" he continued to shout, though none could hear him over the tumult of the crowd, most of which was cheering the removal of James. The other James took one last look at his friends as he was hustled away, but he did not appear to be afraid. Mary began to cry uncontrollably. James was outraged at the decision of Herod and wanted to lash out, but he and the rest of the group were being jostled by the surrounding people and he had a difficult job staying on his feet and attempting to protect his mother.

Suddenly there was a lull in the noise, and the jostling stopped. James looked toward the throne to see Herod standing in front of it, hands held high.

"This has been an educational experience for me," he pronounced, to the delight of the crowd. "I would learn more tomorrow. Simon called Peter, you appear to be of a sharp wit. You will teach us more. Arrest him!" Guards came toward the spot where the apostles were standing to take Peter away, and the crowd cheered exultantly. There were calls that they should all be arrested so that there could be a trial every day for a week, and others that they should all be killed this moment and be done with the trials. James and the others rushed forward to keep the guards away from Peter, but they were not numerous or strong enough.

"Do not fight with them," Peter shouted over the din. "The Son of God will be with me." With that he was lead away through the same side door that the other James had been led out of. At that moment another contingent of guards came to them and pushed them toward the door they had entered through, and then escorted them back through the corridors and out into the street.

First they had no notion of what to do: they would have rushed the building to free Peter to save him from the fate that had apparently befallen the other James, but they could not have dealt with the small contingent of guards which faced them across the gate; protesting to the guards would have been a useless endeavor, and there was no one else handy to scream at in frustration.

So they milled about the gate for a few minutes, attempting to decide what they ought to do next. The problem was that they did not know what would happen to Peter, nor did they know when. The guards finally sent them away, and they crossed the street and walked down a block so as to be out of ear shot.

They agreed that they needed to know what would happen to Peter and when, and they all turned to James for that answer. In his ministering to the faithful of the city he knew where many of them worked, and it was hoped that he would have a contact inside the palace who could find something out. He could think of no one at the moment, but agreed to look into the matter, and hurried off for that purpose. Andrew was detailed to stay behind in hopes of hearing or seeing something of Peter, and the others went about their business.

James scavenged about among the people he knew best, and was at last told that there was a woman among the faithful who did some laundry in the palace of the king. He was pointed in the direction of her home, and found her there by the purest chance. He explained the situation to her, after ascertaining that she would be in a position to learn something of use, and she readily assented to spy as the opportunity presented itself. She hustled back to the palace without having finished the meal she had come home for, leaving James in sole possession of her home. He closed the door after himself and then went about his rounds.

It was only now, when he finally had no action that he could take and nothing else he could do but walk by himself, that he had time to consider the death of the other James. He had been afraid that something of the sort might happen to one of them, and had considered the possibility that it could be him, but it was painful now that it had happened, to think that it had been the other James who was the first to suffer.

He felt that impotent rage welling up inside himself again, as it had at the trial and at the gate after they had been escorted out of the building without Peter. His bile toward the Romans and the Sanhedrin, who as far as he knew had nothing to do with the death of the other James, was limitless. He wanted something or some one to punish for this miscarriage of justice - someone to make pay for the fact that James had been treated so cavalierly. He looked around him as he walked, and there was no one save the innocent inhabitants of the city going about their chores under much the same burdens as he, and knowing nothing of the recent trial and murder. He wanted to pray to calm himself, but he could not overcome his temper. He wanted to scream where he stood, but did not want to appear insane to those who would hear him. Instead he picked up his pace gradually, finally settling into a trot, a pace which he kept up until he was outside the city gates and in the grove of trees where he had first seen Jesus after the resurrection. There he screamed and howled at the top of his lungs, and threw stones at trees until he could lift and hurl them no more. It was not as primal a performance as that on the morning when he had first seen Jesus alive, but it was close. When fully spent from his physical exertions, he sat down under one of the trees to cry.

After about two hours, when he could sit no more, he raised himself and dusted his clothes, and then went back into the city. News of the apparent murder of James and the arrest of Peter spread among the faithful like a plague, and soon James found himself asked about it at every turn and by every person that he happened to meet. The people were full of concern and worry, and there were not a few tears among the women.

Matthias replaced Andrew in the late afternoon, and the others sat down to a late meal long after dark without any hope of enjoyment. What little they ate they ate quietly, and the room was as like a tomb as James ever remembered it being. While he looked around at the others, wondering what they were all thinking, the sound of a small wagon being pulled down the street caught their attention. There was no reason why it should have, since it was a common enough occurrence in the area, yet they all looked up at the same time, as if they all had the same feeling that it had something to do with them. They waited expectantly, all looking at each other, as they heard it stop in the street below. Footsteps followed up the stairs, and in a moment Matthias entered. "Come down with me, brothers," was all he said, and then he retreated out the door again after taking a torch down from the wall.

The others rose and followed him, all fearing the worst. James had no idea what he was about to learn, but knew that either the other James or Peter was at the heart of it. Below, in the darkened street, they found the wagon that they had heard. A shapeless form was lying in it, covered with a cloth. They gathered around it in a foreboding manner, and Matthias lifted a corner of the cloth and held the torch under it so they might see. What they beheld was the body of a man, obviously that of James because of the clothes that were still on him. What James did not notice at first was that while the head was there, it was not attached to the body. There were moans and curses among the men, and tears from Mary.

"What has happened to him?" asked Andrew.

"He was apparently taken outside immediately and beheaded with a sword in a courtyard behind the palace," said Matthias. "The spy that James sent came to me only minutes ago and told that they were casting about for a way to do away with the body when she offered to take it. They belittled her unmercifully but gave her the body, since it relieved them of the problem, and she promptly came to get me. I borrowed the cart from a member of the faithful that I know of, and here we are. We must bury him immediately."

As they set about deciding how to do this, James felt revulsion at the Romans for the way that the other James had died. It would not have been as painful as the death of Jesus, but it would not have been swift and painless either. James prayed for eternal rest for him, and then set about helping the others. Matthias returned to the jail to stand guard.

Much later in the evening when they had all laid down, though none had gone to sleep, James heard the sound of footsteps in the street below. He had been lying awake thinking of the loss of James and the effect it might have on the group, and he could not sleep for fear of the events of the day. It was unusual to hear people walking about in the middle of the night, but James had the foreboding feeling that the walkers were coming to see them, and that they had news of Peter. These thoughts passed through his head before he could sit up, and he nudged Andrew who was laying beside him. When he heard the footsteps Andrew got up to rouse the others, and James went to the door to see who might appear.

After a moment there was a knock on the door, and, seeing in the moonlight that there were only two men standing on the landing, James opened the door. As he did so one of the others re-lit one of the torches to reveal the bedraggled but very much alive Peter and Matthias. There was an audible gasp of astonishment in the room, and then they all rushed forward to embrace and welcome him. There was such a confusion of voices and demands for explanations that Peter could not answer them all. They bade him sit down in his accustomed place in the center of the room nearest the central upright supporting the roof, and tell them how the king had come to let him go.

"Brethren," said he, when there was enough quiet, "it is entirely possible that the king does not yet know that I am free." There were cries of "What?" and "How can this be?"

"You remember how it was that we found ourselves free from prison when we were all arrested at once? Well, so it has been again. I was asleep in my cell, after being given nothing to eat or drink all day...yes, I will have some of that bread and lamb, thank you.... when I was suddenly awakened by a bright light in my cell. I was chained hand and foot, and slept between two guards, yet they did not awaken. I did not think that the same thing would happen again, so I immediately assumed that the Romans had come to take me for a midnight trial. I admit that the thought crossed my mind that this is how they treated our Master. But it was not the Romans, but a single man dressed all in white - blinding white it was - for I soon saw that he carried no lamp though my cell was lit as though it were mid day. He commanded me to throw off my chains, and they fell to the floor, and then to throw off the prison cloak, which I did. The door to my cell was open, and he led me through it, past the outer guards, whom I took to be sleeping, and finally out into the night. He held the gate for me - the very one that we stood by this morning, and I passed through. But when I turned to thank him he was gone. I have not seen him since."

"Was it the same man who led us all out of jail?"

"I cannot tell. I saw his face clearly, and yet I cannot describe it to you, and I am not sure that I would recognize him again if I saw him. I do not believe that the Lord intends for us to know him."

They puzzled over this for a few minutes, wondering who the lieutenant from on high might be, when James was stuck with another thought.

"Perhaps you should make haste to leave the city. When Herod finds that you have escaped he is sure to send after you."

"But there is no where that I can reach at this hour that would put me out of his reach. Wherever I can run, he can follow, and much faster. No, I do not think that we should risk the safety of the faithful by putting them in the position of hiding me. I know that they would do it gladly, but there is no reason to bring them into this affair. No, I will stay here and see what developments there will be. The Master did not run, and told us that we would be blessed if we suffered for his name's sake. I will not be the first to run when we are threatened. By the way, what have we heard of James?"

They told him the news in short order, and Peter took it hard. James could see anger, and then resentfulness and then sadness pass over his face, and it was a few minutes before he was able to speak.

"We have all prepared ourselves for this, and yet it is difficult to believe that James is gone. It is as though I have lost my right arm, so close was he to us all. When Judas left us we were glad to see him go, and the Master was never really one of us, since we are not worthy to tie his sandals. But James is a painful loss, and I shall not get over it soon." Heads all nodded at this.

They talked over the subject of the death of James for a few more minutes, and then covered the miraculous release of Peter, and then laid down once again to try to sleep.

They all laid down half expecting to hear the ominous tread of soldiers' feet in the street below at any minute, but they heard nothing for the rest of the night, and most were awake to hear it if it came.

When they gave up on sleep shortly after sunrise they discussed the possibility that they might find Peter gone in the morning and then come for him, and so they expected to have their morning meal interrupted at any time. But there was no sound of soldiers in the street below, no thump of horses hooves heralding the approaching wrath of the king, no spy from the palace warning them of the coming of the authorities. They waited in the room until mid morning before venturing out, and when they did they were not accosted by the soldiers they met as they expected to be. All was quiet in the city, and it appeared to be business as usual between the new Christians, the Romans, and the Sanhedrin.

They mulled this lack of development over at the evening meal when they had all gathered, and none could account for it. At the very least they expected that Peter would be arrested to salve the pride of the king, but Andrew put an end to the speculation when he commented that it had been hard enough for the powers that be to explain the escape of all twelve of them on the previous occasion. They could not like the prospect of having to do so again.

James had other reason to worry. In the only failure to obey his brother since his conversion, he had never allowed his mother to become the charge of the apostle named John. Jesus had commanded such from the cross, but James reasoned that that had been before James had joined the movement, and that his subsequent doing so obviated the need for Mary to live with John.

So they had been together all these years, and now Mary was aged and infirm. She still did what she could to care for the men in the group who might be in town, but she could no longer keep up with the work that was required. Other women from the community helped her when they could, and it now fell to the men who lived in the room to care for her more of the time than she cared for them. James was sorry to see her deteriorate so - sad to see her in any less than the perfect health that had been her habit all her life.

CHAPTER 17

James had made the familiar walk many times, and he liked to think that doing so had helped to keep a relative peace between the Jews and the Christians, as they now called themselves. Now, in the middle of the week, he had had a messenger come to him at the room asking that he go to the house of Ananias, priest and member of the Sanhedrin.

He and Ananias had remained friends over the years, though he could hardly deny that they were not as close as they had once been. Ananias' rise in fortunes in the Sanhedrin had coincided with James' increasing devotion to the cause of his brother and his subsequent impoverishment. James resented none of this, but he did resent the implication, based on what usually happened at meetings like the one he was going to at the moment, that it was solely the responsibility of the Christians to keep the peace.

Ananias had his heart set on occupying the seat of the High Priest, and had been cultivating the good graces of the Romans in order to get it, at least according to the infrequent accounts that James had formerly received from Joseph of Arimathea, who had recently died. To this end he had taken it upon himself to keep the Christians quiet, and in his mind this included seeing that there were no open conflicts with the Jewish community. He therefore called James in now and again when there had been an incident that alarmed him and with which he wanted James' help. James sometimes had an inkling of what the incident was before he was summoned to Ananias, and sometimes did not. Whenever he heard of an incident that might raise an alarm he knew to expect the call, but he knew of no incident this time, and so was prepared to be surprised.

James was usually forced to wait in the anteroom, where he had waited the day Jesus was crucified, but when he entered this time he found Ananias waiting for him.

"James, my friend, how have you been?" he began, and then continued without waiting for a response, "I suppose you have heard of the incident by the pool of Siloam last night?" James had not.

"There was a dispute among some of your people and some Jews over the use of the pool, and it turned into a fight that was eventually broken up by Roman soldiers." Ananias appeared to be at an end, but James said nothing.

"We have had this talk many times before, and I do not call you here to tell you things that you already know, but we cannot have the Romans believe that they must come between Christians and Jews in the city. It will not help the reputation of the Sanhedrin - which I know does not concern you, though it should - if it appears that we cannot keep order. We do not want to

give the Romans the idea that they must take more power to themselves."
Still James said nothing.

"I believe that I have made myself clear," said Ananias, with some asperity. "Is there something else which you wish to know?"

"Only what it is that you expect me to do about the matter. I am sorry that some of the Christian flock would resort to fighting, and for that I will reprimand them. As always I will remind them of the need to keep the peace, which they ought to do as Christians anyway. But it is true that I cannot be expected to prevent every disagreement in the city. I suppose you cannot tell me whether or not the fight in question was the only fight in the entire city last night? Or the only time this week that Roman soldiers have been called to break up a dispute? No? Then why are we concerned about this fight by the Pool of Siloam more than any other? Surely you are not suggesting that other groups may fight, but not Christians. Or that it is only Christians who can cause enough trouble to bring the Romans?"

"Before the start of this cult that involves your brother, there was peace in the city. Our only enemy was the Romans. It was a nice, clean way to go about business - we knew who we could count on and who we could not, and we presented a united front to the Romans. Now you and the others like you divide Jew from Jew so that every Jew must watch both his brethren and the Romans. It should not be this way. I have relied on you over the years to help keep the peace, but I find that you are becoming less and less reliable."

"It is not in my power to keep the peace. There are too many people in this city for a simple, poor disciple to keep them all in order. If I may say so, it is not the Christians who are the problem. We are not in positions of power. We cannot arrest you, we cannot harass you, we can do nothing in this city save hope that we be allowed to worship on our own without interruption. I repeat my point: not all of the problems in this city are related to Christians; why have you chosen to pick on us? Have you tired of using the Gentiles as your scapegoat?"

"We have no need of scapegoats, and we harass and pick on no one...."

"Then why were a number of us arrested a few years ago, brought to the jail, and all scourged? Because we did not pay taxes? I hardly think so. Why was James, one of our number, arrested, tried and murdered on the same day? And please spare me the story that he was a threat to the Romans. I am not clear to this day who talked the Romans into that, but it was clearly a member of the Sanhedrin. No, no, it won't work. Do not protest your innocence. James had been saying the same things in the same streets for years and the Romans heard him and paid no attention. Why should they have suddenly become concerned? Only because someone whispered in their ear. They would pay no attention to anyone else in the city other than a member of the Sanhedrin."

"We have no need to fear the likes of a band of zealots who worship a man who was punished for the crime of being a blasphemer. Why should we trouble ourselves? But when that band of zealots comes among our people and attempts to trick them into joining the zealots, then we have cause to be concerned. Do not tell me that you would not care if the members of your group were to begin abandoning you and coming back to the faith of their fathers. Of course you would."

"It is happening to us, and we are doing nothing. At least you admit that there are people who see the wisdom taught them in the name of the risen Jesus, and come to it of their own free will. But there are those who come to us and do not like what they find, and we do not hold them; we do not find ways to persecute them into staying with us; we have no power to do so even if it were our desire. We have tried very hard to live with you, but it is you who will not accept us, and not us who will not accept you."

"You accept Gentiles and tax collectors into your midst. They are polluted people and it is our duty to protect ourselves from them."

"The city is full of tax collectors and Gentiles, and yet you do not attempt to rid the city of all of them. You attack only those who have become Christians. There is no way for you to defend yourself: it is Christians who are the target of your wrath, and it is because of our faith, and for no other reason, that you attack us. We have never asked anything other than to be left alone, and even this has not been granted us."

"You have not asked to be left alone; you have asked us to stand by while you spread vile lies about a blasphemer being the son of God and urge otherwise faithful people to join you. You have torn at the heart of our faith by claiming that Jews have killed the son of God and have attempted to turn people against the God of Abraham, Isaac and Jacob. It is our right and our duty to fight back. What kind of faith do we have if we will not defend it?"

"Then let us carry out the battle in the minds and hearts of those we would call our own. Let us leave each other alone, and see how many people come to join the followers of Jesus. Let those we would preach to be the judge of our message."

"There can be no peace in the city if rival religions fight over the possession of the loyalty of the people. How then would we oppose the Romans? I did not ask you here - and note that you were asked, not forced - to discuss once again the difficulties of faith. I ask only that you continue to help me in keeping the two sides apart."

"I do not know what happened at the pool of Siloam last night, but otherwise it is not I who should be keeping the sides apart - it is you. We are not the aggressors - it was not our mob that stoned Stephen outside the gates of the city, or that insisted that Jesus be crucified, for that matter. We haven't the power or the numbers to be able to threaten you, and we have not done so."

"But you have threatened us. You wish to start a cult in the middle of faithful people, and draw them away from the faith of their fathers."

"But we do not do this with force, or with violence, and we are not drawing them away from the faith of their fathers: we are drawing them to the culmination of it. You laugh and sneer, but there are many who believe, and they believe with their hearts and minds, not because we have forced them to do so."

Ananias stared at James for a moment. "There was a time when I had no closer friend in the world than you, but your brother has come between us. There is no point in discussing his status any more; I will not convince you, and you may be certain that you will not convince me. All I ask is that you help ensure that there are no more incidents like that of last night in the city. Help us keep the peace among ourselves so that we have no one to oppose but the Romans."

"That is a reasonable proposition, and I promise that I will do what I can in this matter when I have some assurance that we will be allowed to live and worship in peace; that there will be no more contrived arrests on the part of the king; that there will be no more murders in the name of peace." When James finished speaking it immediately occurred to him that he must look a comical sight: a ragamuffin in threadbare clothes telling a well dressed member of the Sanhedrin, in the member's house, his conditions for keeping the peace in the city.

Ananias stared as vehemently as it could be done. "Get out," he hissed finally, "and never darken my door again." He wanted to be mad, but James, who studied his eyes carefully, could see that there was a hint of sadness there as well. James also felt the pain of the end of the friendship, though it had been eroding for some time. There had always been that hope that they could rekindle their former feelings for each other, but that now appeared to be at an end. James turned to the door and left the house, never to return.

He considered the problem on the way back to the room, but found that he could not feel very sad about the business. If the end of their friendship had come more suddenly it might have been more difficult, but James had known for some time that it must come to this. They had hardly spoken in recent years, even though James had worked hard to ensure that there was no schism between the Jews and the Christians, but it now appeared that the schism was complete, at least for he and Ananias.

James was still concerned for the rest of the Jewish people and for the Gentiles who joined the new church. He would attempt to limit the distance the Christians put between themselves and the Jews to the best of his ability because he did not want open warfare and because he did not believe that Jesus meant for there to be any momentous changes.

James repeated the conversation to those of the brethren who were present at the moment, in this case only Andrew and John, and Mary. None of them thought much of it, though Mary did mention that it looked as though James and Ananias would see little of each other in the future, but this was because none of them had ever placed any faith in staying close to their Jewish roots. They still observed the law as they had been taught, but they were quicker than James to distinguish between those who accepted Jesus' nature as the Son of God and those who did not. After enduring a chorus of "I told you so" from Andrew and John, James sat down to work on the letter that he had been urged by Peter to write.

He had learned to read and write as a boy, but had had little practice when Peter, soon after James had become the head of the church in Jerusalem, suggested that he should put the lessons he had learned down for those who would come after them. Peter and some of the others were doing the same thing, though in most of their cases they wrote to the people of towns and cities that they had visited. James resisted the idea at first, claiming that since he had not heard Jesus preach very much he was not qualified to undertake the task. Peter rejected this, saying that James had learned from the other apostles, that he had heard one sermon, and that he could draw on his own experience in faith and that of the people that he ministered to in the city. They had discussed the matter many times, but James found that Peter was more unbending than he on the subject, so he finally agreed to make the effort.

He found that he progressed slowly. His lack of experience made it difficult for him to organize his thoughts properly, and he feared, once he did begin to write, that he might contradict what the others might be saying or writing. He was particularly fearful that he might run afoul of Paul, who was already famous for the writing that he did back to the cities that he had visited. James was concerned that they all present a united front on matters of faith, and he took care to consult with the others when he had an opportunity, including going so far as to establish a correspondence with Paul. After years of effort, many starts and stops, and much soul searching, he decided to focus his work, and he meant for it to be short, on the practical side of faith in Jesus, and the difference that it ought to make in the lives of the faithful.

This, he decided, other than the fact that they had spent more time with his brother than he, was the principal difference between himself and the other apostles: he spent his time with the people of Jerusalem, rather than preaching to them, converting them, and then moving on. James had steadfastly refused to preach over the years, citing the same reason that he did not want to write the letter in the first place: he did not know enough about the teachings of Jesus. He absorbed what he could from the others, and attempted to help the locals apply it to their daily lives. He was only now, after years of effort, finally to the point where he was satisfied with what he had written, and was able, each time he sat down to write, to pick up from where he had left off.

His inclination in the beginning had been to defer to the opinions of the others when they commented on what he had written, and it was this tendency which caused much of his re-writing. But he saw that he did not progress, and that there were disputes among the others on various subjects. It was this lack of consensus among them that convinced James to limit his theological efforts to the practical applications. When discussing the matter with Peter he had expressed some belief that he had finally figured out what he ought to do, though it would have been easier if Peter had never insisted on the effort in the first place.

"James!" Peter had exclaimed, "The effort must take place. You must see the position we are in: we are the first and the only men to be privileged to travel with the Savior. Think of it! That in all of the world and in all of the times God should send his son here, amongst us, and that we should be given the sight to see him for who he is. We might have been among the many ignorant who refused to believe in him, or we might have lived five years earlier or later, and so missed him. We have been truly blessed. But now we are all that is left, and it is up to us to pass on his teaching to those who will come after us, so that his memory will not disappear from the world. It is up to us to establish his church here on Earth so that men may come to know him and to worship him. All of us must contribute to this, James. If even one of us fails to leave a message, then we have not done the duty that is left to us. Yes, yes I know there are others who are writing nothing, and believe me I will not let them rest in peace. But you have made the start, and now the Lord is with you: he has shown you how to use the knowledge you have gained as the leader of the church in Jerusalem. Do not fail me or those Christians who will come after us."

Peter had apparently discovered that James could be reached with such personal appeals, and this case was no different.

Among the many subjects that James and the other apostles disagreed on among themselves was the still simmering question of the proper entrance into the church for Gentiles. There were those among them who believed that all who joined the church should obey all of the laws of Moses, including the requirement that all men be circumcised and that certain foods be avoided. Others felt that such requirements could not be applied to Gentiles. It was conceivable that they could be circumcised, but it was more likely that such a requirement, since it did not mean anything to the Gentile, might give them the wrong idea about the priorities of the church. For most it was already too late to obey the laws concerning food, since they had been eating food the Jewish people considered unclean all of their lives.

The problem had been present for some time, but it had lately come to a head because of the success Paul was having baptizing Gentiles into the church, and his refusal to attempt to enforce the law of Moses. Reports had reached Jerusalem over the years that Paul was not even teaching the law of Moses to the Gentiles who would enter the church, and there had been some correspondence between Paul and the other apostles on the matter, but it had never been resolved to the satisfaction of all. It was now some sixteen years since the death of Jesus, and the killing of James proved to the apostles that they could not wait forever to have the matter settled. Peter therefore decided that there should be a conference on the matter in Jerusalem, and he wrote for Paul to attend so that he might speak his peace. At the same time he wrote to where he thought the other apostles who were not in the city might be, asking that they all return for the meeting.

It took some time for the messengers to find all of the apostles, and for the apostles to arrange their affairs so that they could return. They trickled back into the city over the period of a few weeks, and settled down to await the arrival of Paul. James was mildly afraid that the arrival of all the apostles at the same time might tempt either the Romans or the Sanhedrin to toy with them, but they did not.

The missive sent to Paul asking that he come for the meeting suggested that he sneak into the city and let no one there know of his presence. He had not been back since he had snuck out with the help of the apostles fourteen years before, and while there had been no great hue and cry over him at any time since, it occurred to James and the others that his presence might tempt someone to act against him.

Paul sent a note back to the apostles saying that he would come to the meeting, but that he would not sneak into the city. While he would not arrive behind crashing horns and cymbals, he wrote, nor would he act as a common thief again. After so many years it was time for the Sanhedrin to forget the matter and allow him to live like any of the other Christians in the city.

Paul and his associate Barnabas finally came into the city. They were warmly greeted by all, notwithstanding the differences they were about to discuss, because it was common knowledge that Paul was a gifted speaker and writer, and that he had brought the most new members into the church. Paul brought with him copies of the letters that he had written to the churches he had founded, and handed them over to James, at his request. They allowed Paul and Barnabas a day to rest from their journey, which had been the longest, and then they convened a conference that made James very uneasy.

The issue was a basic one: should the Gentiles have to obey the laws of Moses, as the Jewish members of the new church had done all their lives? James knew the intransigence that dominates some people when the subject is religion, and he was afraid that a failure to resolve the problem might result in the splitting of the church into two factions. This, he felt, would be fatal to its long term survival. He had voiced this opinion to Peter and some of the others, and they had the same fear, but they, and Peter especially, believed that the church could not survive if the issue were not resolved. "Believe me, James," Peter had said, "the meeting will not end until we have resolved the matter in a way that is satisfactory to all. It may not be the perfect answer that we devise, but it will have the approval of all who attend the meeting."

They met in the room that the apostles lived in for lack of any other space large enough to hold them all. All of the twelve apostles were there, as was James, Paul and his associate Barnabas, and another teacher by the name of Silas. It was cramped for it was a small room, but it was not as hot as it might have been since they were meeting in the early evening. James was amused to note that they would decide the issue without any Gentiles present.

"Brethren, brethren, please," said Peter, holding up his hands for quiet. "It is time for us to begin the discussions that will solve the issue of observance for the Gentiles. It has dragged on for too many years. I will re-state the case so that we may have a common ground to begin. It is this: those of us who are faithful to Jesus, the son of God, but who are also Jews and therefore sons of Abraham, continue to observe the law as handed down to us by Moses, who in turn was given it by God. This law has served us well for many generations, and Jesus himself told us that it would not pass away until all is fulfilled. But he also sent us out to preach to all nations, including the Gentiles, and he made it possible that men of all nations should hear and understand us, and those men have been joining his church ever since his death. But those Gentiles have never obeyed the laws of Moses - in fact they have never heard of them, and so in our eyes they are unclean. How then, to welcome them into the church without making ourselves unclean with them? Is this not the issue?" There was general murmuring among the small assembly that it was, and James was surprised that there was no dissent. "It is Paul who has brought the matter to crisis because of his success in converting Gentiles to the faith of Jesus. We will begin by letting him speak."

"You make it hard for a man, Peter," said Paul, when he had risen. "On the one hand you pay a compliment by saying that I have brought many Gentiles into the church, and then in the next breath you say that I have brought on a crisis by refusing to see to it that the Gentiles obey the law of Moses. I hope that on balance the good will outweigh the bad that I have done."

"You are the most successful of us all, Paul, and you have done as much as anyone to further the work of the Lord. I am sure that there is a place reserved for you with him." The others in the room all nodded their assent, and this seemed to please Paul. He had sidled up to James before the meeting began, since it was James who had introduced him to the apostles fourteen years before, and asked what was the attitude of the other apostles toward him. James had told him that he was universally admired in everything that he did, save the one area of the Gentiles and the law.

"Brethren, I will be brief," he continued, "which I know will please and surprise you all. I know that Jesus said that not one part of the law would pass away until all had been fulfilled, but it is my belief that his life and death fulfilled the law." There were murmurings and shaking and nodding of heads at this, with one or two saying that they were not in a position to decide such a thing. Peter called for quiet.

"Consider: what are the scriptures but the story of the chosen people of God, and their constant disloyalty to him? Is not the first story that of how the first man and woman turned their backs on him in his own garden? Did he not wipe out all the people of the Earth with the flood, save some of the family of Noah, because all people were evil? And it was then that he promised that he would not do such a thing again, and that he would send his son to recall all men to him. Moses then gave us the law as a way to stay close to God until that son should appear. But we have not always obeyed the law, and it was for this reason that the prophets were sent to us, that we might be reminded of the duty that we have to God. But all of the prophets and all of the scriptures have been fulfilled: Jesus, the son of God, came among us, taught us, died for us, and then rose again from the dead, as he said he would do, to prove his power over life and death. We are no longer related to God because we have laws about what kinds of food we may eat or whether or not we are circumcised, but we are related to him by our faith in his son Jesus. It is through Jesus that we come to God now, not through the law of Moses. Jesus told us as much: 'No one comes to the Father but through me,' he said, and it is this which we are teaching those who will listen to us.

"For those of us who are Jews, there is nothing wrong with continuing to obey the law. I obey it in every way, though I would talk to you about the law as I am now. But what are we to tell the Gentiles who receive the gift of faith? That their faith is less than ours because they do not obey the law of Moses? That they will not see God because they are not circumcised? Is this what Jesus taught? And what is the meaning if they were to begin obeying the law? They have already eaten of pigs and of fish without scales, and all their lives they have been uncircumcised. Will they suddenly become clean by obeying the law, or are they doomed, according to our understanding of the law, to always be unclean? Do we not invite them into the church only to then tell them that they shall never have the same status as we because we have always obeyed the law of Moses? What kind of invitation is that? And who will accept it?

"Consider what must be the response of the Gentiles to such a teaching. We tell them that it is faith in Jesus which will bring them to the Father. What is their first response then, if we tell them that they must obey all of the old law? They will say that we lie to them, or that we do not understand our own teaching. On the one hand we say that all that is required is faith in Jesus, and on the other that, even though Jesus has come and fulfilled all that the prophets said, we must still obey the law that preceeded him. It is not a consistent message, my friends: either faith in Jesus is enough to bring us to the Father, or we must also obey the law of Moses. It cannot be both.

"No, brethren, we have been called anew by Jesus, the son of God, to come to the Father through faith in the son. That is all that is required of any man. He has fulfilled all that was foretold in the scriptures, and he has given us new commandments. Let us not say to the Gentiles that Jesus has called only those men who are willing to obey the law of Moses, but that he has called all men."

At this Paul paused, then apparently decided that he was finished, and sat down next to Barnabas.

Peter rose again. "Paul, I can see why you have brought so many into the church. But let us hear from one who would still have us obey the law. Andrew, I believe, would like to address the group."

Andrew rose as Peter re-seated himself, and began. "I will never allow Paul to speak before me again - I cannot help but sound the simple minded fool. But Paul has not considered all that is to be considered. When did the Master tell us that it was no longer a symbol of man's devotion to God to be circumcised? When did he tell us that the flesh of pigs and unscaled fish is now clean? At no time, and I have been with him since the beginning, did he tell us that the law, given us by his Father, was now changed.

"What would Paul have us believe? That God has thought better of the law that he gave to Moses so long ago, and that that law no longer matters to him? If this were to be the case, why would he have given it to us? If we are now to ignore the law, how is God to see us next to our predecessors? Are they more worthy than we because they obeyed the law that God gave them, or are we more worthy because we ignored the same law? What kind of God gives some generations one law, and later generations another?"

And so it went all day and on into the night. There was no clear consensus one way or the other, and it appeared to James that the apostles were divided approximately evenly on the question. No compromise was offered that would solve the problem for them, and it did not appear as if anyone in the room was thinking of a compromise. They argued and discussed the matter until well into the morning before finally laying down to sleep where they sat. The only consolation that James could take from the evening, as he lie there thinking it over, was that they had not come to blows.

They took the subject up again the next evening, but got no farther in their deliberations, notwithstanding the fact that they talked almost as long. Finally, in one of the few lulls in the discussion, Peter stood up in the center of the room and said to them: "Men, brethren, you know that in former days God made choice among us, that by my mouth the Gentiles should hear the word of the Jesus and believe. And God, who knows men's hearts, gave testimony giving unto them the Holy Spirit as well as to us, and put no difference between us and them, purifying their hears by faith. Now, why do you tempt God to put a yoke upon the necks of the disciples which neither our fathers nor we have been able to bear, but by the grace of the Lord Jesus Christ we believe to be saved just as they are saved?"

At this Peter looked about the room for a moment, and then sat down. There was quiet among them for a moment, and then Paul seized the situation.

"This is the truest thing that has been said among us these two days. God has called us all to him through his son Jesus, even those who have never heard of the law of Moses. If he did not mean for them to come to him, why would he have made it possible for Barnabas and I work so many signs among them?" Here he and Barnabas mentioned a few of the signs that they had performed among the Gentiles they had taught, including healing the sick and the lame. Others among the apostles pointed out that they had also performed such signs among the Jews that they had taught, which played right into Paul's hand: "Yes you have! That is it exactly! The very signs that God has made it possible for you to perform for the Jews he has made it possible for us to show the Gentiles. Is that not proof that he loves them as he does us, and that if they come to him he will accept them whether they have ever eaten the meat of a pig or not?" They wrangled some more on the subject, though it appeared to James that those on the side of Paul appeared to have the upper hand. James' greatest fear was that the meeting would see the church split into two camps: he believed that unity within the guidelines of Jesus' teaching was the paramount concern for them, and to that end he decided to propose the compromise that he had formed in his mind the night before. The next time there was a quiet moment, he spoke up.

"Brethren," he said, "hear me. Simon has related how God first visited to take of the Gentiles a people to his name. And to this agree the words of the prophets. They have written: 'All these things I will return and will rebuild the tabernacle of David, which is fallen down: and the ruins thereof I will rebuild. And I will set it up: That the residue of men may seek after the Lord, and all nations upon whom my name is invoked, said the Lord, who does these things.' To the Lord was his own work known from the beginning of the world. For this cause, let us not disquiet those among the Gentiles who come to the Lord, but let us write to them that they should refrain themselves from worship of idols, from fornication, and from things strangled and from blood. This letter will reach them all because the law of Moses is read every Sabbath in the temples."

There was quiet for a moment when James had finished speaking, when suddenly Peter leapt up to support him saying, "That is the answer that will come closest to satisfying all in the room, brethren: we cannot do better. Such a position would force them to obey the laws of Moses that are the most important and which must be obeyed by those of faith, while not forcing them to obey those that they have never heard about in their lives and which, if they were to suddenly adopt them, cause them to have been unclean all of their lives."

There was more debate on the matter, with frequent calls for James to explain this point or that, and James was gratified to see that he appeared to have arrived at something that would suit most of them. He was especially gratified to see that he had the enthusiastic support of both Peter and Paul, the two men in the room whom he respected and admired the most. With those two pushing his idea upon the others it soon carried the day, and they all went to bed agreeing that they could not do better, and agreeing unanimously to accept it. James, as always seemed to be the case for the person who volunteered information, was detailed to begin writing the letter in the morning.

He slept very little that night, and arose early in the morning, as soon as there was enough light, to begin drafting the letter that had been his idea. He worked on it all day, attempting to find just the right words that would satisfy the whole company, and presented a draft to the gathering that evening when they had all settled down again. It was haggled over somewhat, but much less than James thought it might be, and with some pride he made the changes finally agreed to, and, while the others conversed on other matters, wrote out the final copy, which read thus:

"From the apostles and the ancients, to the brethren of the Gentiles at Antioch and in Syria and Cilicia, greetings. We have heard that you have been troubled by the words of some of those of us who have taught among you - but they have had no commandment about what they should teach you. It now seems good to us, being assembled together to discuss this matter, to choose men to send to you along with Paul and Barnabas - men that have given their lives for the Lord Jesus Christ. We have sent therefore Judas and Silas, who themselves also will, by word of mouth, tell you the same things. For it has seemed good to the Holy Spirit, and therefor to us, to lay no further burden upon you than these necessary things: that you abstain from things sacrificed to idols and from blood and from things strangled and from fornication. If you can but stay from these things, you shall do well. Farewell."

Once it was decided that this letter solved the problem for the churches made up primarily of Gentiles, it fell to James to make additional copies of it so that all of those who departed Jerusalem to teach might have it with them. This done the conference broke up once again. When James had finished making the copies they were given to all who would teach, and the group broke up once again. James saw them off with the words of Peter ringing in his ears: "You have done a good weeks' work, James. You may have saved the church from the schism that would have destroyed it, and rendered all our effort for naught. Never let me hear you say again that you are not a qualified teacher, or that you have little to say on matters of faith."

CHAPTER 18

Sometimes, it seemed to James, he was older than his years, and he was an old man at 60 years of age. It had now been 29 years since his brother Jesus had been crucified and then risen from the dead - 29 years since James had done anything other than serve the brother he had once scorned. He used to believe that the life of the religious was easy - that they had little to occupy themselves with but an occasional service and study - but he found the existence grueling, and now and then, in spite of the certitude that he was doing the right thing and that his half brother really was the son of God, he felt as if he could not go on.

It was many years since the other apostles had more or less abandoned Jerusalem for their ministries in other parts of the world. The other James was already long dead, but the others had spread out as far east as India, as far north as Scythia, as far south as Persia, and farther west even than Rome. James heard of them now and again from travelers, but often the news was years old.

He was still in Jerusalem himself, head of the church there, and much admired by those who were his congregation. James did not like to reflect on his popularity for fear that it would turn his head from Jesus, but there were many people in the city who had taken to referring to him as "James the Just" to distinguish him from the other James' in the city. The name had been carried up from Nazareth by those who knew him, and it had taken hold.

He had finished the letter asked of him by Peter and had sent a copy of it off to Rome for Peter to see, and kept one for himself. Many of the Christians in the city knew of the existence of the letter and had asked to see it, and James allowed them to read it if they asked. The original intention of Peter was that the letter be read aloud at services, but James could not bear the thought of reading his own words to the crowds. He much preferred to let them read it for themselves, or have it read to them if they could not manage themselves. He was happy to discuss it with those who might be interested, but only after telling them that it had the blessing of both Peter and Paul.

The years since the death of his brother had been years of constant and increasing conflict with the Jewish and Roman authorities, and there was little that could be done about it. None of the parties involved would surrender their faith or, in the case of the traditional Jews and the Romans, their power for the sake of peace.

It was in this atmosphere of increased tension and anxiety that James learned that Paul was coming to Jerusalem. He heard as much from a traveler who had seen Paul some days before, but had arrived before Paul because Paul was stopping along his way to collect contributions for the church in Jerusalem.

While James admired Paul he did not want to see him in Jerusalem at this moment, given the acid tongued comments fired at him by Ananias. But the traveler told James that Paul was only days behind him so James decided that it was not worthwhile to attempt to dissuade him from coming at all. At the time of the meeting thirteen years before Paul had been warned to keep a low profile, and he had done little in that regard. James amused himself by thinking that he might wait outside the gate of the city for Paul so that he could warn him of the conditions therein, but he could not know which gate Paul would use nor when he might come, and so gave up such a vigil as hopeless. He was not surprised, two days after hearing of his approach, to have Paul standing the in the room with him.

"James," said he, "it has been too long. You really must get out more!"

"I have my work as you have yours, and it keeps me where I am needed. It is not I who should get out, but you who should come in." After settling themselves on the floor and making a plate of food available for Paul, James continued, "I had news of your coming from a traveler but two days ago."

"Yes, it has been a slow progress, but you were aware that I was taking up a collection among all the churches for the Jerusalem church, and such things take time. I hope you can make use of the results."

James laughed. "You know that we can. It will not be long before we are forced to change our system here in the city. Our communal habits have become too expensive."

"Well, well, this will tide you over in the meantime," answered Paul as he presented James with a small bag of money, all in different denominations. "Do not be alarmed that such a small sum is all that could be had. In order to foil the thieves I have broken up the funds into several parts and had them brought to the city by various messengers. They should all be coming in over the next several days. I am glad that I am the first to arrive, or you might have been faced with quite a mystery."

"I thank you with all my heart," said James, enthusiastically. "I cannot think what might have happened to our undertaking if you had not come to us. Little did we realize what valuable work we were doing when we spirited you out of the city so many years ago."

"Perhaps, if I have been of service, I was called for that service. Let us not fail to give the Father enough credit. He called all of the early members of the church so that the church might survive. Where would we be if he had not called his own brother to oversee the church in Jerusalem? Would the Holy City have a church?"

"It is hard to say, but the fact is that it does have a church, and that church is in increasing conflict with the Sanhedrin and the Romans. I was lectured by Ananias - yes, the high priest - just days ago on all of the evils that we have brought upon the city, and you were cited as among the worst offenders."

"I believe that I have been honored with a compliment. Next time you see him, express my thanks to him."

"It is entirely possible that it is you who will see him next, and not I. There is little good will in the city between us, and I am afraid that if they discover your presence, you might be arrested."

"There is no cause for concern on that, because I was seen by many as I walked through the city today on my way here. I was not accosted, but I saw many people that I believe I recognize, and there can be little doubt that the word is already back to the Sanhedrin. I will just have to face the consequences. It is a testament to the power of faith, no matter the persuasion, that I am still considered the enemy after nearly thirty years."

"Forgive me for being crude, but I hope that there are no consequences to be suffered, or, if there, are, they are limited to only a few of us."

Paul looked at James in a quizzical way for a moment, and then the light came on in his head. "You hope that I do not bring down evil on the other Christians in the city. You are quite right - that is my hope as well. But if things have come to such a pass, that my appearance is enough to set off the mob, then that mob will be set off by something else, if not by me. Fire is happy for any spark." James could only nod in agreement.

They talked late into the night, but James had little luck in suggesting that Paul keep out of sight. Paul agreed that he would not look for trouble and would not preach to the people publicly, but that was all that James could wrangle from him.

James offered Paul what counsel he could on his relations with the Sanhedrin, since it seemed safe to assume that the Sanhedrin knew that he was in town.

"They are offended, among other things, that you bring the Gentiles into the church, and suppose you to mean by this that the law of Moses is no longer valid. Of course they do not care who may join us, since to them we are heretics, but they are concerned with your apparent assumption that the law of Moses is no more. You must be prepared to placate them on this matter for the sake of peace. You must tell them, if they raise the subject with you, of the accord we reached here years ago, which is that the Gentiles will refrain from certain things that Jews would consider unclean."

"I appreciate your advice my friend, but I am afraid there is little I can do to make peace with the Sanhedrin. It may be that they are upset with my practice of preaching to the Gentiles, and my offense on this score may be lessened somewhat if I do as you say, but they will always be offended by the fact that I was one of them, and now I am not. There is nothing that can be done on that score. I will act and talk as you say if the subject comes up, but I doubt that they will be satisfied."

"When you go to the temple for oblations, take four of the Gentiles who came with you. They may stand outside as testimony to that fact that you respect and obey the laws of the temple."

"James! My good friend! I did not know that you had such a nose for symbolism! How theatrical you have become!"

"It is not so much for the symbolism as for the fact," James replied, with a smile. "The fact that they are outside will illustrate that you do not have contempt for the law of Moses, as they assume you have. Just as important, it will tell the others in the crowd the same thing. It would also be helpful if you would cut your hair as the law requires before you go."

"I will indulge you, my friend, but do not pin all your hopes on such things."

"I pin my hopes on keeping peace with the officials here in Jerusalem. You are welcome here of course, I believe the same things as you, and I am glad to have you, but when you are gone the rest of us will remain. It is better if we do not come to blows over relatively minor matters."

"Believe me, I will keep as low a profile as it is possible for a man to do."

Paul, James and four Gentiles went to the temple at the end of the seven days oblation. It was bright, sunny and hot without a breath of wind stirring. While James and Paul went inside the other four waited across the street from the temple gate. James did not see anything to alarm him on the way to the temple: it did not appear that anyone recognized Paul or that anyone took notice of their little group. But when they entered the temple all of the alarm bells in James' head went off.

The temple was crowded with others there for the same purpose as themselves, and James feared that in such a multitude there was no way that Paul could fail to be recognized. James found himself scanning every face to see if it recognized Paul and intended to do anything about the fact. Sure enough, they had not been inside but a few moments when James saw a man stare long at Paul and then scurry off - no doubt to tell someone of high rank.

But they continued uninterrupted for a few more minutes, and they had just found a small open spot on the floor in which to stop and pray when James noticed three or four low ranking members of the Sanhedrin suddenly appear on the floor, all in the tow of the man who had stared at Paul. They stood regarding him for a moment, and then, much to James' surprise, they suddenly dispersed, and James lost them in the crowd.

For his part Paul kept his head low and his hands high as he prayed, in an attempt to hide his face without appearing to do so. James could not pray now, though he still held his hands high. He continued to look about the temple for the members of the Sanhedrin that he had seen earlier. He felt certain that they would find a way to make mischief.

He finally spotted one of the group that he had seen earlier, talking to another man, and it was obvious that they were talking about Paul. The member of the Sanhedrin was staring at Paul, and appeared to be pointing him out to the other man. The other man also stared intently at Paul, discussed the matter with the Sanhedrin member again, and then remarked to his neighbor on what he had seen. As he did so the Sanhedrin member pointed out Paul to another man standing on his other side, and the same sequence of events followed. Even at a brief glance James could see that the circle of onlookers was ever widening. He looked about the rest of the area that he could see for the other members of the Sanhedrin but could not spot them immediately. There could be little doubt that they were causing the same trouble. Now James really did pray - for the presence of mind to do the right thing in the crisis that he felt certain was coming.

As James looked up again he felt that he and Paul were the center of attention for a small knot of people that had gathered around them in the course of only a few moments. James looked at the faces in the immediate vicinity to attempt to read their intent, but he could see nothing other than that they were about to speak.

Sure enough, one of the men in the crowd said "Are you not Saul of Tarsus?"

Paul looked up at the man slowly and said, "I am, though now I am called Paul."

"Oh? Do the Christians force you to change your name when you join them? You have been spending too much time with this man," said the first, indicating James. This brought mild laughter from the immediate crowd.

Paul smiled at the man and then bowed his head again, as though he would resume his prayers. But another man from the other side of the circle that had gathered around them said, "I am surprised that you would come here to pray with us, since you have found your calling among the Gentiles." There was some grumbling among the crowd. "In fact," the man continued, "I am surprised that you did not bring Gentiles into the temple with you." There was some laughter and more grumbling at this, but Paul attempted to ignore the man. "Why do you not answer?" the man continued, "or have you ceased talking to your own people?" This brought more laughter from the crowd, and James was alarmed to note that the crowd surrounding them appeared to be growing.

"I would gladly speak to all who will speak to me," said Paul, "particularly those most in need of being enlightened." James winced at this less than tactful answer while admitting, to himself only, the provocation. The man was angered and would have advanced on Paul, but he was held back by the man at his side.

"So you do have a tongue," the man continued. "I was afraid that perhaps the carpenter that you worship had cut it out." There was much laughter at this, and barbs were flying in at Paul from all over - so many that James could not even hear them all. Paul did not lose his composure, but attempted to continue with his prayers.

The first man took advantage of the first break in the crowd noise to say, "If you will worship a carpenter, you should adore me: I am a trader, and ever so much more important." This brought gales of laughter from the still growing and closing in crowd, and James began to feel physically menaced. He took Paul's arm and attempted to steer him toward the exit, but the crowd would not part for them.

They backed off into the middle of the small circle that was left for them, which could now not be more than a man's height across. The crowd seemed to be willing to allow them to have that much space for it did not close in any more, but it did seem to grow more intense in its threats to Paul. James noted, quickly in passing, that he did not seem to interest them very much, except that he was the companion of Paul. Whatever his own offenses against them might have been, the crowd either did not know of them or was not interested.

There were intermittent calls for Paul to be thrown from the temple, to be stoned and to be beaten, amid jokes about his parentage, his clothes (which were nearly as threadbare as James) and the walking stick that he carried with him at all times. In all the tumult James noticed that there was talk of Gentiles and Gentiles in the temple, demands to see the Gentiles and for the offender who had brought them in to be stoned. There were no Gentiles in the temple as far as James knew, and none had come in with he and Paul. The talk earlier (only moments ago, but it seemed an age) of Paul being with Gentiles must have triggered the talk, and it had now come back to them as fact.

Some of those in the front took up the call about the Gentiles as well, and James could hear some of the crowd accusing him of being the Gentile who had defiled the temple precincts. Others claimed that no, James was Jewish, and certainly not a Gentile, and others claimed that James was now a Christian and so had probably defiled himself along with the Gentiles. There now began to be some talk of taking James as well as Paul and dealing with them both in the same manner, and James began to fear for his own safety for the first time.

But it appeared that, in his case at least, the calmer heads prevailed and convinced the others that James was not a Gentile, and that, furthermore, he was not a recruited of Gentiles as Paul had become.

Paul noticed the talk of Gentiles as well, for he began to assure the crowd at the top of his lungs that he had brought no Gentiles with him - for proof they could look outside where his friends stood. Had the situation not been as dire as it was, James might have smiled at the use of this defense, which Paul had laughed at only a short time before. James wanted to appeal to the Sanhedrin for defense, but he could see none in the crowd now. If those who started this riot were still around, they were not in a position where they could be appealed to by James and Paul.

There were demands that Paul explain why he should be worshipping in the temple if he had become a Christian and if it was true that he consorted with Gentiles and recruited them to his church. Paul could not answer even one of the accusations because of the noise and confusion, and it appeared to James that, even if Paul could make himself heard, there was little Paul would be able to do about this mob. Paul roared for silence from the crowd so that he might speak, but his requests only egged them on more. At each attempt of Paul's to speak the ringleaders in the front of the mob screamed all the louder to drown him out, and their threats only became worse and more graphic. James wanted to tell Paul to be silent, but he could not make himself heard above the din.

Finally a large man near them made himself heard above the rest, and demanded of Paul whether or not he had contaminated himself with the practices of the Gentiles. Paul screamed back at him that such things did not matter any more because the word of the prophets had been fulfilled in Jesus Christ. This enraged the man so that he grabbed Paul by the cloak and began to shake him, and with that the entire crowd surged forward around them.

They were pushed this way and that, pummeled with fists, sticks, canes and other implements that James could not identify. Still the crowd could not decide what should be done with Paul, and, suddenly, the whole undulating mass of people began to move slowly toward the exits, apparently having decided that stoning was the proper measure for him, though he had not yet had any sort of trial. James felt the pressure on him ease off, though this did not mean that the crowd ignored him. Where it dealt maliciously with Paul, beating him, hitting him, driving him to the exit, it seemed content to jostle and push James, though he could do nothing but follow the flow of the crowd to the exit. To attempt anything else at that moment would have meant risking a fall and being trampled by the crowd. He tried to stay as near Paul as possible, finally latching on to his cloak for that purpose. There was such a thick crowd around them that James did not notice the condition of Paul's clothing - James' clothing was nearly gone - but he could see that his face was bloodied. Paul, like himself, was struggling as best he could against the crowd, but to no avail other than further infuriating the mob.

As they neared the exit the speed at which they were traveling slowed somewhat so that the crowd could fit through, but the pace was inexorable and finally James and Paul found themselves at the door of the temple. Outside and leading down the steps the way was cleared by the crowd, as though they anticipated that more open space would be needed. As they got outside those who had been tormenting James, and they were few in number though James did not feel it so, left off to watch what would happen to Paul, and James had a moment to get control of himself. But as soon as Paul emerged from the temple the crowd pushed him down the stairs to the next landing. Once again the crowd set upon him, and it appeared to James that he might be killed. It was clear that the mob had lost its collective temper. But at that moment he happened to notice a disturbance on the further reaches of the crowd near the bottom of the steps, and saw the plumed helmets of Roman soldiers fighting their way through the crowd.

It seemed to James as though it took forever for the Romans to finally reach the center of the mob, and when they got there they were none too friendly. Rather than escorting James and Paul out as James hoped they would do, they promptly put Paul under arrest. They tied his hands behind him, to the delight of the crowd, which had initially been upset at the interference from the Romans.

The tribune who lead the Romans was a very young man, and James wondered whether he would have any influence on the crowd. He rose to the occasion. "Silence!" he called to the crowd, and after about the third try he was granted his wish. He then turned to Paul, who was standing with his hands tied behind his back between two of the Romans who had to support him after the beating he had received, and said, "Who are you, and what have you done that this crowd should threaten you with death?"

Paul opened his mouth to answer, but he was drowned out by the mob before he could make a sound. There was an immediate uproar, with some claiming that he was a blasphemer, others that he brought Gentiles into the temple, others that he was a Christian, and finally all of the yelling and screaming melded into one, and no one could be understood. The Tribune saw that he would get no satisfaction in front of the crowd, so he commanded the two soldiers supporting Paul to take him to the Tower of Antonia, a fortress on the north side of the temple that the soldiers had come from.

This they began to do, but the crowd followed, demanding that he be put on trial, that he be stoned immediately, that he be given back to them and other things that James did not care to dwell on. Paul was so weak from his ordeal that he could not navigate the stairs leading into the tower that were shown to him, and the soldiers began to carry him up, to the delight of the crowd. But at the top of the stairs Paul rallied himself, and James, who followed along as near the front of the crowd as he could manage, saw Paul talking to the Tribune. He saw the Tribune nod toward the mob, and Paul turned to face them, obviously to speak.

The stairs were not tall, and Paul's feet were at the level of the heads of the crowd. When they saw that he would speak to them, they suddenly quieted down, much to the amazement of James, who thought that the abuse would increase. Paul waited just a moment to allow the quiet to settle over the whole crowd, and then he began.

"Men, brethren, fathers, hear the account that I give you. I am a Jew, born at Tarsus in Cilicia, but brought up in this city, at the feet of Gamaliel, taught according to the truth of the law of the fathers, zealous for the law, as also all you are this day; I persecuted those, now called Christians, who did not obey the law, binding and delivering into prisons both men and women, as the high priest and all the ancients are my witnesses. From the high priest I received letters to go to Damascus that I might bring the Christians bound to Jerusalem to be punished. But as I drew near to Damascus, at mid-day, suddenly from heaven there shone round about me a great light, and falling to the ground I heard a voice saying to me: 'Saul, Saul why do you persecute me?' And I answered, 'Who are you, Lord?' And he said to me: 'I am Jesus of Nazareth, whom you persecute.'

"And they that were with me saw indeed the light, but they not the voice of him that spoke with me.   "And I said: 'What shall I do, Lord?'

"And the Lord said to me: 'Arise and go to Damascus, and there it shall be told you all things that you must do.'

"But I was left blind by the brightness of the light, so that I was led by the hand of my companions to Damascus and to the home of Ananias, a just man of the law, according to all who dwelt there. And he said to me, 'Brother Saul, look up.' And I did, and saw that my sight had been restored.

"But he said, 'The God of our fathers has ordained that you should know his will and see the Just One and hear the voice from his mouth. For you shall be his witness to all men of those things which you have seen and heard. But why do you lie here? Rise up and be baptized to wash away your sins, and invoke his name on you.'

"Then when I came again to Jerusalem and was praying in the temple, I went into a trance, and I saw him saying to me: 'Make haste and get quickly out of Jerusalem, because they will not receive the testimony concerning me.'

"And I said to him, 'Lord, they know that I cast into prison and beat in every synagogue those that believe in you. And when the blood of Stephen your servant was shed, I stood by and consented, and kept the garments of those that killed him.'

"But he said to me, "Go, for unto the Gentiles afar off will I send you.'"

Paul paused here for a moment, and James could not tell whether he was through, but the mob did not give him a chance to begin again. There were cries that he should be stoned, that he was not fit to live, and that the Romans should turn him back over to them. During all this tumult James worked himself forward in the crowd so that he stood at the feet of Paul and the Tribune. The Tribune, seeing that he would not be able to calm the crowd, told the guards to take Paul into the tower where he should be scourged until he told the truth about his doings and why the crowd should wish so lustfully for his blood.

With that the knot of people disappeared into the palace, and James was left alone in the crowd. James feared lest they turn their wrath on him, since he was now the only available target, but beyond some additional verbal abuse they left him to his own devices as they split up. James hurried back to the room to regain his composure, and on the way decided that he would have those in the community ask around among all their contacts for news of what had happened to Paul.

This time, unlike all of the others over the years, James had no one to report his news to. All of the other apostles were out of the city preaching the word of Jesus, and he had the room all to himself. He was unaccustomed to having that much space, even though it was only about 20 cubits by 15 cubits, or that much quiet. He longed to pass on the news as in the old days, and discuss what was to be done with those who had been in the church longer than he, but it could not be. He sat in the room by himself to eat some cold meat and bread.

He also prayed, thanking God for his own deliverance and asking for that of Paul. In all the time that he had been in the service of his brother he had never felt any personal danger until this day. He had seen other scenes of violence, but he had never been the center of attention in any of them, and he had never really had to defend himself against the crowd as Paul had done. Even this day it had been Paul who had borne the wrath of the crowd and not James, though some of the attention of those who could not get close to Paul had been directed at him. He thanked God that while he had been afraid his courage had not failed him, and that he had not tried to run and leave Paul to the crowd.

He set off after his short meal and reflections to talk to those in the city who might be able to find some information about Paul. He knew the occupations of all the members of the church, and there were several that worked in the palace of the governor in menial jobs that the Roman's would not do themselves. It had been past the dinner hour when Paul had been arrested, and James had gone back to his own room to get over his fright, so it was now dark and the people he hoped to see at home. None knew of the arrest of Paul, which James thought strange, but he encouraged them to find out what they could on the morrow. James walked by the palace himself that evening, but it was dark and the guard at the gate would tell him nothing.

He went about his rounds the next morning hoping that someone would bring him news of Paul, and he found that he was lucky. It was from the wife of Ezra, a laborer in the palace, who found him on his rounds.

"James!" she called out to him when she spied him on the street. "I have been looking all over for you," she said, breathlessly. "I thought perhaps that you might be at your room since it is midday, but I did not find you there. I then set off for the north side of the city because I have heard others say that that is often the direction you take in the middle of the week. But I met my friend who said that perhaps you were at the palace awaiting news. I thought this possible and ran there to look for you, but again could not find you. Then I....."

"Yes, yes, Martha, you are as good and dedicated as they come, and I would not have important news such as this entrusted to any one else at all. Now, what is it?"

She gave him a blank stare for a moment, and then said, "Oh! The news! It is that Paul is to stand before the council this morning to be examined!" James did not wait for more, but rushed off instantly for the council chambers.

When he arrived there was a tumult outside as the priests and council members were still filing in, some wanting to know why they had been summoned. James did not know any of those he saw standing outside, but he managed to insinuate himself among them, fearing that he would not be allowed inside if they had time to get organized, and went in with them.

He stood to the rear of the large room behind a pillar so as not to attract too much attention, but he was somewhat comforted to see that there were others in attendance who were obviously not part of the council. He waited in this spot until he heard one of the scribes call for quiet, and then he walked out slowly and quietly to see what was to happen.

The room in which he found himself was large, possibly 100 cubits on a side, and square, with a high ceiling supported by the aforementioned columns. On the far side from where James stood there was a large stone chair, apparently for the use of the High Priest. All of the other walls were fronted with four rows of stone benches save at the door where James had entered, where there was room for a few spectators. The benches were full of the members of the Sanhedrin, including the Pharisees and the Sadduccees, but the chair for the High Priest was as yet empty. There was a throng of perhaps thirty people surrounding James, and when he realized that Ananias would be able to see him from where he would sit in the large chair, James moved a little further to the back.

At just that moment there was a bustling noise at the far end of the hall, and Ananias himself entered. There was a respectful silence while he made his way to his chair where he made himself comfortable.

"Brethren," said he, when silence that suited him reigned, "you have been called here to consider the case of Saul of Tarsus, whom you know as a traitor to the faith of his fathers. He was threatened by a mob in the temple yesterday, and arrested by the Romans for his own safety. They have held him all night, but they cannot hold him longer without charges, and that is our purpose: to determine if he has committed any crime for which he could be legally arrested by the Sanhedrin. You know that I am no friend of the Christians, as they call themselves, if for no other reason than that they have cost me a dear friendship" (James' heart sank) "but we will be fair in this matter. Like you I am alarmed at the dissension and jealousy they have caused in this city and other places throughout Judea, Samaria and parts north, but we will not judge as they judge, but give the man a fair trial, and see what there is to be learned from him. Has anyone anything to say before we bring him in?"

One priest on a bench to James' left rose and asked, "For what offense was he accosted in the temple yesterday?"

"It was feared by some of those present that he had brought Gentiles into the temple. He has been seen about the city in the company of Gentiles, and he is known to have caused a rift in the Christian movement with his ideas about the Gentiles. So the mob was not without grounds for suspicion, even if it turned out that they were wrong. The only person with him at the time he was assaulted by the mob was my one-time friend James of Nazareth whom you all know to be the local leader of the Christians and the brother of the man Jesus whom they worship as the son of God." At this there were mutterings among the bystanders and the priests, and Ananias had to demand silence once again.

"Unless we can prove that he has committed blasphemy like his son of God, we will not try him on his faith. We all know that it is misguided, but it is not illegal" (again mutterings and calls that Paul should be made an example of) "unless he or one of the others claims to be the next son of God." This brought laughter from the assembly, and Ananias let them laugh. "If there is nothing else we will bring him in, and hear what he has to say."

He then nodded to one of the lackeys standing near him, who in turn ran over to the door through which Ananias had entered, and disappeared through it for a few moments. He came back followed by a Roman soldier, who in turn was followed by Paul - his hands tied behind his back - and another Roman soldier. The Roman soldiers escorted him to the center of the room, immediately in front of the chair, and stood on either side of him.

The High Priest stared down at him for a moment, as though contemplating how a person should have caused so many headaches for so many people, and then said, "Well, Saul of Tarsus...."

Paul interrupted immediately. "I am now called Paul."

The High Priest eyed him condescendingly and then said, "Well, Saul of Tarsus," to the delight of the throng, "we meet at last. I have not spoken to you since you departed for Damascus so many years ago. If I am not mistaken, you owe us restitution from that trip. We sent you there to bring the Christian movement back to the true faith, and instead you converted yourself. That is not just return on our investment in you." There were chuckles about the room, and Ananias waited for Paul to respond, but he said nothing.

"I have heard," Ananias continued after a moment, "that you are quite the eloquent speaker among the Gentiles, inviting them all to help you worship the son of a carpenter of Nazareth whom you call the son of God." More laughter from the onlookers. "But you have nothing to say to us today. That is quite disappointing. I had hoped to be the beneficiary of your abilities so that we might understand how you can talk so many people into following you."

"I do not ask them to follow me: They follow the Lord Jesus."

"Oh, yes. The son of the carpenter of Nazareth," said Ananias nodding his head and appearing to give the matter some thought, drawing another round of laughter from the crowd. "But it is true that you invite Gentiles to join your church?"

"The Lord welcomes all those who believe in him, even as the shepherd loves his black sheep."

"Come now, this is better!" said Ananias. "I like this much better. So. You invite the Gentiles to join your worship of the son of the carpenter - he was not actually a carpenter himself, I understand? - and many are accepting your offer. How many Jews have left the faith of their fathers, as you have done, and joined your new church? Not many, I believe. This is why you have branched out among the Gentiles: better to have Gentiles giving to the plate than no one at all." Again there were gales of laughter from the onlookers, and James was angered at the cavalier way that Paul and their new church, as Ananias called it, were being treated, but he felt as if there was little he could do to help. He had not the oral gifts that Paul had, and he would look foolish standing there in front of the crowd attempting to answer their taunts. The other possibility was that he would be thrown out if discovered, and then he would not know the outcome of the trial.

"But let us hear what your religion has to say on the law of Moses. You are aware that there are many dietary and physical rules, such as circumcision, that must be obeyed and which the Gentiles cannot hope to obey because they have been unclean all their lives. Have you decided that the laws of Moses are no longer worthy of our attention, or have you decided that God and his son have changed their minds and that the Gentiles do not need to obey?"

"We have reached a compromise on the matter that we believe settles it."

"Oh, you and your friends have compromised on the law of God given directly to Moses, have you?" Again there was laughter and catcalls from those watching, and James could not see anyone that appeared to be sympathizing with Paul. "It appears that we should be joining you as well, if you are capable of making such decisions, because we admit that we haven't the wisdom for it."

"We admit that as well," said Paul.

Ananias caught the dig and James could see that he was angry, but he calmed himself almost immediately. "Well, well," said he, "I suppose that if we can give such lip to you we must be able to accept it as well. So, you are willing to compromise on the laws of God with the Gentiles if they will just join your church. I suppose that is your right, if you choose to do so, but do you not think it a bit much to insist that we also compromise?"

"I do not understand your meaning."

"I mean that if you wish to compromise on the law of God without consulting God, you may do so, and good luck to you when you finally face him, or the Messiah." Ananias paused here to see if Paul would understand the dig. It was evident that he did, but he said nothing. "But you should not compromise on the law on our behalf without consulting us first. For example, we still believe, though I know it is antiquated fashion, that Gentiles should not be allowed into the temple - they are unclean and not fit to be there." Ananias said this last in a voice that was rising in intensity and pitch. "And yet," he continued, in a mocking voice, "there are reports that you, in your compromising mood, brought Gentiles into the temple with you yesterday."

"That is not true. I entered with James, the brother of Jesus, and no one else."

Ananias was taken aback at this, but he recovered quickly. "You entered with James, the brother of the son of God?" More laughter from the galleries. "You are well connected, are you not?" Still more laughter. "Well, it may surprise you to learn that I am prepared to believe that you did not bring any Gentiles into the temple, if only because I believe you are a prudent man, and would not take such a risk, particularly given your former position and the place you must know you have in all our hearts." Laughter again. "But what I am not prepared to accept is the chaos that your little church has caused us, and the rift it brings between us and the Romans. Are there not enough problems in the area that you and others like you must attempt to convert people from the true faith, and attempt to mix them with Gentiles? Can you not leave well enough alone? If you had brought Gentiles into the temple yesterday, and not had the Roman guard there to rescue you, I believe you would have received only that which you and the others like you deserve."

"I have heard that you consider yourself the peacemaker," said Paul.

"You must have heard as much from my old friend James, the brother of the son of God. It is hard for me to believe that at one time he was my closest companion, even though we did not live near one another, and that my father offered him a chance to study here in the temple. And now he is considered the head of the Christian church in the Holy City, consorts with Gentiles, and believes that his own flesh and blood is the son of God."

"He does not believe that his own flesh and blood is the son of God," corrected Paul. "He believes that the son of God was sent to us through his mother, by the power of God, that he might share our humanity. He does not claim to be related by blood to Jesus."

"That is very generous of him," said Ananias, perturbed. "I am happy to hear that he is among the crowd of wise and generous men who know how to work out compromises with God on his law." James could sense Ananias' anger rising, but he could also not help but notice the strange feeling that came with standing in the back of the room and hear the people there talk about him as if he were not there. He looked around to see if anybody was looking at him, but no one was. He wanted to pull his cloak further over his head, but feared to lest by that act he might attract undesirable attention. When he returned his attention to the floor in front of him, Ananias was still speaking.

"No, you are too wise a man to bring a Gentile into the temple, though I suppose one could say that you brought the next best thing - James the brother of the son of God. Perhaps you hoped to meet the resurrected son of God?" More gales of laughter from the crowd, anger from James and Paul, but only Paul offered any resistance.

"James is a faithful man who observes the law as you do, if not with a more pure heart." Ananias reddened in the face at this. "But James, like the rest of us, believes that the prophets have been fulfilled in Jesus." At this there was an uproar in crowd, some insisting that Paul had blasphemed, others that he ought to be stoned, others that while he was not blaspheming himself he worshipped someone who was and ought to be arrested on those grounds alone, and much shouting and catcalling.

Ananias raised his arms for silence, but it was some moments before it was granted him. When at last he could be heard he looked at Paul and said, angrily, "You are not afraid to antagonize the council? Consult your conscience and see whether this is how you wish to be remembered by those who knew you - making a fool of yourself for all to see. Tell me that, out of respect for the council, you have spoken rashly and wish to retract what you have said."

"Men, brethren, I have spoken with all good conscience before God up to this day."

Ananias rose from his chair with an angry look on his face, and, without taking his eyes off of Paul, said to the soldiers next to him, "Strike him for that! We will take the insolence out of him." With that each of the soldiers hit Paul once in the face with their fist, leaving him sprawled on the ground and bleeding through the nose and mouth. Through it all his hands were still tied behind his back.

A rush of both anger and fear went through James at this, but he did not dare rush forward - there was nothing he could do. He watched wide eyed as Paul lay on the floor for a moment, watched by the entire crowd in utter silence, and then began to bring himself to his feet. When he had recovered his feet and cleaned the blood from his mouth as well as he could, he looked at Ananias and said, "God will strike you! Do you dare to judge me according to the law and then, contrary to the law, command other men to strike me?"

There was an immediate shout from the gallery that Paul should not be allowed to talk in this manner to the High Priest, and that he should be struck again, amid all manner of insults. Ananias raised his hands again for silence, but when it finally reigned it was Paul who spoke. "I would not speak evil against the High Priest, for it is written 'You shall not speak evil of the prince of your people.'" At this there was more tumult, and more demands that Paul be dealt with sternly, but it seemed to James that Ananias's countenance had soften just a little.

When quiet was restored once more, it was Paul again: "Men, brethren, I am a Pharisee, the son of Pharisees, and yet concerning the hope and resurrection of the dead I am called in question. See that he mocks the resurrection, in favor of the Sadduccees!" At this there was a moment of silence, and then an angry uproar began between the factions of the Sanhedrin who believed in resurrection in the next life (the Pharisees), and those who did not (the Sadduccees). Insults flew back and forth across the room, and James began to fear that there might be violence among the council. Ananias raised his hands yet again for silence, but it would not come. Paul had touched a nerve in the assembly and there was no bringing the peace back at the moment.

He stood there between the soldiers, all three of them looking around the room for some sign as to what they should do. James happened to look over at the tribune and saw him beckon to the guards around Paul. When they saw him, they each took Paul by the arm and led him off of the center floor to the door near which the tribune was standing. When they arrived at that spot the tribune opened the door and led the way through it. Ananias had watched the entire scene, but he was powerless to do anything about it - he could not make himself heard over the near riot in the council room. James saw that it was a good time for him to make his escape before anything else happened, and, with a quick glance to either side to ensure that he was not watched, he turned to the door and left the room. The halls leading to the outside were empty, and James had no trouble regaining the street.

He stopped by the homes of people he knew to be both Christian and excellent spies, told them the story of the trial, and told them to be on the lookout for any information they might hear of Paul. On the way back to the room he congratulated Paul for being able to set one side of the house against the other and thereby save himself, at least for the moment, but on the other hand he could not help but feel that such a trick was beneath him.

It was two days before James heard anything else of Paul. He was brought news on the evening of that day by a young man that he did not know. He was tall and dark, with bright eyes that reminded him of someone, but he could not place the face.

"I am Simon," said the man, when James had admitted him. "Are you James?"

"I am."

"I have news from my uncle Paul that he desired me to pass on to you."

"You are the nephew of Paul of Tarsus?"

"I am. Because of a threat on his life, he has been sent to Caesarea."

"Who threatened his life?"

"Some Jews from the city and some members of the council. The plan was that the council would ask the tribune to bring Paul back for more questioning since his first trial was inconclusive, and while at this trial he would be killed by men who have sworn not to eat until he is dead."

"How was he saved from this plot?"

"A Christian heard it spoken of in the street and passed it on to me, and I to my uncle. He sent me to tell the tribune, and the tribune, after telling me to tell no one, called for an escort and Paul left for Caesarea that night."

James considered this news for a moment and then smiled at the man. "But I see that you have broken your vow to the Tribune by coming to tell me the news."

"My uncle told me where to find you, and to tell you as soon as he was out of town."

"Are you a Christian?"

"I am. I live in Tarsus still, but have come this way on business. I have heard that you are the head of the Christians here in the city."

"I have been honored with such a title, but I am really their counselor. I lead them nowhere except to try to live a life that they could emulate."

Simon shared some food with James and then went his way, leaving James to ponder the ways of God.

CHAPTER 19

Little was heard of Paul thereafter, though some pieces of information did appear now and then. It appeared that Ananias himself and a delegation went to visit the governor Felix and make their case against Paul, going so far as to ask that Paul be sent back to them for trial. The governor refused this request, and while he did not hand Paul over, neither did he free him. Paul apparently did fall back this time on his status as a Roman citizen and insisted that his case should be heard by the Emperor, as was his right.

Paul was kept a prisoner in Caesarea for two years, and at the time when Felix was relieved as governor by Festus, he was still being held. A second delegation was sent to Caesarea by the Sanhedrin to attempt to have him released to them, but was rebuffed again. As a result of this second meeting Paul was sent on to Rome according to his request, and the delegation returned to Jerusalem angry.

James knew they were angry because he felt that wrath himself soon after their return. He was informed by his network of spies that they had left, and when he heard that they had returned without Paul he realized that they would be disappointed at best, and vengeful at worst. Vengeful turned out to be the answer.

He was awakened from his sleep one night by men on the landing outside the door to the room he still occupied alone, and upon opening the door to them was told that we would have to come with them. They were not dressed in any uniform that he recognized, but he also realized that to resist would be foolish and fruitless. Even if he did escape this night, there would be another until the person summoning him was satisfied. Better to have the matter out now. Plus, he was in his sixties. What could he do?

He suspected, following the men down the silent streets of the city, that Ananias was the one behind this summons, and he had his suspicion confirmed when he was deposited at the now familiar house. This time he was not allowed to wait in the anteroom for the master of the house to arrive, but was shown into a smaller room in the back that appeared to be set up for a trial. He was left standing in this room by himself for a few moments, and then Ananias entered.

He was fully dressed and had obviously not been to bed as James had been, but it was also clear that he was not rested and refreshed. He was angry and harsh, and James began to wonder if he had been among the delegation to Caesarea that had just returned that day. Ananias seated himself behind a small table, but did not invite James to sit.

"I have today come from Caesarea where your friend Saul is being held. The Romans will not release him to me that he may come back to this city for his trial. It is unconscionable that they should interfere in what are essentially internal matters of this nature, but there is little I can do. Your courageous friend hides behind his Roman citizenship, and is now, or soon will be, on his way to Rome to appear before the Emperor. I cannot believe that a man such as the Emperor would have time for his petty complaints, but there you have the Romans. They can subjugate the entire world, but they cannot tell one of their own to abide by the rules of the place where he lives...."

James interrupted. "You sneer at his courage, but it was you who forced the Romans to send him to Caesarea in the first place. They sent him there to be safe from the plot on his life."

"You know nothing of such things. And it is none of your affair."

"I know more than you think, and I can imagine the enmity of the Sanhedrin toward a man like Paul, who has forsaken them for the Christian faith. I find it hard to believe that, if the Romans had released him to you, he would have made it back to this city alive. I tend to think that he would have met with some unfortunate accident on the way."

At this Ananias lost his temper. "You are a vile creature," said he, snarling. "There is no insult to which you will not stoop, no step you will not take to offend those who adhere to the faith of your fathers. Saul would have had a fair trial...."

"Like Jesus? Arrested in the middle of the night, without any particular charge against him, tried immediately so that none of his supporters would know, and then sent off to be crucified so you could be home in time for the Sabbath?"

"Jesus got better than he deserved. Look at the headaches that he caused, and that his followers continue to cause."

"On what grounds would you have tried Paul, if you had managed to bring him back here? He did not claim to be the son of God, he assaulted no one, he broke no laws. He was assaulted in the temple during the simple act of prayer to the same God that you worship, and nearly stoned. If it had not been for the interference of the Roman tribune you would have been spared all this worry over Paul because he would have been arrested, tried and executed by the same mob." James paused for a moment, but then added, as Ananias was about to speak, "A mob, I might add, that I believe was stirred to action by members of the Sanhedrin, whom I saw whispering among the crowds immediately before the mob formed."

Ananias had attempted to interrupt once or twice during this speech, but James had not allowed him to do so. "Silence!" he screamed. "I do not have to tolerate this sort of language from you. All of these years I have born the wounds I have suffered from you and your new religion in silence because you were my friend. But that has been over for some years now, and still I have allowed you to go your way, out of respect. But I will tolerate this abuse no longer. From now on you are nothing but another troublemaker, and that is how I shall treat you, brother of the son of God. Ha! I laugh even to say it. Now get out, and never darken my door again."

"You had me brought here in the middle of the night to tell me to get out, and never darken your door again?"

"I brought you here to tell you that the Sanhedrin will be less forgiving of the Christians and their efforts to convert those of good faith to their new sect. It would have been part warning and part advice to a man I once admired. Now it is nothing but warning. I no longer care what happens to you any more than I do any of the others of your group. But you are the leader, brother of the son of God, and you know what can happen. Any other blood that is spilled will be on your head. If you do not find some way to control your people, we will do it for you."

James regarded Ananias for a moment, and then turned and walked away, finding his own way out of the house and into the street.

Only three days later, while James was in the room by himself, eating a spare noon time meal, there was a commotion outside in the street, and he heard the sound of feet rushing up the stairs to his door. When he opened it he found two of his flock there, a man by the name of Elihu and his wife, Mary.

"James, James, there is a disturbance in the temple! Come quickly!" James ran out of the door without even closing it, and followed them down to the street. He could not follow as fast as they would have liked, due to his age, but they tried to stay back with him and explain what was happening.

"Some of us and some of our former brethren began exchanging words in the temple courtyard....no, I do not know who started it or what was said....but soon there was a large crowd gathered, and people were arguing and throwing stones back and forth! When we came to get you the Christians were lined up on one side of the courtyard facing the others, and it looked as though they would come to blows!"

This was the worst incident that James had ever heard of. All tales of disagreement in the past had been among very small groups of people and there had not been much to fear in the way of a larger conflagration. But it sounded as though there was a sizable crowd involved this time, and, what was worse, it was apparently happening in the temple courtyard, where it would be right under the noses of the Sanhedrin. It was not difficult to predict who would be blamed for this incident.

Fortunately the situation had not deteriorated too far by the time James arrived. When he entered the outer courtyard of the temple he saw that there were indeed two camps, though the Jewish group was at least five times larger than the Christian group, and they were separated by a narrow corridor of perhaps a few feet between them, and this corridor was occupied by members of the Sanhedrin who were unknown to James. There may have been six or seven hundred people present, divided into two camps. James immediately entered this narrow pathway and advanced on the nearest Sanhedrin member to see what was up and what was to be done about it, but he found himself cheered by the Christian side and jeered by the other, and for a moment he could not make himself heard above the crowd. He had not realized he was so well known to those outside the Christian community.

The man that James approached was not in the mood to discuss how to disperse the crowd, but began to berate the Christians and James as troublemakers. James listened patiently, attempting to interrupt now and again to suggest that they should put aside their differences for the moment and disperse the crowd. Another member of the Sanhedrin who walked up to them agreed, but he and James did not know what to do about a crowd this size, other than to tell it to go home.

Soon the small group of leaders, the Sanhedrin in fine robes and James in tattered remnants of the clothes of others, was joined by Ananias. His appearance caused the Jewish side of the debate to cheer loudly, and the Christians to become more quiet.

"So, this is how you heed my warnings," he snarled to James.

"I have had nothing to do with this matter," said James. "I have only just arrived myself."

"But they are your people causing the disturbance. Did I not warn you that this might happen?"

"Yes, but you failed to warn me about what might happen if it were Jews who started the trouble, and not Christians. What should I have done to prevent this?"

"Who is the cause of this?" asked Ananias of one of the other Sanhedrin members who had been talking with James.

"I do not know, and I have not been able to find out how it started."

"It is an ugly crowd. What are they arguing about?"

"It would appear that some of the Jews resent the presence of the Christians here, since they profess a Messiah who has not yet come, and the Christians refused to leave."

"Once again it is the carpenter son of God who is at the heart of the matter. Well, let us see what we can do about it," said an obviously angry Ananias. "Bring him along," he said to two of the temple guards who had accompanied him, nodding to James.

The guards surrounded James and forced him to walk into the temple in the wake of Ananias and his entourage. They walked down hallways and up steps until they emerged into the sunlight on the roof of one wing of the temple. Ananias led the small crowd of guards, prisoner, and entourage to the edge of the roof looking down on the angry crowd below. As they waited for the crowd to notice them, Ananias spoke to James.

"I am about to give you an opportunity to right all the wrongs that you have done over the years, to me and to the faithful sons of Abraham. There is a mob down there that is about to come to blows over your carpenter son of God. Send your followers home - tell them that they no longer have any business here, and that from now on you will all keep the peace by staying out of the temple."

"That is impossible, and you know it. They are also the sons of Abraham, and they have as much right to be there as anyone. They are worshipping the same God."

"The temple of Solomon is no place to be invoking the name of a carpenter's son who was crucified for blasphemy. Tell them that you will all build your own temple, and that you will stay out of this one."

"I will not."

"Then you will suffer the consequences."

James said nothing.

"I am tired of the attitude of you and all your followers. You act as though you had some insight to God that none of the rest of us have, as though he had chosen you from among the chosen people for special favors. But you are nothing of the kind, yet there is a mob down there about to erupt because you and others like you cannot keep your mouths shut and allow other people to worship as they see fit. Rather than focusing our attentions on the Romans you have forced to us fight on two fronts: on the one side against the Romans and on the other amongst ourselves because some of us would rather worship a blaspheming son of a carpenter than follow the law of Moses." Ananias was becoming more angry by the minute, and James could see that there was no placating him.

Gradually the crowd became aware of their presence, and, as Ananias signaled with his hands for silence, it slowly obeyed. Before Ananias spoke to the crowd he turned to James one more time and said, under his breath, "If you do not disown Jesus of Nazareth as the Messiah now, at this instant, I promise that there will be a purge the likes of which the world has not seen." He then turned to the crowd and continued.

"People of Jerusalem!" he shouted. "See who is here to speak to you. It is James, often called the Just, who would talk to you of Jesus of Nazareth and his meaning." Then half turning to James, who was standing next to him, he said, loud enough for those below to hear, "Tell us James, the Just, because we should believe you, about Jesus. Who is he that we should know him and have peace among us?" Ananias then stepped back a little, a clear sign for James to advance closer to the edge and speak. James, discovering for the first time that he was afraid of heights, and this appeared to be about 60 cubits from the ground, and a sheer drop from the edge. It was difficult to look down because of the height, but it appeared to James that there may have been 1,000 people below him, though only 100 or so were followers of Jesus.

At his introduction by Ananias there was a tumult below as the members of the crowd reacted to him in their own way. His own compatriots were drowned out in their cheers by the much more numerous and vocal Jews, who demanded that he be removed from the temple, among other things.

He waited for them to quiet themselves again, and then began simply. "Brethren, why do you ask me about Jesus, the son of Man, who is in heaven and sitting at the right hand of his father?"

At this there was another great uproar in the courtyard below, and James could feel the tension building. He stole a quick glance at Ananias and saw that he was beside himself with rage. Just as James glanced at him he saw Ananias nod to the guards behind him. James then felt two sets of hands grab him by the arms and the clothes on his back, lift him off his feet, and throw him over the edge of the roof.

James felt an immediate surge of fear, but it hadn't the time to last, because he hit the ground with a sickening thud within a second. They had pitched him over the edge roughly head first, and when he landed it was on his right shoulder and the back of his head. The pain as he landed was excruciating, and he could both hear and feel bones break in his body. He ended laying on his right side, facing away from the temple and toward the crowd which had backed off far enough for him to land.

He was in great pain and found that he could not move. He also felt warm liquid welling up into his mouth and then leaking out through his lips, and he guessed that it must be his blood, but he could not move to verify his supposition. He could hear, though the noise around him seemed to homogenous - like a long, indistinguishable roar - but he could hear people calling for him to be stoned. He could feel heavy objects began to hit his body and land on the ground near him. As they landed in front of him he could see that they were stones, but, strangely, he felt no pain as they landed on him. He prayed, saying, "Father, forgive them." At that moment a strange peace came over him, and he stopping struggling to rise, laid his head down and closed his eyes to await his fate.

But just as he came to this resolution, the rocks stopped falling. James opened his eyes, looked ahead, which is to say toward the crowd, and saw that a pair of muscular legs were standing between him and the crowd. He turned his eyes to the left, which had the effect of looking up, and saw the broad back of the fuller known to him by the name of Ezra defending him with the fuller's club that he used to beat laundry. He could see the crowd fall back as Ezra advanced toward them wielding the club over his head, and then advance again as he fell back toward James. James saw one or two people throw stones, and saw that the fuller attempted to fend them off with his club. The fuller was screaming at the crowd to go away and leave James alone, but the crowd would not obey him. This enraged him the more, and he advanced on them, but as he moved forward those on his sides had more room to throw stones, so the fuller had to fall back and stay close to James.

This happened several times, and James wanted to stop the man, both for the man's sake and for his own, because he felt that he would not live anyway. He attempted to call out to the man, but could not form words and so had to content himself with loud groans. The fuller apparently heard him because he fell back, stepped backward over James, and knelt next to him. He then leaned forward over James, shielding him with his body, and looked into his eyes.

James could barely manage to croak, "Let them send me to my brother," and the effort caused him to cough and then choke on the blood that came up. The effort racked his body in pain, the pain caused him to cough up more blood, and this in turn caused the pain to increase. He knew that the end must be near. The fuller's eyes filled with tears, and he felt the crowd closing in once again, so he rose to chase them away. He ran at them in all directions, wielding the club over his head, swinging it at those who would not give way, and roaring at them all to stand back. He then backed carefully to James again and looked down on him from the front, while keeping a wary eye on the crowd. James could say nothing, but saw that the man was in great emotional pain. It seemed to James that the man's temper broke at that moment, and he made another frenzied rush on the ever encroaching crowd, darting this way and that, swinging his club over his head, slashing this way and that to frighten back the mob. He managed to land a couple of glancing blows on people who could not fall back fast enough because of the crowd behind them, but as soon as he fell back on James again the crowd moved back in as well, though more cautiously than before.

At last the fuller could see that he would not win the battle with the mob, and stood over James, openly weeping. He knelt close to James again and leaned over him, still facing the crowd, and James found the strength to croak once more, "Let them send me to my brother." The fuller advanced on the crowd again in a rage, swinging the club wildly. He then fell back once more, stepping over James so that he could glance down at him without turning his back on the crowd. James could do no more than moan. The fuller appeared to be in the last stages of indecision, but he seemed to take resolution finally, took a step further back, raised his club high over his head and, with a single crushing blow to James' head, sent him to be with his brother.

Made in the USA
Monee, IL
20 August 2024

64297028R00187